Praise for the bestselling novels of Madeleine Wickham

SLEEPING ARRANGEMENTS

"A delightful story . . . surprises abound . . . Wickham does a bang-up job."
—*Publishers Weekly*

"Wickham's [*Sleeping Arrangements*] has a different tone than do her Shopaholic tales, but it's an equally engaging yarn, sure to please her many fans and gain her new ones."
—*Booklist*

THE GATECRASHER

"Memorable characters who are as unpredictable and multi-faceted as they are stylish."
—*Publishers Weekly*

"Wickham [is] an observant and engaging storyteller."
—*Kirkus Reviews*

"[A] witty and deeply biting novel of modern manners and morals."
—*Library Journal*

"Wickham knows her characters well and the story never drags . . . an enjoyable read."
—*Booklist*

"Wickham has a shrewdly malicious touch with her characters."
—*Atlantic Monthly*

ALSO BY MADELEINE WICKHAM

A DESIRABLE RESIDENCE

Madeleine Wickham

St. Martin's Paperbacks

For Henry

Originally published in Great Britain by Black Swan, a division of Transworld Publishers, Ltd.

This is a work of fiction. All of the characters, organizations, and events portrayed in this novel are either products of the author's imagination or are used fictitiously.

A DESIRABLE RESIDENCE

For information address St. Martin's Press, 175 Fifth Avenue, New York, NY 10010.

Library of Congress Catalog Card Number: 96-35455

ISBN: 978-1-250-00324-9

Printed in the United States of America

St. Martin's Press hardcover edition / June 2010
St. Martin's Griffin edition / June 2011
St. Martin's Paperbacks edition / February 2012

St. Martin's Paperbacks are published by St. Martin's Press, 175 Fifth Avenue, New York, NY 10010.

10 9 8 7 6 5 4 3 2 1

Warmest thanks to Araminta Whitley,
Diane Pearson and Sally Gaminara,
and to Clare Pressley

CHAPTER ONE

There wasn't much point, Liz told herself, in getting upset. It wasn't his fault, poor man. The estate agent had finished talking, and was looking at her concernedly, expecting a response. To gain time, she glanced out of the sash window of the office, the panes bright with the sun and raindrops of a confused September's day. There was a little courtyard garden outside, walled, with a white wrought-iron bench and tubs of flowers. It must be nice in the summer, she thought, forgetting that this still was, to all intents and purposes, the summer. Her mind always worked at least half a term ahead.

'Mrs Chambers . . . ?'

'Oh yes, sorry,' said Liz, and turned back. 'I was listening.' She smiled at the estate agent. He didn't smile back.

'I did warn your husband at the time the property went on the market,' he said, 'that this might happen. I advised a price rather lower than your asking price.'

'I know you did,' agreed Liz. She wondered why he felt it necessary to remind her. Was he feeling defensive? Did he experience a need to justify himself; explain why their house had been on the market for ten months with his agency and had failed to sell? She studied his young, well-shaven face for signs of I-told-you-so; if-you'd-listened-to-me . . .

But his face was serious. Concerned. He was probably, she thought, not the sort of person who would countenance recriminations. He was simply pointing out the facts.

'And now,' he was saying, 'you must make a decision. You have, as I see it, two realistic options.' And a few unrealistic ones? Liz wanted to ask, but instead she looked intelligently at him, leaning forward slightly in her chair to show she was interested. She was beginning to feel rather hot; the sun was beating brightly through the panes of glass onto her cheeks. As usual, she had completely misjudged the early-morning weather and dressed for a brisk autumn day. She should perhaps remove a layer of clothing. But the thought of taking off her unwieldy jersey—which would necessitate first removing her spectacles and Alice band—to reveal a crumpled denim shirt, which might or might not be stained with coffee, seemed too much to contemplate. Especially in front of this smooth estate agent. She glanced surreptitiously at him. He didn't seem to be too hot; his face was tanned but not at all flushed and his cuffs looked crisp and cool. Starched, probably, she thought, by his girlfriend. Or perhaps, bearing in mind how young he looked, his mother. The thought amused her.

'Two options,' she said, more agreeably than she had intended.

A flicker of something like relief passed across his face. Perhaps he had been expecting a scene. But before Liz could react to it, he was back into well-grooved, grown-up professionalism.

'The first option,' he said, 'would be to put your house back on the market and drop the price considerably.' Of course, thought Liz. Any fool could have told me that.

'By about how much?' she asked politely. 'Realistically speaking,' she added for good measure, stifling a sudden, inappropriate urge to giggle. This conversation was unreal. Next thing she'd be saying, Let's have the cards on the table, or, Would you run that by me again . . . Pull yourself together, she told herself sternly. This is serious.

'Fifty thousand pounds. At least.'

Liz's head jerked up in shock. The giggle rising up inside her suddenly subsided; she felt shamefaced. No wonder this boy's handsome face was so concerned. He was more worried about her situation than she was. And, to give him his due, it was worrying.

'We've already reduced it by twenty,' she said, noting with slight horror that her voice was shaking. 'And that's less than the mortgage.'

'I know,' he said. He looked down at the papers on his desk. 'I'm afraid the market has dropped considerably since you bought.'

'Not that much. It can't have.' Belated worry made her belligerent. Of course she had seen the headlines in the papers. But she'd always skimmed them with her eyes; assumed they had no relevance to her. She'd avoided the chat of friends, some overtly anxious, others smugly triumphant. The property market this, the property market that. For heaven's sake. Stupid phrase, anyway. *The property market* . . . It made her think of rows of market stalls covered in tiny houses, each with a price label tied around the chimney.

'We can't sell it for so little,' she added. She could feel her cheeks growing even more hot. 'We just can't. We won't have enough to pay back the bank, and we only got the mortgage for the tutorial college on the basis of selling the house. We had some people interested in it then; they actually made an offer.' She stopped. A tide of humiliation seeped through her. How much older than this young man was she? And here she was, blurting out all her money worries; looking to him for an answer.

But he didn't look as though he had one. His fingers ruffled the papers on his desk anxiously; he avoided her eye. 'I'm confident that if you reduced the asking price by the amount I suggested, we would have a sale within a very reasonable time-scale,' he said. He sounded as though he was reading from a prompt card.

'Yes, but we need more money than that!' cried Liz. 'We've got a mortgage to pay off. And now we've got a business to run. And what's a reasonable time-scale anyway?' Too late, she realized her error. The estate agent's head shot up, an unmistakable look of relief on his face at having been given a question he could answer.

'Ah, well, these things always take a certain length of time,' he began. 'We'll be promoting the house afresh, highlighting the reduced price, targeting a different purchaser altogether.'

As his voice droned on, happily outlining the benefits of local advertising and colour photography, Liz's gaze wandered. She felt suddenly drained, worried and fearful. She had not, she realized, taken the sale of the house seriously enough. When the first buyers had pulled out, she had almost been pleased. She could hardly bear the idea of strangers in their home, using their bathroom, their kitchen, sunbathing in their garden. Even though she had been the driving force behind the move in the first place.

Of course, Jonathan couldn't understand that. One night, several months ago, she had broken down in a torrent of weeping at the thought of leaving the house for good, and he had stared at her in amazement.

'But you were the one who wanted to do all this,' he had said, almost shouted. 'It was your idea to buy the tutorial college in the first place.'

'I know it was,' she wailed, tears streaming hotly out of her eyes. 'But I still don't want to leave this house.' He gazed at her for a few seconds in stupefaction. Then his expression changed.

'All right, darling, then we won't.' His voice suddenly firm, he lifted her chin and looked into her teary eyes, in a gesture straight out of a 1940s film. 'We'll stay here. We'll stay where we're happy. I'll phone the solicitors tomorrow.'

'Oh Jonathan, why are you so stupid!' Liz jerked her chin out of his grasp impatiently. She wiped her nose with her hand and pushed it exasperatedly through her hair. A second wave of tears, feeble and benign, squeezed their way onto her cheeks. 'You never understand anything. Of course we're not going to stay here.'

She had given a huge, shuddering sigh, and got up to close the window. When she returned to bed, Jonathan was facing the other way, not out of resentment, she was sure, but out of complete bewilderment. And she had realized that she really wasn't being fair on him. Jonathan was inherently cautious; naturally unambitious. It had taken a lot of her enthusiasm to persuade him into this enterprise. And here she was, weeping distressingly at him, worrying him unnecessarily.

'Sorry,' she had said, taking his narrow hand, watching his shoulders relax. 'I'm just tired.'

Since then, she had gone to the other extreme; maintaining a blithe, positive approach that swept them all along, through the documentation, delivery vans and detritus of the move; into the shabby little flat that they were now to live in; out of safety and into precarious uncertainty. While Jonathan paced anxiously about the small, dusty rooms of their new home, searching for plug sockets; while Alice shuffled around blackly, in conspicuous, unspecified teenage gloom, she had been the one to smile, and throw open tea chests and sing Beatles songs, cheerfully mismatching tunes and lyrics. She had been the strong one; the face of reassurance. But now reassurance seemed to have slipped adroitly away from her, as though recognizing too great an adversary in the tidings of this fresh-faced, droning messenger.

'A good interior makes all the difference,' he was saying, as Liz's senses snapped back into focus. 'There's a lot of competition out there; people with Jacuzzi bathrooms; conservatories . . .' He looked at her expectantly. 'I don't suppose you'd consider installing a power shower? It might help attract buyers.'

'Instead of dropping the price?' said Liz, in slight relief. 'Well, I don't see why not.'

'As well as dropping the price, I meant,' said the estate agent, in a tone of almost amusement. It was that tone which suddenly touched her on the raw.

'You want us to drop the price *and* install a new shower?' She heard her voice screech; felt her face adopt the expression of outrage which she usually reserved for her most thoughtless pupils. 'Do you realize,' she added, slowly and clearly, as though to a class of sulky sixth-formers, 'that we are selling our house because we actually need the money? That we haven't decided to go and live in a tiny poky flat because we *want* to, but because we *have* to?' She could feel herself gathering momentum. 'And you're telling me that because *you* haven't been able to sell our house, we've got to put in a new shower at a cost of goodness knows how much, and then we've got to drop the price by—what was it?—fifty thousand? Fifty thousand pounds! Do you have any idea what our mortgage is?'

'Yes, well, it's quite a common situation you're in,' the young man said quickly. 'The majority of our clients have found themselves to be in a negative equity situation.'

'Well, I'm afraid I don't give a toss about your other clients! Why on earth should I care about them?' She wouldn't, Liz decided as she listened to her own voice crescendo, let Jonathan know that she had yelled at the estate agent. He would only get cross and worry.

Perhaps even phone up to apologize, for heaven's sake. A spurt of indignation at her husband's humility fuelled Liz further. 'We put our house on the market nearly a year ago,' she shouted. 'Do you realize that? If you'd sold it then, like you were supposed to, we wouldn't be talking about new showers. We wouldn't be lowering the price by such ludicrous amounts. We'd have paid off the mortgage, we'd be fine.'

'Mrs Chambers, the property market—'

'Sod the property market!'

'Hear, hear!' A rich, easy, expensive voice joined the ensemble. The estate agent started, forced a smile onto his face and swivelled in his chair. Liz, who had been about to continue, took a deep, gasping breath and looked round instead. Standing in the doorway of the office was a man in a tweed jacket, with dark brown eyes and crow's-feet and an amused grin. As Liz watched, he took a couple of steps into the room and then leaned casually back against the door frame. He looked at ease; urbane and confident, unlike the young estate agent, who had begun twitchily rearranging the papers on his desk. The man in the tweed jacket ignored him.

'Do carry on,' he said to Liz, giving her a quizzical smile. 'I didn't want to stop you. You were saying something—about the property market?'

Jonathan Chambers was sitting by the window in the grim little office of the Silchester Tutorial College, going through the last year's business accounts. Miss Hapland, the former owner of the tutorial college, had done the books herself for thirty years in a manner which had become more and more idiosyncratic as the years progressed. In the months since her death, a nephew had perfunctorily taken care of the business side of things until the place was sold, and now the books looked even more confused than before.

Jonathan frowned as he turned a page, and involuntarily wrinkled his nose at the rows of figures before him. It was a dull and wearisome job, this, which he had been tackling methodically at intervals since they had finally taken over the tutorial college that summer. He peered at the column headings and tried to ignore the odd ray of sunlight which played alluringly on the paper in front of him. This was the perfect afternoon for a walk or bicycle ride—and the temptation to give up and go outside for some fresh air was tremendous. But he had told Liz he was going to spend the day sorting things out, and it wouldn't be fair to let her down. Not when she was out doing a day's dreary shopping and tackling Witherstone's about the house.

He paused in his thoughts, pen poised over a column of figures, and wondered how she was getting on. A sudden vision of a smiling estate agent popped into his mind. *Yes, Mrs Chambers, I was going to phone you today. We had an offer on the house yesterday. The buyers would like to complete as quickly as possible.* Some chance. As far as he was aware, nobody had even deigned to look round the house in recent weeks. Let alone put in an offer. No one was interested. It was going to remain unsold. Mortgaged and unsold. The thought sent a small shiver of panic up Jonathan's spine.

They had only been given such a large mortgage to buy this tutorial college on the basis that their house would be sold within months; that they would soon be able to pay off one mortgage completely. But instead of that, they now had two mortgages. The size of their total borrowing was horribly huge. Sometimes Jonathan could hardly bear to look at their mortgage statements; at the monthly repayments which seemed to loom so large on the horizon of their monthly budget, and yet eat so little into the outstanding debt.

It had never entered his mind, at the start of all this, that they might get to the stage where they had bought the college but not managed to sell their house. They had always taken the sale of the house for granted; had even worried that it would sell too soon, before they were ready to move out. They'd put it on the market as soon as they'd decided to have a go at buying the tutorial college; and an offer had come along within weeks, from a young couple with a toddler and a baby on the way. A good offer; enough to cover the mortgage with some over. But they'd hesitated. At that stage they weren't certain whether they'd be able to raise enough money to buy the college. Was it wise to sell the house prematurely? Jonathan wasn't sure what to do; Liz thought they should wait until their plans were firmer. So Jonathan stalled the buyers for a week while they thought about it. And during that week, the young couple found another house.

In hindsight, of course, they should have grabbed the offer while they had it. But how could they have known? thought Jonathan. How could they have predicted the dearth of interest in their house that had followed? He tried to be philosophical about their predicament. 'The house will sell eventually,' he often said to Liz, trying to convince himself as much as her. 'It will. We only need one person interested. Not twenty. Only one.'

'We only need one, and he's been unavoidably detained,' he once joked, trying to jolly things up. But Liz wasn't interested in jokes any more. For her, the sale of the house seemed, in the last few months, to have taken on a new significance. It wasn't simply the money. In her mind, it almost seemed a yardstick; a sign that they would succeed. It was she who had insisted, as the new autumn term approached, that they should move out of the house and into the tutorial college, as they had always planned. She was almost superstitious about it. 'If we don't move now, we'll be admitting defeat,' she'd wailed, when Jonathan said that in his opinion it was no bad thing that they had a bit longer in the house, just while they got used to running a business. 'We've got to stick to the plan. We've *got* to.' Even though, as Jonathan pointed out several times, the plan was based on the assumption that by now, their house would be sold. And even though Liz loved the house more than any of them.

There was a streak of fatalism in Liz which Jonathan found, on occasion, rather alarming. But experience had taught him not to argue with it. So they had moved out of their house and into the little flat above the college, and left the house empty, waiting to be sold. Liz had been, during the days since the move, almost maniacally cheerful, as if to prove to herself and everybody else that they'd done the right thing; Jonathan already dreaded the tumble in her spirits, which would surely come.

For himself, Jonathan really didn't know whether they'd done the right thing or not. They'd both given up steady teaching jobs, a comfortable life and a secure future, to take on a business which, while not exactly declining, had certainly seen better days. If Liz was right, they would, between them, easily kick-start it into vitality, growth and profit. If Jonathan's occasional pessimisms were right, it was foolish for the two of them, with no business experience, to take on such an enterprise. But since they'd moved in, he had only once confided his worst fears to Liz. She had reacted savagely, as though he were accusing her of dragging them down into ruin; as though he were blaming her for a disaster which hadn't even happened.

'For God's sake, Jonathan,' she'd shouted. 'Why do you have to be so negative? I mean, you wanted to buy this place, too, didn't you?'

'Of course I did—'

'And now all you can do is worry about money all the time. Oh God!' Liz gave the tea chest she was un-packing a little shove with her foot. 'This is all hard enough, without you being miserable the whole time.'

And so Jonathan had postponed telling her that he was going to have to take out an extra loan. The original loan they'd been given to get the business going was running out, and they still hadn't ordered all the equip-ment they wanted. They needed money for the begin-ning of term. They needed a bit extra for emergencies. Another five thousand should cover it. Or maybe ten, to be on the safe side.

The bank had agreed immediately, pointing out in the same smooth letter that the interest rate on such a loan would necessarily be, as Mr Chambers must be aware, higher than that on the previous loan. *Whilst we are confident in your ability to pay back this loan, we would point out that your total debt is now far in excess of that originally agreed. In particular, we are concerned that you are still maintaining two mortgages. Perhaps you could update us on the proposed sale of your property in Russell Street?*

Jonathan clenched his pen slightly harder, and stared out of the window. If only he could. If only he could get shot of that house, once and for all.

Liz could feel her cheeks burning hotter and hotter. Both the young estate agent and the older man in the doorway were looking at her expectantly, obviously waiting for her to explain her outburst. She glanced at the twitchy young estate agent to see if he was going to say anything, but he was staring morosely downwards. It was up to her.

She looked up, and smiled shamefacedly at the man in the doorway. 'I'm sorry I shouted like that,' she said.

'Don't be silly,' exclaimed the man in the doorway. 'Sod the property market! I couldn't agree more. What do you think, Nigel?'

'Well yes, perhaps it would be nice,' said the young estate agent, a craven half-smile appearing on his face. 'Sod the lot!' He began to laugh, then abruptly stopped, and cleared his throat.

'And now,' said the man in the doorway, turning to Liz, bestowing on her a charming smile, 'do tell me: were you just making a general observation, or did you have something specific in mind?'

'Mrs Chambers—' began Nigel.

'Can tell us herself what's on her mind,' cut in the older man.

'Yes,' said Liz hurriedly, before she lost her nerve. 'I'm sorry I got so cross,' she began, 'but really, it seems an impossible situation. We put our house on the market ten months ago and it hasn't sold, and now we've moved and we really need to sell, and . . .' What was the boy's name? Oh yes, Nigel . . . 'Nigel tells me that we're going to have to drop our price by fifty thousand and put in a power shower to attract buyers. But, I mean, we can't afford to do that. We've just bought a business, you see, and we promised the bank we'd pay off the mortgage on the house by the end of the summer. And here we are in September . . .' She spread her hands out helplessly. If she hadn't been distracted by Nigel's obvious growing discomfiture, she might have burst into tears.

'What I said was—' began Nigel, as soon as she stopped talking. The older man cut him off with an up-raised hand.

'We'll return to the power shower in a minute, Nigel. Awful things, don't you think?' he added confidingly to Liz. 'Like sticking needles in your back. Give me a good old-fashioned bath.'

'I've never been in a power shower,' admitted Liz.

'Well, my advice is, don't bother. Now, tell me, what is this business you've bought?'

'We've bought Silchester Tutorial College,' said Liz, unable to stop her mouth curving into a smile. They had actually bought a tutorial college. They were the owners of a business. It still gave her a thrill to articulate it; to watch for the reaction on people's faces. This time it was even better than usual.

'No! Really?' The debonair, amused expression slipped from the man's face, to be replaced by a disarming enthusiasm, and his eyes focused on Liz anew. 'I was crammed for my O levels there. Wonderful place.' He paused. 'Actually, what am I saying? I still failed them all. But I'm sure that was my fault. I was a hopeless case.' He smiled reminiscently. 'I was taught English by Miss Hapland herself. I think she hated me by the end of it.'

'She's dead now,' said Liz cautiously.

'Really?' His face fell briefly. 'I suppose she must be. She looked pretty ancient even when she taught me.'

'It only happened last year,' said Liz. 'That's why the tutorial college was put up for sale.'

'And you bought it. That's wonderful! I'm sure you'll have a much better calibre of pupil than I was.'

'But you're a graduate. You're a qualified surveyor,' objected Nigel, who was leaning back in his chair, staring gloomily at the ceiling. A cloud had passed over the sun; suddenly the room seemed colder and darker.

'Oh, I got a few exams eventually,' said the older man impatiently. 'Anyway, that's not the point. The problem here is what to do about your house. Where exactly is it?'

'Russell Street,' said Liz.

'Oh yes,' he said. 'I know. Nice family houses. Got a garden, has it?' Liz nodded.

'Well, from what you've said, I would have thought one of your best bets might be to try and rent out your property for a while, just until prices pick up. Are you on a repayment mortgage?' Liz nodded. 'Well then,' he smiled, 'the rental income should cover at least part of your monthly repayment. Maybe the whole lot, with any luck!'

'Really?' said Liz, feeling a flicker of hope rising inside her.

'And there's no shortage of prospective tenants at the moment, especially for a nice, well-located house like yours.' He gave her a warm smile, and Liz felt suddenly overcome, as though his compliment were to herself. 'We can handle all the arrangements here, draw up a shorthold tenancy agreement, and then, when the market seems right, try and sell again. I certainly wouldn't be tempted down the route of power showers,' he added, flicking an almost imperceptible grin at her. *It's you and me against that idiot Nigel,* his look said, and Liz gazed back at him, feeling ridiculously warmed.

'I only suggested installing a power shower in the context of my first mooted option,' said Nigel, clearly not quite daring to adopt the defensive tone he would have liked. 'I was about to proceed onto the rental option.'

'Yes, well, perhaps you should have mentioned that first,' said the older man, a steely note creeping into his voice. Nigel's back stiffened, and Liz wondered for the first time who this stranger was. Someone important, obviously. 'In fact,' the man added, turning back to Liz, 'I might even know some people who are interested. A very sweet girl and her husband. She does PR for us— you know Ginny Prentice,' he said to Nigel, who nodded. 'Lovely girl, husband's an actor. I'm sure she said she was thinking of taking a place down this way. Your house would do them perfectly.'

'Gosh, that would be wonderful,' said Liz. 'But actu-

ally, I'm not sure about renting it out. I mean, we're supposed to be selling to pay off our mortgage. The bank
might not like it if we have a mortgage on the house and
a mortgage on the business as well.' She stared at him,
mutely pleading, willing him to pull another rabbit out
of the hat. He looked down at her consideringly. There
was a moment's still silence.

'Who's your lender?' he suddenly said.

'Brown and Brentford.'

'Main Silchester branch?'

'Yes.' There was a pause, and Nigel looked up, a look
of utter disapproval on his face.

'I'll see if I can sort something out,' said the man.
'No promises, of course. But I'll try.' He looked kindly
at her, and Liz gazed back, pink-cheeked, gratitude filling her body like a balloon. She suddenly wished, foolishly, that she had bothered to put her contact lenses in
that morning. Then abruptly the man looked at his
watch. 'Christ. Must fly. Sorry, I'll be in touch. Nigel
will give me your details.' He gave her another crinkle-
eyed conspirator's smile.

'But wait!' cried Liz, her voice sounding shrill to her
own ears. 'I don't know your name!' A look of amusement passed afresh over his face.

'It's Marcus,' he said. 'Marcus Witherstone.'

As Marcus proceeded down the corridor to his own office, he was filled with a glow of benevolence. It was so
easy to help people, he reflected; really, very little effort
for the reward of such self-satisfaction. Sweet woman;
she had been so touchingly grateful. And it had been

worth it just to put that dreadful Nigel in his place. Marcus frowned as he pushed open the door to his office. It was his cousin, Miles, who had hired Nigel—poached him from Easton's, the rival estate agency in Silchester. Said he was a young dynamic talent. Well, perhaps he was. But no amount of talent, in Marcus's opinion, made up for that horrible nasal voice and smug young face.

Nigel was just another of the topics on which Marcus and Miles disagreed. Only that morning, Marcus had spent a fruitless half-hour trying to persuade Miles that they ought to be branching out into property abroad. Setting up an office on the south coast of France, perhaps. Or Spain.

'All the big boys are doing it,' he said, waving a collection of glossy brochures in front of Miles. 'Look. Villas worth half a million, a million. That's the kind of business we should be handling.'

'Marcus,' said Miles, in the dry, deliberate voice that he'd had since he was a small boy, 'what do you know about French property?'

'I know that it's an area we should definitely be going into,' said Marcus with determination. 'I'll go over there, make some contacts, suss out the market, you know.'

'I don't think so,' said Miles firmly. He spoke in much the same way as he had when, aged seven, Marcus had tried to persuade him to climb out of the window of their grandparents' house and go to the village pub to buy Coke and crisps for a midnight feast. He hadn't had any guts then either, Marcus thought crossly. And just because he was three years older, he wielded a tacit authority over Marcus that neither of them could quite abandon. Even though they were supposed to be equal partners.

He stared angrily at Miles, so bloody staid, in his ridiculously old-fashioned three-piece suit, puffing away at his stupid pipe. A pipe, for God's sake.

'Miles, you don't live in the real world,' he said. 'Expansion's what it's all about. Diversification.'

'Into areas we know nothing about? And at which we're bound to fail?' Miles took his spectacles off and began polishing them on his handkerchief. 'I think it's you who doesn't live in the real world, Marcus.' He spoke kindly, and Marcus felt a series of angry retorts rising. But he kept his mouth closed. If there was one thing Miles couldn't tolerate, it was conspicuous family rows at the office. 'This is the time to be consolidating,' Miles continued. He replaced his spectacles and smiled at Marcus. 'If you want to go to France, why don't you go there on holiday?'

Now Marcus looked aggrievedly at the glossy brochures still sitting on his desk, tantalizing him with photographs of blue skies, swimming pools, bougainvillaea. And his own inspired jottings: *Witherstone's Abroad. Spread your wings with Witherstone's. Weekending abroad with Witherstone's.* He hadn't even had a chance to show his slogans to Miles. But perhaps it was just as well. He opened his bottom desk drawer and stowed the brochures inside. Maybe he would bring the subject up again in six months' time. But now he had to go. He glanced at his watch. Five twenty already, and he had promised to pick up Anthea and the children from outside the library at half-past.

He glanced hurriedly at the fluttering yellow Post-it notes decorating his desk. They would just have to wait till tomorrow, he thought, gathering up his briefcase, stuffing a few random papers inside. But as his eye ran automatically over the messages, one suddenly stood out and grabbed his attention. He stared at it silently for a minute, then looked around as though afraid of being observed, and sat casually down on his leather swivel chair, from where he could see it better without actually touching it. It was written in the same innocent, rounded handwriting as all the others, in the turquoise ink that was the trademark of Suzy, his secretary. It sat benignly between a request for details of small country estates by a Japanese businessman and a cancelled lunch appointment. And it was unremarkably short. *Could you please ring Leo Francis, tel: 879560.*

Marcus looked at his watch. Shit. Nearly twenty-five past. Anthea would probably already be standing outside the library, looking anxiously up the road, wondering loudly to the boys whether Daddy had forgotten to leave the office early. He looked at the phone for a torn, undecided second. Either way, the longer he sat there, the later he would be. But the thought of leaving it; of spending the whole evening wondering whether Leo had phoned about *that*—or for some other, innocuous reason; listening to Anthea's chatter while a secret anticipation filled his mind and body—was unbearable. With a small surge of excitement, he picked up the receiver and dialled the number.

'Francis, Frank and Maloney.'

'Leo Francis, please.' God, even his voice was shaking.

'I'm sorry, Mr Francis has left for the day. Can I take a message?' Marcus stared at the phone for a moment. Leo wasn't there. He would have to wait until tomorrow to find out. A sudden, surprising sensation of relief went through his body.

'Just say that Marcus Witherstone called,' he said, and put down the phone. Shit. Oh shit. What was he getting himself into?

He closed his briefcase with slightly trembling hands, peeled the post-it with Leo's number on it from his desk, folded it in two and put it in the breast pocket of his jacket. He would get rid of it in the kitchen rubbish bin at home. Although why on earth should he not legitimately have a message from Leo on his desk? Leo was, after all, a well-known local solicitor with whom Witherstone's had often done business. He was being paranoid, he told himself firmly as he closed his office door behind him. And anyway, he hadn't actually talked to Leo yet. He could still change his mind.

Feeling calmer, he strode through the outer office, nonchalantly pushing a hand through his hair, saying a cheery good night to the remaining staff, smiling kindly at a young couple sitting in the waiting area, leafing anxiously through a pile of details. Outside, he nearly bumped into a woman unlocking a bicycle from the forecourt railings.

'Oh, hello!' she said, giving him a slightly tremulous smile.

'Hello there,' said Marcus in a jovial voice, bleeping open the locking system of his Mercedes.

'I just wanted to say thank you,' she continued in a rush. Marcus turned round to look at her again. Of course. It was the woman from Nigel's office. She gazed at him in beseeching gratitude, and brushed a few locks of dark hair from her face.

'Don't mention it,' he said, in his charming, all-part-of-the-service manner.

'No really,' she insisted. 'It was terribly kind of you to take an interest. And I had no idea who you were,' she added, glancing up at the illuminated 'Witherstone & Co.' above the office. 'I'm sure you don't normally go around organizing people's problems for them.'

Marcus shrugged disarmingly. 'I'm just an estate agent, like all the rest of them.'

'Rubbish. You're nothing like most estate agents!' Marcus let out a laugh in spite of himself.

'That's about the biggest compliment you could give me,' he said conspiratorially. 'But don't tell anyone I said so.'

'OK,' she grinned back, and wheeled her bike down to the pavement. 'Bye-bye, and thanks!'

Marcus was still smiling as he got into his car. It just showed. People like Nigel, however bright and talented, simply weren't popular with the customers. He would relate the whole story at the next weekly meeting, he decided, including the comment from the customer that he, Marcus, was nothing like most estate agents. That would get Miles worked up, all right. Not to mention the precious protégé. 'I've decided, Nigel,' he would say, in a kind voice, 'to oversee the rest of this case myself. I'm not convinced you've grasped the best manner of dealing with the client. We can't afford to have our customers upset, you know.' He grinned to himself. That was precisely the reprimand Miles had used on him years ago when he told that obnoxious old couple they wouldn't be able to sell their bungalow because it smelt disgusting. It would be highly satisfying to see Miles's face as he said exactly those words to Nigel. And the best thing was that Miles was so hidebound by ideas of family loyalty, and presenting a united front to the staff, that he probably wouldn't say a word in Nigel's defence.

Liz arrived home with bright eyes and a bag of doughnuts.

'Time for tea,' she said, planting a kiss on Jonathan's head from behind. 'Time to stop working and have a doughnut.'

'Did it go well, then?' said Jonathan, following her to the kitchen. 'Have we sold the house?' Liz was filling up the kettle. When she turned around, her face was triumphant.

'We don't need to,' she said. 'We're going to rent it out.'

'What?'

'The rent we get will probably cover the mortgage repayments. It'll be completely self-sufficient.'

'Says who? The estate agent?' Jonathan sounded sceptical, and an impatient look crossed Liz's face.

'Not just any old estate agent,' she said. 'The top estate agent. Mr Witherstone himself.'

'How does he know about it?' Liz glared at Jonathan.

'Can't you stop asking questions? Honestly, I'd have thought you'd be a bit more pleased.'

'I am pleased,' protested Jonathan, picking up the

bag of doughnuts and putting them onto a plate. 'I think. But I can't quite see how it's going to solve all our problems. We're supposed to be selling the house to decrease our mortgage.'

'Yes, well, we don't need to if we've got a rental income, do we?' said Liz impatiently. 'I mean, it'll be just as if we don't have that mortgage any more.'

'I'm not sure the bank will see it quite like that,' said Jonathan cautiously.

'Well actually, I think you'll find they will,' said Liz triumphantly. 'Mr Witherstone's going to speak to them.' Jonathan stopped, doughnut in hand.

'Liz, are you joking?'

'No, I'm not.' A tinge of pink crept into Liz's cheeks. 'He said he'd talk to them. Pull some strings. You know.'

'This all sounds very dubious to me,' said Jonathan. 'Can't we just go ahead with selling the house? I mean, do you know what our total debt is? It's going to be hard enough to keep up the repayments on the tutorial college, let alone the house too.'

'For God's sake, Jonathan! It'll be fine! We'll get some tenants in and they'll cover the mortgage and there'll be nothing to worry about.'

Yes, but what if they don't, Jonathan was about to say. And what if the bank doesn't agree? Then, looking at Liz's flushed face, he thought better of it. The kettle came to a noisy boil, and Liz poured the scalding water into the teapot.

'Anyway,' she said belligerently through the steam, 'it has to work. Otherwise we'll have to drop the price of the house by fifty thousand. That's what they said. We won't sell it otherwise.'

'What?' Jonathan suddenly felt weak. 'Fifty thousand? That's impossible.'

'That's what I said,' retorted Liz. 'I mean, if we did that, we'd never pay off the mortgage, would we? It would just hang over us.' Jonathan looked at her. She was reaching into the cupboard for a couple of mugs, and almost seemed to be avoiding his eye.

'You don't seem very worried,' he said, trying not to sound accusing.

'Yes, well, that's because I'm not worried,' said Liz quickly. 'It's all going to be sorted out. I told you.'

'Yes, but what if this great plan doesn't work?' Jonathan could hardly bear to think about it. The extra loan was worrying enough. But this was worse. If their house was worth fifty thousand pounds less than they had thought, then that debt would always be there, even after they'd sold. Fifty thousand pounds. He compared it in his mind with the yearly salary he had received as a teacher at the comprehensive, and gave a small shudder. How could they even begin to pay back that kind of money? Even if they did start making a profit?

'Here's your tea,' said Liz. She looked at his face and frowned. 'Oh, come on. Don't be such a misery.' Jonathan roused himself, and gave her a small smile. Liz took a huge bite of doughnut and looked at him balefully. 'I've had a really hard day,' she added.

'I know you have,' said Jonathan, automatically adopting a soothing voice. 'Well, why don't you go and sit down, and I'll bring you a piece of toast.'

'OK,' said Liz grudgingly, taking another bite of her doughnut. 'Where's Alice?' she added, in a muffled voice.

'She went out earlier on,' said Jonathan. He opened a drawer and took out the bread knife. 'She didn't say where she was going.'

The house looked just as it always had done. Solid. Familiar. Home. Gazing at it from her strategic viewing position across the street, Alice thought that if she'd walked past it in a hurry and looked up, she might even have believed it was still home and that if she went inside she would find her mother in the kitchen or in the sitting-room watching *Summer Street*, her father playing classical music in the study, the smell of food in the air and Oscar asleep in front of the fire.

Alice bit her lip and frowned and hunched her narrow shoulders in her old brown suede jacket. They'd had to give Oscar away. To Antonia Callender, of all awful, awful people. *What a gorgeous cat! I bet you'll miss him. You can come and see him any time, you know.* Stupid bitch. There was no way Alice was going near Antonia's house. She had hated her ever since they sat next to each other on the first day in the upper third, and Antonia asked Alice what her favourite drink was and laughed really loudly when she said Lilt. Of course, Antonia's was gin and tonic. And then everyone else in the class had said theirs was gin and tonic, too, except the real squares. Now she kept asking people if they'd got stoned at the weekend, and last term she'd gone on about how she was going to stay with her cousins, who were really cool and smoked joints in front of their parents. Alice reckoned she made it all up. When they'd gone to her house to deliver Oscar, Antonia's mother had offered Alice orange squash. But she hadn't felt able to drink anything.

They'd taken him there in the car, in his travelling basket, which he hated. Alice could still remember the precise feel of the wicker on her knees, weighted down unevenly by Oscar's pacing paws. He'd scrabbled heavily against the sides most of the way there, as if he couldn't wait to be let out. But when they'd opened the little gate, he'd looked around nervously, and then retreated back as far as he could go. They'd had to tip the basket up to get him out, and then he'd crouched down, looking panic-stricken, before streaking across the rug and under the sofa. Then he'd made a mess on the carpet. Hah. That served them right . . .

An old lady with a shopping basket pushed past Alice, interrupting her thoughts.

'Excuse *me*,' she said crossly, and gave Alice a suspicious look. Alice stared back rudely. This was still her street. She'd grown up here; she still belonged here. Not in Silchester shitty Tutorial College.

She'd just had to get out of that place this afternoon. Her father was trying to sort things out downstairs, in the classroom bit, and kept shouting upstairs to the flat, asking her to come and help move desks around. Then he'd told her to turn down her music, then he'd told her she should really be a bit more helpful and lots of girls of fourteen had Saturday jobs, and all he wanted was half an hour of her time. The more he said things like that, the more she wanted to be as unhelpful as possible. So she'd shrugged on her suede jacket and made sure her cigarettes were in the pocket, and stomped noisily down the stairs. She couldn't bring herself to say anything at all to her father—to have him smiling hopefully at her was even worse than hearing him shout—so she hadn't told him she was going out. Anyway, it was pretty obvious.

It was getting cold, and drops of rain were starting to fall on her head. She fingered her lighter, and wondered what to do. She hadn't really intended to come back here. She'd just thought she would go somewhere for a cigarette, maybe sit on the grass in the Cathedral Close. That was one tiny little good thing about living at the tutorial college, she thought grudgingly. At least they were nearer the centre of Silchester. But although she'd started off going there, she hadn't ended up in the Cathedral Close. At some point on her journey she'd stopped concentrating, and had automatically started walking west, the way she used to go home from St Helen's when she was little. And here she was, back in Russell Street.

It was really weird—to think that she'd walked where her legs told her and not where she was intending to go. Like being hypnotized, or sleepwalking, or something. She would tell Genevieve in her next letter, she decided. *It was so weird*, she would begin. Or, no, *It was so spooky*. Genevieve always said everything was spooky. Now she'd be telling the people in Saudi Arabia how spooky everything was. Probably she'd be telling them how spooky *they* were. An image sprang into her mind of Genevieve, standing in the desert in her cut-off Levis, telling an Arabian man in a white dress he was really spooky, and she gave an involuntary giggle.

Her cigarette lighter had been a goodbye present from Genevieve. She'd put it in a carved Indian box and wrapped it all up and actually given it to her in front of both sets of parents. Alice had nearly died when she opened the box and saw what was inside. And then, of course, her mother had gone on about what a lovely present, and could she have a look, and Alice had glared at Genevieve, who couldn't stop laughing and said, 'Oh yes, Alice, show your mum, go on.' In the end, she'd had to scrumple up the wrapping-paper and shove the lighter inside it when no-one was looking and then retrieve it from the waste-paper basket the next morning.

And now it lay warm in her hand, silver and chunky and rounded. Alice looked surreptitiously up and down the street. She would, she thought, go and have a quick cigarette in the garage. There couldn't be anything wrong with that; it was still their garage. It was still their house come to that. She should have brought a front doorkey with her; then she could have gone and smoked in the kitchen if she'd wanted. Or the sitting-room. Anywhere.

Trying to look as casual as possible—although surely she wasn't doing anything wrong—she crossed the road to number twelve. The gate gave a familiar squeak as she pushed it open, and the rose bushes halfway up the path would have snagged her new black leggings if she hadn't automatically dodged them. She skirted quickly across the front lawn, feeling stupidly guilty, and unlatched the gate to the back garden.

Of course her parents hadn't got round to mending the lock on the back door of the garage. She knew they wouldn't have. Heaving her shoulder against it, she pushed it open and walked quickly into the familiar darkness. The piles of newspapers that used to make a comfortable seat for her and Genevieve had gone, but one corner was still dry enough to sit down. She fumbled for her cigarettes, cupped her hand around the smooth contours of her lighter, lit up, leant back and took a deep, long, comforting drag.

CHAPTER TWO

Jonathan cleared his throat and looked around the room, an anxious smile hovering on his face.

'As you can see,' he said, 'we've changed a few things.' He paused, and looked around again. The staff of Silchester Tutorial College looked back at him. One or two gave nods of encouragement but none of them smiled. They were assembled in what had been the staff room at the tutorial college—a long, light room at the back of the building, which overlooked the small garden. In Miss Hapland's day, this had been a charmingly furnished sitting-room with faded chintz armchairs, coffee maker and television, in which the staff had relaxed between lessons. Now it was a businesslike classroom, with brand-new white board, overhead projector and bookshelves.

The members of staff had each come in that morning, clearly expecting to flop down in the usual armchairs with cups of coffee—and their looks of shock at the transformation of the room had not helped Jonathan's confidence. It was crucial to get the staff on their side, he thought, beginning to feel rather flustered; perhaps he and Liz should have let them all know in advance about the new arrangements.

'As you can see,' he repeated, 'we've changed a few things. For example, the staff room. From now on we're going to use the old languages room on the first floor.' He hesitantly gestured upwards; a few pairs of eyes dutifully followed. Others exchanged glances.

'I wouldn't have thought,' came a deliberate voice from the corner, 'that the languages room was big enough for all of us.' Mr Stuart, head of maths, looked challengingly at Jonathan.

'Well, no,' conceded Jonathan, 'perhaps not. But then, the staff room is only meant to be for those who aren't teaching in a particular period. Which should mean you aren't all in it at once!' He gave a little laugh. 'And we thought that a lot better use could be made of the space.' He paused.

Go *on*, thought Liz, sitting supportively beside Jonathan. Why was he pausing so often? Every time he stopped speaking, she could see members of staff looking at each other; he really needed to galvanize their attention. She smiled at him encouragingly, willing him to get going. He looked down at his piece of paper.

'So this room will become the new languages room,' he said. 'And we're intending to install sound systems so that students can work with earphones. We want to make language teaching a priority.' He cleared his throat. 'Liz is a qualified teacher in four languages, as some of you will already know. Or perhaps all of you.' He paused again, as though considering this. Liz couldn't bear it any more.

'We want to make Silchester Tutorial College a centre for languages as well as simply a crammer,' she said rapidly. 'Languages have never been more important for students, and if we can offer first-class teaching in the major European languages, as well as specialist languages on demand, we feel we should be able to attract more than simply retake students. Eventually we'll market ourselves to companies which need good language training, and possibly organize children's holiday courses. To achieve that, we'll need absolutely first-class language facilities, and high-calibre teaching. I'll be seeing the language tutors in a separate meeting to discuss resources and study programmes. All ideas welcome.' She stopped, and gave a quick glance around the room. There was no doubt, she'd got their attention now. The faces she recognized as belonging to language tutors were looking animated; the others were looking variously indifferent, wary and hostile.

'Does this mean,' said one of them, 'that you'll be phasing out other subjects?'

'Oh no,' said Liz. 'This will all be as well as the mainstream teaching. But our aim is to make this college far more efficient, so that we've got time and resources to do both.' She took a deep breath and didn't look at Jonathan. 'To put it bluntly, this whole place needs shaking up. Part of the reason for moving the staff room is that we want less sitting around drinking coffee and more teaching.'

There. She'd said it. Jonathan wouldn't be pleased. They'd had an argument about what they were going to say at this first meeting. He had said they must be gentle and diplomatic; avoid ruffling the feathers of the staff. Liz had retorted angrily that their feathers deserved ruffling, they'd had such a cushy life up until now. Swanning in and out; teaching as and when; even using the premises for their own private coaching sessions. It was quite obvious from looking at the books that Miss Hapland had let the business side of things lapse almost completely during the last five years. She'd liked to see the staff around the place; liked to come down and chat with them as they reclined on the sofas she'd provided and drank the endless free coffee.

But she hadn't needed to make a profit like they did. She hadn't had a huge mortgage on the place. She'd seen the tutorial college, certainly in the latter part of her life, more as an agreeable social enterprise than a business. For Liz and Jonathan it was different. They needed to rationalize; to start making profits and paying back their debt. And that had to start with the staff. OK, they were all very sad about Miss Hapland's death. Of course they were. But that didn't mean, as Jonathan seemed to think it did, that they should all creep around for the first term, pretending nothing had changed. It was better if they started as they meant to go on.

And although there were disgruntled faces, raised eyebrows and exchanged glances around the room, as Liz waited for her statement to sink in, she thought she could detect something else in the air: an alive, positive feeling. She risked a glance at one of the younger tutors, a sweet young girl who taught German. Her face was bright; her eyes fixed on Liz, waiting for her to continue.

'It should be a very exciting project,' said Liz, looking straight at her. 'I'm sure you'll all have your own thoughts and suggestions on what we should do, and I'm very much looking forward to discussing it.' The girl blushed, and Liz smiled at her. There. She had at least one ally. And these others would come round when they realized there was more teaching in it for them.

She risked a little look at Jonathan. He was smiling miserably. Clearly the disgruntled faces had fazed him. For heaven's sake, couldn't he get a grip? Why couldn't he just ignore them, like she did? He was the boss, after all. 'We also have plans for the Common Entrance coaching department,' she said, in an encouraging voice. 'Don't we, Jonathan? Lots of exciting plans?'

Later on, when they'd all gone, she made him a cup of instant coffee and took it to him in his classroom.

'I'm sorry,' she said.

'What for?' He was leafing through a book of Latin prose, selecting the first piece to give the five Latin A level retake candidates starting that term. *Gallia est omnis divisa in partes tres*, thought Liz, as she always did when confronted with a page of Latin. That was the first line of her O level Latin set text, which she'd learnt off by heart for the exam, and was almost the only Latin she could remember. It was really amazing, she thought vaguely, peering over Jonathan's shoulder at the dimly familiar words, that so many young people still chose to learn a dead language when there were so many living, vibrant languages in the world. Then, no, of course it wasn't at all amazing, she corrected herself hastily. That was the kind of thoughtless, ignorant comment that drove Jonathan mad.

'What a wonderful language,' she said guiltily; feeling an obscure need to prove herself. 'I can always see the Italian in it.' Idiotic remark. What was she trying to say? Oh yes. 'Jonathan, I'm sorry for taking over at the staff meeting,' she said, putting a hand on his shoulder. 'I didn't mean to monopolize it.' He looked up at her; his eyes benign and surprised.

'Oh, my lovely, don't apologize. I thought you were wonderful. Tremendous stuff. You did it much better than I could have done.' He gave her the wide, lopsided, entirely natural grin which had always charmed schoolboys and parents alike, and Liz's insides contracted in a strange mixture of affection and relief. Of course, she was surprised to find herself thinking. That's why I love him. I knew there was something . . .

Daniel Witherstone knew his mother would be waiting eagerly for him as he came out of school on the first day of term. He lingered in the cloakroom for a while with Oliver Fuller, who walked home and could leave when he liked, and would have liked to stay longer in the companionable atmosphere of shoe bags and radiators, playing on Fuller's Nintendo. But there was always the danger that his mother would come and find him, as she had that memorable day when he'd borrowed Martin Pickard's Walkman and forgotten what time it was. She'd completely flipped, and thought he'd been run over or abducted, and got all hysterical and gone to find

Mr Sharp. When they'd arrived in the cloakroom and she'd seen him, curled up on the bench, completely absorbed in Michael Jackson, she'd nearly burst into tears, according to Pickard. Daniel had always been grateful to Pickard after that, for not telling everyone about it and making it into some big class joke. But he never wanted it to happen again.

So after a while, he tore himself from level three of Mortal Kombat and mooched slowly out of the cloakroom, up the stairs, through the hall and out into the drive of Dene Hall. His mother's car was parked near the school building, and Andrew, his younger brother, was already strapped into the back seat. Daniel preferred it when Hannah, their housekeeper, came to pick them up. She was really cool, and played tapes really loud and swore at people in her Scottish accent when they got in her way. But he'd known his mother would be there today. She always came on the first day of term. And besides, she'd want to hear about the scholarship class.

Just thinking about it gave Daniel a secret, elating feeling of pride. It was the way Mr Williams had said, so casually, 'And, of course, Witherstone. You'll be sitting a scholarship of some sort, I should imagine.' He'd given Daniel a little smile—that showed he knew how chuffed Daniel was but wasn't going to say—and then told everyone to get out their maths books. And all day, Daniel had carried around a little glow inside him. Even when Miss Tilley told him she couldn't fit him in at any other time, and he'd have to come for his clarinet lesson at eight-thirty on Monday mornings, he'd smiled, and said that was fine. It was as if nothing could go wrong.

But now he was going to have to tell his mother. He looked at her face, smiling at him questioningly through the windscreen. At least she knew enough not to get out of the car, like she used to, and call out really embarrassing things like, 'How did your spelling test go?' But she would still want to know whether Mr Williams had said anything about scholarships. And then he'd have to tell her, and then the glow would be gone.

It wasn't that she wouldn't be pleased. It was that she'd be too pleased. She'd talk about it too much, and ask him all about it, and ask how many other boys were in the scholarship class, and what had Mr Williams said to him exactly, and then tell her again, start from the beginning, and tell her which lesson they were in when he said it, and had they mentioned which schools they might sit and was anyone trying for a scholarship at Bourne?

He'd have to tell her all about it, and talk about it all the way home, and then hear her tell Hannah, and his father, and probably everyone else in the world as well. It would be like the time he won that clarinet competition, and she'd told every single mother in his form. It was really embarrassing.

As he neared the car, she leaned back and opened the rear door for him.

'Jump in,' she said. 'Good day?'

'All right,' he muttered.

'Did anything happen?'

'No. What's for tea?'

'Hannah's doing it. Something special, I'm sure.' She backed the car smoothly out of its parking space, and out of the school drive. A few moments' silence elapsed.

Daniel stared doggedly out of the window. Andrew was reading a comic that he must have borrowed from someone at school. Daniel glanced at him.

'Can I read that at home?' he said, *sotto voce*.

'OK,' said Andrew, without looking up.

'What's that?' said their mother brightly.

'Nothing,' said Daniel. His mother hated comics; she said they should be reading books, even though she spent the whole time reading big shiny magazines with more pictures than words. He shouldn't have said anything; maybe she would look round and ask Andrew what he was reading. He sat very still and tried to think of something harmless to say. But it was no good.

'And so . . .' she said in a bright voice. Daniel looked out of the window; perhaps she wasn't talking to him. 'Daniel?'

'Yes?' he said discouragingly.

'Did you have Mr Williams today?' Perhaps he should lie. But that never worked. He went bright red and his voice shook and she always found out.

'Yes,' he said reluctantly.

'Oh good!' She turned round briefly to flash him a bright smile, and he felt the glow begin to fade. The whole point was that it was a *secret* glow. He stared at the passing houses and furiously remembered the exact smile Mr Williams had given him; the exact thrill of hearing his name out loud like that; the way Xander, his best friend, had looked at him—kind of casually impressed . . . But her voice cut through his thoughts inexorably, breaking them up and spoiling them. 'And did he say,' she paused to negotiate a roundabout, '. . . did he say anything to you about the scholarship class?'

———

By eight o'clock, Marcus was sick of the subject of scholarships. He had arrived home from work to find Anthea in a triumphant mood, even though, as far as he could make out, nothing had actually happened beyond some teacher at Daniel's school saying he could try for a scholarship. Well, big deal. It was hardly surprising, given the number of times Anthea had mentioned scholarships to Daniel's teachers. They must have realized their lives wouldn't be worth living unless they recommended Daniel for the scholarship class. She was completely obsessed by the idea. Marcus, meanwhile, was ambivalent, and resolved, almost unwillingly, to say something to her about it.

After supper, he made a jugful of strong, dark coffee—decaffeinated, at Anthea's insistence—and took it into the drawing-room. The boys had volunteered to help Hannah stack the dishwasher, which meant they could hang around the kitchen, breathing in illicit cigarette smoke and Radio One, Marcus shrewdly realized. He had to return to the kitchen for a jug of milk, and as he went in, he saw them both sitting on the kitchen floor reading comics—strictly forbidden by Anthea. Daniel jumped, with a startled, deer-like movement inherited from his mother. Andrew, meanwhile, looked up calmly from his copy of the *Beano*, ignoring his older brother's frantic signs, and said, 'Don't tell Mummy about the comics.'

'That's no way to talk!' chided Hannah, drying her hands on a cloth decorated with green apples. She draped it on the heated towel rail by the sink, pulled an elastic band from out of her hair, and let the furious, aubergine-coloured tangle descend slowly from its pony-tail, around her shoulders. A few plaited strands fell heavily around her face, weighted down by coloured beads. These had appeared after last year's Glastonbury Festival and had stayed put ever since.

'You know you're not supposed to read comics,' she continued. 'If your mum finds out, that's your own fault.'

'I told you,' whispered Daniel to Andrew, turning agonized eyes on his father. Marcus felt it was his turn to speak.

'Now, really, boys,' he said, trying to inject a tone of disapproval into his voice. 'What did Mummy say about comics?' Daniel hung his head, and half closed his comic, as if trying to hide the evidence.

'Well, can we just read them tonight?' Andrew looked engagingly at Marcus. 'I've nearly finished, but Daniel wants to read this one next.'

Marcus watched, half amused, half pained, as Daniel blushed pink at Andrew's words and looked down, fronds of dark hair falling over his forehead. He felt at a bit of a loss. As far as he was concerned, comics were utterly natural reading matter for boys of that age. At prep school, he'd been a keen subscriber to about five comics himself, he remembered. But he'd been over that particular argument enough times with Anthea to know that he was defeated. And, as a matter of principle, he backed up all her decrees to the children, whatever he thought of them.

Andrew was displaying not a morsel of guilt, he noticed. In fact, his eyes had dropped to the page again, as though to take in as much cartoonery as possible before it was confiscated and, as Marcus watched, he gave a little chortle. Daniel was also looking down, but miserably, clearly waiting for his father's wrath to fall. A flash of irritation crossed Marcus's mind. He really needn't cower on the floor like that, as if Marcus were about to hit him.

Then, almost immediately, the irritation vanished. He took in Daniel's bowed head, his resigned eyes, his ink-stained fingers. He'd probably had a hell of a day, what with all of this scholarship nonsense. A bit of comic reading was probably just what he needed.

'I'll tell you what,' he said. 'Just this once, as you've done so well, Daniel, you can finish the comic you're on before you go to bed. But that's all. And tomorrow you give them back to whoever gave them to you.'

'OK.' Daniel gave his father a sheepish smile. 'Thanks.'

'Thank you, Daddy,' said Andrew cheerily. 'Would you like to read them after us?'

'Er . . . no, thank you,' said Marcus, catching Hannah's eye. She grinned back at him.

'I'm taking the boys to school tomorrow. I'll make sure they're given back. Or thrown in the bin,' she added threateningly to Andrew.

'Thanks, Hannah,' said Marcus. 'Now, I came in for some milk . . .'

'Here you are.' Hannah reached over to the fridge. She handed him a carton.

'Thanks,' said Marcus. 'Actually . . .'

She sighed. 'I know. Put it in a jug.'

'Mummy hates cartons,' said Andrew conversationally.

'Yes,' said Marcus firmly. 'And so do I.' He ignored

Hannah's quizzical look, and took the porcelain jug of milk into the drawing-room.

The floor-length curtains were cosily drawn, and the lamps around the room gave out a warm light. Anthea was sitting on a yellow brocade sofa, frowning at a book entitled *Improve Your Child's IQ*. Her chin was cupped in one hand, and as she read, she unconsciously tapped her teeth with a palely manicured nail. As Marcus poured the milk into her coffee, he glanced over her shoulder. At the top of the page was a cartoon of a child and parent, grinning at each other over an open book. The caption read, *These reasoning exercises will help both parent and child develop their powers of argument.*

Marcus gave a little shudder. As far as he was concerned, Anthea's powers of argument were already quite developed enough. She'd always had a pincer-like mind, able to seize deftly on the flaws in her opponents' theories and demolish them with disconcerting ease. It had been one of the things that most excited him about her, back in the days when she was a rangy, long-legged, serious-minded undergraduate at Oxford. He'd taken her home gleefully to family parties, sat back, and waited for the heady thrill as he watched her throw back her long red hair, coolly look at whoever was speaking, and completely destroy their argument. Particularly when it was his cousin, Miles. Miles had been astounded by Anthea from the beginning. 'She's a bloody teenager!' he had exclaimed, the first time Marcus brought Anthea home to show off.

'Nearly twenty,' Marcus had replied, with a grin. 'She's young for her year. But very bright. Extremely bright, in fact.'

And that, of course, had been the attraction. Living in Silchester, settling down to his life as an estate agent in the family firm, doing everything that was expected of him, by his late twenties Marcus had begun to experience a discomforting feeling of mediocrity. A comfortable, provincial, well-heeled existence seemed to be all he was ever going to achieve. And, in some obscure way, this had worried him. With an enthusiasm he'd never felt as a student, he'd begun to visit London night-clubs at the weekend, take a few drugs, try to experience the intensity of life that he'd missed out on. And there he'd met Anthea: young and beautiful and clever, dancing at Stringfellow's with a crowd of undergraduates. With her pale face and long red hair, she'd attracted him even before he discovered what she did. And when she told him, matter-of-factly, that she was eighteen and a maths scholar at Oxford, a surge of excitement, of awe almost, had gone through him. Here was intellect. Here was excellence. The first time he'd visited Oxford, she'd arrived at her room late, from some function, and as he'd watched her running across the quad, long miniskirted legs emerging from a billowing black gown, he'd experienced a growing surge of sexual energy that he could barely control.

During the weeks and months that followed, he would sit in his dreary Silchester office, gazing out of the window, imagining her sitting in the Bodleian Library, surrounded by piles of books, or taking high-powered notes in a huge panelled lecture hall. When she took her finals, he drove up to Oxford every night to hear how her papers had gone; on the last day, he waited outside Schools with an enormous bunch of flowers and a diamond engagement ring.

'I'll move to Oxford so you can carry on with research,' he'd declared. 'Or London. Or the States. Wherever you want to go.'

'Really?' She eyed her newly sparkling left hand thoughtfully. 'I'm not sure yet what I want to do. Perhaps we could start off in Silchester and see what happens.'

'Of course,' he'd replied heartily. 'Great idea.'

And so Anthea moved into Marcus's house in Silchester, and for a couple of years they kept up the charade that she was carrying out important maths research from home. Marcus took out subscriptions to a number of weighty pure mathematics journals which he left lying around prominently in the drawing-room, bought a sophisticated computer system, and frequently referred to Anthea's work in conversation. But it was apparent even from the first week that she wasn't really interested.

It now struck Marcus that she'd never actually been interested in the subject at all. Her aim had simply been to be the best in the year; achieve the highest marks; beat her contemporaries. Mathematics had only been a vehicle for success. And when the spirit of competition was taken out of her work, it ceased to appeal. Now she never referred to maths except in the context of the boys' homework.

She looked up as Marcus poured the milk into her coffee, and smiled. Her hair, still auburn but tinted slightly darker than its natural colour, was cut short in an elfin crop which had dismayed Marcus as soon as he'd seen it. Especially as she had given him no warning that she was to have it done. That was six months ago, and the sight of it still sometimes upset him. He couldn't explain why it affected him so much, to think of that lovely hair lying on the floor of the hairdresser's salon; to see Anthea's thin neck exposed suddenly to view. But after that initial, debilitating argument, he hadn't mentioned it again, except to reaffirm how much he liked it, now he'd got used to it.

'I told the boys it was OK to read a comic before bed,' he said, as soon as he had sat down. He knew there was no point expecting the boys to be discreet and not tell their mother. Andrew, in particular, would no doubt be bubbling over with the doings of Dennis the Menace when they went in to say good night.

'Really?' Anthea's skin was so thin and fair that, although she was still young, every slight frown produced the thinnest of lines on her brow. 'Where did they get them from?'

'Someone at school.' Marcus tried to downplay the matter. 'Anyway, it's good news about Daniel, isn't it?' As soon as he said the words, he realized he didn't mean them. 'Although I was wondering,' he continued, feeling his way cautiously, 'whether there was actually any need for him to sit a scholarship. I mean, we don't really need the money, and it seems to be an awful palaver.'

'Honestly, Marcus.' Anthea's voice snapped at him; too high pitched and defensive to be entirely natural. Marcus suddenly wondered whether she had been expecting him to say something like this. 'The money's not the point. It's the achievement. It'll set him up for life. A scholarship to Bourne. How many people can put that on their CV?'

'Yes, well, I'm sure Daniel will have quite enough on his CV by the time he's finished without scholarships here, there and everywhere,' said Marcus.

'Bourne College isn't here, there and everywhere,' retorted Anthea. 'It's one of the most prestigious public schools in the country.'

'I do know that,' said Marcus testily, suddenly feeling like an irate old man. 'I did go there myself.'

'Well then.'

'But I didn't have a scholarship. I didn't need a scholarship.'

There was a short silence, during which Anthea pointedly said nothing.

'Look,' said Marcus eventually, in calmer tones, 'I just want what's best for Daniel. If that means him trying for a scholarship, well, fine. But I think he's under enough pressure as it is.' He paused, then generously said, 'We should both try to lighten up a bit.' As soon as he said it, he knew it was a mistake.

'Oh, don't pretend you really mean that,' snapped Anthea. 'What you really mean is I should lighten up a bit.'

'No,' protested Marcus weakly.

'What would you know about what's best for Daniel? You've no idea how hard it is out there, how important it is to be able to compete in the world. You've never even had to find yourself a job, have you?'

'Well, no,' admitted Marcus. *And neither have you*, he refrained from adding. 'I just don't want to see Daniel get into a state about it,' he said instead. 'You know what he's like. Gets worried about everything.'

'Yes, well, there's no need for him to get worried,'

said Anthea shortly. 'Not if he does all the work he's supposed to. He's a very clever boy. You don't seem to appreciate that.'

'I do,' said Marcus indignantly. 'I'm sure he can get a scholarship anywhere in the country if he wants to. I'm very proud of him,' he added, in gentler tones. He drained his coffee, stood up, and reached for the cafetière. Anthea gave him a half-smile as he poured more coffee into her cup, a sign of temporary reconciliation.

And as he sat down again, he realized that it would be really quite irrational to expect Anthea to behave in any other way. Her academic success; her scholarship to Oxford; all the things that had attracted him to her in the first place, had been achieved with exactly the pushy determination that she was now displaying over poor old Daniel. It would be impossible for her to act otherwise. And in many ways, it would make all of their lives easier—at least in the short term—if he were just to leave her to get on with it.

CHAPTER THREE

A week later, Alice finally remembered to bring up the subject of the school skiing trip, which had been mentioned at assembly on the first day of term. She was eating breakfast in her school uniform at the time, sitting uncomfortably on a chrome and mock-leather stool in the tiny kitchen above the tutorial college.

It was a grim little room, with an ancient brown lino floor, grey-doored units and no space for a table. Really, it would have been more sensible for them all to take their breakfasts next door to the sitting-room, where at least there was a small dining table. But, as a family, Alice, Liz and Jonathan were used to breakfast in the kitchen. At Russell Street, there had been a big pine table and comfortable wicker chairs. Here, there was none, so they unquestioningly arranged themselves every morning on whichever stools and surfaces were to hand. Jonathan had taken to wedging himself in beside the fridge, from where he could reach the toaster on the peeling Formica counter opposite. He was a prodigious breakfast-eater, cramming in as many as eight or ten slices of toast every morning—and still, as Liz often complained, keeping his thin, bony shape. Alice had inherited his skinny figure, and ate similar effortless quantities of food. Liz, on the other hand, was getting quite concerned about the width of her hips. This morning, she was leaning against the sink, carefully munching a banana, and trying not to exclaim as Alice helped herself to another huge bowl of cereal.

It was as she poured milk over her second lot of Grape Nuts that Alice remembered about skiing. Closing the carton, she suddenly said, with no preamble, 'Can I go skiing with the school? It's in January,' and began spooning cereal into her mouth. She had no particular desire to go skiing, which she imagined, rather abstractly, to be an effortless and boring slide down a hill. But they had been told to ask their parents about it, so she did. Jonathan put another piece of bread in the toaster and looked at her.

'Is it very expensive, Alice?'

'Six hundred pounds.' Jonathan drew in his breath sharply.

'Well, we'll have to see,' he said. 'Mummy and I will talk about it. You know we haven't got an awful lot of money at the moment. But if you really want to go—'

'What do you mean?' Liz's voice cut across his. 'What's there to talk about? It doesn't matter if she wants to go or not; we can't afford it. Sorry, Alice.'

'OK,' said Alice.

'We may be able to, for something special.' Jonathan raised meaningful eyes to Liz's. He looked exhausted, she thought. And she felt shattered herself. The first week of term at the Silchester Tutorial College had been a frantic round of lessons, administrative hiccups, meetings with parents, and unforeseen hassles.

'Don't be silly, Jonathan. We haven't got a spare six hundred pounds. And a skiing holiday is hardly a priority at the moment.' Jonathan ignored her.

'Are all your friends going?' he asked Alice. Alice shrugged.

'Dunno.' She wasn't entirely sure who her friends were, now Genevieve wasn't there any more. At the moment she was spending her break-times hesitantly hanging out with the crowd that she and Genevieve had sometimes dabbled in. But really, they'd been Genevieve's friends, not hers. And she was beginning to think she might prefer to go around with a couple of the others. But their set was already pretty much established. And she wasn't part of it. It was all a bit difficult.

'This could be a real opportunity for Alice,' Jonathan was saying to Liz.

'Rubbish,' said Liz brusquely. 'An opportunity to learn how to ski? Send her to a dry ski slope, then.'

'S'all right,' said Alice. 'I don't really want to go. I just thought I'd tell you.'

'It won't be like this for ever,' Jonathan said to Alice, in what seemed to Liz an unnecessarily weary-sounding voice. 'I promise, you'll be able to go skiing next year. When we've sold the house.' He shot a look at Liz. 'Or whatever it is we're doing with it.'

'You know perfectly well what we're doing with it,' said Liz, in a voice which sounded more assertive than she felt. 'We're letting it out until the market picks up.'

She stopped, and racked her brains for something else to say. Every time they talked about letting out the house, she tried to recall the confident phrases which that nice estate agent had used; tried to think of words which would inspire Jonathan with the same enthusiasm for the plan. But they seemed to have vapourized, leaving her with only the bare facts to cling to. They were going to let the house out. Beyond that, nothing. She had heard no word from the estate agent since their first meeting; the tenants whom he had promised had so far failed to materialize. Even she was beginning to have sneaking doubts about the project.

Jonathan was deliberately silent. He took a piece of toast from the toaster, and began to butter it carefully. Liz watched in mounting exasperation. Eventually she could bear it no longer.

'Stop looking like that!' she exclaimed.

'Like what?'

'Like, I'm not going to say anything, even though I'm thinking what an idiot my wife is.'

'I'm not thinking that,' protested Jonathan.

'Well then, what are you thinking?'

'I'm going to school now, all right?' interrupted Alice quickly. She pushed back her chair with a speedy urgency and, without looking either of her parents in the eye, clomped out of the kitchen.

'All right,' said Liz, momentarily deflected. 'Have a nice day, darling,' she called to Alice's retreating back.

'We shouldn't argue like that in front of Alice,' said Jonathan, when they'd heard the front door slam below.

'Nonsense, she's fine,' said Liz. 'We're not arguing,

anyway. We're having an animated conversation. Which you're trying to get out of.'

'I'm not trying to get out of it,' said Jonathan. 'It's just—'

'What?'

'Well, this business of renting out the house. I mean, you just come back here and announce that's what we're going to do, without bothering to ask me, or talk about it, and you know, that's fine by me, as long as it works out.'

'But?' Her voice sounded rattled to her own ears.

'But, well, it doesn't seem to be working out so far. I mean, does it? Here we are, after more than a week, and we haven't heard anything. Where are these famous tenants you said the agent had up his sleeve?'

'I don't know. I expect he's working on it.' Liz stood up with a sudden movement and began piling bowls and plates together with angry little clashes. 'I'll ring him this morning, all right? Or do you want me to call the whole thing off?'

'No, no, of course not!' Jonathan spread his hands in a self-deprecating manner. 'I mean, what the hell do I know about it? It just seems to me that we should be either trying to sell the house or renting it out, and at the moment we're doing neither. But I'm sure you're right. I'm sure it'll get sorted out before long. Still, it might be an idea to ring the agent. He's probably put our details at the bottom of his pile.' He gave her an encouraging smile, and began to clear away the breakfast things.

Oh, blast you, Jonathan, thought Liz, watching him calmly stack the plates up, put the cereal packets in their cupboard, run a cloth over the Formica counter. She turned away to the sink, began to run the hot tap into the washing-up bowl and squirted a long, thick stream of washing-up liquid under it; then plunged her hands into the scalding water in an obscure need for some sort of penance. Why do you have to be so bloody reasonable all the time? she thought to herself crossly. Why can't you shout and yell and get angry? And, more to the point, why on earth do I always have to be such a stroppy old cow?

At the first opportunity she got that morning, she dialled the number of Witherstone & Co. It seemed almost presumptuous to ask for Mr Witherstone himself. But she didn't want to risk being put through to the dreadful Nigel again.

'Which Mr Witherstone?' asked the receptionist, in an unhelpful voice. Liz, standing in the cramped office of the tutorial college, was momentarily flummoxed.

'I'm sorry, could you—'

'Mr Miles Witherstone or Mr Marcus Witherstone?' Liz thought furiously. She knew it began with an M. But that didn't get her very far.

'Marcus, I think,' she said eventually.

'I'm afraid Mr Marcus Witherstone is out of the office this morning,' said the receptionist immediately, in tones, Liz was sure, of some triumph. 'Would you care to leave a message?'

'Yes please,' said Liz robustly. 'Could you say that Mrs Chambers called regarding her property in Russell Street, wondering if any tenants had been procured yet.' She gave the number of the tutorial college, and put the receiver down, feeling pleased with herself. The use of the word 'procured' had been especially satisfying. And now she could stop feeling guilty about the house. It wasn't her problem any more; it was Marcus Witherstone's.

Marcus was at that moment driving along the main road of Collinchurch, the village in which Leo Francis lived. He had begun his journey that morning with a brisk feeling of adrenalin at the thought of his meeting with Leo. This, however, had faded away during the rigours of negotiating the Silchester ring road, to be replaced eventually by a growing sensation of panic.

He could scarcely believe he was really doing it. Taking up Leo's carefully worded invitation; agreeing implicitly to . . . what? As his mind scanned vaguely over any number of possibilities, he felt a tremor run through him, a blurred feeling of fear pierced by sharp exhilaration. And, already, guilt. Even though he hadn't set foot in Leo's house yet; hadn't even listened to what he had to say. He was, so far, innocent.

Except that he'd already lied to Miles. Trusting, honest Miles, who had asked Marcus to have lunch with him that day. He'd asked in a conciliatory way, which meant that he felt bad at having brushed Marcus off so peremptorily the week before. He'd suggested Le Manoir. He'd intimated it would be his treat. And Marcus, who usually jumped at Le Manoir and, on principle, never turned Miles down, had panicked.

'Sorry, Miles. I'm seeing a client. That rental case I told you about. Another time, perhaps?' And he'd put the phone down, shaking slightly. Now he winced at the memory. Why the fuck had he said that? Why not admit he was meeting Leo Francis? An informal meeting between two local professionals: estate agent and solicitor. Nothing could be more respectable.

Except . . . except. Oh God. A twinge of anticipation rose in Marcus, filling him with a mixture of horror and delight. Was he really doing this? Marcus Witherstone, of Witherstone's? Better not think about it. Better just get there, and have a stiff drink or two.

It was now three months or so ago that Leo had sidled up to Marcus, at a rather dull party, and murmured a few discreet, ambivalent phrases into his ears. Phrases whose meaning could be taken in either of two ways. Phrases which Miles, for example, would have deliberately—or even unknowingly—misunderstood.

Marcus, however, was not Miles. Nothing like Miles. He'd listened to Leo's bland, innocuous, double-sided words, then, playing for time, put his glass to his lips. It occurred to him that if the rest of the guests present knew what Leo was indirectly proposing, they would be shocked. Horrified, even. And part of him was also shocked at Leo's seedy suggestions. Of course, he knew this kind of thing went on, but he had never really thought he would come across it. It was the sort of thing other people did. Not respectable professionals like himself.

But that, of course, had been part of the appeal. The idea that he could combine the safe, predictable veneer of a well-established, middle-aged estate agent with something more dangerous, more lucrative, more exciting in every way. Or at least less boring. For life at Witherstone's was, Marcus had suddenly realized, clutching his drink and taking in the implications of Leo's words, boring him beyond belief. He had done all the learning he was ever likely to do; he had tried out all the new plans and ideas he was ever likely to think of. His position was safe; his work not arduous; he was able to pick and choose his clients. There was nothing to aim for; nothing new to try.

Impetuously, he had swallowed his mouthful of wine, turned to Leo, and in a suitably muted voice, murmured, 'I'm extremely interested in what you're saying.' He hadn't actually winked, but he'd certainly given the air that he knew what was going on; that he was a man of the world. And for the rest of the party, he had gone around the room with high spirits and a kind of internal swagger.

Of course, by the next morning, both the high spirits and the swagger were gone, and he was inclined to think he had entirely misconstrued Leo's invitation. He almost felt tempted to tell Anthea the whole story; probably would have done, if he hadn't been convinced she would completely miss the point. And as the weeks passed, and he heard nothing from Leo, he'd persuaded himself that the whole thing had been utter fantasy on his part.

But it wasn't fantasy. It was actually happening. Oh God. It was actually happening.

As he neared Leo's house, Marcus could feel himself almost involuntarily slow the car down, until it was proceeding at a ridiculously snail-like pace. A young mother pushing a pram on the pavement opposite overtook him, and gave him a curious look as she passed. Shit. He was drawing attention to himself.

'Fuck off,' said Marcus quietly. 'Don't look at me.' He pushed his foot down on the accelerator and sped past her, only to brake immediately as he saw the gates to Leo's house on his left. He signalled, with unnecessary diligence, and slowly turned into the drive, crackling the gravel satisfactorily underwheel as he descended the incline into Leo's forecourt.

He got out of the car and slammed the door shut with what he hoped was a hearty gesture. He took a deep breath and gave a confident smile to his reflection in the glass. Then, as he turned round to stride jauntily to the front door, he saw the girl with the pram peering at him from the other side of the road. His heart began to beat a notch faster.

He gave the girl a craven smile, and she immediately began to push the pram away. Marcus turned and walked, rather flustered, to the house. He wanted to get inside as quickly as possible. As he rang the bell, he tried to stand as close to the heavy wooden door as possible, as if somehow to blend into it. A couple of dogs barked warningly from the recesses of the house; gradually the tapping of feet became audible. Then the door was flung open.

'Marcus!' Leo's cry of welcome seemed indecently loud, and was augmented by the welcoming yelps of two English setters which began to frolic about Marcus's knees. The whole ménage immediately filled Marcus with dismay, and he found himself shrinking very slightly back into his jacket. But Leo seemed to notice nothing amiss. He held out his pudgy hand in greeting, and, as they shook, gave Marcus the slightest of winks. Marcus forced himself to grin knowingly back.

'I thought we might as well be comfortable,' said Leo, as he led the way down a flagstoned corridor. 'Come on in.' They entered a large, bright sitting-room, and Leo gestured to a couple of dark green button-backed chairs. Marcus looked apprehensively around. At one end of the room was a long row of windows looking onto the street.

'Sit down,' said Leo cheerily. 'I've asked my daily to bring us some coffee.'

Marcus sat down, gingerly, on one of the chairs. This was not at all how he had imagined their meeting. He had envisaged a small, discreet room, tucked far away from the eyes of the outside world, preferably locked and bolted before they began talking. Here, in this large, exposed room, he felt vulnerable and uneasy.

'So,' he said, more abrasively than he had intended. 'What's this all about?' As he spoke, he glanced involuntarily towards the window. The sooner this meeting was over, and he was out of the house, the better. He turned back, and stared at Leo, willing him to start talking.

But Leo, sitting on the opposite chair, simply smiled, and placed the tips of his fingers carefully together. He was younger than Marcus by about five or even ten years, but corpulent and already middle-aged looking. Sandy curls waved around his pink face, and as Marcus watched him, his full lips drew back in a smile, revealing small, pearly teeth.

'Well now,' he said eventually. His voice was high, with fruity overtones, and seemed to bounce around the bare-boarded room. There was a moment of silent anticipation.

I could just leave, thought Marcus. I could just get

up, quickly, before Leo says another word, tell him I'm ill, forget the whole thing. He tried experimentally to move his leg, to flex his muscles as if preparing for a quick departure. But his whole body seemed comfortably weighed down in the chair, heaped with inertia. And as he leaned back again resignedly, watching Leo's complacent smirk, temporarily closing off his professional conscience, he became aware of a new sensation. Right in the base of his stomach, almost hidden underneath the murky layers of unease and guilt, began to thump a small, bright beat of excitement.

That day, Alice had a double free period after lunch. She was supposed to spend it in the senior library, doing her prep and starting on her background reading lists. The week before, because they were now starting their GCSE courses, they'd all spent a lesson being shown how to use the library by sixth-formers. The teachers had chosen the most lumbering, conscientious prefects for this task, who had explained laboriously how to use the filing system, and what to do with returned books. While she trailed around, pretending to listen, Alice had seen girls sitting at each gleaming wooden table, writing out neat essays, or frowning over lists of vocabulary. The atmosphere had been tranquil and ordered and obviously designed to be conducive to work. But that was all wrong for Alice. She liked doing her homework curled up awkwardly on the floor in her bedroom, or at the kitchen table with the radio on, or, best of all, in front of the television, so that any free moments between writing or working out problems could be spent looking at something interesting, not just the wall.

Besides, only the real losers did what they were supposed to and went to the library. A gaggle from her year spent all their free periods behind the trees at the end of the rounders pitch, sitting on the leaves and whispering and smoking. Another lot would bunk off and go to the nearest McDonald's. They'd already once been frog-marched back to school by a teacher, but they still went. A few people went to the music study room, where you could listen to compact discs through earphones. They were supposed to be classical, but no one ever checked.

As Alice queued up for lunch with her tray, she considered each of these options. But none appealed. It wasn't so much doing those things, it was doing them with the people who did them. Alice pictured herself sitting on the leaves with Fiona Langdon flicking her hair everywhere, and shuddered. She would really have liked to hang out with a couple of girls who were in her English set. She didn't know them very well, because they were in the other form. But they seemed OK.

As she sat down with a plate of lasagne, an apple, and a glass of water, one of them, Charlotte, walked past.

'Hey, Charlotte,' said Alice, 'are you free after lunch?'

'No fear,' said Charlotte. 'Bloody double biology. Dissecting the worm.'

'Gross,' said Alice. Charlotte walked off to find a place, and Alice dug disconsolately into her lasagne with her knife.

She stared ahead, and munched, and eventually supposed that what she was feeling was lonely. *I'm lonely*, she thought to herself, with a certain gratification at having identified the experience. It had always surprised her that people gave names to feelings so easily. How did they know everyone felt the same?

She could remember once sitting in the back of the car on the way to a birthday party with jitters in her tummy, and saying, 'What's it called when you're not looking forward to something and you think it's going to be awful? What do you feel?' 'Depressed,' her mother had replied. So Alice had said, 'I feel depressed.' But of course she had meant she felt nervous. And for ages after that, whenever she felt nervous, she'd said, 'I feel depressed.' She couldn't remember when she'd discovered her mistake, but she must have done sometime.

And now she definitely felt lonely. She prodded around her feelings. Not bad enough to want to cry, but heavy-making around her head and eyes. What she felt like doing was curling up in front of the television, or better still in bed, with a cup of hot chocolate. Her thoughts circled comfortably around images of pampered cosiness at home, taking her briefly out of the school canteen clatter and bustle, into the sitting-room with a fire burning and a good film on the telly.

Then she realized her mistake. Stupid. She'd been thinking of Twelve Russell Street. But that wasn't home any more. Home was the Silchester Tutorial College. She pictured in her mind the small, dark, uninviting sitting-room in the flat above the tutorial school. Her grotty little bedroom, still cluttered with boxes of stuff. And all those awful classrooms downstairs.

She'd already made the mistake last week of going home during the day to pick up some music she'd forgotten. As she'd gone through the gate, she'd suddenly realized that the tutorial college would be in action, and they'd be having lessons everywhere. Before that, she'd only ever seen the classrooms empty, full of a musty holiday smell and posters peeling off the walls. But as she stealthily turned her key in the lock of the front door, she could hear voices and sense people everywhere. Behind the frosted glass of classroom doors, she could see blurred faces; from one she heard her own father's voice, intoning some Latin phrase. She had run quickly, quietly, and with a mounting sense of panic, up the stairs to the flat and into her own room, irrationally terrified of being spotted by someone, of having to explain her presence. Even though this was her own house.

Now she had taken to leaving the house in plenty of time every morning, so that she didn't risk overlapping with the arrival of any of the students or teachers. And in the afternoons she dawdled home, usually stopping off for a cigarette or two. Draining her glass of water, Alice felt for the reassuring cardboardy feel of her cigarettes in her pocket. She would go and have one on her own.

As Marcus drove back to Silchester, he felt invigorated and energetic. He sped along the motorway with the radio on loudly, humming along, slapping the steering wheel from time to time, and marvelling to himself how easy it was all going to be. The meeting with Leo had been a doddle. All he'd had to do was sit there, listening to Leo speaking. At intervals he'd given a nod, or made the odd affirming sound, but otherwise he had contributed practically nothing to the meeting. And yet now, after no particular effort on his part, he was firmly inveigled in an arrangement which, in all honesty, could only really be described as . . . as . . .

As the word 'fraud' flashed across his mind, he felt a small, predictable shock leap through his body, which he firmly quelled. It wasn't such a big thing, really. In fact, fraud was far too strong a word. It was just a business arrangement. Out of which he should do very nicely. On this one deal, he should make at least a couple of hundred thousand. Easy money.

But then, the money wasn't really the point—for either of them, Marcus suspected. Everyone knew Leo had been well set up on his father's death. And Marcus wasn't exactly short himself. It certainly hadn't been the thought of financial gain which had made him listen when Leo first made his invitation. And even now, thinking about the deal, it wasn't the money which excited him. It was the thrill. The novelty of the illicit. Anyone can play by the rules, he thought. But how many people have the brains, the nerve, the gall to do what he and Leo were planning?

As Marcus slowed down on the approach to the ring road, the whole car seemed filled with his thumping adrenalin. He'd actually done it. He'd said yes to Leo. He was into another world; a different league. The thought made him feel powerful and confident. Cosmopolitan and sophisticated. And energetic. Far too energetic to go back to the office. He felt like striding around a few fields. Or even striding around a property. Anything, rather than going straight back to provincial little Witherstone's.

The thought of sitting in his dreary office, leafing through interminable bits of paper, filled him with a sudden horror. And then, of course, there was Miles to consider. Miles, who would quite possibly come into his office that afternoon and ask how the meeting had gone. The so-called meeting with the client. At this thought, Marcus felt a stab of something that was suspiciously like alarm and he irritably shook his head. It was pathetic. A sophisticated player like him shouldn't worry about what his parochial cousin might think. He was above all of that, for Christ's sake; he was into a new league. Big business; his own boss; unaccountable to anybody.

But on the other hand, it might be useful to have some sort of story ready. Just in case. Marcus indicated, and pulled onto the ring road, trying to recall the details of the client he'd given as an excuse. The rental woman. Perhaps he could go and have a look at the house now. It was something he needed to do, anyway, having promised to look after her case. He couldn't remember her name, but he recalled perfectly the expression on her face when he'd volunteered to sort it out for her. She'd been so grateful, and he hadn't actually done anything about it. An irrational wave of guilt went through him, and he tried to remember where it was. Somewhere in West Silchester . . . His mind went blank.

But it would be on the updated property list he'd slung into his briefcase the night before. Leaving one hand on the wheel, he groped with the other for his briefcase, twisting his wrist awkwardly to open the clasps. He scrabbled for the paper, and eventually wrenched it out, a little crumpled. Diverting his eyes from the road, he scanned the list. He would recognize it when he saw it, he thought, running his eyes down the page. He would recognize it when . . . Yes! Twelve Russell Street. That was it. And, fortuitously, the turning was just ahead.

As he parked the car outside number twelve, Marcus thought he saw a smallish figure disappearing down the side of the house, towards the garage. He got out of the car, took a few steps forward and squinted at the passageway. But whoever it was had gone. Probably someone local taking a short cut. Or his imagination. He turned to survey the house itself. A rather nice family semi-detached Victorian villa. Not huge, but big enough. Big enough for Ginny Prentice and her husband, he was sure. And she'd definitely said she was thinking of renting a place in Silchester. There seemed no reason why she shouldn't take this house.

He pushed open the gate, and made his way cautiously up the garden path. He'd have to come back with the keys; have a proper look round. But at least now he could get an idea of the place. He walked slowly round, peering in through dusty sash windows. The predictable knocked-through double-purpose reception room, with two fireplaces, possibly period, possibly reproduction. Plain white walls; dark red carpet. Not bad. Round to the back, and a nice-sized kitchen. Harmless pine units; stripped wood floor extending out into the hall. No doubt there was a little study on the other side of the staircase. And upstairs there would be, what, two or three bedrooms. And a bathroom or two. In fact, probably only one bathroom, he decided. But that was OK.

He turned round and studied the garden. Grass and a few bushes. Nothing fancy. Still, that was ideal for renters. And a useful garage. He wandered over, and gave the door a hearty thump. The lock seemed to be broken, but the door still held surprisingly fast. The wood had probably got damp and stuck, he thought. They'd have to sort that out. And tidy the place up a bit. But from first impressions, the house seemed perfect. Perfect for Ginny and that actor husband anyway, he thought. He would phone her as soon as he got back to the office. It gave him something to take his mind off the other stuff, anyway.

Alice waited until she'd heard the car start up and drive away before she relaxed her position, braced against the garage door. She didn't know who had been poking around their house. But the idea that whoever it was had got so close to her without even realizing she was there gave her a certain satisfaction. She looked at her watch. Only twenty past one. She had until twenty past three. And no one even knew where she was.

CHAPTER FOUR

'"A desirable family residence, situated in a sought-after West Silchester street."' Ginny Prentice looked up from the piece of paper she was holding, and giggled. 'I'm sorry,' she said. 'But I don't think West Silchester is remotely sought after.'

'I bet it is,' said Piers. 'Among the lower echelons of society. You've spent too long talking to hacks at *Country Life*, that's your problem.' He leant luxuriously back on his chair, pulling the folds of his dressing gown around him, and took a sip of coffee from the hand-painted Italian mug in his hand. 'Go on, what else does it say?'

'"A spacious Victorian semi-detached house, benefiting from a large reception room and many period features. The property has a good-sized kitchen-breakfast room, three bedrooms and an attractive Victorian-style bathroom." Well, that doesn't sound too bad.'

'It sounds great,' said Piers. 'Let's take it.'

'"To the rear is a lawned garden, with several mature shrubs, and to the side is a single brick garage."'

'Great. Mature shrubs. Just the thing. Phone them up today and tell them we'll have it.'

'I'll tell them we'll *look* at it,' said Ginny in mock reproval. 'I've got to go down to Silchester on Tuesday for a meeting, anyway. You can come down too, and we can go round it.'

'I don't need to go round it,' said Piers nonchalantly. 'I know what it's like. Three bedrooms and a Victorian bathroom. It'll be one of those huge baths with claw feet and room for five people.'

'No it won't,' said Ginny. 'It'll be tiny and cream coloured, with gold taps and wood panelling.'

'Great,' said Piers. 'I love gold taps.' He grinned annoyingly at Ginny.

But Ginny was not in the mood for feeling annoyed. It was a bright, crisp October day, and she was feeling slim and energetic. And it looked as though they really were going to move to Silchester. She beamed at Piers, who was sitting languidly in the bay window of their *bijou* London kitchen in a pose she recognized from a production of *Les Liaisons Dangereuses* two years ago, and poured herself some more coffee. She was dressed for the office, in smart shoes, and tights, and a new amber-coloured suit, which went rather well, she thought, with her wavy blond hair. Piers, meanwhile, was attired for loafing. He would, Ginny knew, dress at some point in the morning, and with some care. But with an entirely free day stretching ahead of him, it was hardly reasonable, she supposed, to expect him to compress the dressing process into a snatched five minutes.

Ginny, on the other hand, had a full day ahead, conducting a big press trip to a new property development some way out of London. She snapped open her briefcase to check everything was in order: the agenda for the day, the list of journalists who had promised they would attend, the shiny press packs. She checked the pile of photographs, fanning them out quickly to check that each attractive feature of the development was represented. The landscaped gardens. The picture windows. The built-in fireplace seats.

Clarissa, her business partner, had been particularly scathing about the fireplace seats. She never touched modern developments, and couldn't understand how Ginny could bear to spend a day enthusing about them to the press.

'Little boxes, for little executives,' she'd mocked, in her tiny, clipped, baby voice. 'Full of drip-dry suits.' But Ginny had smiled, and looked at the pictures, and immediately conjured up an image of herself, the happy wife of just such an executive, keeping the carpet hoovered and making jam tarts and even wearing a flowered pinny. A nice, cosy, unexciting sort of life.

'It's not so bad,' she'd said to Clarissa. 'And they're a very good client.'

'Well, I don't know how you can,' said Clarissa.

'Neither do I,' said Ginny.

But Ginny did know. She knew that she had somehow a strange ability to find an attraction in almost any kind of residence, be it a tiny flat or a manor house. Confronted with the meanest little house, she was always able to construct in her own mind a charming hypotheti-

cal life there, imbuing on it a vicarious, often quite unde-
served appeal. Scores of journalists would listen
entranced as she stood at the gates of a dull rural development, painting a glowing picture of country family
life, or in a hard hat on the site of a derelict city ware-
house, enthusing about open-plan apartments and a London existence so fast-paced there was barely any need to
build in a kitchen. It was really, she supposed, a gift, this
ability of hers. And it made her ideally suited to a job in
property PR.

The Mozart stopped, and the pips began. Ginny came
to, with a little flurry.

'Right,' she said. 'I'm off.'

'Have a good one,' said Piers.

'I'll try,' Ginny said brightly. She'd given up asking
Piers what he thought he might do during the day. He'd
begun to think she was getting at him; they'd actually
had a row about it. She kissed him quickly, then stood
up straight, brushed down her jacket and checked her
tights for ladders.

'Ginny,' Piers said suddenly, catching her offguard.
He had an extraordinarily deep, resonant voice, which
he used to great effect in shops and in restaurants, causing old ladies to back away nervously and waitresses to
blush, and scribble more quickly.

'Yes?' she faltered. His voice still, ridiculously, could
make her feel quite lightheaded, even after four years of
marriage.

'Tell them we'll both be down to look at the house in
Silchester.' He grinned at her, and pushed his dark,
springy hair back off his forehead. 'I'd love to see it.'

'Oh, brilliant.' Ginny's natural enthusiasm bubbled over. 'It'll be a day out. We'll go and have lunch somewhere nice, shall we? I'll have to go into Witherstone's for my meeting, of course, but you'll be able to find something to do in Silchester, won't you?'

'I bloody hope so,' said Piers. 'If we're going to live there.'

Prentice Fox Public Relations was based in a tiny office in Chelsea, just about walking distance from the flat which Ginny and Piers were currently renting. As Ginny picked her way through the sodden autumn leaves on the pavement, she wondered how to break the news to Clarissa that she was looking at a house in Silchester on Tuesday. She had already warned Clarissa that she was thinking of moving out of London; that she'd had enough of the city; that she'd fallen in love with Silchester . . . but Clarissa had scoffed at her.

'You'll never move,' she'd asserted. 'You'd miss London too much.'

'But I spend half my time out of London anyway,' Ginny had pointed out. 'Nearly all the clients I look after seem to be in Silchester. Witherstone's is a really big account now, and there are those two property relocation companies near by.'

'What about Brinkburn's? They're in London. And what about all the journalists? They're all in London.'

'I know,' said Ginny. 'But I can always come up a couple of times a week. People commute from Silchester, you know. And, I mean, I could do all this equally well from home, couldn't I?' She gestured around the little office at the computer terminals, the filing cabinets, the piles of property details and press releases waiting to be sent out.

'But you can't just leave me!' wailed Clarissa. 'We're a team!'

'I know,' said Ginny, soothingly. 'And we still would be a team. I just wouldn't be here all the time. But anyway, don't worry about it. We probably won't go.'

Now she tried to prepare tactful phrases in her mind. There was no point trying to conceal from Clarissa the fact that they were going to see a house. Even if Witherstone's hadn't been a client of theirs, Clarissa would have picked it up in no time. Not for nothing was she one of London's foremost property PR consultants. She had generations of family connections with one of the country's biggest estate agents, an engaging manner and an ability to wheedle gossip out of people who barely realized they had anything interesting to relate. She was also one of Ginny's best friends and it would, Ginny realized, be a real wrench to leave their cosy office companionship and giggles.

But she couldn't spend the rest of her life giggling in an office. It was all right for Clarissa—she had a rich, cosseting father and a rich, cosseting husband, and a secure future mapped out. According to her, this included a baby at age thirty-two and another at thirty-four and an extra-marital fling at age thirty-six. 'To prove to myself I haven't lost it,' she'd explained to Ginny in her tiny, brittle voice. 'And to keep myself in shape.'

They'd shared a thirtieth birthday party the year before, at which Clarissa had confided to Ginny that she was seriously thinking of postponing the first baby until age thirty-three. Or even thirty-four. 'Then I'll have to have the fling at thirty-eight,' she'd said, swaying drunkenly on Ginny's shoulder. 'But that would be OK, wouldn't it?'

For Ginny, the future was certain only insofar as it existed within the four walls of her career. Several years of marriage to an actor had taught her that a steady job was not, after all, simply an interminable sentence of boredom; an endless dragging millstone to which all the tedious little people of the world chose to manacle themselves. It was a future; an income; in fact, it was a release.

For the two years before they'd married, Piers had been almost constantly in work. He'd followed a series of badly paid, well-reviewed plays with a stunning television success as Sebastian, the hapless upper-class recruit in the police series *Coppers*. It was a popular programme, and by the time of their wedding, he'd almost, but not quite, reached celebrity status.

But then Sebastian started to find police training too hardgoing, and eventually committed suicide. This, admittedly, came as no surprise to anyone, since it had been planned from the start—although it still grieved Ginny that they had not decided to make him a permanent fixture. But after leaving *Coppers*, Piers didn't know quite what to do. He was by now, as Malcolm his agent had explained to both of them, slightly too well known to do extra work, but probably not quite well known enough yet to be approached by producers. It might be best if he stuck to stage work for a while.

Which was all very well, thought Ginny, turning the corner into the street where her office was. But the little company that he'd always worked with had gone bust while he was playing Sebastian. There seemed to be no work around. The parts he did get were invariably terribly paid, or, even worse, profit share. And, for the last six months, there had been nothing at all.

Ginny was, she thought, entirely reasonable in her demands of life. She didn't particularly want to be rich. She didn't hanker after a huge flat in Knightsbridge like Clarissa's, or a flashy car, or a moneyed life of leisure. But she did want a house and a garden. And a few years at home, in which to have some children, and bring them up, and not feel that they couldn't still afford nice clothes and food and the odd treat. Other people seemed to be able to manage it, she pointed out to herself, as she mounted the steps to the front door of the building. Other people had houses, with lots of room, and loads of children and still went on holiday every year.

But then, other people, a small voice whispered in her ear, weren't married to actors.

By eleven o'clock, Piers had had a bath, got dressed in jeans and a T-shirt, and watched an hour of morning television. He was engrossed in a studio discussion on the subject of dangerous dogs when he heard the sound of the post thudding onto the hall floor. It was a sound which always foolishly made his heart leap, even though everything was done over the phone or fax these days.

He carefully strolled over to the pile, quickly established that there was nothing in it of any interest, and turned his attention to his weekly copy of *The Stage*. It was laughable to think there could be anything for him in it, of course, he thought, shaking it open. All the best parts were inevitably tied up, through the agent mafia in which his own agent, Malcolm, didn't seem to figure. The familiar thought that he should really try to get himself a new agent flew briefly through his mind and then vanished, leaving behind a vague, lingering loyalty to Malcolm. After all, Malcolm had got him the part in *Coppers*. But that was too long ago now. Far too long. And, really, someone like him shouldn't be having to scan the wanted columns at the back of *The Stage*.

To prove to himself that he wasn't really reading it for the advertisements, Piers carefully turned to the front of the paper and began reading an interminable account of an in-house Equity row. Even when the phone rang, he looked up as though in annoyance at having been disturbed, glanced down at the page again, and finally got up and went over to the phone, still holding the paper.

'Darling! Have you seen what I've seen?' It was the unmistakable voice of Duncan McNeil, the only friend from drama college that Piers had kept up with. Short and camp and excitable, he lived around the corner from Piers and Ginny, just as he had done when they lived in Islington and also when they lived in Wandsworth.

'It's the *zeitgeist*,' he had said plaintively, when they discovered he was planning to follow them for a third time. 'Something inside me just said, "It's time to move to Fulham." All the best people live there, you know.'

Now his voice was even higher and more agitated than usual.

'What are you talking about?' said Piers patiently.

'In *The Stage*. I take it you have received your requisite copy?'

'Yes. And?' In spite of himself, Piers felt his heart begin to beat more quickly. 'Is there something interesting?' he added casually.

'Well, if you're that blind, I'll have to come and point it out to you myself. See you in a sec.' The phone line went dead, and Piers turned feverishly to the back of the paper. He scanned each page of advertisements quickly, then turned back and scanned them all again. There was nothing remotely suitable for him. Fucking Duncan. This would be one of his stupid jokes.

The buzzer sounded, and he went to let Duncan in, feeling suddenly weary.

'What the fuck are you talking about?' he said sternly, as soon as Duncan's bullet-shaped head appeared round the door.

'Right here, dumbo.' Duncan took the paper and pointed to a large box in the centre of the page. 'All parts in new West End musical. Open audition next Monday and Tuesday.'

'Yes, and have you seen what it says here? Strong dancing required, bring shoes and music.' Duncan shrugged.

'Oh well, if you're going to believe everything they tell you . . . I thought I'd go along, anyway. I've never tried for a musical. It might be my forte.' Piers looked meaningfully at his plump frame.

'I thought you were serious,' he said accusingly.

'I was,' protested Duncan. 'I am. Well, half serious. Heaps of people in musicals can't dance, anyway. We could always just shuffle around at the back together . . . OK.' He broke off at the expression on Piers's face. 'I'm not entirely serious. Shall I make the coffee?'

'There's no milk.'

'OK then, shall I pay for coffee?'

The Italian coffee bar which they always went to was beginning to fill up with young mothers and pairs of elderly shoppers.

'Quick,' hissed Duncan in a penetrating whisper. 'Nab the window table before that old bat gets there.' A few moments later, he came over to join Piers, bearing two frothy cups of coffee. Draping his leather jacket and scarf creatively over the two spare chairs at the table, he sat down, took a sip, then looked up, his top lip covered in a white moustache.

'So, what's new?' he said.

'We're moving to Silchester.' In his annoyance with Duncan, the words came out more brusquely than Piers had intended. He and Ginny had deliberately refrained from discussing their Silchester plans with Duncan, reasoning that it might upset him, that he might try to dissuade them, and that, anyway, it might not happen. Probably wouldn't happen. Piers, in particular, was fairly ambivalent about the whole thing. Sometimes he thought it was all madness, to move away from London and the hub of the arts world; other times he imagined a carefree provincial existence, and reminded himself that they hardly ever went to the theatre in London anyway.

'What?' Duncan's voice cracked slightly, and he gazed at Piers with a shocked expression. Piers reminded himself furiously that Duncan had always been good at the ashen, innocent-betrayed look.

'It's not definite yet,' he said. 'But we're going down there to look at a house next week.'

'I see.' Duncan looked down miserably into his cup. Piers stirred his coffee awkwardly. Then Duncan looked up, with an expression of animation on his face.

'Did you say Silchester?' he said. 'How extraordinary. I was thinking to myself only yesterday that if I ever moved out of London, it would definitely be to Silchester. Don't you think that's curious?'

'Duncan . . .'

'Really, I've never believed in coincidences, but this one is just incredible. Don't you think?'

'Incredible,' said Piers, giving up. Time enough to tackle Duncan when the time came. If it ever came. He got up to get another two coffees and a pair of almond croissants. When he got back to the table, Duncan clearly had remembered some gossip.

'I take it you've heard about Ian Everitt?' he said, before Piers had even sat down.

'What about him?' The intense jealousy which Piers had once automatically experienced whenever their old classmate's name was mentioned had, over the years, fallen to a muffled pang. He could even watch him playing his part in the tri-weekly episodes of *Summer Street* without feeling his insides twist up in a morass of envy and regret and missed opportunity.

Ian Everitt was, like Piers, tall and dark and moderately good-looking. He had taken a tiny, short-term part in a fairly new soap opera, *Summer Street*, at about the same time that Piers had started on *Coppers*. But while Piers's part had blossomed and then withered, Ian's part had steadily grown and then been made permanent.

Summer Street was now the most popular soap in the country, and Ian Everitt had reached exactly the heights of stardom that Piers had so closely missed. But the worst thing of all was that Piers had himself been offered Ian Everitt's part and had turned it down for *Coppers*.

'Hollywood is calling his name,' said Duncan.

'What, films?'

'Apparently. Rumour has it they think he's going to be the next Hugh Grant.'

Piers snorted. 'Oh, right. Of course he is.' Duncan shrugged.

'He's leaving *Summer Street* in the spring.'

'What are they going to do? Kill him off?' Duncan was silent for a moment, chewing on a piece of croissant and running his spoon delicately around the rim of his cup.

'Apparently,' he said eventually, not looking at Piers, 'they're considering recasting the part.'

'Shit.' Piers gazed at Duncan for an incredulous second. 'Are you serious?'

'Word on the street. Or, rather, in the Duke's Head.'

'Oh shit. How can I find out?' There was a short silence, during which Piers gazed distractedly around the coffee shop. When he looked back at Duncan, he saw a small grin beginning to form at his lips.

'What's the joke?'

'I've just remembered something,' said Duncan airily. 'I always knew there was a good reason for reading *Rural House and Potting Shed*, or whatever it calls itself. Do you know where Ian Everitt's charmingly decorated Georgian country home is located?'

'Fuck knows.' Piers looked impatiently at Duncan for a few seconds. Then his expression changed. 'What? Not . . .' Duncan shot him a look of triumph.

'Of course,' he said. 'It's the *zeitgeist*. All the best people live in Silchester.'

CHAPTER FIVE

They had been running the tutorial college for nearly a month now, but Liz was still unsure precisely how she felt about it. She veered continually between a heady, sparkling feeling of power; of boundless energy and control—and a crushing conviction that the enterprise was far too ambitious; that it would ultimately overwhelm, sink and ruin them. On good days she strode about the building proprietorially, making confident snap decisions, speaking with a clear, well-articulated voice, marvelling at the way the place almost seemed to run itself, and even wondering whether they should not think eventually of expanding. On bad days she had to force herself out of the flat, into the exalted, exposed position that she occupied as co-principal, and longed to be, once again, a simple teacher; an employee, with a well-defined, limited remit and no responsibility outside the classroom.

Jonathan, meanwhile, kept an even keel. He had

matter-of-factly shouldered this project, for good or for bad, and he took each day as it came; neither reaching Liz's heights of rejoicing, nor sinking with her into her pits of despair. This evening, Liz was in rejoicing mood, after a particularly successful meeting with the modern languages tutors. Her eyes were flashing, her cheeks flushed with exhilaration. She had begun to peel the carrots for supper, but after she put the knife down for the third time in order to describe, with waving hands, her plans for a trip to Italy, Jonathan quietly took over.

He was filling the saucepan with water when the phone rang. Liz, in her freshly confident mood, didn't hesitate, but grabbed the receiver.

'Hello?'

'Mrs Chambers?' It was a male voice which she half recognized.

'Yes, speaking.' Was it one of the tutors? Or the students?

'It's Marcus Witherstone here. From Witherstone's.' Liz's heart gave a little jolt.

'Oh, hello,' she said, adjusting her voice to a more friendly pitch. She felt Jonathan raise questioning eyebrows at her, and for some reason, which she would think about later, she turned casually away from him. She shook back her hair and gave a little smile to the cork pinboard in front of her.

'I've got you some tenants.' He sounded animated and rather pleased with himself. 'Ginny and Piers Prentice. The couple I told you about.'

'How nice,' said Liz. She allowed herself to dart a triumphant look at Jonathan's back. 'That's wonderful news. When can they move in?' Jonathan swivelled

round, a surprised look on his face, but Liz turned
away again before he could catch her eye.

'Sooner than I thought,' Marcus was saying. 'Apparently they can leave their place in London in a couple
of weeks. And Ginny, the girl, will be in Silchester tomorrow. She wondered if we could meet to sign the
contracts and talk about furniture. We thought the best
place would be the house itself, some time in the afternoon.' Liz felt a lurch of disappointment. She was teaching all afternoon.

'Yes, that would be fine,' she found herself saying.
'Three o'clock. See you then.'

Without looking at Jonathan, she quickly dialled the
number of Beryl, an elderly languages tutor who only
worked mornings.

'Beryl? It's Liz Chambers. Listen, could you take a
couple of classes for me tomorrow afternoon? From
three o'clock. Something's come up. Yes, I'll fill you in
over lunch. Really? Oh, Beryl, that's great. Yes, of
course, usual rates. Of course. Bye!' She replaced the
receiver, and turned to face Jonathan.

'We've got tenants for the house.' She felt her eyes
glitter and her face flush.

'So I heard,' said Jonathan. 'That is good news.' He
went to the door. 'Alice!' he called. 'Come and lay the
table!'

'Is that all you can say?' demanded Liz. Her voice
sounded guiltily truculent to her own ears. 'After giving me all that pressure about where are these famous
tenants?'

'Of course not.' He turned back and grinned at her.
'I'm sorry I was a doubting Thomas. I take it all back.

Excuse me!' He reached past her to the shelf for the tomato ketchup, and Liz had a sudden urge to slap him. She stared at him, at his mild forehead, and narrow shoulders, and bony hands, and felt a mounting frustration fill her body with an unchannelled, pulsing energy.

The kitchen door opened, and Alice shuffled in. 'Hi,' she said, in a discouraging voice.

'Knives and forks, Alice,' said Jonathan. He opened the oven door and peered inside. 'Who wants two pieces of fish?'

There was silence. Alice sat down on the chrome stool and began to examine her fingernails. Liz turned her attention away from Jonathan's thin, jersey-clad back, and gave Alice a wide, motherly smile.

'Hello, darling,' she said. 'How was school?'

Alice pretended not to hear. She couldn't stand it when her parents started asking questions. And that was the stupidest question of all. What was she supposed to say? There was nothing about school that was of any interest, except things her parents wouldn't understand. She stared doggedly down, unconsciously grinding her teeth, waiting for the inevitable moment when she would have to give in, look up and reply.

'Alice?' Liz ruffled Alice's silky dark bob, and Alice tried not to flinch. 'We've had good news,' she said gaily. 'The agent's found someone to rent the house.'

'Oh, right.' As Alice spoke, she felt as though the words were being torn from her. She tilted her face very slightly away from Liz, so that there wasn't any danger of meeting her eye. Sometimes she felt as though she could hardly bear to occupy the same space as her parents.

'I'm going to meet them tomorrow,' Liz continued, in a too-loud voice. 'The tenants.'

'Tomorrow afternoon, wasn't it?' said Jonathan, carrying a jug of water past. 'You know, I don't have any teaching tomorrow afternoon. I could have gone. Alice, where are the knives and forks?'

'Really?' said Liz casually, watching Alice haul herself sulkily to her feet. 'Oh well, it's arranged now.'

The next afternoon, Liz twice found herself uttering complete gibberish to her students. When her first lesson was over, she dashed upstairs to the flat and threw her books down on the double bed in their gloomy bedroom. She went over to the window and stared at herself in the mirror. If she put on some make-up, she would look more attractive. But she might also look as if she'd made too much of an effort. Visions of well-groomed women who thought nothing of wearing full make-up every day went through Liz's mind in quick succession, as though gliding past on a catwalk. But she had left it far too late in life to join their ranks. And, more practically, it was already ten to three. For a panicked instant she stared, immobilized, at her reflection. Her face was full of rosy colour, at least. And she had put in her contact lenses. And her hair would look all right if she gave it a quick brush in the car before she got out.

But as she turned into Russell Street, she saw the estate agent already leaning against the gate of number twelve. He peered at her car, then gave a cheery smile. Liz smiled back, and hoped he couldn't see her hairbrush lying on the front seat. She parked neatly and quickly in front of the house in a series of familiar manoeuvres, lining herself up instinctively with the end of the brick wall that bordered their garden; opening the car door with automatic care, to avoid bashing it against the steeply rising pavement. Everything looked the same, she thought, getting out. It was almost as if she'd never left. Except that in front of her, gleaming obtrusively, was an expensive-looking Mercedes. And there, beside it, was Marcus Witherstone. He was holding a bottle of champagne.

'Hello, Mr Witherstone,' said Liz. She closed the car door and tried briefly to assess her appearance from a fleeting reflection in the window.

'Please, do call me Marcus,' he said, giving her his crinkle-eyed smile. Liz smiled back nervously.

'And I'm Liz,' she said, forcing herself to let go of the car door handle and walk forward naturally. A sudden picture of herself and Marcus standing together in the street popped into her head, and for the first time in her life she wondered what the neighbours would think if they were watching. Certainly, she felt very noticeable. The street seemed strangely empty, and her voice sounded thin and high to her own ears. She looked hurriedly away from Marcus and up at the house.

'Well, this is it,' she said.

'Yes,' said Marcus, kindly. 'I suppose it's a bit strange for you, letting out your old family home.'

'Well, yes,' said Liz. 'But it's better than selling it . . .' She stopped, and blushed, suddenly remembering her outburst at the hapless Nigel. 'I mean, we really did have to do something with it. But I prefer it this way.' She gave Marcus a hesitant smile. 'It was very good of you to fix all this up.'

'Not at all!' Marcus waved the champagne bottle at her cheerfully. 'All part of the service.'

'But finding tenants so quickly!'

'No trouble.' He smiled at her, an easy, relaxed smile, and Liz gazed back in admiration. She wanted him to keep talking; to transfer some of his effortless assurance to her; infuse her with the same airy confidence. He was holding his bottle of champagne with an impressive casualness; no doubt he would be the sort to open it with one deft movement and not a drop spilled.

Marcus saw Liz's eyes on the bottle, and gave a start of recollection.

'What am I doing still holding this?' he exclaimed. 'It's for you!' Liz's fingers closed over the cold bottle neck in bewilderment. 'It's a new custom at Witherstone's,' he explained. 'A bottle of champagne for every sale.'

'But . . .'

'In your case, since we failed so dismally on the selling front, I thought this could count.'

'Goodness!' Now Liz felt even more noticeable. Russell Street wasn't the sort of place where champagne bottles passed without comment. Nor strange men in expensive cars. You're being ridiculous, she told herself. He's not a strange man, he's an estate agent. She eyed Marcus surreptitiously. But in his smooth tweed jacket and polished shoes, he looked nothing like an estate agent. He had resumed his leaning position against the gate, eyes narrowed against the wind. From where Liz was standing, his broad shoulders obscured completely her view of the front door. His hand rested confidently on the front wall. She didn't quite dare look at his face.

A few moments' silence passed, and Liz began to feel awkward. She cast around in her mind for something to say.

'That's a very smart car,' she ventured at last, then immediately chastised herself. *Oh what a boring, unsophisticated remark.* But Marcus turned and looked at his car in agreeable surprise, as though he'd never really noticed it before.

'Nice model, isn't it?' he said. 'I do prefer it to the new one, I think.' He looked questioningly at her, as if expecting her to disagree. But Liz was stumped by the subject of car models. She transferred the freezing-cold bottle from one hand to the other and wondered what she could say next.

'I wonder where Ginny is.' Marcus looked at his watch and smiled apologetically at Liz. 'I'm sorry to keep you hanging around like this. If you'd rather go, and leave it to another day, I'm sure Ginny would understand.'

'Oh no,' said Liz breathlessly. 'I mean, I might as well wait, now I'm here.' She looked at her own watch. 'It's only quarter past.' She put the champagne bottle on the pavement and rubbed one icy palm against the other. Despite the over-bright sunshine, the afternoon air was getting colder and colder, and a chill breeze had begun to blow. 'But if you like,' she added slowly, 'we could always go and wait inside the house.'

'Of course we could! Why didn't I think of that?' Marcus suddenly took in Liz's ungloved, chafing hands.

'You look freezing!' he exclaimed. 'I'm terribly sorry, keeping you out here. Of course we should be waiting in the house.' He pushed open the gate and led the way up the path.

Liz groped in her pocket for the doorkey. She felt automatically for the ridges as she pulled it out, put it in the lock and heaved up before turning in one, seamless, unthinking movement. The door swung open with the familiar creaking moan that she'd stopped noticing years ago; the smell of floorboards came rushing out at them, and Liz, to her utter horror and surprise, burst into tears.

At four o'clock, Alice came silently into the kitchen, opened the fridge and took out a yoghurt. She reached past Jonathan, who was pouring out a cup of tea, to get a spoon from the drawer, and he jumped in surprise.

'Alice! Just in time for tea.'

'I hate tea.' Alice hovered noncommittally by the door, unable to decide whether the indignity of staying in the kitchen with Jonathan was worse than the aloneness of taking her yoghurt off to her bedroom. She watched as he carefully poured milk into his cup, put the bottle back in the fridge and wiped the surface with a jay-cloth. Both her parents, she had noticed, were always cleaning this kitchen, and sweeping crumbs off the floor and arranging the mugs neatly. As if they could make it look any nicer by keeping it tidy. In their old kitchen at Russell Street, everything had just mounted up in a cheerful profusion until someone decided to clear up, usually Jonathan. But then, even when that kitchen was tidy, it had always been full of stuff; of plants and books and

Oscar's basket and his toys all over the floor. There was only room for one plant in this kitchen, and that was already looking pretty dismal.

Jonathan turned round and smiled.

'You're home early.' Alice chose to take this as an accusation.

'No I'm not.'

'Home by four?' Alice rolled her eyes and sighed loudly.

'I had a free lesson. We're allowed to go home. I can show you my timetable if you don't believe me.'

'Of course I believe you.' Jonathan carried his tea through into the sitting-room, and Alice followed, unwillingly, at a distance.

'A free lesson,' mused Jonathan, sitting down on the sofa, next to a pile of essays. 'How can it be called a lesson if it's free time?'

'Lesson,' said Alice, through gritted teeth. 'Lesson. Like, lesson on a timetable. Not lesson where you learn things.'

'I see,' said Jonathan. 'But you do have some lessons where you learn things, I take it?' He gave her an amused smile.

'Of course we do.' Alice gave her father a scathing look. Sometimes he behaved as if she was still about nine.

'And tell me, how's your Greek going?' Alice spooned yoghurt into her mouth, and thought of her Greek lessons, of the strange symbols and rhythmic incantations. *Alpha, beta, gamma, delta.* She had only been doing the subject since the beginning of the term, but already she was enchanted by it. Her teacher had marked her first piece of homework Very Good, and said in class, 'Do give my regards to your father, Alice, and tell him I think you're doing very well.' But the thought of relaying any such message filled Alice with a horrified embarrassment. She shrugged her shoulders and looked away.

'S'all right,' she said, and scraped noisily at the bottom of the plastic pot. When she had finished, she leant back on the sofa and reached for the television remote control.

'You will throw that pot away, won't you?' said Jonathan.

'Yes,' said Alice irritably. Why did he have to tell her? Why couldn't he have just waited and seen if she threw it away herself? She flicked on the television, and a cheery voice greeted her fractionally before the picture cleared to show a man with blond hair wrestling with a furry puppet.

'And now,' he gasped to the camera, 'it's quarter-past four, and time for *Nina's Gang*.' The screen was filled with psychedelic graphics, and a loud guitar riff began to wail. Jonathan winced slightly, and got up.

'Quarter-past four,' he said. 'I expect Mummy's on her way home.' He bent down, and picked up the yoghurt pot. 'I'll go and make some more tea.'

Liz was not on her way home. She was sitting on the floor in her old bedroom, propped up against the wall. On one side of her was the champagne bottle, now half empty. On the other side of her was Marcus.

It was Liz who had insisted on opening the bottle.

Although her tears had only lasted for a momentary flurry, she still felt upset and shaky as she walked around the house, explaining in a wobbly voice that they'd left the pine table behind because there was no room for it at the tutorial college, and that the cat flap had been for their tabby, Oscar, but they'd given him away when they moved.

'And this is our bedroom,' she'd said, opening the door onto a sunny room at the front of the house, with a large square mark in the middle of the carpet to show where their double bed had rested. 'Was our bedroom.' She squinted at the shafts of light which pierced the dusty air, and landed on the dark red carpet in pools of pink. 'We took our bed with us,' she explained, unnecessarily. 'There was one in the flat already, but we didn't want to leave ours behind.'

'I'm not surprised,' said Marcus. 'I think a bed is the most important piece of furniture in a house.' It was almost the first thing he'd said since entering the house, and as he listened to his words hanging in the still, empty air, he had a sudden strange feeling of surrealism. This appointment was not turning out the way he had expected.

First there had been the tears at the door. Then she had composed herself, but seemed to want to tell him all about the house. He had followed Liz patiently from room to room, listening to her halting, irrelevant explanations; building up a picture of what their family life in this house must have been like. And now, from what he could gather, they were squashed into some appalling little space at the top of that tutorial college. No wonder the poor woman was upset.

'Why did you do it?' he asked abruptly. 'Move away from here?'

'We had to,' said Liz. She turned to him. 'It was too good an opportunity to miss,' she said, with more energy in her voice. 'We've got the chance to really make something of that place. It's got such potential. We're going to expand into modern languages, run courses in the holidays, gradually do the place up so it looks really smart . . .' She ran a hand through her hair with a determined gesture and looked briefly around the room. 'Of course I miss this house,' she said, with a slow emphasis. 'I'm only human. But you've got to think ahead. Things will get better. We won't be in that little flat forever.'

'It must be difficult,' said Marcus cautiously. Liz swept round and fixed him with suddenly burning eyes.

'Of course it's difficult,' she said, her voice rising slightly. 'It's hellishly difficult. And sometimes I wonder why we didn't just stay put, with our nice comfortable lives. But, you know, life's about more than just being comfortable, isn't it?'

'Well, yes,' said Marcus. 'I suppose it is.' He gazed at Liz's bright eyes and animated face, and couldn't help but feel impressed.

She walked over to a patch of sunlight on the floor, and sat down in it luxuriously, like a cat.

'I always liked this room,' she said, closing her eyes. Marcus cleared his throat uncomfortably and walked over to the window.

'I can't see any sign of Ginny,' he said. 'Perhaps I should phone the office.'

'Perhaps we should open the champagne while we wait,' said Liz, still with her eyes closed. Marcus frowned.

'Surely you'd like to keep it, and drink it with your husband? And . . .' What was the daughter's name? 'And with Alice?' Liz opened her eyes.

'What I would really like to do,' she said deliberately, 'is to drink it now.' She held it out to him. Marcus hesitated, and then, giving an inward shrug, began to untwist the metal cap. It was only a bottle, after all. She was entitled to do with it what she liked. And, after that outburst of weeping at the door, it seemed a good idea to go along with whatever she wanted.

So now they sat companionably against the wall of the bedroom, taking swigs from the bottle. Every now and then, Marcus got up to check whether Ginny had arrived yet, but after a while, he gave up. Perhaps she'd got the day wrong, or the address, or had been held up by some catastrophe. At any rate, it was unlikely she would turn up at this late stage. It would have been sensible for them to give up and go home.

But Marcus didn't want to go home. He had begun to enjoy the atmosphere of the tranquil room, the warmth of the sunshine on his face and the cold, sparkling champagne in his mouth. Liz had insisted he share the bottle with her, although he was pretty sure he'd only drunk about half the amount that she had. Nevertheless, it was enough to have given him a pleasant glow. Liz also looked as though she was glowing. Her head was thrown back, her eyes were closed and there were two vivid spots of colour on her cheeks.

Marcus looked aimlessly around the room, and became aware again of the square patch of flattened carpet; a testimony to the marital bed which once lay there. Liz and her husband had slept there and woken up there. Argued there. Made love there. They'd made love just feet from where he was sitting. Liz probably made love with the same vigour with which she talked and argued. And afterwards, she probably lay, head thrown back and cheeks flushed, just as she was doing now. The thought began to excite him. He gave another surreptitious glance at her pink cheeks.

Marcus had promised to be faithful to Anthea, forsaking all others, as long as they both should live. And, in his own mind, he had kept that promise, more or less. He did have a longstanding arrangement with an old girlfriend of his, also married, which involved one or perhaps two brief but satisfying reunions a year. And he had also made the mistake, a few years ago, of bedding a secretary at Witherstone's. The liaison had only lasted a couple of weeks, but the hassle afterwards had gone on for months, and culminated with him finding her, at her request, a job in a prestigious estate agency in New York.

All in all, though, Marcus considered himself to have kept to his side of the promise. He had never had what he would consider to be a proper affair. To be honest, he hadn't really had the opportunity to have one. Most of the women he saw from day to day were colleagues or old friends or chums of Anthea's. The clients he saw were generally rather grand and, more often than not, male. And the sorts of well-groomed women he did occasionally find himself ushering into his office were, in his opinion, almost too perfect to be attractive.

But this woman, with her flushed, unmade-up face, and her flashing eyes, and her infectiously energetic manner, was stirring in him an attraction which was as powerful as it was surprising. As though drawn by an invisible string, Marcus found himself silently leaning nearer to Liz. She seemed unaware that he had done so. He moved closer, tantalizingly closer still, and looked at her eyelids for signs of reaction. Her lashes flickered slightly. But her eyes remained closed. Surely she could feel his breath on her cheek? Surely she could hear the rustle of his jacket? Was she asleep?

Liz sat perfectly still, and willed Marcus to come closer. The champagne had robbed her of enough responsibility to let her sit in a happy stupor and wait and see what would happen. It wouldn't really be her fault, she thought hazily, if she kept her eyes closed and pretended she didn't know what was coming.

She could feel him moving towards her; could sense his face looming up in front of hers, and imperceptibly, she tilted her face towards his and very slightly parted her lips. Nothing happened, and for a second she thought she might have been completely mistaken. Perhaps Marcus had got up to check for Ginny again; perhaps he'd even left the room.

But then, suddenly, with no warning, she felt a strange pair of lips landing roughly on hers, and a hand cupping her cheek, and the exhilarating, shocking sensation of a warm, sweet, utterly unfamiliar mouth opening up and exploring her own. For a few delicious, seemingly endless moments, she responded blindly and pleasurably to his kiss; her mind blank and her body tense with delight.

His hands began to move down her body, and she began to shiver with pleasure. But the more his hands moved, the more her stupor faded, giving way to a hard, cold feeling of misgiving.

'Actually,' she murmured, as a hand began to circle her right breast; 'actually . . .' The hand stopped. Liz opened her eyes. She was looking at Marcus's left ear.

'Is something wrong?' he whispered. His breath was hot and moist against her neck, and suddenly Liz felt constricted. She struggled out of his grasp, and leant back against the wall, with a damp patch cooling beneath her ear and her hair uncomfortably askew.

'No, nothing's wrong,' she said, and had a sudden desire to giggle. She looked at Marcus. He was panting slightly, and looked concerned. 'It's just that, I don't know . . .' She made a helpless gesture with her hands. 'I just feel a bit strange, doing this. Apprehensive.'

'Don't be.' Marcus spoke firmly. 'We're not hurting anyone. You mustn't feel guilty.' He spoke almost as though he was trying to convince himself. Liz thought about this for a few moments.

'Actually,' she said, 'I don't think I do. Feel guilty, that is. I think I deserve this.'

'Well then.' Marcus bent his face over hers again, and Liz moved to meet his mouth eagerly. His hand found its way beneath her jersey, unzipped the top of her skirt and began to finger the top of her tights. Liz gasped, and sat bolt upright.

'I'm sorry,' she panted. 'I don't know what's wrong with me.' She gave a frustrated wriggle. 'Everyone else seems to do this with no effort at all. You know, *suddenly we found ourselves making love.*' She swallowed and pushed her hair back. 'I don't think I could ever just *find* myself making love. I think I'd have to decide to do it. And . . .' Marcus gazed at her with an impatience tempered by curiosity.

'What's wrong? Is it this room?' Liz shrugged hopelessly.

'Maybe. I think it's more the thought of you seeing what I'm really like. Under all this.' She tweaked her jersey disparagingly. 'I bet you're used to women with perfect bodies. Not all droopy like mine.'

'Rubbish,' said Marcus. His mind flicked abstractly to Anthea's slim figure; her small, well-shaped breasts, her smooth, pale skin and elfin shoulders. Making love to her was making love to a thing of beauty; an aesthetic experience as much as a sexual one.

'I wasn't exactly expecting to be seduced this afternoon,' Liz was saying. 'I expect I've got my grottiest bra on.'

Marcus stared at her, mesmerized. He couldn't believe how much he wanted to undress her, there, down to her old bra, and no doubt unglamorous knickers. He wanted to cup the pendulous, ripe curves of her breasts, and run his hands over the folds of her stomach, and bury himself inside her.

'I don't give a fuck what you're wearing,' he said, in a voice husky with desire. 'I've just got to have you.' Liz stared back at him, her eyes wide, her breath coming quickly, a delicious anticipation rising inside her.

'Hello! Is anyone there?' A cheerful female voice calling from outside broke the silence, followed by the sound of the doorbell. Marcus and Liz stared at each other for an agonized second. Then Marcus spoke, in a hissed, angry whisper.

'Fuck it! It's Ginny.' He struggled to his feet, and

smoothed back his hair. Liz felt like crying. Marcus strode to the window and leant out.

'Hello there! We've been waiting inside.'

'Marcus, I'm so sorry! Is Mrs Chambers still there? Have you been waiting long? I can't believe how late I am!'

'No problem,' replied Marcus slowly, as he retreated inside.

He looked at Liz, pushing his hand back through his hair in shaky disbelief. 'We'd better go and let her in,' he said.

'Oh God,' said Liz. She pressed her hands to her flaming cheeks. 'Am I looking very red?'

'No,' began Marcus. 'Well actually, yes. You are a bit.' He grinned wickedly at her, and Liz's legs started to feel shaky again.

'I can't get in! The door's closed!' It was Ginny's voice, wafting up to them from outside.

'I'll go,' said Marcus quickly to Liz. 'You come down when you're ready.'

'No!' said Liz. 'That'll look really obvious.' She smoothed down her skirt. 'We'd better go down together.'

As Marcus opened the front door, Ginny burst through like a puppy ready for a walk. She kissed Marcus on both cheeks, and smiled in a charming, shamefaced manner at Liz.

'Mrs Chambers, I'm so sorry! Oh my goodness, you must be freezing, waiting here so long!'

'Oh no,' said Liz gaily. She felt dishevelled beside this glossy girl. 'We had a bottle of champagne to keep us going,' she added, foolishly.

'Really?' Ginny looked from Liz to Marcus with bright eyes. 'How nice! Is there any left?'

'Sorry,' said Liz. 'It's all gone.' She gave a sudden giggle, and Marcus quickly took Ginny by the arm.

'We always give our clients a bottle of champagne when a deal goes through,' he said firmly.

'Yes, I knew that,' said Ginny, eyes sparkling. 'But I didn't realize you always drank it straightaway.'

'We don't normally,' said Marcus tetchily. Ginny looked at him, and back at Liz. She gave a little grin.

'Well, no,' she said. 'I don't suppose you do.'

CHAPTER SIX

On the third Saturday in October, Ginny and Piers collected the keys to Twelve Russell Street, and supervised the arrival of the removal van containing their things. It took an hour to unload the futon, the kilims, the huge wrought-iron candlesticks, the chests full of clothes, CDs, pictures, and books. Then, leaving everything piled up in the sitting-room, they locked the door and went off to Wales for a week, where Piers was filming a tiny part in an obscure children's fantasy drama.

By the next Saturday, Alice still hadn't noticed anything different. She had pared down the route from the school gate to the door of the garage to an efficient minimum, and, with her Walkman pounding loudly in her ears, she rarely looked right or left. She would have had to peer hard in at the window of the sitting-room in order to see the pile of boxes on the floor; the rolled-up rugs against the fireplace. And, despite having been told the good news by her parents, it had not actually registered with her that the house had been let out. Conversations at home about the tenants moving in had passed as effortlessly over her head as did the morning radio news bulletins which her parents put on every breakfast so that she would grow up aware of current events.

The garage was quite cosy now. She'd bought a couple of cushions from a charity shop and put them in the corner, and she'd taken the spare torch from home and rigged it up on a shelf so it was almost like a lamp. There wasn't a heater in the garage, and it was getting colder and colder in there as the weeks went on. But just sitting there, listening to music and smoking and munching on sweets and sometimes trying to read a magazine, she felt a strange happiness; an obscure sense of achievement.

As soon as she had pulled the door behind her, she took out a Marlboro from the packet in her top pocket, pulled out her lighter with her other hand and flicked the tiny flame alive in a familiar, instinctive action. She'd got into the habit of always lighting up before she sat down. It was almost a matter of principle; a superstitious routine.

And coming to the garage was also a routine. She was there nearly every day now, usually between school and supper. Her parents sometimes asked what she'd been doing, but not in the sort of way that meant they really wanted to know. The only time she'd bothered to come up with a convincing story, her mother had interrupted her when she was still speaking, to say something boring about the tutorial college.

The tutorial college. Alice's train of thought paused scathingly; she was even less cheerful about it now than she had been when they moved in. And now it wasn't just that they had to live in a grotty little flat. The week before, she had arrived back for supper to see a girl she knew from school coming out of the front door. They'd given each other a dismayed smile, and said Hi, and then Alice had blushed bright red and rushed past, up the stairs to the flat.

'What was Camilla Worthing doing here?' she'd demanded of her mother, who was sitting on the sofa in the sitting-room, staring blankly at the television.

'Camilla Worthing? Oh yes, extra coaching for her Maths GCSE. She must have stayed late.'

'Extra coaching?' A thumping sense of panic began to fill Alice's chest. 'What, like, after school?'

'Yes, of course after school,' said Liz shortly. 'We haven't gone quite so far as to poach pupils from their school lessons.' Alice wasn't listening.

'Do lots of people come? For extra coaching?' she said.

'Not yet,' said Liz. 'It's a bit early in the year. But they will. At least, we hope they will. A few have put their names down for next term.'

'From my school?'

'Some, yes.'

'And what about next year?'

'What about it?'

'Will you do GCSE coaching then?'

'Of course we will.' Liz changed channel, and the title music of *Summer Street* blared out of the television.

'But I'm doing GCSEs next year!' wailed Alice. 'It'll be people in my year coming. It'll be so embarrassing.'

'Don't be silly,' said Liz brusquely.

'But I'll see them coming here! It'll be awful!'

'Oh for Heaven's sake, Alice! Grow up!'

Grow up, they said. Be more mature. Alice stared resentfully into the darkness of the garage. They said all that, and then they treated her like a child. Just that afternoon, she'd had to spend hours and hours trailing around Silchester with her father, putting leaflets through doors. As if she didn't have anything else to do.

Her father was an active member of ECO, a local environmental society, and Alice was a junior member. That didn't amount to much, since she refused to attend the weekly meetings. But it somehow went without saying that she always helped her father when there were leaflets to give out. She didn't usually mind doing it; didn't mind walking in companionable silence round the outskirts of Silchester, always trying to finish her side of the street before he finished his without looking as though she was making an effort. And her mother always bought something nice for tea, as a reward.

But today she'd felt scratchy and put-upon. They shouldn't just assume she was free to do things like this; they should ask her first; they should be grateful. They didn't treat her like a proper human being. She'd shuffled blackly along the streets, kicking the leaves with the toes of her Doc Martens, shoving the leaflets grumpily into letterboxes. And she'd averted her eyes from the words on the front of the leaflets; unwilling to show any interest in the subject, even by accident. It was all about the awful Christmas environment parade, that happened every year. If they tried to make her go on that again, they really had to be joking.

They'd finished up in the furthermost reaches of West Silchester, each with two empty carrier bags and a list of streets ticked off and a collection of rubber bands which had gone round the bundles of leaflets.

'Good work, Carruthers,' said Jonathan, which was what he said every time. 'Now let's get back to headquarters for hot chocolate and rations.' Alice twitched in annoyance.

'Actually,' she said, before she could think about it, 'I've got to get some things. I'll see you later.'

'Oh.' He sounded taken aback, and Alice felt a pouring sensation of guilt and irritation at herself. So what if they traditionally went back home for a huge tea after the leaflets? It wasn't such a big deal. She felt a pinkness in her cheeks; an imminent embarrassment; the sort she used to have at school whenever she was about to put up her hand.

'See you at home,' she muttered, beginning to walk off.

'Yes, of course,' said Jonathan. 'Well, thank you, darling. You were a big help.'

Alice pretended not to hear, and strode off before her father could ask what she needed to get or suggest coming along with her. It was almost worse being praised for doing something than actually having to do it.

She'd arrived at Russell Street in a few minutes, and gone straight into the garage. Now she looked around, exhaling a cloud of smoke, waiting for her customary feeling of satisfaction. But the garage seemed even colder today than it normally did. As she sat down dolefully on the cushions, staring out through the crack in the door at the darkening sky, she felt a strange sense of gloom come over her. She'd been so anxious to get here; so anxious not to go home with her father. But now . . . it wasn't so great. She looked at her watch. Ten to six. She pulled her jacket around her, and sat rigid, staring sternly ahead. She would stay for another twenty minutes, she promised herself. And she would have two more cigarettes. And then she would go.

Ginny, Piers, and Duncan arrived back at Twelve Russell Street at six o'clock. After a morning spent unpacking and arranging, they had gone into Silchester to get some food and look around. Duncan had insisted on buying a long list of exotic ingredients for that evening's supper, which had inevitably meant trekking about until they eventually found a delicatessen, which was about to close. It had taken all his persuasive powers to get them an extension of ten minutes, during which he asked for brands which the salesgirl had never heard of and fingered packets and bottles with an air of slight disappointment.

'Well, if this is the provinces . . .' he said expressively, as they came up the garden path. 'I mean, their range of olive oils was pitiful.'

'Duncan,' said Ginny threateningly. 'Piers, have you got the key?'

'I know, I know, I'm sorry,' said Duncan. 'It's all lovely. I'm going to adore it here.'

It had been Piers who suggested Duncan should rent a room from them in Silchester for a while. After all, his lease in Fulham was coming to an end; he didn't have any work; they could do with the money. Duncan had stood in the kitchen, not quite hiding, while Piers threw these arguments at Ginny. She was tired, she'd just come home from work and she had wet feet from the rain. She'd agreed without really taking in what was being said.

Now she stood, and looked appraisingly at Duncan waiting on the path.

'You're not going to be trouble, are you?' she said.

'Trouble? What kind of trouble?'

'I don't know.' She looked at him sideways, affection not entirely masking a growing suspicion. 'Just remember, you're on probation.'

'Oh yes, I know. I'm going to be good, I promise.' He paused. 'By the way,' he added casually, 'I asked Ian Everitt over tonight. As a sort of housewarming.'

'Duncan! You didn't!'

'Oh, for God's sake, Duncan!'

Alice heard raised voices from inside the garage, and cautiously went to the door. She opened it enough to poke her head out, and looked carefully round the corner. At first she couldn't hear anything, and thought it must just have been people on the street. But as she was drawing her head back inside the garage, she heard, with a stab of recognition, the familiar groaning sound of the front door shutting.

Her immediate thought was that it must be burglars, and she had a sudden vision of being discovered in the garage, beaten up and dragged off to her death. She would be on the telly. *Silchester mourns for tragic Alice*. For a few seconds, she stood still, transfixed by the idea of her sad face peering out of the screen into all her friends' living rooms.

Then the kitchen light went on. It couldn't be burglars. It must be . . . it must be . . . She stood still, frowning, her hand on the door. And then it came to her. The tenants. She paused abruptly in her thoughts, amazed at her powers of deduction. The tenants. It was a phrase which had buzzed around at home for the last few weeks, and she had taken it in at the shallowest level, without bothering to digest what it really meant. But now various phrases and conversations between her parents began to swim belatedly into her memory. And now she realized, for the first time, exactly what they'd been talking about.

Her heart began to thud. If other people lived in their house now, perhaps she was trespassing. She quickly looked out of the door again, at the lit-up kitchen. A hand appeared at the window, turning on the tap. A kettle was thrust under it. Then the hand disappeared. Alice counted to ten, then put one foot outside the door. Then her other foot. She made her way slowly along the wall of the garage, moving sideways with one stealthy foot over another.

As she reached the front garden she paused. The sitting-room was lit up, and she was suddenly filled with curiosity to see other people's stuff in it. But as she edged cautiously towards the window, a man came into the room. She gasped, and retreated, feverishly concocting a story in her mind. But he was shouting something out of the door; his attention was away from the window. She had to go now, before they all came into the room and she was stuck there. Without looking back, she ran quickly and lightly over the lawn, down the path, fiddled furiously with the gate for a second, and then was safely outside, on the innocuous pavement. She quickly walked a few paces along for good measure, then risked a backward look. She couldn't see anyone. They hadn't seen her. She was OK.

Ginny couldn't decide if she was more angry than excited, or more excited than nervous.

'For Heaven's sake, Piers,' she said, dragging a couple of empty tea chests into the hall and staring at them distractedly. 'Look at the state this place is in.'

'What?' said Piers. 'It looks lovely.'

'With empty packing cases everywhere? And piles of books all over the place?'

'It looks Bohemian,' said Piers. 'Artistic.' He caught her eye. 'You're not getting too worked up about this, are you?'

'Of course not,' said Ginny briskly. 'I just want the place to look tidy. That's all.'

He caught hold of her, and drew her near, bringing her face up so that she couldn't avoid his gaze.

'Look,' he said quietly. 'I'm not even sure if I want the part yet. I mean, I didn't go through years of dramatic training just to end up in a soap opera.' Ginny opened her mouth to speak, and then closed it again. 'I'm just going to play it by ear,' continued Piers. 'Now, calm down and relax. As if a few packing cases have got anything to do with it, anyway.'

'OK,' said Ginny, as he released her wrists. 'I'm calm. I'm so calm I'm falling asleep.'

'That's more like it,' said Piers. 'How about a drink?'

'After you've taken those tea chests out to the garage,'

said Ginny. She raised a hand before Piers could protest. 'Now I've got them this far, you might as well. And Duncan's bike. He's *not* keeping it in the hall!'

'All right,' said Piers agreeably. 'I suppose that's fair enough. And then a drink.'

'And then a drink,' conceded Ginny.

As Piers began to drag the chests along the floorboards of the hall, Ginny waited for a few seconds, then bounded upstairs. She went into the bathroom, shut the door and stared at her reflection in the mirror. Her cheeks were flushed, and her eyes shining. 'Calm down,' she instructed herself rather hopelessly, and she tried to adopt a relaxed expression. But a sparkling excitement was filling her body with pulsing adrenalin, and she could barely stand still.

Ever since Piers had first told her about the *Summer Street* part, she had tried desperately not to let him know how much she wanted him to get it. She had sat casually nursing a cup of cocoa while he and Duncan told her between them just how much Ian Everitt was reputed to earn, and how talentless he'd always been, and how they *must* be looking to recast and how perfect Piers would be. That evening, they had all been consumed with an air of hilarity; of boundless optimism and hope.

By the next morning, of course, Piers had completely changed his mind. They would probably get rid of the role altogether, he said gloomily; if they didn't, there would be incredible competition; and the current producer hated him—he'd already once turned him down for something else. After several years of marriage to Piers, Ginny knew better than to contradict him or display unwanted optimism when he was in this mood. But in her own mind it was too late to go back. Her mind was entirely overtaken by the part; she could think of nothing else.

On the way to work the next day she'd calculated the mortgage they would be able to afford on that kind of salary, and she'd spent the rest of the morning looking through details of big country houses with a mounting exhilaration. Since then, she'd begun to scour the papers for mentions of *Summer Street* and its stars; had noted with a jolt the appearance of Ian Everitt among the guests at the latest minor Royal wedding; had gazed, consumed by envy and wishes, at a glossy colour spread of a female *Summer Street* star and her new baby.

'That could be us,' she said quietly to her reflection. 'That will be us.' Her reflection smiled back knowingly at her. She sat down on the edge of the bath, closed her eyes and briefly indulged in her favourite fantasy. She would switch on the television, she would hear that famous, catchy, unavoidable tune, she would see the familiar credits . . . and then she would see Piers on screen. A delicious, glowing sensation stole over her. He would be perfect. He would look gorgeous. He would steal the show. Thousands of people all over the country would fall in love with him.

But she wasn't allowed to think about it too often. She had to be sensible. She knew the rules. If you want something too badly, you probably won't get it. If you tell anyone you want it, you certainly won't get it. Ginny stood up, took a deep breath and pressed her burning cheeks against the cold pane of the mirror. She had to cool down; calm down; put on a casual front.

Piers already thought she mentioned *Summer Street* too much. She would have to be careful, stop herself from bringing it up. And it was especially important to be nonchalant tonight.

Oh God, tonight. She could hardly believe Duncan had had the nerve to invite Ian Everitt round. Only he could be so . . . so brazen. But perhaps he knew what he was doing. Perhaps this would turn out afterwards to be the night that changed everything. They would recall it when Piers wrote his autobiography. Oh God. Oh God. Stop thinking about it.

Ignoring the bounding feeling of excitement in her stomach, Ginny opened the bathroom door with a confident gesture. She sauntered to the banisters, looked down at the empty hall, and hummed a few throwaway lines of a cheerful tune; checking first that she wasn't about to sing the theme to *Summer Street*. Then she walked unhurriedly and carelessly down the stairs, one casual foot after the other, swinging her hair unconcernedly; practising a nonchalant expression for the rest of the evening.

Alice didn't discover that her lighter was missing until it was after supper and she'd gone to her bedroom for a quick cigarette out of the window. She patted the pockets of her jacket, then felt inside each one; first methodically, then with alarm. Her lighter wasn't inside her jeans pockets, neither was it in either of the carrier bags she'd carried all the way back home. She must have left it in the garage.

At first she told herself she could go and find it the

next day. It would be light then, and those people probably would have gone out, and she'd probably see it
straightaway. She had a vague recollection of seeing it
lying on one of the cushions; whether that was from
today or some other time, she couldn't be sure. At any
rate, it had to be there. And it wasn't as if anyone was
going to pinch it in the meantime.

But the thought of it worried and worried at her. It
was all very well to tell herself she'd find it more easily
tomorrow. But she wanted it now. She wanted its smooth,
comforting contours in her hand. She wanted its familiar
weight in her pocket. And she wanted to get rid of the
slither of fear in the back of her mind, which persisted
however hard she tried to get rid of it; the niggling, pan-
icking thought that she might perhaps have lost it for
good.

'I'm going out,' she said at the sitting-room door,
avoiding her parents' surprised looks; trying to sound as
if this was just confirmation of something they should
have known already.

'At this time?'

'Where are you going?'

'I'm meeting some people from school. In McDonald's. Just for a milkshake.' She paused. 'Like I used to
with Genevieve,' she added, in a pathetic voice. She saw
her mother give what was supposed to be a secret look
to her father, then turn round and beam at Alice.

'That sounds lovely,' she said. 'Do I know them?'

'No,' said Alice vaguely. She fingered the door frame.
'So I'll see you later,' she said.

'Yes. Be back by eleven, won't you?'

'Do you need some money?' added her father, feeling for his wallet.

'Do you want a lift?' Her mother sat up suddenly. 'I'll run you into town, if you like.'

'No. No!' Alice's voice came roaring out. 'Thanks,' she added. She could feel her face turning pink. Why were they being so *nice* all of a sudden?

When she got to Russell Street, Number Twelve was lit up from the inside. The curtains were drawn and, as she crept cautiously over the grass towards the garage, she could hear music playing in the sitting-room. She edged down the side of the house, quietly pushed open the garage door and walked confidently into the blackness. She knew the garage so well, by now, she could have walked straight to her pile of cushions and sat down without opening her eyes.

Which was why the howl she gave when, a couple of seconds later, she tripped awkwardly over an anonymous bicycle lurking in the darkness, was as much from affront as it was from pain. For a few moments, the sheer outrage of being taken by surprise like that prevented her from moving. She sat helplessly, tangled beneath the unforgiving metal shape, until it fell further down on top of her, bashing her shin and causing her to yelp. Suddenly she was filled with a panicked claustrophobia. She began to struggle furiously with the bicycle, trying to work out which way it went; grunting with annoyance as she reached for what she thought must be the handlebars only to find her hand falling on a softly spinning wheel. If only she had a torch; if only she'd waited until it was light; if only—

'Hello there.' A deep voice interrupted her thoughts. Alice jumped in genuine terror, and then gasped as one of the bicycle's brakes went sharply into her ribs. For a moment she considered freezing; if she played dead perhaps whoever it was would go away. Like grizzly bears. 'I wouldn't bother if I were you,' the voice continued, in ironical tones. 'It's not worth very much.'

'What?' Alice turned round in a fury of indignation. 'Do you think I'm trying to steal it?'

The door of the garage was open, and a silhouette was standing just outside. Alice couldn't see his face, but she had an uncomfortable feeling that he might be able to see hers.

'I'm not a thief,' she added for emphasis.

'Oh really?' Alice felt herself blushing red; her bravado was about to slip away. She had to admit to herself, she must look a bit weird.

'I'm just getting something,' she said, looking away. 'I used to live here.'

'Aha.'

'I did!' she exclaimed. 'I'm Alice Chambers. I used to live here. Ask anyone.'

Suddenly a torch flashed on, and wavered over her face. She screwed up her eyes and gave another push at the bike.

'Oh dear.' The voice was amused. 'You are in a bit of a state, aren't you? Here.' The silhouette loomed towards her, and she felt a strong hand under her arm, hauling her free of the bike. It fell with a clatter to the ground, and suddenly she was standing up, next to the voice.

'Are you OK?' he said. The torch flashed over her face again. 'No, you don't really look like a bike thief.

So, what were you after? I didn't think there was anything in here.'

'My lighter,' muttered Alice.

'What, cigarette lighter?' His voice held surprised amusement. 'How old are you?' Alice was silent. 'All right then, what does it look like?'

'Silver. I think it's over there.' She pointed, and his torch beam followed, picking out the saggy brocade of her pile of cushions, the old magazines, the Mars Bar wrappers littered around her corner.

'Looks like you were quite at home in this place,' he said conversationally. Alice said nothing, but followed the path of the beam anxiously. She couldn't have lost it, couldn't . . .

'There!' Her voice rang out with an excitement she would rather have hidden. 'On that ledge. Beside the torch.' And suddenly, as though she'd known all the time, she remembered putting it there while she fiddled with the nozzle of the torch, trying to get it to point downwards.

The figure beside her stepped forward, reaching effortlessly across the piles of stuff that were now blocking the path to Alice's corner, and retrieved the lighter.

'Thanks,' she said, as her hand clasped its friendly shape. 'God, if I'd lost it . . .'

'Your mother would have killed you?' he suggested. Alice giggled, and looked up. She could just about distinguish dark hair, dark eyes, not much else . . .

'Well, thanks again,' she said, and began to make a move towards the door.

'Not so fast.' A hand clamped on her shoulder and a sudden burst of panic ran through Alice's body. This was what rapists did. She'd seen it on the telly. They pretended to be friendly and then suddenly they changed. 'You don't get away that easily,' he continued. 'I want you to come inside and say hello. Since you used to live here.'

'I've got to get home, really,' muttered Alice, thoughts of escape fluttering around in her mind.

'Everyone would love to meet you,' he insisted. 'They sent me outside to see what the noise was and if I come back empty-handed they'll be most unimpressed.'

'Well, I dunno.' Actually, he sounded as if he might be normal. But perhaps that was the trick.

'And I'm sure you'd like a cup of coffee. Or a glass of whisky?'

Alice paused, and glanced at the shadowy face. There were other people in the house. She'd heard them. And if he tried to rape her, she'd flash her lighter in his face and scream really loudly.

'All right,' she said slowly.

'Good!' They began to walk towards the house, and Alice's fears started to recede as they approached the familiar back door.

'I'm Piers, by the way,' the man was saying. 'And you're Anna, did you say?'

'Alice.'

They went swiftly through the kitchen, through the hall, and into the sitting-room. There they stopped, and Alice blinked, and looked bemusedly around. It was the same room as before, with the same walls and the same fireplace and even the same sofa. But now it was full of strangers, and it smelt different, and somehow it looked foreign. There was a strange rug on the floor, and there were loads of candles everywhere, and there was a high-tech-looking sound system in the corner.

'This is Alice,' Piers was saying, in an amused voice, 'who used to live in this very house and, to my great regret, wasn't trying to steal your bike, Duncan.' A man sitting on the floor gave a sort of high-pitched squeal, and Alice jumped.

'That's Duncan,' Piers began to say. 'Don't take any notice of him. And this is my wife, Ginny, and . . .'

But Alice wasn't listening. She was staring at the man sitting on the sofa. His face was so familiar, she gave a sort of sigh of relief, and all thoughts of rape went out of her head. She knew him from somewhere. But where? School? He wasn't a teacher and he was too young to be a father. Did he live in Russell Street? Was he one of those neighbours they'd never really got to know? Suddenly his name came into her head.

'I know you,' she began. 'You're Rupert . . .'

She stopped, gasped, and reddened. As she said his name, she suddenly knew where she recognized him from. In spite of herself, she began to tremble, and a sense of unreal awe percolated through her body. It was him. Rupert from *Summer Street*. Sitting there in front of her, smirking complacently at her. Oh God, he must think she was so stupid.

'I'm sorry . . .' she mumbled.

'My dear girl!' He sounded a bit different from the way he spoke on television, she thought confusedly. But it was definitely him. 'Don't apologize. And do call me Ian.'

'You will stay for a drink,' said the girl sitting in front of the fire. She smiled warmly at Alice, and Alice gazed in silent admiration at her shiny blond hair and tight white T-shirt and big leather belt holding up torn Levis. 'It's lovely to meet you. I've met your mother, of course.'

'What do you want?' interrupted Piers. 'We're all on the whisky, I'm afraid. But I could make some coffee.'

'Have a whisky,' piped up the stocky man sitting on the floor. 'It's good for you.'

'And sit down here beside me,' said Ian-Rupert. He smiled winsomely at her, and Alice crossed the floor in a trance. She couldn't believe this was happening to her. Any of it.

CHAPTER SEVEN

The first time Liz and Marcus made love, Liz insisted that the lights stay off all the way through. The second time, she allowed one heavily shaded bedside light to remain on. The third time, Marcus sprang on her un-awares in the bath, and there was no time for her to lunge at the light switch. He hauled her, sopping and protesting, out of the geranium-scented bubbles, onto the thickly carpeted hotel bathroom floor, and shut her cries up with a firm pair of lips on her mouth and a firm hand between her legs.

Afterwards, Liz sat happily at the dressing-table, smearing body lotion from a small, complimentary bottle all over herself, and ignoring the thought that although it was free, it was also disappointingly thin, and smelt rather nasty. When Marcus came and put a proprietary hand on her shoulder, she looked at his re-flection in the dim, glowing dressing-table mirror, and smiled. She enjoyed his proprietary air, just as she enjoyed his easy, confident driving, his assured voice, his expensive overcoat, and even, perversely, his utter ignorance of and lack of enthusiasm for modern languages.

They had first visited the hotel the week before, ostensibly for dinner. When Liz discovered, during the course of the evening, that Marcus had also thoughtfully booked a room with a four-poster bed, she had been amazed and exhilarated.

'What if,' she'd demanded, later on, as they drove back to Silchester, 'what if I'd just eaten my dinner and said thank you very much, let's go home now?'

'Then,' Marcus replied calmly, 'I would have paid the bill and taken you home.' He paused, and put out one hand to caress the nape of her neck. 'But I was pretty sure that wouldn't happen.' Liz tingled briefly at the touch of his fingers, then sank back blissfully into the cushy seats of Marcus's Mercedes. She felt warm, cherished, and protected.

Now she put down the bottle of body lotion, and looked at the picture the two of them made in the mirror. Marcus was broader built than Jonathan, with thick dark hair on his legs and chest, and sturdy arms and wrists. He stood upright, with a relaxed, unconcerned posture, and Liz found herself making a brief disloyal comparison with Jonathan, who would always hunch unhealthily over his books until he suddenly remembered to sit up straight and jerked his shoulders back with an abrupt movement.

'We'll have a drink before we go,' said Marcus, stroking her shoulder. 'I've got to get back by midnight.' They met eyes briefly, then looked away from each other.

A trail of white lotion was still running down Liz's arm, and she began to rub it briskly into her skin. She had carefully avoided thinking about Marcus's wife; his family; the clichéd, shadowy characters that threatened at any moment to spoil her treat.

For that was how she thought of Marcus. He was her treat. She deserved him, she reckoned, after all her hard work, after being faithful and cheerful and making such an effort with the tutorial college. She deserved something nice for all of that. And Marcus—as well as being tall and strong and enthusiastic, albeit not particularly imaginative, in bed—had the delicious air of a luxury item. Just sitting in his car, listening to the cocooned sound of the stereo; just watching as he casually signed the bill for dinner; just leaning against his expensively cotton-shirted chest and breathing in the delicious smell of his aftershave, was enough to make a broad smile of contentment spread slowly across her face. Words like infidelity and betrayal didn't come into it. This was just her special treat, nothing to do with Jonathan. And sometimes she even persuaded herself that if he knew about it, he would be glad. For her sake.

Not that he would ever find out. When Marcus had asked her out to dinner, Liz had hit upon the idea of telling Jonathan she was thinking of resuming her Italian conversation classes in Frenham Dale, a good twenty miles from Silchester. He had no idea that Grazia, who used to run them, had moved back to Italy; nor did he ever ask where they were supposed to be taking place. And he couldn't have been more supportive of the idea. Liz remembered, with a slight twinge of guilt, his exclamations of delight; his encouraging

smile. He really thought she was doing it all in aid of
the tutorial college. Stupid fool.

She had not asked Marcus what he had told his wife.
She didn't want to think about it; didn't want to remind
him. But sometimes she wondered if he was thinking of
her. Now she surreptitiously eyed Marcus as he buttoned
up his shirt. He looked serious. Grim, even. The horrible
thought came to her that he might be thinking of his
wife, and regretting what had happened. He might even
now be considering how to extricate himself from all
this. She imagined his face, telling her this was the last
time, screwed up in an attempt to be kind but unequivo-
cal. And then they'd never see each other again, and
there would be no more dinners and no more hotels and
no more rides in that lovely car. She'd be back to her
unutterably dull life with Jonathan. She couldn't bear it.

She peered at Marcus's face again, trying to read his
expression. But she couldn't tell what he was thinking
about. Was it her? Or was it his wife?

Marcus was not thinking about his wife. Nor was he
thinking about Liz. In fact, he had almost forgotten
that she was in the room. His frown of concentration
was due to the fact that the next day he was intending
to begin, for Leo, the valuation of Panning Hall.

It should be a simple job. It was a good-sized estate,
a fair way out of Silchester, with nearly twelve hundred
acres, a manor house, several more houses dotted
around the place, and good riding facilities. He'd at-
tended a charity event at the house once, years ago, and

as far as he could remember there were no unusual features; no zoos or recording studios; no surprises.

He'd met Lady Ursula, then, too. Painfully thin, and elegant, despite her age. One of the few owners of country estates he'd met who actually seemed at home in a huge country house. So often these places were inhabited by largely absent businessmen and their ill-at-ease wives. Drawing-rooms lay empty while the wife watched television in her bedroom. Dining-rooms grew chilly and unwelcoming, while the children ate fish-fingers every night in the kitchen. But Lady Ursula had known how to live in such a large house. She'd grown up in it. She'd had the right style. Marcus had felt an admiration for her then which lingered even now. Even now that she was dead.

It had been a bit of a shock when Leo casually mentioned, towards the end of their meeting, that the estate he was talking about was Panning Hall. Marcus hadn't heard of Lady Ursula's death, and his immediate feeling was one of shock.

'That's awful!' he'd blurted out.

'What is? What, did you know her? Is there some sort of problem?' Leo's eyes scanned Marcus's face. 'She wasn't a friend of yours, or anything, was she?'

'Well, no,' said Marcus. 'It's just that I met her a few years ago. And I didn't realize she'd died.'

'Alas, yes,' said Leo gravely, adopting a solemn face. Then his expression changed. 'But, frankly, the rest of her family is a shambles. They don't want to have the estate; they're only interested in the money. And that's all going straight up their noses.'

'Really?' Marcus felt nonplussed. Leo fixed him with a shrewd eye.

'I wouldn't like you to think, Marcus, that what I'm suggesting is my normal practice with all my clients.'

'Oh, er, no,' said Marcus. 'Of course not.'

'I specifically asked you, Marcus, to help me out on this one, because I trusted your judgement.' Leo leaned forward slightly and gazed into Marcus's face. 'I credited you, Marcus, with a certain vision. I hope you won't disappoint me.'

And Marcus had felt confused, flattered and exhilarated all at once. Leo had chosen him. He'd spotted his potential; seen that the constraints of provincial estate agency were stifling him; realized that Marcus was a man who could face a challenge head-on.

That was now a few weeks ago. And since then, everything had gone, Marcus thought, swimmingly. He'd set up the usual procedures impeccably. In his filing cabinet at work he had a bland letter from Leo, informing him of the owner's recent death and requesting a valuation for probate with a view to selling as soon as was convenient. The letter was addressed to Marcus at his work address, but Leo had actually sent it to him at home, to avoid the danger of anyone else at Witherstone's seeing it and deciding to do the valuation themselves. It had been easy for Marcus to bring it into the office, slip it into a file and sit quickly down at his desk again before Suzy, his secretary, came in.

He'd debated for a while whether to tell Suzy where he was going that day; whether a mysterious absence would draw more comment than the words *Panning Hall* scribbled across the diary page. People were so nosy: his cousin Miles would be sure to want to know all about the valuation if he found out about it; might even suggest coming along to see the place.

So in the end, he'd written in the diary, himself, the carefully ambiguous phrase: *Valuation – Panning.* Panning was itself a large village with a number of good-sized properties. And, as everyone was all too aware, there was a great trend at the moment for people to request valuations without having any intention of selling. If anyone asked where he'd been, he could make up some appropriate story about a client who had confessed at the end of their meeting that she didn't really want to sell. No one would bother to pursue it. And meanwhile, having a reference to Panning in the diary might be useful in the future. Just in case anyone ever suggested he hadn't put this case through the usual channels or that he'd tried to keep it quiet. Heaven forbid.

Marcus was trying, as far as he could, to lull himself into a normal frame of mind for this valuation. He would be professional about it, he would follow his usual procedures; he would carefully note the features of the main house and the state of the outlying buildings; investigate the river frontage and areas of woodland. He would undertake the job conscientiously, without skipping bits or cutting corners or taking anything for granted.

Marcus's hands tightened as he tied up his shoes; his breath quickened slightly. And then, at the end of the valuation, when he'd taken all factors into consideration, he would come up with an overall figure which would be, give or take the odd thousand, one million pounds short of what it should be.

Easy. A piece of cake. What was it his son Andrew always said? No sweat.

By five o'clock the next afternoon, Marcus was feeling very sweaty indeed. He had arrived at the manor house at ten, to find an elderly man in a navy blue anorak and wellingtons waiting outside in a Range Rover.

'Thought you'd be along soon,' he said, in a comfortable local voice. 'I'm Albert, used to do work on the estate for Lady Ursula. Thought you might like someone to show you about.'

'It's quite all right,' said Marcus in a cheerfully polite voice. 'I wouldn't like to trouble you.'

'No trouble,' replied Albert, grinning at Marcus. 'I suggested it to Mr Francis last week, and he said you'd probably be glad of someone who knows the place.'

'Did he indeed?' said Marcus, feeling annoyed. Bloody Leo. Why did he have to say that?

'Well then,' he said, carefully modulating his voice to avoid suspicion. 'I'd be glad of your help.'

As they walked around the main house, Albert kept up a continual flow of chatter.

'Suppose they'll be selling then?' he said. 'Those daughters?'

'I believe so,' said Marcus.

'Drug addicts, both of 'em,' added Albert, surprisingly. 'Used to smoke those cigarettes in one of the stables. "Oh Albert," they says. "Don't tell Mother." Don't tell Lady Ursula, indeed! I was straight up to see her that very afternoon. And they went to see her and started weeping and crying, and said they wouldn't do

it no more.' He clicked his tongue. 'Just found somewhere else to do it, that's all.' He sniffed, and looked
around. 'No wonder they ended up in America.'

Marcus wasn't listening. He was staring at the fireplace in front of him. If it was, as he suspected, an
Adam piece, then it would add, what, maybe fifty thousand to the value of the house. If not, then he could already discount the value by that amount. His hands
trembling slightly, he scribbled in his notebook 'attractive fireplace.' He looked at the words for a moment,
then briskly added a full stop and looked up. Albert
nodded approvingly.

'That's a fine fireplace,' he said disconcertingly. 'Must
be worth something on its own, that.'

'It's an attractive piece,' said Marcus in an off-putting
voice.

'I was watching the *Antiques Road Show* once,'
added Albert. 'Fireplace just like that one got a hundred
thousand pounds!' His voice rolled lovingly round the
words and he looked impressively at Marcus. 'Think that
one's worth the same?'

'I doubt it,' said Marcus crushingly. He tried to think
of some impressive jargon which would shut this man
up. 'The medallions at the corners are all wrong, for a
start.' He mustn't mention Adam. 'And the scagliola
work looks completely inauthentic to me,' he added for
good measure.

'Is that so?' said Albert. 'Fancy.' He looked beadily
at Marcus, who felt a sudden urge to hit him.

'Anyway, let's move on,' he said briskly, moving towards the door.

'After you, sir,' said Albert, moving aside with an

air of deference. Marcus eyed him suspiciously. In his state of unease, he was almost prepared to believe that this Albert character was a plant; that he would report straight back to the authorities; that the way was being paved for a sudden arrest; a fraud charge; dismissal and disgrace. Perhaps he had been sent as a spy from the district surveyor. Oh Christ. Marcus gazed at Albert and felt a cold shiver run down his spine, even though Leo had assured him that there was nothing to worry about on that front.

'The district surveyor's an old school chum,' he'd told Marcus smoothly. 'He'll rubber-stamp anything I put in front of him.' And Marcus had felt a stupidly naïve shock, followed by a feeling of astonishment that this sort of thing really did happen. 'What else?' he'd wanted to ask Leo. 'What else goes on in this town that I don't know about?' Now he rather felt as though he didn't want to know any of it. Albert was striding confidently down the corridor ahead of him. Marcus suddenly imagined him turning round and looking at Marcus with an appraising, knowing gleam in his eye. Oh shit. How much of this scam was obvious? How much had he given away already?

'Something wrong, sir?' Albert turned around, and Marcus jumped. He hastily adjusted his facial expression, and took a deep breath. He had to carry this off. He had to appear convincing.

'So,' he said, following Albert down the corridor, his voice bouncing off the acres of polished wooden floor. 'Lady Ursula lived here for many years, I believe.'

'Lived here all her life, more or less,' replied Albert knowledgeably. 'Grew up here, moved away, inherited the house and moved back. Eighty years or so, she lived here.'

'And she never thought of selling?' Marcus kept his voice light and casual, but listened carefully for Albert's reply. It would be awkward if she had had a recent valuation made—although one could always blame everything on the market.

'Never,' said Albert in shocked tones. 'Saw it as a family house, she did. Would have liked one of those daughters to come back and live in it, too. But they weren't interested.' He paused. 'I suppose they'll do very nicely out of the sale, though.' His eyes, gleaming with speculation, swivelled to meet Marcus's.

'Well, it's hard to say,' said Marcus discouragingly. 'The property market's taken a tumble, you know. Particularly among large estates. They're actually worth much less than you might imagine. Much less,' he repeated with emphasis. The last thing he needed was for Albert and his cronies to start bandying stupid prices about the village.

'Oh,' said Albert, with an air of slight disappointment. 'But still, they'll do nicely.'

'Oh yes,' said Marcus, reassuringly. 'They'll do nicely.' He looked at his watch. 'I don't want to keep you,' he said. 'If you need to get off—'

'Oh no,' said Albert cheerfully. 'I'll show you around properly, sir. Don't you worry.'

In the end, Albert had trailed round with Marcus for the whole day, accompanying him to the village shop to buy a sandwich for lunch, and taking him to see the manor farm in his Range Rover.

'So, you'll be coming back tomorrow?' he said,

as Marcus wearily got into his Mercedes at the end of the day.

'I'm not sure,' said Marcus. 'Maybe.'

'I'll be at home if you need me,' Albert said. 'Mason's Cottage. Ask at the shop.'

'I will,' said Marcus, summoning up his last reserves of good humour in order to smile at Albert. 'And thank you so much for all your help. It really was tremendously useful.' Albert shrugged.

'Any time,' he said, and got into his Range Rover. There was a pause, as each waited for the other to leave, then, impatiently, Marcus put his foot down, and roared off in a trail of spitting gravel.

As he drove home, he thought gloomily about how much there was still to do if he was to carry out a full valuation. He had covered only a fraction of the property. Would it be possible, he wondered, to find some impressionable junior who would do some of the legwork for him without asking questions? But even as the thought entered his mind, he knew the answer was no. The latest bunch of juniors in the office were pushy, ambitious creatures, who were uniformly desperate to attract attention and further their careers. They worked late, volunteered for extra tasks, and had the temerity to look askance at Marcus when he sloped off early to pick up Anthea and the boys. Any old-fashioned deference to senior status seemed to have vanished from this lot; any opportunity for personal gain was grabbed with glee; loyalty was an alien concept. He would be safer doing the whole thing on his own. And certainly, as far as the cut he would receive from Leo went, it would be well worth it.

He was working out in his mind how long the whole affair was likely to take as he pulled up to a set of traffic lights in outer Silchester—and when he heard a sudden knocking on the car window, a spasm of foolish terror went through him. He looked up in guilty alarm, almost expecting to see the face of a policeman. But it was the smiling face of Ginny Prentice.

'Marcus!' she cried. 'Can I cadge a lift into town?' Without waiting for an answer, she opened the passenger door and clambered in. 'Oh, sorry, I'm on top of your papers. Shall I move them?' Marcus made a grab for the Panning Hall papers.

'I'll do it,' he muttered, shoving them on the back seat. Christ. This was all he needed.

'What luck to see you!' Ginny was exclaiming, as she settled into her seat and put on her seat belt. 'I've been showing a load of journalists round that new development in North Silchester.'

'Oh really?' Marcus forced himself to pay attention. 'New developments aren't really my line.'

'No, well . . . This one's really nice. As they go. And I think the journalists liked it. We gave them all champagne in the show house,' she added inconsequently. 'That's why I couldn't take my car. I've had rather a lot of champagne. I was going to take a taxi.' She giggled, and looked at her watch. 'Are you going back to the office? I promised to go in and see Miles. But it's a bit late now, isn't it?'

'I suppose it is,' said Marcus. He was trying desperately to think of an alternative topic to that of work. Anything. As long as she didn't ask him where he'd been . . .

'So, where have you been?' said Ginny conversation-ally. 'Skiving off?' Marcus could feel his neck growing warm.

'Oh, nowhere in particular,' he said, trying to keep his voice light. 'Just a meeting. Very boring.'

'That's the trouble with you lot!' exclaimed Ginny. 'How am I supposed to provide interesting stories for the press if you describe everything as boring? I bet you've just been to see some lovely house . . . it didn't have a ghost, did it? One of the nationals is doing a story on haunted houses, and we don't seem to have any!'

'No,' said Marcus. 'No ghosts.'

'Are these the details here?' said Ginny, reaching be-hind Marcus for the Panning Hall papers.

'No! No, they're not,' cried Marcus. 'That's some-thing else.' This was unbearable. He put his foot down on the accelerator and increased his speed. He had to get into town and Ginny out of the car.

'Oh, OK,' said Ginny. She dropped the papers and gave him a curious look.

'How's your house, anyway?' said Marcus abruptly. Ginny paused.

'Oh, it's fine,' she said. 'Lovely. Actually, we met the daughter the other day. Alice Chambers. The daughter of the woman letting the house out.' She eyed Marcus carefully.

'Oh right,' said Marcus abstractly. Thank God. They were onto another subject. 'Nice, is she?' he added, for good measure.

'She's a lovely girl,' said Ginny, and gave Marcus another side-long look.

They passed the rest of the journey in silence. Ginny looked out the window, and remembered the faces of Marcus and Liz on the day when she'd first visited the house in Russell Street. She'd thought it odd at the time, for them to have waited so long together, and to have been drinking champagne. And now, Marcus had obviously spent the afternoon doing something he didn't want her to know about. Something must be going on between those two. It must be.

Marcus sat still, and willed Ginny not to ask any more questions about that afternoon. Of course, there was nothing wrong in telling her he'd been carrying out a valuation. Perfectly legitimate work. And with anybody else, he might have done. But not Ginny Prentice. Ginny wasn't in public relations for nothing. He'd never met anyone with such a fertile imagination; such an eye for a story. If she caught even a whiff of what he'd been doing, she'd put together all the other pieces in no time.

As they approached the first major junction before Russell Street, Ginny gathered up her bag and pile of folders.

'Drop me here,' she said. 'That's completely brilliant.' She flashed him a smile. 'Thanks, Marcus! One less taxi fare to charge to Witherstone's!'

'Don't mention it,' said Marcus, forcing a smile to his lips. And as he drove off, he reflected that he really meant what he said.

At home, a row was in progress. When Marcus stepped in through the front door, he found Anthea, Daniel and

Andrew still standing in the hall. Daniel's face was bright red; he looked bunched up and uncomfortable in his blazer and school rucksack, and he was speaking in a raised, distressed voice.

'Everyone's been laughing at me all day,' he was saying, as Marcus entered.

'Nonsense,' said Anthea briskly.

'It's true,' said Andrew dispassionately. He had taken off his blazer and was sitting under the huge, heavy oak hall table, running a car idly up and down the legs. 'They were laughing at him.'

'What's all this about?' said Marcus in a hearty voice. 'Hello, darling.' He kissed Anthea, took off his coat and hung it up in the hall cupboard. 'Daniel, why don't you take off your blazer? You'll feel better then.'

'No I won't,' muttered Daniel, but he allowed his father to take his rucksack off his back, and began to unbutton his blazer, with rough, jerky movements.

'Now, come on, Dan,' said Marcus, when Daniel was unbuttoned and looked a bit calmer. 'What's gone wrong?'

'Everyone's been laughing at me at school because Mummy told all the other mothers that I always translate all my homework into French for fun.' His voice trembled. 'For fun!' he repeated, on a rising note. 'Edward White's mother told him and he told the whole class and they kept laughing and pretending I can't understand things if they're not in French, and calling me Danielle.'

'Well then, they're very immature and stupid,' said Anthea. 'Just ignore them.'

'You always say that! It's not fair! And it's all your fault! Why did you have to tell them that?'

Yes, why did you? Marcus wanted to repeat. He eyed Anthea suspiciously, then changed his expression to a supportive smile as she turned to face him.

'It's all nonsense,' she said, in a defensive voice. 'I was just having a conversation about homework with some of the other mothers, and I must have mentioned that time when we had Jacques Reynaud's children over. Do you remember? They were gabbling away in French all evening. And they did translate Daniel's homework into French.'

'Yes, but that was a game!' shouted Daniel, his chest heaving in frustration. 'And it was only once! You told them I did it all the time because I found it fun.'

'I didn't tell them anything,' said Anthea sharply. 'I expect Edward White's mother wasn't listening properly.'

'Could you have given them the wrong impression?' said Marcus carefully.

'Of course not!' Anthea was sounding rattled. 'This is ridiculous. If those other boys want to make fun of you, it's because they're jealous, that's all. Now, go into the kitchen. Hannah's got your tea.'

When the boys had left, Daniel resentfully slouching, Andrew trailing his car happily along the wall, Marcus looked sternly at Anthea. He knew exactly what she was like in the company of the other mothers at the school gate: unable to stop herself from boasting about the boys' prowess; unable to let another parent's story go without capping it, even if that meant embellishing the truth. She couldn't help it; it was bigger than her.

'What did you say to those mums?'

'Nothing! I said nothing.' Her eyes fluttered round. 'It's not my fault if a lot of silly boys decide to pick on Daniel.'

'They seem to pick on him rather a lot. And it's often because of something you've said.'

'What do you mean?' A fiery spot of colour appeared in each of Anthea's cheeks. 'What are you accusing me of?'

'I just think you should be more careful of what you say. Daniel's under enough pressure as it is at the moment, without being made the laughing-stock of the class.'

'I see. So you think I'm deliberately trying to make him a laughing-stock, do you?' Anthea's eyes flashed at Marcus.

'Of course not—'

'Do you know how much I do for him? How many hours I spend helping him with his homework, listening to him practise, ferrying him around?'

'I know you do!' said Marcus, suddenly pushed to the limits of frustration. His day had been stressful enough, without all this. 'Well, maybe you should do a bit less!' Anthea paused, for a shocked second, then turned slowly away, bowing her head slightly. Oh fuck it, thought Marcus. He'd played right into her hands.

'Look, I'm sorry,' he said. He went over, and put a hand on her bony, cashmere-covered shoulder. He felt the muscles relax; felt Anthea begin to give a little. Then suddenly into his head popped a twin vision of Liz's well-covered generous shoulder, warm and naked apart from a blob of lotion. He flushed slightly, and shook his head to dispel it. Christ. Who was he to lecture Anthea? 'I'm sorry,' he repeated. 'I've had a hard day. Let's just forget it, shall we?'

She turned to face him, and he saw the unmistakable light of guilt in her eyes. She had been boasting to the other mothers. And she knew she had. But something in her would refuse to allow her to admit it. It was a familiar pattern. When she was in this mood, she would deny any charge until she was in a state of hysteria. Marcus shuddered at the memory of previous arguments; scenes of increasingly wild accusation on his part and shrieking denial on hers. He always gave in first; always would give in first. It simply wasn't worth doing anything else. And so they all had to carry on, allowing her the pretence that she was innocent; suggesting other explanations; letting the ripples of arguments die down without identifying a satisfactory cause. The boys would learn soon enough that the easiest route was always to go along with her; to fudge the truth for a quiet life.

But it wasn't fair. Like a small boy, Marcus found himself repeating the words to himself, even as he began to massage Anthea's shoulder; even as he cupped her face affectionately in his hand. *It's not fair. It's not fair. It's not fair.*

Later on that evening, he went to say good night to Daniel, who was propped up in bed, avidly reading a Biggles book. Marcus sat down on the edge of the bed.

'I hope this whole French thing will have blown

over by tomorrow,' he said honestly. Daniel shrugged mutely and turned pink. 'I hate to say it,' added Marcus, 'but Mummy does have a point when she tells you to ignore it. You must know what it's like if you're teasing someone. If they ignore you completely, it gets boring.' There was silence. Daniel gave no impression of having heard. Marcus waited.

'She did say it,' said Daniel suddenly, in a low, aggrieved voice. 'I know she did.'

'Well, maybe she said something without meaning to,' said Marcus placatingly. 'The trouble is,' he continued, 'that Mummy is so proud of you, she finds it difficult not to tell everybody when you do well.'

'I know,' said Daniel despairingly. He glanced up at his father. 'We don't tell her things, sometimes, because all she'd do is tell everybody straightaway.' He paused, and looked at his father for a reaction. Marcus felt unable to speak. 'Andrew got a star in his comprehension last week,' continued Daniel, 'and he didn't tell Mummy. And he made me promise not to either. We told Hannah, instead.' Marcus looked at Daniel's earnest face, and felt a creeping sadness in his chest. Had it really come to this? That in order to get along as a family, they all had to have secrets from each other? That the only person they could confide in was the housekeeper?

'Well, I can see why you might want to keep things like that quiet,' he said eventually. He fingered Daniel's blue-and-white-striped duvet, and a smell of fresh-laundered linen rose up in the air. 'And I think—' He broke off and looked at Daniel. 'I think you might be wise.'

He got up abruptly and paced to the other side of the room, picked up a model car on the mantelpiece, and turned it over idly in his fingers. 'But, you know,' he said, suddenly, not quite looking at Daniel, 'Hannah isn't the only person you can tell things to.' He put the car down, and came back to the bed. 'I won't go running to Mummy,' he said softly. 'If you do well at something, either of you, you must tell me.' Daniel looked at him solemnly.

'OK,' he said.

'And Andrew too,' said Marcus.

'All right,' said Daniel.

'And I won't say a word to Edward White's mother,' said Marcus in serious tones. He caught Daniel's eye, and they both started giggling. 'I don't even know Edward White's mother,' added Marcus. Daniel's giggles got louder; his face turned scarlet and he disappeared under the duvet.

Anthea appeared in the doorway.

'What's funny?' she said. Marcus noticed that she had an automatic note of disapproval in her voice. Was that new? Or had he never picked it up before?

'Nothing important,' he said. 'Right, it's time to go. G'night, Dan.'

'G'night,' said Daniel, emerging from the duvet, still with a gurgle in his voice.

As Marcus passed Anthea in the doorway, she gave him an anxious, mildly suspicious glance. He ignored it, and strode away down the corridor. Behind him, he could hear Anthea's voice asking Daniel rather petulantly if he'd brushed his teeth.

Leave the boy alone, he thought grimly. Leave him alone. But try saying that to Anthea, and he'd regret it. Try saying anything to Anthea, these days, and he'd probably regret it.

CHAPTER EIGHT

Piers gave an enormous, self-conscious yawn, looked out of the window, and tried to stop a huge smile from spreading across his face. He was sitting, alone briefly, in the office of Alan Tinker, the producer of *Summer Street*. The phone had rung a couple of minutes ago, and Alan had grimaced to Piers as he picked up the receiver.

'Bugger,' he said as he put it down again. 'That bastard McKenna. Look, Piers, you won't mind if I pop out for a few moments?' He gestured around the office. 'Make yourself some more coffee if you want to; do what you like. Watch some telly!' He'd flashed a conspirator's grin at Piers, and disappeared out of the room, leaving Piers alone to sit as calmly as he could, and try to ignore his growing sense of elation.

The meeting was going well. By any standards, it was going well. Alan Tinker had met Piers in reception himself, had taken him casually into the main canteen for a cup of coffee, had introduced him to a number of people. A number of really quite important people. And although he hadn't actually said, 'This is Piers who's taking over from Ian'—the way he was talking, it seemed as though . . .

Piers forced himself to break his train of thought. He'd been here before; too often to allow himself the self-indulgence of assuming everything was OK. He had only met the guy, for God's sake. It wasn't as if he'd even done an audition yet. There was really nothing to get excited about. And yet, as he stared deliberately blankly round the room, taking in the bank of four television screens mounted on the wall, the framed awards, the rows of books and magazines, the piles of folders and papers and scripts, he felt his heart thudding with an incipient exhilaration. Alan Tinker was an important man. He was a head producer. If he liked someone, he had the power to make them big. If he liked them.

'We know you can act' had been almost his first words. Piers stared down at the pale blue carpet of the office and allowed a secret, painful thrill to run through him. Alan Tinker knew he could act. Alan Tinker had *told* him he knew he could act.

'But all of this isn't just about whether you can act or not,' Alan had added impressively. Piers nodded intelligently.

'Of course not,' he murmured, then wondered if it was a mistake to say anything.

'What we really want is commitment,' said Alan. Piers looked straight back at him, trying to adopt his most committed expression. 'We don't want someone who's going to disappear after six months to do, I don't know . . .' Alan waved his arms airily '. . . a juicy part in the West End.'

'Of course not,' said Piers again. Some fucking chance, he thought bitterly.

'You've been doing a lot of stage work recently, haven't you, Piers?' Alan gave him a penetrating look.

'Yes,' said Piers. He thought desperately. 'But I'm very committed to working in television as a long-term aim.'

'Is that so?' Alan raised his eyebrows at Piers, who remembered, too late, the announcement in the latest edition of *The Stage* that Alan Tinker was setting up his own theatre company. Fuck it. He just couldn't win. But Alan relented. 'Good, good,' he said encouragingly, and leant forward. 'Now, Piers, we on *Summer Street* like to think of everyone, cast and crew alike, as part of a team. A family. If you're working as hard as we do, there's no time for not getting along with this person, or thinking yourself better than that person. You're just a part of the machine. A cog. Do you see what I mean?'

'Yes, yes,' said Piers, trying to sound as convincing as he could. 'Everyone working towards the same goal.' What was he saying? The guy would think he was taking the piss.

'Many actors,' Alan continued, 'consider themselves too important to blend in with a lot of others. After all, you have to be pretty self-centred to be an actor in the first place.' Piers wondered whether to dispute that. Was this some elaborate test to see whether he had any character; whether he could stand up for himself? He eyed Alan's face. But Alan looked in deadly earnest.

And he'd always heard that the guy had some weird ideas.

'So what we like to do,' said Alan, 'as well as, obviously, a screen test, is to let each contender for a part come into the studio for a couple of hours, and rehearse a few scenes with the rest of the cast. That way, if anyone is obviously not going to get on with the others, isn't going to blend in easily, then we realize it straight away.'

'Good idea,' Piers had said heartily. 'That really makes sense.'

Now, left alone, he rose to his feet, too keyed up to sit still. He paced over to the window, allowing his eyes to skim the papers on Alan's desk for anything interesting, then adopted a relaxed but elegant pose by the side of the window. Rupert, the character he would be playing in *Summer Street*, was, if not exactly camp, then certainly not hearty—and it would do no harm to try to show Alan that he could look the part.

The door opened, and Piers turned his head unhurriedly. There in the doorway was a woman dressed in a pair of crushed-velvet leggings and suede boots up to her thighs.

'I'm sorry,' she said, 'but Alan asked me to tell you that he's been held up. He'll be in touch later this week.' Piers stared at her, blankly, stupidly, for a moment, and then realized what she was saying.

'Oh, I see,' he said. 'So I'll go now, shall I?'

'If you wouldn't mind,' said the woman, in tones that weren't quite sarcastic. 'Alan did ask me to apologize. But he's terribly busy at the moment.'

'Oh, no!' said Piers, hurriedly. 'That's fine. We'd

finished our meeting, anyway.' The woman didn't look convinced.

'I'll show you out,' she said.

Piers followed as she marched along the carpeted corridors, nodding to people as she passed but neither looking at Piers nor speaking to him. By the time they reached the entrance, he felt rather deflated.

'Well, goodbye,' he said, trying to summon up some cheer. 'Thanks for showing me the way.'

The woman didn't smile, but said, 'Could you give back your visitor's pass please?' and Piers handed over the white card feeling as though he'd been found infiltrating the building under false pretences. He pushed open the swing door, and threw his head back to a blast of chill winter wind. Who gives a fuck anyway? he thought to himself. They can keep their crappy little part.

But by the time he was on the train to Silchester, his initial excitement had returned. So what if some secretary had made him feel stupid. It was Alan Tinker who counted. And Alan Tinker had said he knew he could act. Now Piers sat staring out of the train window, running down the list of cast members in his mind. The characters of *Summer Street* were mainly young, laid back, his kind of people. He would get on with them fine. He'd bloody well have to.

It was dark when the train arrived, and even colder than before. Hurrying along the streets, Piers wondered idly if it might snow. He was not normally one to rejoice at snow; Ginny's inevitable raptures at the sight of even one snowflake usually amused and sometimes irritated him. But even he had to admit that a snowy Silchester might be quite pretty. And it was certainly cold enough. Bloody freezing. As he strode along, he pictured in his mind the comforting image of a roaring, crackling, log fire. A glass or two of mulled wine. Perhaps even some mince pies. It wasn't quite December, but Christmas had been apparent in Silchester's shops for quite a while. He should be able to get hold of them. He looked at his watch. Half-past four. He would take Duncan along with him to the supermarket. Duncan would know what to put in mulled wine.

But as he neared Twelve Russell Street, he saw that the windows were darkened, and a sense of disappointment came over him. He was in a mood for people and noise and celebration; the house would be cold and dark and empty. He was almost tempted to head back for the bustle of the town centre.

Then he saw a pair of feet poking out from the doorstep. His first thought was that it must be Ginny or Duncan, locked out, and he began to hurry towards the house. Ginny, in particular, was not good in the cold; if she had been sitting there for long, her fingers would be blue and she would be miserably snappy. He began to wonder if the water was on; if he would be able to run her a bath straight away and get a fire going downstairs. As he neared the gate, however, he saw that the legs were skinny and clad in thick tights, and that the feet were shod in incongruously large boots. It couldn't be Ginny. Of course. It was the kid. Alice.

He opened the gate, and she looked up, with a pale, startled face. She was sitting wedged up against the door, with her shoulders hunched up in her jacket and a pair of earphones on her head.

'Hello there,' he said cheerfully. 'No one home?'

'No,' she said hesitantly. She reached inside her jacket pocket and turned off her Walkman. 'I wasn't going to wait long. I just thought I'd see if anyone came.'

'And a good thing you did,' said Piers heartily. In principle, he thought they were seeing a bit too much of this kid. She seemed to appear nearly every day, awkwardly popping her head round the kitchen door, or arriving in the front garden, waving at them through the sitting-room window. She never rang the bell; sometimes he wondered whether there were times when she'd failed to catch anyone's attention and had simply gone quietly away again. 'Now you can help me,' he continued. 'I need someone to come shopping with me to buy stuff for mulled wine. You know what to get for mulled wine, don't you?' Alice thought frantically. It was spices. She didn't know what sort. But she couldn't say no.

'Yes,' she said breathlessly.

'Good,' said Piers. He put his key in the lock. 'Now, come in for a sec. I want to get out of this jacket and put on something warmer.' He looked at her suspiciously. 'You look freezing. Do you want to borrow one of Ginny's sweaters?'

'No, no,' said Alice, 'thanks.' She blushed, but Piers was opening the door and didn't see.

'Right,' he said, bounding up the stairs. 'Won't be long.'

Alice hovered in the hallway and hugged herself, half from cold, half from an unspecified nervousness. Even though she'd been coming round to see Ginny and Piers and Duncan quite a lot, she hadn't really ever spent any time with Piers. He unnerved her slightly; his voice was so loud, and sometimes she wasn't sure if he was being serious or not.

Ginny and Duncan were much easier to get along with. They always seemed pleased to see her, and made her cups of tea, and asked what had happened at school. Which was, in a way, Alice admitted to herself, just what her parents did—but with them it was completely different. When she told Ginny and Duncan about things, it all suddenly seemed far more interesting than before. Duncan always listened really intently, and made loud exclamations all the time, and called it the Unfolding Saga of St Catherine's. And Ginny always knew what she meant and understood why things were important, not like her mother, who always said things like, *But if you've got a free period, why can't you spend it getting some of your homework done?*

Sometimes Ginny would tell her to come upstairs, and show her some clothes she'd bought, or some perfume, or make-up. Once, she'd made Alice up to look really glamorous, and another time she'd actually given her a brown jumper which she said she couldn't wear and would look stunning on Alice. Sometimes she brought stuff home from work and asked Alice to give her a hand, folding up press releases and putting them in envelopes, or labelling photographs of big country houses. She'd promised that when Alice had to do work experience for school, she could come and work in her office, and actually go on a press trip with real journalists.

Duncan didn't ever seem to do any work, but he

always had funny stories about what he'd done during the day and about what he called the Good Burghers of Silchester. At first Alice thought he meant Burger King and McDonald's, but then she'd realized he actually meant all the people he met in the town centre. He seemed to go into town nearly every day, and he always saw something exciting or weird or revolting, or had a long conversation with a complete stranger. He never seemed to do normal things.

Sometimes Alice wondered whether she went round to see them all too much. Once or twice, when she'd arrived, Ginny had said kindly, 'Actually, Alice, this isn't a great time,' and Alice always felt like running away and never ever going back. But then Ginny always said something like, 'But how about tea on Saturday?' or 'You will come back tomorrow, won't you?' And so she always did.

And, really, she couldn't bear to keep away. When she was with them, everything seemed exciting and glossy and fun. It made home seem even more drab and boring. Once, Ginny suggested that they should invite Alice's parents round for a drink to meet them properly.

'They're very trusting,' she said, 'letting you spend all this time with a bunch of people they hardly know. Why don't you bring them round sometime?' Alice wriggled uncomfortably on her chair, and said her parents were very busy, and never went out, and they didn't mind where she went, honestly. In fact, that wasn't quite true. When she'd eventually told Liz and Jonathan where she was spending all this time after school, Liz had immediately suggested that Ginny and Piers come round for supper. Alice gasped in horror.

'They're really busy,' she said, 'and they never know when they're going to be free. But I'll ask them,' she added hurriedly, as she saw her mother opening her mouth to protest. 'I'll ask them.'

Ask them! Alice shuddered at the thought of it; of leading Ginny and Piers and Duncan through the empty passages and classrooms of the tutorial college; of taking them up the narrow stairs to the tiny flat, of expecting them to sit down and eat shepherd's pie and talk to her awful parents. Her mother would pretend to be really hip, as if she knew all about acting, and her father would say things like, 'Which one is *Summer Street*? Is it the one in Australia?'

Alice now knew all about *Summer Street*. She knew that Ian Everitt was leaving the series, that they'd definitely decided to recast his part and that they'd asked Piers to audition for it. And she knew that he simply had to get it.

A few weeks ago, she and Ginny had spent the evening together alone while Piers and Duncan were seeing a play in London, and after a few glasses of wine, Ginny had told her all about it. How Piers hardly had any work any more, and how wonderful it would be if he was in *Summer Street,* and how then they could afford to move to a big house in Berkshire and have lots of children and Alice could come and stay with them every summer. She got really excited about it, and so did Alice, and then they opened another bottle of wine and phoned up for some pizza and watched all the videos of Piers in old episodes of *Coppers*.

Alice had never seen Piers on television before, and

she was amazed. Amazed at how good he was, just like a proper famous actor, and amazed at how spooky it was, seeing him on the screen. And how weird she felt when she saw the bit where he kissed one of the police girls. She wanted to ask Ginny what she felt like when she saw that, but didn't quite dare. So they both sat, hugging their knees, watching in silence, as Piers slowly undressed the girl, and murmured things against her neck, and kissed her all over, and then the next thing it was morning and Piers and the girl were in bed together.

And then Ginny looked at Alice really strangely, and started asking her about her parents. Things like how long they'd been married, and wasn't it really hard for them running a business, and did her mother get much chance to have a social life. Alice had never really thought about either of her parents having a *social* life before. But she answered all Ginny's questions as best she could. And then suddenly Ginny leant over and gave Alice a big hug, and said, 'Oh, poor little Alice!'

Alice thought it was all a bit odd. But when she shyly told Duncan what had happened, he said that was just like Ginny, the old lush. And then he explained what a lush was, and then he somehow ended up being Sir Toby Belch for the rest of the evening.

'Right then!' Alice gave a startled jump as Piers appeared by her side, now wearing a huge cream aran jersey under a Barbour. 'Let's go shopping!'

They headed off down the street, Piers striding along briskly, Alice scuttling beside him; taking three steps for every two of his. For the first few minutes they proceeded in silence. Alice tried frantically to think of something to say. At one point she actually opened her mouth, but then thought better of it. It was only when they got to the short cut that she spoke.

'Actually, this way's quicker.' She flushed, as Piers stopped in his tracks.

'Really? Down there?'

'It's a short cut. I mean,' she floundered as his gaze fell on her, 'we don't have to go that way. We could carry on. It's just—'

'Of course we'll go that way.' Piers bestowed on Alice a charming smile as they began to walk again. 'Aren't I lucky to have had you with me? I would never have thought of looking for a short cut.' Alice glowed silently with pleasure.

'I went to see the producer of *Summer Street* today,' said Piers suddenly.

'Really?' Alice looked up at him in awe. Piers had never said anything to her about *Summer Street*, only Ginny.

'It's all looking quite good,' Piers added. 'He's going to set me up with an audition in the New Year.'

'Wow. That's so cool. Will you meet, like, all the people?'

'Yes.' He looked down at her. 'In fact, that's part of the audition. I've got to get along with the cast. Be part of the team.'

They had arrived at the supermarket now, and Piers held open the door for Alice. He picked up a basket and looked around expectantly.

'Now come on,' he said. 'What do we want? Cinnamon sticks? Cloves?'

'I think so,' said Alice vaguely. She had just spotted

Antonia Callender on the other side of the shop, with her mother. It would be so cool if she could just walk past with Piers, and kind of nod to Antonia. She tossed back her hair nonchalantly and risked a friendly smile at Piers. Antonia might even think Piers was her boyfriend.

'I think the spices might be that way,' she said, pointing to the other side of the shop.

'OK then.'

As they approached Antonia, Alice could feel her cheeks becoming pinker. She clenched her hand in her pocket and squeezed the lining material tighter. Any minute now, Antonia would see them and . . .

'Hi, Alice!' Antonia's voice rang across the aisle. Alice waited for a second, then casually looked up at Antonia's eager face. Antonia's gaze shifted to Piers, and then back to Alice. Her eyes were bright. Alice gave her a blank look, almost as though she didn't recognize her. Then a bit of a smile.

'Hi, Antonia,' she said shortly. Antonia looked at Piers again and blushed.

'Oh, hello, Alice.' It was Antonia's mother, coming over from the frozen fish counter, looking disapprovingly at Piers. 'Doing some shopping for Mummy?'

'No, actually, we're buying some stuff for mulled wine.' Piers's voice resounded through the shop, confident and arresting. 'Is it cinnamon we want? And cloves?'

'Well, it depends.' Antonia's mother looked at Alice again. 'The way I usually do it is to stick some cloves into oranges. And add brown sugar and water.'

'That's right,' exclaimed Piers. 'I remember now. And lots of brandy.'

'Well,' said Antonia's mother. 'It depends how strong you want it. It depends who's going to be drinking it.' She looked meaningfully at Alice. Antonia shifted uncomfortably from one foot to the other.

'Oh, I think we want it as strong as possible,' said Piers cheerfully. 'Don't you, Alice?'

'Oh yes,' said Alice joyfully. She grinned at him and forced herself not even to look at Antonia. 'Had we better go?' she added bravely.

'Yes, we'd better crack on.' Piers smiled charmingly at Antonia and her mother. 'So nice to meet you,' he said. 'And thank you for the cookery tips.' His voice held just the faintest tinge of mockery, and as they walked away, Alice could hear Antonia wailing at her mother, 'Mummy, why did you have to *say* that?'

'Friend of yours?' Piers asked, as they rounded the corner.

'Enemy,' said Alice succinctly.

'Thought so,' said Piers. They grinned at each other, collaborators' grins, and Alice felt a sudden pull of yearning in her stomach. She looked at Piers, and felt herself growing hot. Somewhere, dim and distant in the back of her mind, resided permanently the silhouetted image of a couple kissing each other passionately. The girl was Alice; the man had always been faceless. But now, in spite of herself, she could see the face of the man. And it was Piers.

When they got back, Ginny and Duncan were sitting on the floor, playing Scrabble. Ginny's head shot up as they entered.

'How was it?'

'What, the supermarket?'

'The meeting! *Summer Street!*'

'Christ, yes. I'd almost forgotten about it.' Piers grinned and began to shrug off his Barbour.

Ginny sat perfectly still and waited. She mustn't say anything; mustn't start hectoring him. But a throbbing feeling, somewhere between excitement and dread, was nearly driving her mad. It couldn't be bad news, surely. Not with Piers looking so cheerful. Now he was going out to hang his Barbour on the banisters, and she nearly squeaked with annoyance. Why couldn't he chuck it onto a chair like he usually did?

'It went really well.'

'What?' Her head jerked up.

'I think he likes me. He said, get this, "We know you can act."'

'He said that to you?' Ginny's eyes lit up. 'Alan Tinker?'

'It was practically the first thing he said.'

'And what did you say?'

'I can't remember. I think I just sort of nodded.'

Ginny drew her knees up, and hugged them tight, trying to quell her pounding exhilaration. *We know you can act.* Her mind lingered lovingly on the phrase for a few moments, then firmly put it away in the back of her mind, to be brought out and savoured in the future.

'And then what happened?'

'Then he said he'd fix up an audition after Christmas, and that the most important thing is being able to get on with the rest of the cast.'

'What?' Duncan looked up. 'What's that supposed to mean?'

'Oh, you know. The usual bollocks. Team work and stuff. I guess they don't want some prima donna.'

'Oh well, you won't get the job then,' said Duncan. 'Everyone knows what a bitch you are to work with.' Ginny gazed at Piers with anxious eyes.

'How do they decide that bit?'

'I spend an afternoon working with the cast. Something like that.'

'And what are they like? Will you get on with them all right?' Too late, Ginny realized how worried she sounded.

'I would hope so,' said Piers, with a hint of tension in his voice. 'Unless I'm being my usual charmless self.'

'Of course! I didn't mean—'

'Of course he will,' said Duncan easily. 'Piece of piss. Now come on, you two, join in our game of Scrabble.' He waved his rack of letters at Piers and Alice, so that the pieces scattered all over the floor.

'We've got stuff for mulled wine,' said Piers. 'And I'm going to light the fire.' He dropped a kiss on Ginny's shiny blond head. 'Do you know how to make mulled wine? We bought cloves and stuff.' Ginny looked up at Piers, and gave him a penitent smile.

'That sounds lovely. I could do with some mulled wine. And I'm sorry, Alice, I haven't even said hello to you yet. How are you?'

'Alice helped me buy the cloves,' said Piers.

'And now she can help me make the mulled wine,' said Duncan quickly. 'I am the world's leading expert on mulling, as you might be aware.'

'And the world's worst fire-maker,' added Piers. 'We know.'

Half an hour later, they resumed the game of Scrabble in front of the beginnings of a fire, armed with glasses of steaming, aromatic mulled wine.

'Bloody hell!' said Piers, as he took a sip. 'What's in this?'

'About three bottles of brandy,' giggled Alice. She and Duncan had already had several glasses, and she could feel herself getting drunk.

'My go,' said Duncan. He stared at the Scrabble board. 'Oh bugger. I can't do anything.' He paused, scratched his head and took a few sips from his glass.

'Is there such a word as X-Y-N-E?' he said eventually. 'Xyne. I'm sure it was in Shakespeare.'

'I don't think so,' said Ginny. She sat comfortably with her back against a chair, tilting her face to the glow of the flames. Piers's fingers were linked with hers, and with every sip of mulled wine she could feel herself relaxing. 'I think you've just made it up.'

'Xyne,' said Duncan musingly. 'Xyne. Isn't it a form of meditation? Xyne karma.'

'Never heard of it,' said Piers.

'Philistine,' retorted Duncan. He sighed hugely. 'Oh well, I can't go then.'

'Of course you can,' said Ginny. 'What about Yen?'

'Oh yes, I suppose that would do,' said Duncan brightly. He looked at his pieces and put them down. 'But I wanted to use my X. I'm sure Xyne's a word. It's very unfair.' He looked severely at Alice. 'What are you sniggering at?'

'My go,' said Ginny. She stared at her letters and

took several sips of mulled wine. Then she giggled. 'I've got one.'

'D-I-C-K,' read Duncan as she put the letters down. 'Dick. You can't have that. It's a name.'

'No it's not!' retorted Ginny. 'It's a thing.' She gave a snort of laughter.

'Is it?' Duncan looked about with raised eyebrows. 'Is it? Could you tell us what it is, please? I've never heard of it. And neither has Alice. Have you, Alice?' He winked at Alice, who was still shaking with giggles. Ginny ignored him.

'Piers, it's your go.'

'No, let Alice go first.'

Alice felt blissful. She was all warm and cosy and drunk, and surrounded by the beautifulest, coolest, funniest people she'd ever met. She controlled her giggles and stared at her row of letters. If only she could think of something funny to put. But as she gazed, her mind went blank. She couldn't see a single word.

'Let me have a look,' said Duncan helpfully. He leant over and whistled. 'Oh dear. Oh dear, oh dear. Crap-letter alert.'

'Is there really nothing?' said Ginny.

'Completely, absolutely noth . . . Wait!' Duncan's voice rose to a squeal. 'I've seen something.' Slowly and ceremonially, he placed each of Alice's letters down on the board in a row. Ginny read them out as they went down.

'J-E-C-C-S – Duncan, is this really a word? – Q-B. Duncan!'

'Jeccsqb,' said Duncan confidently. 'Come on, you're not going to tell me you don't know that one.' He beamed at Alice, whose laughter was now uncontrollable. Her stomach hurt; she couldn't speak. 'Well done! You get a fifty-point bonus for using up all your letters. And another glass of mulled wine.'

Alice's elated mood lasted all the way home. She bounded up the stairs to the flat, feeling euphoric and witty. She had never laughed so much in her life; even now, remembering some of the things Duncan had said made her erupt into a half-giggle. She burst into the sitting-room, a huge grin on her face, to find her parents watching television.

'I've left some supper for you in the oven,' said Liz. 'Vegetable lasagne.'

'Thanks,' said Alice. Suddenly she felt very hungry. Piers and Ginny and Duncan often seemed to just drink, without having any food, and by the time she got home she was always ravenous.

She came back into the sitting-room and sat down, balancing her plate on her knee. The final few minutes of a documentary were playing, and when the title music had finished her father silenced the screen with the remote control. He looked up and smiled at Alice.

'Did you have a nice time this evening?'

'Brilliant,' said Alice, her mouth full of lasagne. 'We played Scrabble.'

'Scrabble! What fun. We haven't played that for ages.' Jonathan looked at Liz. 'Do you feel like a game of Scrabble?'

'Oh, I don't know.' Liz spoke in a bored voice. Then she smiled. 'No, actually, that would be nice. Get the board out.'

When he returned, Jonathan was carrying a piece of paper.

'I've got my sponsorship form for the ECO Christmas Parade,' he said. 'Will you sponsor me?'

'How much?' said Alice. She felt grown-up and generous.

'You should be going on the parade, Alice, not sponsoring it,' objected Liz. 'Aren't you supposed to be a member of the society?'

'Yes, well, I gave out leaflets, didn't I?' said Alice. 'I'm not dressing up as a bloody tree again.'

'It's birds this year,' said Jonathan, 'and don't swear. We've been doing a lot of interesting work in the local woodland. The number of species that manage to survive, just around Silchester, is incredible. But some of them are terribly at risk.' He felt for his glasses. 'Anyway, you can fill in the form later. Let's get on with the Scrabble.'

The sight of the little square pieces in her rack made Alice want to laugh out loud again at the memory of Duncan. She rearranged them for a second or two, then looked up expectantly.

'Who's going first?' she said, in a voice that sounded too loud in this little room. 'I will.'

'Have you forgotten?' said her father, smiling at her indulgently. 'We all pick a letter out of the bag to decide that. Go on.' Alice watched in frustration as her father deliberately picked a piece from the bag, then passed it on.

'I'm first,' announced Liz. She looked at her pieces. 'Hmm. What shall I put?'

Alice gazed at her as she peered at her letters, picking one up, putting it back down again, frowning and cupping her chin in her hand. Then she looked at her father, busily drawing up a chart for the scores. He was actually using a ruler. A *ruler*, for Christ's sake!

'Here we are,' said Liz eventually. 'Temple. Not very exciting, I'm afraid.'

'Well done,' said Jonathan. 'How many's that?' There was a silence while he notched up the points. Alice felt like screaming. All the sounds in the room seemed magnified: the clinking of the pieces, the rustle of the bag, her mother's breathing and her father's Biro.

'Alice,' he said. 'Your turn.'

Alice stared at her pieces, willing something exciting to happen.

'Can I have Pete?' she said eventually.

'P-E-A-T?' said her father.

'No, P-E-T-E,' said Alice. She looked challengingly at her father.

'That's a proper name,' he said. 'Not allowed. Try again!'

'What about Teep? I'm sure there's such a word as Teep!' Her voice sounded slightly hysterical to her own ears, and she looked at her mother for a bit of support. She could at least laugh. But her mother was gazing moodily into space and didn't even seem to have heard her.

'Really, Alice!' Her father looked at her in surprise. 'You must be able to do better than that. Let me have a look.'

Alice passed her letters silently over to him, and felt a crushing sense of misery fall over her. She didn't want to be sitting in this poky, silent little room. She didn't want to be here, playing Scrabble with her awful, boring parents. She wanted to be back at Twelve Russell Street, playing with Ginny and Duncan and laughing and drinking, and glancing up every so often to see whether, by any remote, delicious chance, Piers might be looking at her.

CHAPTER NINE

Early on the morning of the ECO Parade, Anthea drove into Silchester and came back with two big boxes.

'Boys!' she called as she came in through the door. 'Come here and see what I've got!'

They arrived in the hall still in their pyjamas and dressing-gowns, munching on Weetabix. Hannah followed behind, holding a mug of the strong, sweet breakfast tea without which she couldn't function in the mornings.

'Look!' said Anthea proudly, and held out a box to Daniel. He peered at it.

'Owl, ten to twelve,' he read.

'This one's Owl, eight to ten,' reported Andrew. 'I wonder what they are,' he added interestedly.

'Open it and see,' said Anthea. Daniel looked up at her. He had a dawning, awful suspicion as to what might be in the boxes. But dutifully he began to tug at the ties which held the lid on. Andrew got there before him.

'It's feathers!' he said.

'It's a costume!' said Anthea. Daniel finally got the lid of his box off and looked inside. An owl's face looked back at him. With slightly shaking fingers, he picked it up. It was a whole hollow head, made out of brown feathers and furry material. There were two big yellow eyes with eyeholes punched in them, and an orange plastic beak. And curled up inside the box was a furry, feathery owl's body.

'It's got wings that you can flap as you walk along,' said Anthea in a pleased voice. Andrew and Daniel exchanged glances.

'Do we have to wear them?' asked Daniel. 'Couldn't we just have face paint like last year?' Anthea looked surprised.

'No,' she said sharply. 'Don't be so silly. Now, when you've finished your breakfast you can go and put them on. We've got to leave at eleven.' She looked from Daniel's glum face to Andrew, who was staring thoughtfully at his costume. 'Come on, both of you,' she exclaimed. 'Look a bit more cheerful! This parade's going to be fun! And you'll both look splendid.' She glanced at Hannah. 'Won't they, Hannah?'

'Splendid,' echoed Hannah in indeterminate tones. Anthea peered suspiciously at her, then started to walk briskly up the stairs.

'Now hurry up with your breakfast,' she said over her shoulder. 'We don't want to be late for the start of the parade.'

When she had gone round the corner, Daniel turned agonized eyes on Hannah.

'We can't wear these!' he said. 'We'll look like complete nerds!'

'It won't be so bad,' said Hannah. 'No one will know it's you inside.'

'They will,' said Andrew. 'They'll know it's us because Mummy will tell them.' Hannah started laughing.

'You've got a point there,' she said. She looked back at Daniel, who was miserably fingering his costume. 'Look, Daniel,' she said kindly, 'put it on when you've finished your breakfast, and if it looks too awful, maybe your mother will say you don't have to wear it.'

'OK,' said Daniel. He dropped the box on the floor and gave it a little kick. 'But I bet she won't,' he added gloomily.

Marcus was sitting at the breakfast table, sipping his coffee, utterly oblivious to the arrival of the costumes. He looked as though he was reading the newspapers spread out before him, but in fact his mind was elsewhere. The night before, Leo Francis had popped round to Witherstone's, ostensibly for a simple goodwill meeting between local solicitor and local estate agent. When the door had closed on Suzy, he had leaned over to Marcus.

'You'll be glad to hear,' he murmured, 'that the Panning Hall estate has been granted probate, and sold privately at the asking price you suggested.'

'Ah, good,' replied Marcus softly, ignoring the nervous thrill that leapt through his chest. 'And your clients were satisfied with that?'

'Wholly satisfied,' Leo said, smirking at Marcus. 'Living, as they do, in the States, they have very little appreciation of the current state of the British property market. I had warned them that the estate might not fetch a great deal, and I believe they were rather pleased with the amount that they received.' Marcus paused, and studied his blotter. He wasn't quite sure how he was supposed to be playing this meeting. Was it done to ask direct questions? Or did the whole conversation have to be carried out as though it were being recorded as evidence against them?

'And the purchaser?' he said eventually.

'The property was bought as an investment,' said Leo smoothly, 'by a small private company.' He smiled at Marcus.

'Aha,' said Marcus, nodding wisely. 'A private company.' Owned by Leo, obviously. He wondered briefly how it was that Leo had the money to make such a huge purchase. Perhaps he was in partnership with someone. Or perhaps he had amassed a fortune from having pulled similar scams in the past. After all, on this deal alone, he stood to make a good million profit from selling the estate on. Minus the cut of twenty per cent that he would give to Marcus.

Marcus smiled at Leo again.

'And will this company perhaps be looking to sell the estate fairly soon?' he said, then wondered if that was too blatant. But Leo grinned even harder.

'Imminently,' he said. He paused, and looked out of the window. 'I understand the market has rallied lately,' he said distantly.

'It has been doing better,' agreed Marcus. 'Considerably better.'

Now his attention was caught by a headline on the front page. *Property Prices Down*. Not in Panning, he thought, and silently smirked to himself. The whole thing had been ridiculously easy. Two hundred thousand pounds, for six days' work. What was that as an hourly rate?

As he was trying to work it out, the phone rang.

'Marcus? It's Miles.'

'Miles, hello.' For some reason, hearing Miles's voice made Marcus feel suddenly guilty. He searched quickly around for something innocuous to say.

'Lovely day, isn't it?' he exclaimed brightly at last. 'The boys are going on that big parade later on. Should be a good event.' Oh, for Christ's sake, now he was gabbling.

'Marcus, I just wanted to ask whether you and Leo Francis had a meeting yesterday.' Marcus's heart began to thump.

'Oh. Er, yes, as a matter of fact we did.' There was a short silence. Marcus forced himself not to plunge in with unasked-for, incriminating explanations. What was wrong with having a meeting with Leo, for Christ's sake?

'Have you been doing business with him?' Marcus flushed.

'Well, you know,' he said. 'The odd bit. Why do you ask?' he added, suddenly feeling annoyed with Miles. What right did he have to phone up like this and start quizzing him?

'I only mention it,' Miles paused in his deliberate

fashion, 'because I thought you might not be aware of Leo Francis's reputation.'

'Reputation?' Marcus could feel his voice edging slightly higher. 'What do you mean? Inefficiency?'

'No, Marcus, not inefficiency. I'm sure he's very efficient at what he does.'

'Well, then, what?'

'I have only hearsay to go on.' Miles's voice came quietly and calmly over the line. 'But general opinion is that Leo Francis may not be completely above board all of the time. George Easton altogether refuses to deal with him. Apparently there was once a case at Easton's in which a junior member of staff was persuaded by Francis into some sort of minor fraud. Nothing was ever proved, but since then—'

'What happened to the junior member of staff?' said Marcus, without meaning to. Oh Christ. What was he saying? There was a startled pause.

'I'm afraid I don't know,' said Miles eventually. 'Marcus—' His voice was drowned by the sound of Daniel and Andrew coming into the kitchen amid a flurry of scuffles.

'Stop it, Andrew!' Daniel was shouting. 'It's not funny.'

'Boys!' Marcus put his hand over the receiver. 'Quiet! I'm on the phone! Sorry, Miles,' he said into the phone. 'What were you saying? There's a bit of hoohah going on here.'

'I won't take up any more of your time, then. But please—'

'What?' Marcus was aware that he sounded childish and belligerent.

'Nothing. I'm sure you know what you're doing.'

As Marcus put the phone down, he felt suddenly fearful and uneasy. Did Miles know something? Was he trying to warn him? If so, he was too late. It had all been done. For a brief, terrifying moment, he imagined that Miles had somehow found out; had overheard their conversation. Then he deliberately thrust those thoughts aside. It was impossible. Unthinkable. He forced a smile onto his face and looked up.

'Hey, what's wrong?' he said. He peered at Daniel's disconsolate face, then glanced at Hannah. She shrugged at him meaningfully and went to put on the kettle. 'Boys? Daniel?'

'Mummy's making us wear these awful costumes,' burst out Daniel suddenly. 'We're going on the ECO parade and she's got owl suits for us.'

'Owl suits?' Marcus gave an uncertain laugh. 'Why owls?'

'You have to be a bird,' said Daniel, sitting down hopelessly. 'It's a parade for birds.' He stared miserably at his half-eaten bowl of Weetabix and pushed it around.

'Well then,' said Marcus jovially. 'I think owl suits sound like fun.'

'No you don't,' retorted Daniel with sudden scorn. 'You'd never wear one, would you?'

'I might,' said Marcus. 'Or perhaps not an owl. I think I'd look good as a moorhen. How about you, Hannah?' He smiled at her with the good-humoured veneer of a television presenter, hoping she would pick up the cue. Hannah was notoriously unpredictable at saying the right thing to the children; on one occasion Anthea had nearly sacked her for making some chance reference to the joys of cannabis.

But now she smiled back brightly at Marcus and said, 'I think I'd be a good penguin.' She looked at Daniel. 'And I think you'll make a brilliant owl.'

'No I won't,' said Daniel vehemently. 'I'll look like a wanker.'

'Daniel!' Anthea's voice rose, outraged, from the doorway.

'What's a wanker?' asked Andrew at once. Marcus looked helplessly at Hannah, who started giggling into her mug of tea.

'Daniel, how dare you use such language!' Anthea neared the table and looked suspiciously at Hannah.

'What's a wanker?' said Andrew again. Daniel blushed.

'I don't want to dress up as a bloody owl,' he said. His face went crimson and he didn't look at Anthea. 'I don't want to go on the parade at all.'

Marcus risked a glance at Anthea. Her mouth was set ominously firm, but her eyes were wavering uncertainly between the assembled faces. Marcus suspected she wasn't quite sure how to deal with the situation.

'Perhaps,' he began in a soothing voice, then wished he hadn't spoken, as Anthea's head whipped round towards him.

'What?'

'Perhaps Daniel needn't go on the march,' Marcus said, in a reasonable voice. 'Perhaps he could stay at home.'

'He's got to go!' Anthea's eyes glittered angrily at Marcus, then swivelled towards Daniel. 'You've got to go!' she insisted. Marcus sighed inwardly and looked away. His suggestion had, he realized, simply given her an excuse for an outburst. He should have kept his mouth shut. 'It's down on your scholarship application form!' Anthea was exclaiming to Daniel. 'It says you're a keen junior member of a local environmental society.'

'So what? It doesn't matter if I don't go on one lousy march!'

'It does! You need to be able to talk about it at your interview. They won't be very impressed if you didn't go on the annual parade.'

'They won't care,' began Daniel.

'And yesterday,' Anthea gave Marcus a glance of self-vindication, 'yesterday, someone told me that the head-master of Bourne College has recently joined the society. I'm sure he'll be there on the parade. You might even get to meet him.' She threw this information down like a trump card and looked around triumphantly. Hannah shrugged, and moved off towards the sink as though admitting defeat.

This bloody scholarship to Bourne College had become, Marcus thought, like the word of the Lord. Nothing and nobody could argue against it. And Anthea had decreed herself the only person who could pronounce on what might or might not affect it. He gave Daniel a surreptitious sympathetic look. Despite his protestations, he couldn't think of anything worse than having to dress up as some stupid bird and march through the centre of Silchester. As if that would affect a scholarship result one way or the other. Anthea was just using it as a way of dictating Daniel's life. He was going to have to talk to her; make her see sense; put a stop to it.

But he'd do it another time. He couldn't face a row just then; not when he was feeling so pleased with himself. Daniel would just have to wear the costume to the parade and they'd all have a quiet life. Ignoring Hannah's raised eyebrows, averting his eyes from Daniel's flushed face, Marcus neatly folded his newspaper and made his way out of the kitchen, down the hall and into his study.

He closed the door, sat back in his chair and dialled the number of the Silchester Tutorial College. If Liz heard the phone ringing from upstairs, she would, if she was able to, run down and answer it. It was safer, she had told him, than ringing the number in the flat. Not that Jonathan was remotely suspicious, she had added, and Marcus had felt a sudden compunction for this trusting man whom they were deceiving so easily. But the feeling had come and gone and been forgotten. Now he sat with his chin resting in his palm, his elbow on the desk, slightly tensed, waiting for the pleasure of hearing Liz answer.

'Hello?' She was panting slightly, and Marcus had a vision of her, red-cheeked and dishevelled.

'You still OK for today?'

'Yes. Why? Are you—'

'I'm still fine. Just thought I'd check.'

'Oh. All right.' Her breathing had subsided a little, and Marcus imagined her leaning against the wall, running her hand through her hair and smiling at the receiver. 'So you've brought me all the way down here for nothing?'

'I suppose so.' He had a sudden thought. 'No, actually, not for nothing. I wanted to ask you a question.'

'What?'

'It's a bit personal.'

'Fire ahead.'

'OK then. Tell me, is your husband going to dress up as a bird for this blasted parade?'

Upstairs in the kitchen, Alice was hurriedly spooning her last mouthful of cereal into her mouth. As soon as she had done so she stood up from her seat on the radiator, still munching. She dumped her bowl in the sink, picked up her half-drunk cup of coffee, and retreated to her bedroom before her father could say anything to her.

She shut the door and stared disconsolately at her reflection in the mirror. She was too pale, she decided, and too thin, and she had awful teeth, all pointy and crooked. She thought enviously of Ginny's white, even teeth; of Ginny's dimpling, infectious smile. Ginny's gurgling laugh. If Alice ever laughed it came out either in a terrible high-pitched giggle or in great guffaws.

She scowled at herself, reached for her black eyeliner and drew a thick line on each eyelid. She drew another line underneath each eye. Then she brushed a glob of glutinous dark mascara onto each set of lashes. She batted her eyes alluringly at herself. Not too bad, if you didn't look at the rest of her face. She tossed her hair back with a film-star gesture and pressed her lips together hard so that the blood would flow into them. 'Hi, Piers,' she said casually. She gave a half-smile and immediately looked at her cheeks to see if they were blushing. But they were still pale and clear. 'You've got such lovely skin,' Ginny had once exclaimed. 'Not a single line.'

Alice thought about Ginny's skin. It looked older than Alice's, of course. But somehow it went with Ginny's face. It went with her shiny blond hair and her wide smile, and the round, large-nippled breasts that Alice had seen a couple of times when they'd tried on clothes together. Alice was utterly unable to relate her own pale, thin, undeveloped body to Ginny's creamy curves. And she knew it wasn't just that she was younger. Never, in a million years, would she look anything like Ginny.

And it was Ginny that Piers was in love with. Or at least Alice supposed he was in love with her. The thought of Piers being in love with anyone, even if it was Ginny, not her, made Alice feel a bit overcome. And the daydream she often had, about him suddenly noticing her and pulling her towards him and giving her a long, passionate kiss—preferably with Antonia Callender watching jealously—gave her a completely delicious feeling that she could normally make last for a whole lesson.

She gave her hair a last flick, checked her back view in the mirror, and pulled on her jacket, giving her pocket a perfunctory pat to check her lighter was there. She did sometimes have a cigarette when she was round at Twelve Russell Street, and Ginny and Piers were fine about it. But she had noticed she was smoking less and less when she was there. The others didn't smoke—except perhaps dope, which they never did in front of her. And somehow it wasn't the same, puffing away on her own, filling up an ashtray with her own solitary stubs.

Today, however, she had decided she would definitely

smoke a few. Everyone looked sexier when they smoked. She would sit on the floor and lean back against the sofa and take deep drags and push a hand casually through her hair. And she wouldn't look at Piers at all.

She picked up her rucksack and went out into the hall, smearing cherry-flavoured lip salve onto her lips as she went. Her father was still in the kitchen, engrossed in a letter. At the sight of his hunched shoulders, Alice felt a sudden guilt that she wasn't going on that stupid parade with him.

'Bye, Daddy,' she said awkwardly. 'Hope it goes well.'

'What's that?' Her father looked up, a distracted expression on his face. 'Oh, yes, thank you.' He looked at his watch. 'I'd better start getting ready, I suppose.' He glanced down at the letter in his hand, then looked up again with a bright smile that didn't look quite right. His eyes fell on her jacket, her rucksack, and the heavy-patterned cotton scarf which she was now swathing thickly around her neck. Ginny had bought that scarf for Alice; she said she'd seen it in the market and couldn't resist it. Alice loved it.

'Are you going out?' her father said.

'Yes,' said Alice, wishing somehow that instead she could say, *No, I've decided to come on the parade with you*. But she couldn't. She just couldn't. She pushed the ends of the scarf into the collar of her jacket, and picked up her rucksack. 'I might see you in Silchester,' she added. 'We might go Christmas shopping.'

'Yes, that sounds a good idea,' said her father vaguely. He didn't seem to be listening to her. Alice gave an impatient snort, and marched out of the kitchen. She couldn't bear standing there a minute longer, feeling guilty and annoyed all at the same time.

She slammed the front door of the tutorial college, and began to stride off down the road, watching her breath turn to steam in the cold air, wondering if Piers would open the door when she got to Russell Street, and agonizing, for the millionth time, over what on *earth* she was going to buy him—and Ginny, and Duncan—for Christmas.

Jonathan remained motionless when Alice had gone, staring into the corner of the kitchen, holding the fluttering white letter in his hand. He was still in this position when Liz came back in.

'Was that Alice I heard charging out?' she said. She smiled widely at Jonathan and, as she went past to switch the kettle on, put a hand out to rumple his hair. Then she wondered whether she was behaving suspiciously. Did she usually rumple Jonathan's hair? Or had she only ever done that to Marcus? While Marcus's thick, glossy locks naturally invited a hand to run through them, Jonathan's hair was thinning and rather dry. She tried to remember rumpling his hair in the past. But the only vision that came into her mind was that of plunging her fingers into Marcus's dark hair as they made love; of caressing his head as they lay companionably afterwards; of tickling the back of his neck as they drove back to Silchester, until he turned his head to smile at her.

This affair with Marcus was, she realized, robbing her of her instinctive, everyday behaviour towards Jonathan. Every gesture she made now was measured; every comment designed to quell suspicion; every tender moment shadowed by the memory of a counterpart with Marcus. She couldn't remember how she used to act before all of this; couldn't judge what was natural and what was false. She felt like an actor with selective amnesia: sometimes everything would come flooding back with accustomed ease; sometimes she would be left stranded, with only a small repertoire of comments and gestures to get her through the moment.

She gave a quick glance at Jonathan. He was still sitting stationary on the stool, staring at nothing. And he probably didn't notice any of it, she thought, with sudden irritation. He had always been hopelessly oblivious to variations in the tone of her voice; to meaningful gestures or raised eyebrows designed to galvanize him into action. He wouldn't wonder why she was suddenly rumpling his hair; he probably hadn't even noticed her doing it.

'Do you want some more coffee?' she said, trying to sound unconcerned. She looked round. 'Jonathan?' He swivelled to face her, his face weary and unsmiling. Oh my God, thought Liz. Oh my God. He's found out.

'Look at this,' he said, holding out the letter. Liz's eyes flickered to it, then rose to meet his.

'What is it?' she asked, hating her voice for faltering.

'It's a letter,' said Jonathan.

'I can see that! Who's it from?' She picked up a mug from the draining board and began, needlessly, distractedly, to dry it.

'It's from Brown's,' said Jonathan. He took a deep, sighing breath and rubbed his hand over his face. 'They've written to us about our mortgage.'

Liz stared at him, unable to respond as she knew she should. She tried to adopt an expression of concern; tried to summon up a shared feeling of alarm. But a little voice inside her sighed with relief. It was only the mortgage. She and Marcus were safe from discovery.

'What's wrong?' she said, wrinkling her brow in what she hoped looked like worry. Jonathan shrugged.

'I don't know,' he said. 'Maybe nothing. It's from the new branch manager. She's carrying out a review of all small business loans. She wants to see us. She says she isn't sure why we've been allowed to carry on with two mortgages.'

'She?' Jonathan looked down at the letter and nodded.

'Barbara Dean.'

'Are you sure it isn't a man called Dean Barbara? People have funny names, you know.' Liz grinned at Jonathan, trying to haul him out of his slough of gloom. But he peered at the letter again.

'Barbara Dean, brackets, Mrs.' He looked up at Liz. 'Close brackets.'

'OK. It's a woman.' Liz began to feel an impatience of the sort that hit her whenever pupils put up their hands to point out that the wrong date was written on the board. 'And what does she say?'

'She wants to see us. To discuss our position, she says.' He read from the letter. ' "In particular, I wish to go over the circumstances which have led to you keeping such a large mortgage on your property in Russell Street, together with a substantial mortgage on your business." '

'Well, that's OK. I mean, it was their decision to let

us keep both.' Liz flushed slightly as she remembered the hand that Marcus had played in Brown's making that decision. Used some old connection, he'd told her. Some friend of the family's. But there was nothing really wrong with that, she told herself. After all, he'd said he would sort out their mortgage situation even before that day in Russell Street; even before they'd . . . She shook her head impatiently, as her thoughts began to swim down familiar, delightful paths, and dragged her attention back to Jonathan.

'I know it was their decision,' he was saying. 'But now they might regret it.'

'Well, we've got the mortgages now. And we're paying them off OK, aren't we?'

'Nearly,' said Jonathan. He pushed a weary hand through his hair. 'Actually, this month, we're in arrears.' Liz stared at him.

'Are we? Why?'

'Because at the moment, we haven't got the money to pay all our bills. Something had to go.' Jonathan stared at Liz, willing her to respond; to show some interest; to apply some of her zest for tackling problems to this, their hugest problem ever. But her eyes met his coldly.

'Well, they'll just have to wait,' she said. 'They can't exactly do anything about it.'

'Can't they?'

'Well, can they?' Liz demanded. Jonathan shrugged.

'I don't know. I really don't know.' He gazed hopelessly down at the letter, and Liz felt a rush of impatient fury. She felt like ripping the page from his hand and telling him to brace up, get a grip, stop being such a wimp. An immediate, utterly unfair comparison with Marcus inevitably sprang into her mind. If Marcus got a letter like that through the post, he would be dynamic and forceful; he wouldn't just accept it; he'd be on the phone immediately, pulling strings and sorting it out.

Of course. Marcus. The realization hit her with a pleasurable shock. Marcus would sort it all out for her. All he had to do was telephone one of his cronies at Brown's and put in a word or two. A feeling of delight spread over her as she considered the power that Marcus had in Silchester; the power that, by proxy, she now had also. She was in another league from Jonathan; poor, sad, worried Jonathan, with his financial humility; his low expectations; his unfailing deference to authority. He had no idea of how the world was really run; he had no idea of the influence that she, his own wife, could wield.

'I wouldn't worry about it,' she said, trying not to sound too flippantly cheerful. The kettle was boiling, and she spooned some coffee into her mug. 'Why don't you go off now and get ready for the parade,' she suggested, 'and we'll go and see this Barbara Dean character next week. There's nothing you can do about it now, anyway.'

'I suppose you're right,' said Jonathan, folding the letter up carefully and pushing it back into its envelope. 'There's nothing either of us can do about it until Monday.' Liz poured hot water over her coffee, took a sip and said nothing.

When she'd gone out, to do some shopping, Jonathan made his way downstairs to his classroom to pick up some marking. On his way, he passed a collection of parcels and packages lying on the landing of the tutorial college. They'd been there almost a week now. Each contained a piece of equipment for the new language lab. Computers, software, cassettes, and workbooks. When they'd arrived, he'd deliberately refrained from tearing them open. They were Liz's; they belonged to her project. And when she'd arrived home that evening, he'd told her to look on the landing, with a small thrill of excitement.

But all she'd said was, 'Oh, good. They've arrived.' She hadn't even bothered to open them. And since then, all that lovely, expensive equipment had just been sitting there. Jonathan wondered whether Liz appreciated how much all this stuff cost. Whether she realized that he'd taken out a costly loan to pay for it. Then it occurred to him that he'd never told her about the loan. Only he knew about it. And the bank. Oh God. Jonathan sat down on a wooden classroom chair and buried his face in his hands. Suddenly he felt very lonely.

As soon as he tried to get into his owl costume, Daniel could feel that it was too small. He struggled about uncomfortably until he was halfway into it, and then stared at himself in the mirror on his wardrobe. His legs were now covered in yellow felt, and an orange cut-out claw flopped on top of each shoe. His body had become an unwieldy barrel of brown feathers and furry stuff. He couldn't bear to think what he would look like when the head was on.

'It's too small!' Andrew's voice rose up behind him, on the landing. Daniel turned round, and saw his younger brother staggering comically down the passage, half in, half out of his owl suit. He gave another glance at himself in the mirror, then went to the door.

'Mine's too small as well!' he called, and went out onto the landing. 'Look!' Andrew turned round and saw him. He began to giggle.

'Far too small!' he exclaimed. 'Size nought, more like. Your one's size nought!'

'Your one's size minus a hundred!' rejoined Daniel. He flapped the wings of his suit comically and Andrew copied him.

'Minus a thousand!'

'Minus a million!' They flapped their wings at each other and giggled hysterically.

'Boys! Quietly!' Anthea was coming up the stairs. 'Let me have a look,' she called. She reached the top step and looked crossly at them. 'Put them on properly!' she exclaimed.

'They won't fit,' said Andrew. 'They're too small.' Anthea looked suspiciously from him to Daniel, who nodded.

'My one's far too small,' he said.

'Size minus five thousand million billion,' said Andrew. Daniel laughed.

'Be quiet!' said Anthea. There was a short silence. Daniel looked at Andrew. He was still mouthing 'billion billion billion billion.' Daniel started to mouth 'trillion trillion trillion' at him. They both started to giggle. Daniel gave a snort.

'That's enough!' exclaimed Anthea. 'Go to your rooms and get those costumes on.' She tugged roughly at Daniel's. 'Look. It does fit. You're just not trying. Take your jersey off and really pull it on.'

Daniel went to his room and closed the door behind him. He dutifully took off his jersey, and hauled at the shoulders of his costume. He screwed up his face and wriggled about until one shoulder was on. Then the other. He took a few cautious steps. The legs wouldn't move very far, and his shoulders felt pinned down. All in all he felt strung-up and uncomfortable. But at least it was on. Experimentally, he put on the owl head. It was all dark and scratchy, and he couldn't see properly out of the eye holes. He felt as though he might be dead. He breathed loudly and miserably at himself for a few seconds, then took the owl head off and put it on the bed. Perhaps he wouldn't have to wear the head bit. But then perhaps that would be worse. He opened his door and waddled out onto the landing.

'Well, that doesn't look too bad!' Anthea's voice was truculent with relief. 'Where's Andrew? Andrew!' she called. 'Come out and show us your costume!'

Andrew appeared at the door of his bedroom, holding the owl suit in one hand. Daniel felt a twinge of shock. Something had happened to Andrew's costume. One wing dangled sadly from his hand, and there were ragged bits of cloth sticking up from it.

'I tore it,' said Andrew unrepentantly. 'By accident. I was trying to pull it on, like you said.' He held out the furry bundle to Anthea. 'It's all spoilt,' he added, as though she might not have understood him. 'I can't wear it in the parade.'

'Andrew! You naughty boy!' Daniel winced at his mother's furious voice, as she held up the poor torn costume. But his immediate, overriding feeling was one of relief. If Andrew's costume was ruined, they wouldn't have to wear them. He caught Andrew's eye, and Andrew grinned at him. He must have really pulled at his costume to tear it, thought Daniel. It was quite strong stitching. Maybe he'd even cut it. But nobody could prove it wasn't an accident. It was a really good idea. He grinned back at Andrew and began to shrug at the shoulders of his costume.

'What do you think you're doing?' Anthea's voice caught him off-guard. 'Put your costume back on!'

'What?'

'Put it back on! You're wearing it to the parade.'

'But . . .' Daniel looked from her scarlet face to the placid expression of his brother, unable to believe his ears. 'But it's not fair!' he cried. 'Why do I have to wear it if Andrew doesn't?'

'Andrew has been a very naughty boy,' his mother said sharply. 'And he will be punished. But that's got nothing to do with what you wear to the parade.'

'It has!' Daniel couldn't believe no-one was going to admit the injustice in this. 'I don't want to wear this crappy costume if Andrew doesn't!'

'Don't speak like that!' Anthea's voice was like steel.

'I'll paint my face,' Andrew suggested sweetly. 'Like last year. Then we'll both be dressed up.'

'It's not the same!' said Daniel savagely. He wrenched

furiously at the seams of his costume. 'It's not bloody well the same! You know it isn't.' With a shudder of horror, he gave up on the seams and looked desperately from Andrew to Anthea.

'It's unfair,' he said. 'It's bloody fucking, fucking bloody unfair.' And before Anthea could react, he swept backwards into his room and slammed the door.

CHAPTER TEN

The Silchester ECO parade always followed the same pattern. At eleven o'clock, all the regular members of the society, plus spouses, children and dogs, plus those members who felt guilty about never going to meetings, plus various hangers on, met at the playing fields of St Catherine's School. They picked up piles of leaflets to hand out, accepted cups of coffee provided by the school catering staff, and then plunged joyfully into a general mêlée of greetings and gossip.

It was normally at least an hour before they could be assembled into any kind of order, and given yelled instructions on the route of the parade, its purpose, and the supportive messages sent by sympathetic members of the town council. This year, Jonathan had been asked to give the instructions, and as he raised his voice above the hubbub, he wondered, not for the first time, whether all this really helped the cause. Half the people here, he thought, casting his eye over the animated faces—most happily chatting and oblivious to his words—had only come for the sociable atmosphere and free mulled wine at the end of the march. They would glance carelessly at the leaflets as they handed them out; they would protest noisily that it was really terrible about all those poor little . . . a hesitation, a glance down at the pamphlet . . . oh, yes, birds. Of course. The poor birds. Criminal, really.

But they had no idea of the real work and ethos of the society. They had no idea of the hours of research carried out by the regular members; of the patient, careful lobbying which went on all year; of the original aim of the founder members to further the environmental cause peacefully. Without force; without polemic—but with reasoned arguments.

This annual parade was almost the antithesis of the original aim of the society, characterized as it was by noisy, ill-informed protestations and, on some occasions in the past, violence. The violence—due mainly to teenage gatecrashers—had been brought under control in recent years, but the whole affair was still riotous and unfocused. Those in the society who periodically suggested bringing the tradition of the parade to an end, however, were shouted down—the society needed a public profile, it was argued. It needed to take the message to the people in the streets.

What message? thought Jonathan, as he surveyed the motley crew in front of him, squinting in the bright winter sun. What message was this lot going to bring to the streets? Some of them probably barely knew what a bird was, let alone an endangered species. His eyes roamed gloomily over the rows of faces, most of which he didn't recognize or only dimly remembered from previous marches. Then his gaze fell, with sudden affection, on two little figures at the side of the crowd. One he recognized as Andrew Witherstone, who had only recently joined the society as a junior member. He was dressed in brown cords and a duffle-coat, and his face was decorated with face paint and a yoghurt pot beak. Standing next to him, holding his hand, was the thin and glamorous Mrs Witherstone, whom Jonathan had never met but only heard about. She was looking down disapprovingly at the other smallish figure, which must be, Jonathan decided, Daniel Witherstone. It was, however, difficult to tell, because whoever it was was wearing a luridly coloured furry owl costume.

Jonathan was fond of the Witherstone boys, particularly of Daniel, who had a stoic approach to life with which Jonathan could sympathize. When he had finished giving out the instructions to the assembly, he climbed down off the makeshift podium and went over to greet them.

'Mrs Witherstone? How do you do? I'm Jonathan Chambers.'

'Hello!' said the woman brightly, her eyes darting about. 'Do call me Anthea.' Her gaze fell on his head. 'Is that a mask?'

'This?' Jonathan tugged at the elastic round his chin. 'It will be when I put it on properly. It's supposed to be a duck.' He smiled at her. 'We've been doing a lot of work this year on the natural habitat of ducks in the area. In fact . . .' Anthea wasn't listening.

'You see, Daniel?' she exclaimed. Jonathan winced

at the sudden strident note in her tone. 'Lots of people are in costumes.' The owl shook silently. Anthea looked up and met Jonathan's questioning eyes.

'You wouldn't believe a boy of twelve could be such a baby, would you, Mr Chambers?' she said, her voice carrying loudly over the heads of the crowd. 'He's made such a terrible fuss about wearing this costume.'

Jonathan eyed the costume and thought that if he were Daniel he would have made a fuss, too. But he couldn't say that to the mother.

'You look very impressive,' he said, trying to catch Daniel's eye through the plastic eye holes of the costume. 'Very smart,' he added. *You look ridiculous,* he added to himself.

Anthea was looking around distractedly.

'I don't suppose you know,' she said, 'if the headmaster of Bourne College is here?' Jonathan raised his eyebrows.

'Geoffrey?' he said. 'I think he said he was going to try to make it. But he's very busy.' He shrugged. 'There are so many people here, he could have arrived and I wouldn't have noticed it. Why? Did you need to speak to him?' Anthea didn't reply. As he had spoken, her expression had changed. Now she fixed him with a suspicious gaze. Jonathan wondered what was wrong. 'Would you like me to give him a message?' he hazarded.

'Do you mean,' said Anthea, 'that you actually know the headmaster of Bourne College?'

'Well, yes,' said Jonathan, in puzzled tones. 'He's become very involved in the society, you know. And then, of course, I used to work with him . . .' His attention was distracted by a shout from behind. 'Sorry,' he said to Anthea. 'I think the parade's about to begin.'

'Oh, don't worry,' said Anthea. She gave him a sudden, unnerving smile. 'We can walk along beside you. That's if you don't mind.' Jonathan looked at her thin, intense face. Then he looked at Andrew, snapping the elastic on his beak, and the miserable owl-form of Daniel.

'Of course I don't mind,' he said. 'It would be a pleasure.'

As they moved off, shuffling in an unsteady mass towards the gates of St Catherine's, Daniel felt as though he was going to expire with humiliation. He felt boiling hot and achy inside his owl head, and although he wasn't actually crying, he knew that if anybody else addressed a remark to him, he would probably start.

It was just so unfair. *So* unfair. It had been Andrew who had been naughty. And it was Andrew who had got the reward of not having to look stupid. A painful shudder of injustice ran through Daniel and he eyed his mother's back with a hateful resentment. He'd been the one who struggled into his owl suit, even though it was definitely too small; he'd been the one to do what his mother said. And it was he who was being punished.

He eyed Andrew, happily walking along, talking to Mr Chambers, secure in the knowledge that he didn't look like a nerd. He was sure Andrew had torn that costume on purpose. Andrew always got what he wanted, even if it meant doing really naughty things; things which Daniel wouldn't be able to bring himself to do. He didn't

ever seem to feel worried about being caught and he
didn't ever feel guilty. At least, not guilty like Daniel felt.
Even when Andrew was in big trouble and really told off,
he cried for a bit and then forgot about it. When Daniel
was in trouble, it haunted him for days. *I'm disappointed
in you*, his mother would say, and his heart would squirm
inside him, and his chest would heave, and he would feel
a slow, dull mortification creep over him.

As they turned into College Road, Andrew came
dancing up to Daniel, who scowled at him before remembering that his face was hidden.

'Mummy's talking about your scholarship,' said Andrew cheerily. 'To Mr Chambers.' Daniel's heart sank.
He didn't want to be reminded of his scholarship. 'She
said if you didn't win, you wouldn't be able to go to
Bourne,' said Andrew. Daniel's head jerked up.

'Really?' His voice shook slightly. 'Daddy said it
didn't really matter.'

'She said the fees were terribly high,' reported Andrew. He gave a little skip, and stretched his yoghurt-
pot beak out from his face on its pieces of elastic.

'D'you think you'll win?' Daniel gave a hopeless
shrug.

'Dunno.'

'Jack Carstairs says his brother is going to win it,'
said Andrew. 'He says his brother can do long division
in his head. Really big numbers.'

Daniel slouched down in his costume, feeling suddenly defeated.

'When I'm in your form,' said Andrew, suddenly
slipping off his plastic beak and swinging it at his side,

'I'm not going to do any scholarships.' They passed a rubbish bin, and Andrew deftly slung the beak into it.

'They'll make you,' said Daniel, without any conviction.

'No they won't,' said Andrew confidently. 'I bet you they won't.' He pulled a piece of chewing-gum out of his pocket and began to unwrap it. As he put it into his mouth, Anthea turned round.

'Andrew!' she called. 'What are you eating? Is it chewing-gum?'

'Yes, Mummy,' called back Andrew politely. 'One of the grown-ups gave it to me.' Anthea gave a doubtful nod, and turned back again.

'Did a grown-up really give it to you?' said Daniel.

'Yes,' said Andrew. 'A shopkeeper gave it to me after I gave him twenty pence.' He began to shake with giggles and, against his will, Daniel found himself unable to help joining in.

Marcus felt bad about Daniel. As he drove out of Silchester, taking care to avoid the roads allocated for the parade, he told himself that he should have stepped in; battled with Anthea; prevented this charade with the costumes from going through. Daniel had looked utterly miserable as he got into Anthea's car; as far as Marcus could make out, it was now only he who was having to wear the costume. Which certainly seemed unfair.

Hannah, like him, plainly thought the whole thing was ridiculous, and Marcus had caught her opening her mouth a couple of times as if to speak. But in the end she had obviously decided it wasn't worth her sticking her neck out for. And he couldn't blame her. If anybody should have said anything, it was himself.

A feeling of guilt assailed him as he parked the car in a side-street and began walking towards the hotel where he and Liz were to meet. If he'd volunteered to go along on the parade, he thought, perhaps he could have done something to cheer Daniel up. They could at least have gone out for lunch or something. He had a sudden vision of a joyful family lunch at the Boar's Head in Silchester; of a happy, relaxed Anthea; of a smiling Daniel; of Andrew playing the fool and making them all laugh.

And instead of that he was here, meeting his mistress in a secret daytime assignation. It was a thought which had filled him with excited anticipation all week. But now his excitement was tempered by a sudden feeling of dismay. He looked distastefully at the chrome-and-glass doors of the hotel as he walked up to the entrance. It had always been his idea to use hotels for their meetings; to choose outfits which were big and impersonal and a fair way from Silchester. Now he regretted his decision. Hotel bedrooms were such sordid places. And today he felt rather sordid himself.

'Afternoon, Mr Witherstone!' Marcus turned in startled horror. Coming up the street behind him was a familiar, grizzled, anoraked man. 'It's Albert,' the man added unnecessarily, as though Marcus couldn't remember who he was. 'You remember me! From the Panning Hall estate.' Marcus flinched, and quickly looked around. No one he knew seemed to be in sight, thank God.

'Hello, Albert,' he said, trying to keep his voice brisk and business-like. 'How are you?'

'Very well indeed, thank you, Mr Witherstone,' said Albert. He paused, and sniffed loudly. 'Haven't seen you in Panning recently,' he added. 'Finished your work there, no doubt.'

'Yes, my work there is finished,' agreed Marcus shortly. He stopped. The entrance to the hotel was just ahead on his left. But he didn't necessarily want Albert watching him go in. On the other hand, the less said about Panning Hall, the better.

'So, how much was the place worth in the end?' Albert's voice rang cheerfully through the air, and Marcus jumped. 'You don't mind my asking?' added Albert. Marcus's heart began to beat faster. This was intolerable. He should have got away while he could. He should have ignored Albert altogether. He should have gone with Anthea and the boys on the ECO parade. He shouldn't be here at all.

'It's just that a few of us in the village were wondering,' Albert was saying.

'Yes, well, I wouldn't wonder if I were you,' snapped Marcus. 'It'll be a while yet until we can finalize things. Strictly speaking, we shouldn't even be talking about it.' He looked impressively at Albert, as though with the full weight of the legal system behind him.

'Oh really?' Albert looked disappointed.

'Yes,' replied Marcus quickly. 'And now, I'm going to have to go, I'm afraid. I have a meeting for which I'm already late. So nice to see you again. Goodbye.' And he strode up the drive of the hotel without looking back at Albert, his heart thumping, and his face sweating, as though he'd survived some sort of near-accident.

Liz had already arrived at the hotel, and Marcus

found her comfortably ensconced in front of the television, sipping a gin and tonic from the mini-bar. A tiny flash of irritation went through him. Of course, he was the one with money; he could hardly expect her to start paying the bills for these rooms. But the reticence which she had once touchingly displayed when it came to the mini-bar and phone and all the other extras had soon melted away. She was learning fast, he thought grimly. Then he chided himself. Was he begrudging his lover one simple gin and tonic?

'Hello there,' he said cheerfully, not quite having to force the smile to his lips. Liz got up and came towards him.

'Hi.' Her lips met his warmly and he felt himself relaxing. 'Drink?' She waved in the direction of the mini-bar with the gracious air of a hostess.

'I think I'll have a whisky.'

Liz picked up the remote control and turned off the television.

'Marcus,' she said seriously, 'I'm afraid we're in a bit of trouble.'

'What?' Marcus whipped round, open bottle in hand. He looked at Liz's face and his heart plummeted. What was it now? Hadn't he had enough trouble already? Several alarming scenarios appeared simultaneously in his mind. She was pregnant. Her husband had found out. Oh fuck. What was it? A vision of Leo's corpulent face appeared inexplicably in his mind. It couldn't be anything to do with *him*, could it? Was Albert's appearance outside no coincidence? Were the police waiting in the lobby? Shit. Shit! He glanced warily at the door. 'What do you mean?' he almost whispered.

'We got a letter from Brown's this morning.'

'What?' Marcus gazed at her in incomprehension for a few seconds. Then his brow cleared. 'You mean "we" as in you and your husband?' he said.

'Yes.' Liz flushed. 'Sorry. I should have made that clear.' Marcus cracked a couple of ice cubes into his drink from the tiny plastic ice tray and came over. He took a huge slug of whisky. A comfortable sensation of warmth and relief spread through his body. But there still lingered a feeling of alarm.

'Cheers,' he said. He wandered over to the window and looked outside. 'It's a nice day,' he said in almost accusatory tones. 'Good weather for the parade.'

'Yes, I suppose so.' Liz didn't want to think about the parade. 'Anyway, Marcus—'

'Come here.' His voice was peremptory, almost brutal. Liz flinched, but went over obediently to face him, first putting her drink down on the television set.

She said nothing when he started roughly unbuttoning her cardigan, without kissing her first. And she gave only a single, surprised cry when he pushed her down on the bed, pulling up her skirt, undoing his trousers and thrusting hastily into her without once meeting her eye.

Afterwards, he left her lying half-clothed on the bed, while he went to make himself another whisky. Liz eyed him warily. He was in a funny mood, and common sense told her to keep her mouth closed. But she couldn't. She had to get this mortgage thing sorted out.

'Marcus,' she began again. She sat up and reached for her cardigan. It was chilly in the room, and, with the windows swathed discreetly in pale netting, rather gloomy. She suddenly craved a warm, crackling fire and a pot of hot, strong tea. But instead she padded over to the silent television and picked up her half-drunk gin. 'Marcus, about this letter.'

'What letter?'

'The one we got from Brown's. It's about our mortgage.'

'Oh yes?' His tone was discouraging, but Liz pressed on.

'There's a new manager. She wants to see us. She wants to know why we were allowed two mortgages. What are we going to say?' Marcus shrugged. He was feeling unhelpful.

'I really don't know,' he said shortly. He drained his glass and opened a packet of peanuts.

'But, Marcus!'

'But what?' He looked up impatiently. Liz stared at him, feeling a strange wariness. This was unfamiliar ground.

'It was you that sorted it all out for us in the first place,' she pointed out in cautious, mollifying tones. 'If you hadn't phoned your friend, if you hadn't pulled strings, they wouldn't have let us keep the two mortgages. They would have made us sell the house. The house in Russell Street,' she added, hoping this would trigger fond memories of their meeting.

Marcus picked up his drink and went into the bathroom. He turned on the taps of the bath and began discarding his clothes.

'Marcus!' Liz followed him to the door of the bathroom, not quite daring to go in.

'What do you want?' he snapped suddenly. 'What am I supposed to do?'

'Well, you could phone Brown's again,' said Liz tremulously. 'Speak to the person you spoke to before.'

'He's retired,' said Marcus shortly. 'I don't know anyone else there.'

'Oh.' Liz paused. 'So what can we do?'

'I don't know, all right? I'm not fucking God! Solve your problems yourself.' He turned away and began to undo his cuff links.

Liz gazed mutely at his back, feeling a shocked panic swelling inside her. She'd been so sure Marcus would sort everything out; so confident in his powers. Above all, she'd really believed he would want to help her. But instead he seemed angry with her. For a moment she wasn't quite sure what to do. She stood at the door, clutching the door frame, wondering in a dazed sort of way whether he'd had enough; whether, in a moment he'd tell her to go. As if she was some sort of call-girl.

A wave of intense misery ran through her, and she began to shake. Suddenly she hated him; hated herself; hated the whole horrible, sordid situation. She thought of Jonathan on his blameless, well-meaning parade; of his leaflets and his duck mask and his trusting smile; and a fat tear began to run down her face. More tears fell, splashing onto her hand, and suddenly she gave a huge sob.

Marcus whipped round.

'Oh Liz,' he said. His voice didn't sound steady. 'I'm sorry. It's not your fault.' At the sound of his voice suddenly sympathetic, Liz's tears increased. Marcus came over, still half in his shirt, and put his arms round her.

'I'm sorry, sweetheart,' he murmured. He gently kissed her forehead.

'It's all right,' snuffled Liz. 'I shouldn't have asked.'

'Yes you should,' said Marcus wearily. 'It wasn't that. It was . . . Other things.' He looked at her. 'All this lying is getting to me.'

'I'm not sure afternoon meetings really suit us,' volunteered Liz. 'I feel really bad about being here.'

'So do I,' said Marcus. 'Perhaps we should make an appearance at the ECO parade.'

'Together,' giggled Liz. 'That really would look suspicious.' She stopped abruptly. Perhaps that was a stupid thing to say. But Marcus's face was still relaxed. He pushed her away slightly and looked into her eyes.

'I'll do what I can at Brown's,' he said seriously. 'No promises . . .'

'I know,' said Liz humbly. 'Thank you.' She looked over his shoulder. 'Your bath is full.' Marcus reached over and turned the taps off. The room seemed suddenly very silent.

'I can't promise anything about Brown's,' he said. 'But I can promise you one thing.'

'What?'

'That before either of us gets into that bath, I'm going to make up for the way I behaved earlier on.'

'No, really, it doesn't matter . . .' Liz blushed. But Marcus bent slowly towards her and began to kiss her with a gentle determination.

'If we're both going to feel bad about being here,' he said softly against her skin, his hand descending between her legs and pushing them firmly apart, 'it's only fair if we both have a turn at feeling good as well.'

Marching into Silchester that afternoon, Alice felt absolutely wonderful. She had arrived at Twelve Russell Street to find everyone outside, drinking steaming coffee in the wintry sun. Piers and Ginny were sitting on the ledge of the open french windows; Duncan was standing on the grass, declaiming melodramatically from a script.

'What do you think, Alice?' he said, looking up as she came round the side of the house. 'Could I get a part in *Summer Street*? I think I'll be . . .' he glanced at the page '. . . I'll be Muriel the grandmother. She's got some tremendous lines. Listen to this, "Oh, Rupert, when will you ever take life seriously?" ' He clasped his hands and looked skywards. Alice giggled.

'Shut up, Duncan,' Piers said lazily. 'Chuck it here.'

'It's the script for Piers's audition,' explained Ginny, as they went inside to get the coffee pot and a mug for Alice. 'It arrived this morning.' She grinned at Alice and, as they entered the kitchen, gave the excited skip she had not permitted herself in front of Piers.

'Wow!' exclaimed Alice, with gratifying awe. 'Is it a real script? Like on the telly?'

'Yes,' said Ginny, beaming. 'Just the same.'

'That's so cool!' said Alice. 'I wish I had one.'

'I know,' said Ginny. 'I'm going to keep it afterwards, and leave it around on the coffee table. Whatever happens.'

'But Piers will get the part,' said Alice, with a surprised conviction. Ginny turned round. Her eyes were sparkling.

'I know he will,' she said. She hugged herself. 'I know he will. I can't wait.'

They had gone back into the garden, warmed by a shared enthusiasm, to find Piers standing up and Duncan throwing his coffee dregs into the flower-bed.

'Christmas shopping!' he announced. 'Come on, Alice, I bet you haven't got my present yet, have you?' He gave her a penetrating stare, and she giggled and blushed.

'Not yet,' protested Ginny. 'I've got things to do first.'

'Well, hurry up!' said Duncan. He clapped his hands. 'We can't sit around all day drinking coffee, you know!'

Eventually they managed to leave the house, Ginny still complaining loudly at Duncan. But Alice could tell Ginny wasn't really cross with him. She seemed too happy to be cross. Everybody seemed happy. And Alice felt especially happy. She was sandwiched cosily between Piers and Duncan, and, as they all strode energetically along towards the town centre, she felt as though it was their steps which were moving her along; as though she wasn't having to make any effort at walking herself. She felt cushioned from the cold air, cushioned from the rest of the world, with these tall male figures on either side of her. Or at least, she amended in her mind, one tall figure and one stocky figure. She knew Duncan didn't mind being called stocky. In fact he quite liked it; he'd once been called 'stocky and appealing' in a review in *The Scotsman*.

But Duncan wasn't the point. It was Piers. It was the fact that she was walking along the road, right next to Piers. She was so close to him that she could feel his jacket through her sleeve, and smell his aftershave, and when they turned the corner a squirm of delight went through her as he put a guiding hand on her arm.

As they turned into Market Square, though, her heart gave a squirm of a different sort. Piling into the square, at the far corner, were the leaders of a bright, noisy, jolly crowd which, she knew, was the ECO parade. She couldn't see her father, but he would be there somewhere. Dressed in some crappy bird mask, handing out leaflets, being all worthy. She would die if they met him.

She looked distractedly around the square, trying to think of some reason for them to leave. But it was difficult. All the main shops were around the square, as well as Duncan's favourite coffee shop. She could see him eyeing it already. And at any moment now, he would notice the parade. She couldn't bear it.

'Which shops are we going to?' she began, in an unnaturally high voice. But it was too late.

'Look!' Duncan's voice rang out above hers. 'Look over there! Who are all those people?' Everyone followed his gaze. Alice scanned the crowd nervously for her father's slight figure.

'Let's go and have a look,' said Ginny. 'It looks like a demonstration.'

'In Silchester?' said Duncan, in mock-surprise. 'My dear!' He looked up at Piers, whose expression was distantly blank, and gave him a nudge with his elbow. 'Wake up, love,' he said. 'Stop thinking about *Summer Street*.'

'I'm not,' said Piers irritably. 'I wish everyone would stop going on about it.' He directed a frown at Ginny and she went pink.

'Come on,' she said hastily. 'Let's go over and see what's going on.'

As they neared the other side of the square, a short

plump woman accosted them. She was dressed in sensible black trousers and a grey anorak, but her reddened, wrinkled face was framed by the yellow beak of a bird's head, clumsily made from papier-mâché. She thrust a leaflet at Duncan, and he gave a little cat-like skip backwards in real or perhaps simulated alarm. Ginny glanced over Alice's head at Piers, and her lips began to quiver. Alice heard Piers give a muffled snort of laughter, and she looked away in mortification. The woman was Mrs Parsons, who used to babysit Alice. It would be so embarrassing if she said anything to her. But at the moment, her attention was with Duncan.

'I'd like you to take this leaflet, young man,' she said. She tried to put a leaflet in his hand, and he firmly put his hands behind his back.

'I'm sorry,' he said politely, 'but I'm allergic to leaflets.' He peered at the leaflet. 'And I'm terribly environmentally unfriendly. Let it all go to pieces, that's what I say.' He beamed at her. 'So it's probably not worth wasting your precious paper on me.'

'Duncan!' exclaimed Ginny. 'He doesn't mean . . .' But the woman was glaring at Duncan.

'You should be ashamed of yourself!' she trumpeted. 'The environment is only on loan to us. We've got a duty to look after it. What would you say to your children if the rainforests disappeared?' She fixed him with a triumphant stare. Duncan appeared to give the matter some thought.

'I'd say, "There used to be rainforests,"' he said eventually. The woman glared at him angrily. Alice turned away, trying to hide her face behind her scarf.

'Let me have a leaflet,' put in Ginny, in mollifying

tones. 'Thank you very much. Duncan!' she hissed angrily as the woman stomped off. 'That was awful!'

'I know,' said Duncan, wrinkling his brow, 'I shouldn't be like that . . . but I mean, *honestly*! Just look at them! They look like extras from *The Muppet Show*.' Ginny looked at the milling, jostling crowd in bird costumes and masks and, in spite of herself, gave a little giggle.

'They're well-meaning people,' she said sternly. 'I bet you've never given up your Saturday in aid of a good cause.'

'I don't call dressing up a good cause,' retorted Duncan. 'I call it work. And anyone who dresses up without being paid for it has got to be a sad, hopeless character. I bet all these people dress up in medieval clothes when they're not being birds,' he continued, looking around at the crowd. 'They go off to some gloomy old castle, and spend the weekend curtseying and saying Begad and thinking they're being cultured.'

Alice listened with an unbearable mixture of embarrassment and indignation. What Duncan was saying sounded all witty and clever, and made her want to laugh. But it wasn't true about her father. He didn't really like the dressing up, he'd always said that. And he'd never ever dressed up in medieval clothes. She stood perfectly still, feeling her cheeks burning, hoping desperately he wouldn't come along; hoping that Duncan would soon get bored with the parade and drag them all off for coffee like he usually did. But he was still watching it avidly.

And then it happened.

'Hello, Alice!' Whipping round to the right, Alice

felt her heart plunge downwards in a fiery trail of mortification. Her father was standing in front of her, wearing a duck mask on top of his head, smiling benevolently at her and holding out one of his leaflets. 'Have your friends all got one of these?' he said, and smiled at Duncan. Alice felt paralysed with embarrassment. She didn't know what to say; she couldn't risk speaking in case she giggled or, even worse, burst into tears.

Ginny glanced at Alice's scarlet face and came to her rescue.

'Hello,' she said brightly, extending a leather-gloved hand. 'You must be Mr Chambers. I'm Ginny Prentice, your tenant. And this is my husband, Piers. And this is our friend, Duncan.'

'Hello, Mr Chambers,' said Piers. His voice resonated confidently round the square, and he gave Jonathan a practised, charming smile.

'Hello,' said Duncan in a strangely subdued voice.

'Hello, all of you,' said Jonathan heartily. 'Do call me Jonathan.' He glanced at Alice and she turned her head away, deliberately avoiding his eye. His smile faded, and there was a short, awkward pause. 'Well, I'll let you get on with your shopping,' he said eventually. 'I hope the parade isn't too much of a nuisance to you.'

'Not at all,' said Ginny warmly. 'We were just admiring it.'

'Oh good,' said Jonathan, a pleased surprise in his voice. Again he glanced at Alice, and her fixed stare hardened. *Go away*, she thought. *Just go away and leave me alone*.

'I like your mask,' said Duncan suddenly, in chastened tones.

'Do you?' Jonathan pulled it down over his face. 'Actually,' he said, his voice muffled, 'I'm not too keen on costumes. But, you know, you have to go along with these things.' He pulled the mask up again and beamed at Duncan. 'If it attracts attention, then it's worth doing, I suppose.'

'Absolutely,' said Duncan earnestly.

Ginny glanced round. Piers's attention was elsewhere, and Alice was still staring tautly at a far corner of the square. 'Well,' she said, smiling at Jonathan, 'we must be getting on.'

'Yes, well,' Jonathan rubbed his hands together, 'I must be going, too.' He looked at his watch. 'Time for some mulled wine.'

'Mulled wine!' said Ginny. 'Lovely!'

'It's a bit of a tradition to finish the parade with mulled wine in one of the houses in the Cathedral Close,' explained Jonathan. 'One of the canons is a member of our society. He was asking after you,' he addressed Alice tentatively. 'Canon Hedges. You remember him?'

'Oh, yeah. Right.' Alice forced the words out like grape pips, and resumed her staring. Jonathan gave rather a crestfallen smile to Ginny.

'Well, I'll be off then,' he said.

'Good luck,' said Duncan plaintively. 'I hope you save lots of birds.'

'Duncan!' Ginny scolded as soon as Jonathan was out of ear shot. 'He'll think you're taking the piss.'

'But I wasn't!' wailed Duncan. 'I feel awful! Alice, why didn't you tell us your father was in the parade?' Alice shrugged miserably. Now that her father had gone, she felt even worse. A painful remorse burned in her chest; an unwanted guilt made her head feel heavy. And yet she still cringed resentfully when she remembered her father's appearance; his jolly voice; his stupid mask.

'That'll teach you, Duncan,' Piers said cheerfully.

'But I didn't mean it!' Duncan grabbed Alice's shoulder. 'Honestly! I didn't mean any of that stuff! I just said it because . . .' He shrugged. 'I don't know why I said it. Anyway, I didn't mean your father.' Alice somehow managed to grin at him.

'I know you didn't,' she said.

'Well, I thought your father was really nice,' said Ginny with emphasis. 'Really nice. Gosh . . .' She seemed about to say something else, then stopped herself. 'Didn't you think he was nice, Piers?' she said instead.

'Oh yes,' said Piers vaguely. 'Good bloke.'

He put an arm round Ginny's shoulders, and Alice's cheeks burned with renewed misery. Ginny and Piers must think she was a real cow to her father, she thought frantically. They'd probably hate her now. They'd probably stop asking her round. She'd never see Piers again. She couldn't bear it. Everything was absolutely awful.

As Jonathan was making his way slowly to the Cathedral Close, he felt a tapping on his shoulder. For a brief, hopeful moment, he thought it might be Alice, coming to have some mulled wine after all. But as he turned round, he saw the thin, bright face of Anthea Witherstone.

'I was very impressed by what you were saying earlier,' she said, regarding him intently.

'What?' Jonathan gave her a puzzled look. 'I'm sorry, I don't quite remember.'

'About the classics,' Anthea said. 'About the superiority of a classical education.'

'I'm not sure I quite said that—' Jonathan began to protest. But Anthea wasn't listening.

'I quite agree with you,' she interrupted. 'There's something so, so . . . *distinguished* about the classics, isn't there? Homer and Plato, and all those Greek gods . . .' Jonathan gazed at her in bemusement as she prattled on. He'd been told that Mrs Witherstone was frightfully clever and highbrow. But she didn't seem to have a sensible idea in her head. Then a phrase suddenly grabbed his attention.

'. . . which is why I'd like Daniel to come to you for extra coaching,' she was saying. He stared at her.

'Sorry, I didn't quite catch all of that.' He gave an apologetic gesture towards the surrounding, chattering crowd.

'I'd like Daniel to come to you for extra coaching,' Anthea repeated, a slight note of impatience in her voice. 'In Latin and Greek and . . .' she waved her hand vaguely, '. . . whatever else. For his Bourne scholarship.' She looked at him suspiciously. 'You do *do* extra coaching, don't you?'

'Oh yes, we do. But . . .'

'But what?'

Jonathan was about to say that, if what he'd heard was correct, Daniel Witherstone was one of the local scholarship candidates least in need of extra coaching. But as he opened his mouth to speak, he realized what he was doing. The letter from the bank was still lying in the kitchen, ready to remind him of their troubles as he walked in. He and Liz had promised that they would increase the income of the college. And this was the first request they'd had for Common Entrance coaching. To turn it away would be a crime. He looked up. Anthea was waiting for him to speak.

'But . . . I'll have to see where we can fit him in,' he said weakly. 'How many lessons were you thinking of?'

'I thought maybe every day, after school,' said Anthea. 'For half an hour, perhaps. Or an hour?' Jonathan's heart began to beat more quickly.

'As it's private tuition,' he said hesitantly, 'it will, I'm afraid, be quite expensive.' Anthea turned an indignant gaze on him.

'I don't mind what I pay,' she said. 'My son's education is worth it.'

At first, Daniel thought Andrew was making it up. He turned round, clutching his warm, sticky glass of mulled wine, and gave his little brother a superior smile.

'Nice try,' he said. 'I'm not *that* gullible.'

'Did you know,' said Andrew, momentarily diverted, 'that they've taken "gullible" out of the dictionary?'

'I told you that joke,' retorted Daniel condescendingly. 'You're the pits, you know that?' His spirits had been lifted by the mulled wine, and the fact that his ordeal was nearly over. He'd already taken off the headpiece of his costume, and was holding it under his arm like a headless owl-ghost.

'I'm not,' said Andrew blithely. 'Anyway, you're the one that's got special coaching.'

'Shut up,' said Daniel in irritable tones. 'You always have to make things up.' He took another swig of mulled wine. He didn't exactly like it, but it was better heated up than it was cold and sour in a glass like wine usually was.

'It's true, it's true,' insisted Andrew, hopping from foot to foot. 'Look. They're talking about it over there. Look!' His voice squeaked in excitement, and Daniel turned reluctantly round, just in time to see Anthea writing something down in her diary, then putting it away in her bag.

'That doesn't mean anything,' he said, as though trying to convince himself. 'They could be talking about anything.' But he watched with a sinking heart as Anthea turned, scanning the room with a slight frown on her face, then caught sight of him and pointed him out to Mr Chambers. She was talking intently about something, and Mr Chambers was nodding, and suddenly, blackly, Daniel knew that it must be true.

He took a gulp of wine, and another. Then, with his empty glass, he made his way over to the drinks table.

'Excuse me,' he said, in his best Dene Hall voice. 'My mother doesn't like mulled wine. Could I have some normal, please?' One of the ladies behind the table regarded him suspiciously. But the other recognized Daniel and smiled as she reached out for his glass.

'This isn't her glass, it's mine,' said Daniel quickly. 'Would you mind if I took the bottle? I'll bring it back, I promise.'

Only a few people were left in the room by the time Anthea had finished talking to everyone. She finished her conversation about road bumps with a local councillor, looked around the room, and sharply called out to Andrew, who was under a table, munching his way through a selection of unwanted bowls of crisps.

'Where's Daniel?' she asked shortly. 'It's time to go.' Jonathan, who had been watching Andrew with amusement, heard her raised voice and wandered over to say goodbye. 'Have you seen Daniel?' Anthea asked him. 'Were you talking to him?' she added hopefully. Jonathan stifled an urge to tell her he had been conversing with Daniel in ancient Greek, and shook his head.

'Perhaps he's outside,' he suggested.

'That's a thought. Stay here while I have a look,' she commanded Andrew, and headed for the door.

Andrew took a few handfuls of crisps. Then he looked up at Jonathan. 'Daniel's drunk,' he said conversationally.

'What?' Jonathan looked, aghast, at Andrew. 'What do you mean, drunk?' he added.

'You know, all wobbly, and can't talk properly and smells all funny,' explained Andrew. 'He's upstairs.'

'Oh God. I'd better go and have a look,' said Jonathan.

'I wouldn't,' said Andrew. 'He said he hates you. And Mummy. And me,' he added, in tones of surprise. 'I can't see what I've done wrong.' He took another handful of crisps and shoved them into his mouth. Jonathan gave him a hard look.

'Are you always this cheerful?'

'I think so,' said Andrew, looking up at him with untroubled eyes. 'I can't remember.' Jonathan sighed.

'Look,' he said. 'Stay here. I'll see what state Daniel is in.' He glanced towards the door. 'If your mother comes back, tell her I've gone to look upstairs.'

Daniel was in Canon Hedges's spare bedroom, still dressed up to the neck in orange fur. He was sitting on the floor at the foot of the bed, a glass in his hand, staring up at the television.

'Look!' he said, as Jonathan came in. His voice sounded blurred. 'It's *Scooby Doo*! That hasn't been on for ages!' His eyes shot uncertainly about the room, and he smiled beatifically in Jonathan's direction. When the music began, his head jerked back towards the television set. 'Scooby-Dooby Doo,' he began to sing along, in a lurching, quavering voice.

'Daniel,' said Jonathan cautiously.

'Yes?' Daniel looked up. His expression changed as he recognized Jonathan. 'I suppose you've come to give me some coaching, haven't you? In bloody Latin and pissy Greek.'

'No, I haven't,' said Jonathan, hiding a smile.

'That's good,' said Daniel emphatically. 'Because I don't want it. That's all I ever do, work, work, work, and then she says I've got to have coaching as well. It's not fair. It's bloody well not fair!' His voice rose to a shout and Jonathan hastily closed the door.

'Daniel,' he said again, 'your mother wants to go home now.'

'Good!' said Daniel, waving the bottle at him. 'Tell her to go home and never come back again.' Jonathan sighed. He looked at his watch.

'Stay here,' he commanded Daniel. 'I'll take you home myself.'

Downstairs, Anthea was eager to be off.

'Daniel's quite keen to come and see the tutorial college,' said Jonathan, ignoring Andrew's torch-beam eyes. 'I thought we could pop along there now, and then I'll run him home.'

'What's there to see?' said Anthea suspiciously. 'It's just a classroom, isn't it?'

'It would be useful if he could have a look at some of the teaching materials before we begin,' improvised Jonathan hastily. 'There's no point wasting time in the first lesson.' Anthea peered at him.

'That seems to make sense,' she said slowly. 'All right then. You know where we live?'

'I'm sure Daniel will be able to tell me,' said Jonathan confidently. 'But perhaps you should give me directions, just in case.'

On the drive to the tutorial college, Daniel sat silently next to Jonathan, with his head thrown back and his eyes closed. His breaths came quickly and his face looked suspiciously green. When they arrived, he muttered, 'I feel sick.'

'Well, we're here now,' said Jonathan, getting out and opening Daniel's door for him. 'You can be if you want to.'

'Can I?' said Daniel. 'Thank you.' And, leaning out of the car, he was quietly sick on the Tarmac of the tutorial college drive.

When both Daniel and the drive had been cleaned

up, Jonathan sat Daniel down in the staff room with a cup of strong, sweet tea, and made himself a mug of coffee.

'I feel awful,' groaned Daniel. He sat hunched forward in his chair until he was almost bent double and his fronds of dark hair brushed against his knees. He was now wearing a pair of jeans that had once fitted Alice; the owl suit waited, crumpled and reproachful, in the corner.

'People generally do,' said Jonathan, 'after they've drunk too much.' He took a sip of coffee. 'It's a sad fact of life.' He surveyed Daniel. 'Actually, you're not looking too bad. We'll be able to get you home soon.'

Daniel scowled, and took a gulp of tea.

'I don't want to go home,' he said. 'I hate my mother.' Jonathan sipped his coffee and waited. 'Why does she have to keep going on about the scholarship?' Daniel suddenly burst out. 'She talks about it all the time. She's told all my friends' mothers I'm going to get it.' He looked up at Jonathan with dark, pained eyes. 'Last week, I dreamt I went into the exam and just wrote Fuck Off on all the papers. It was brilliant.' He looked down. 'I suppose you think that's really awful,' he said.

'Not at all,' said Jonathan pleasantly. 'I think it's completely natural. The great thing about dreams is that you can do things you'd never do in real life. I mean, you don't really want to do that, do you? I have a feeling that, in real life, you'd like to do well.' He looked straight at Daniel. 'Wouldn't you?' Daniel shrugged uncomfortably.

'I dunno,' he muttered.

'The thing to remember,' said Jonathan, 'is that this scholarship is for you, not your mother. If you'd like to do well in it, you might as well try as hard as you can. It would be a shame if you did badly on purpose, just to spite Mum.'

'We're not allowed to call her Mum,' muttered Daniel. 'We have to say Mummy. She says Mum's common.' Jonathan's mouth twitched.

'Well, anyway,' he said, 'I'd hate to see you turning into an alcoholic because of your mother.' Daniel gave an unwilling giggle. 'I'll be seeing quite a lot of you over the next few weeks,' added Jonathan, 'and if ever I smell wine on your breath, or whisky—'

'I hate whisky,' said Daniel. 'Yuck.'

'Or Tia Maria,' said Jonathan, 'or Baby Cham—' Daniel giggled again. 'I'll be right round to tell your mother,' Jonathan finished. He looked seriously at Daniel. 'I mean it.'

'OK,' muttered Daniel. 'Thanks.' He looked up and smiled at Jonathan. 'Thanks a lot.'

'And don't worry,' said Jonathan, going over and putting on the kettle again. 'Coaching won't be so bad. I'm quite human, really. We'll have a good time.' He smiled at Daniel. 'Honest.'

CHAPTER ELEVEN

Piers's audition for *Summer Street* was in the first week of January. Ginny waved him off on the early train to London, then stood on the platform, staring down the tracks, hugging herself in the cold and hoping. She allowed herself a brief mental picture of him arriving back that evening, throwing open the door of the carriage, and, with shining, triumphant eyes, scooping her up in his arms, shouting, 'I got the part!'

A stab of agonized hope ran through her, and for a moment she stood, transfixed by the vision; two tears trembling on her lower lids. Then, as they fell, she turned briskly away and began walking out of the station. She was, she realized, even more tense about this audition than she'd thought she was. They had had a strained Christmas at her parents' house in Buckinghamshire, with Piers increasingly edgy, and her mother following Ginny about the house with questioning, criticizing eyes. The reason for her criticism had become clear late on

Christmas Eve, when she had suddenly launched into a catalogue of the daughters of her acquaintances who had, in recent months, provided their mothers with grandchildren, and then, almost in the same breath, asked Piers what work he had lined up for the next year.

Ginny would have loved it if he could have told her parents that everything was OK; that a big part was in the offing; that they would soon have enough money for five children. But Piers was insistent that they should keep the audition a secret from them.

'If I tell them I'm going for the part and don't get it,' he said, 'I'll never hear the end of it. It'll be a nightmare.' Which Ginny had to admit was quite true. But, then, he was going to get it. He had to get it.

As she turned into Russell Street, she imagined him in the train, perhaps going over the script for a final time; muttering the lines under his breath. Not that he needed to. They both knew that cursed script backwards by now. They all did. She and Duncan, and even little Alice, had been through it so many times, they could say the lines in their sleep. Duncan's game of declaiming a phrase and seeing who could carry on had been gradually honed down until now he merely had to give one word, and the rest of them would all chime in with the rest of the sentence. In the end they'd had to declare a veto on it.

He couldn't have done more preparation. Ginny muttered to herself as she went up the path, trying to build a sense of reassurance. He'd done everything he could. But then, it wasn't the preparation that would get him the job. It was whether they liked him.

She pushed open the front door, and stood in the

gloomy hall, feeling suddenly stranded. Now that it was happening, now that Piers was actually on his way to the audition, she seemed to have lost her focus. There was nothing she could do; no help she could give him. He was on his own.

And so was she. Duncan had gone to Scotland for an extended Christmas break, and although she'd relished the quiet house at first, she was, incredibly, beginning to miss him. Especially today. She could have done with someone there to break the silence; distract her from her own thoughts. She walked into the sitting-room, feeling rather discouraged, and sank into a chair, still with her coat on. She looked at her watch. Only a quarter past nine. The audition wasn't until after lunch. An entire empty morning stretched ahead of her before Piers would even ring. Let alone before they'd hear the result. Oh God. The result. A pang of excitement shot through her, and she got to her feet impatiently. She couldn't stand a whole morning in the house on her own, waiting for the phone to ring. She needed stimulation, distraction, people, light and warmth. She needed office banter. Anything, anything at all, but her own obsessive thoughts.

Marcus arrived at work at about eleven to find Ginny sitting on the floor of his outer office, leafing through a heap of client files. Suzy, his secretary, was sitting watching her and filing her nails at the same time, and a cafetière full of coffee sat snugly on the floor between them.

'Hello, Marcus!' Ginny exclaimed, jumping up and scattering a pile of photographic prints. 'How are you?'

'Fine, thank you, Ginny,' said Marcus, smiling guardedly back at her. Since the day at Panning Hall, he had deliberately seen very little of Ginny. After a few fraught days of jumping every time the phone rang, he had become gradually reassured that she hadn't picked up on what he was doing that day. Now he smiled to himself at the idea. She was a bit of a bimbo, really, he thought, looking at her bright red miniskirt that would have been indecent if her black tights weren't so utterly opaque. She obviously hadn't cottoned on to anything. Her face was totally unsuspicious, her eyes were sparkling, and she seemed even more lively than usual.

'Don't mind me,' she said. 'I'm not here to quiz you. I just thought I'd get some stuff together for general press releases.'

'Good idea,' said Marcus heartily. 'Let me know if you need any more information.'

'Oh, I will,' said Ginny. 'Don't worry.'

As she sat down and picked up another file, she remembered the conviction she'd once had that Marcus and Alice's mother were having an affair. Could it have been true? She glanced at Marcus, walking towards his own office, and tried to imagine him in bed with Liz Chambers. But even as she conjured the image up, it floated out of her mind, to be replaced by an image of Piers, who would be off the train by now, perhaps already in a taxi to the television studios. Perhaps already *at* the television studios. Oh God . . . Ginny's stomach twinged with painful nerves, and she forced her attention down to the file in front of her.

Marcus made his way into his office, sat down at his desk, and pressed his intercom in order to remind Suzy, humorously, that he would like some coffee too, please. Then his eye was caught by the open drawer of his filing cabinet. He released the intercom, and walked quickly over to it. The drawer was empty. The drawer of client files.

A small exclamation came from the outer office and Marcus went swiftly to the door. His heart began to thump. Ginny was holding the Panning Hall estate details. She looked up and beamed at Marcus.

'This is a good story!' she exclaimed. 'Just right for the New Year.'

'What's that?' said Marcus, adopting a falsely jovial manner. He felt a rather sick smile cross his face.

'A chance to buy a property on a country estate!' said Ginny. 'Or even the manor house itself!' She beamed at Marcus. 'I'll do a load of separate press releases. The weekend sections will love it.' She looked down again. 'And look at these lovely low prices! I always thought anything in Panning cost the earth.'

'It's a very realistic valuation,' snapped Marcus before he could stop himself.

'Is it?' Ginny looked once more at the details. 'I'm amazed. I mean, Panning is such a pretty village. I'd love to buy somewhere there myself.' She flipped idly through the papers again, and Marcus felt a sudden urge to whip them from her grasp. The door of the office was open; Ginny's voice was loud and insistent; anyone might wander in. Tiny waves of panic began to run through him.

'The thing is,' he said, in an elaborately casual voice, 'that the estate's been sold.'

'Really?' Ginny looked up in dismay. 'Gosh, that's quick! Oh, what a shame. It would have made a lovely feature!'

'Yes well,' said Marcus briskly. 'Never mind. I'm sure we've got lots of other things on our books that would make interesting press releases.' He held out his hand for the papers. But Ginny, infuriatingly, was still leafing through the details. And he didn't dare interrupt her with Suzy sitting there. Suzy wasn't the brightest of girls, but even she might start to wonder why he was so bothered about one set of property details. She might take it upon herself to mention it to Miles. Or, even worse, Nigel. He leaned casually against the door frame and forced himself to smile at Ginny.

'I love Panning,' she said dreamily. 'If I ever had a lot of money, I'd definitely think about moving there.' She looked down again, and a pink tinge crept across her face. 'I mean,' she said, 'look at this lovely farmhouse. Only a hundred thousand pounds.'

Marcus clenched his fists. That farmhouse was worth at least half as much again. But he'd had to scale everything down a bit. Perhaps he'd been too drastic.

'Yes, well,' he said quickly, 'the market has dropped. As well you know.'

'Who bought it?' said Ginny abruptly. 'Perhaps we could interview them.'

'No!' shouted Marcus without thinking. 'I mean,' he added, 'I don't think they'd be very keen on the idea. There were some complications. I think you'd better forget all about it.' He leant over, and, fighting the urge to snatch, gently lifted the Panning Hall papers from Ginny's hand.

'Could I have some coffee please, Suzy?' he managed to say, before disappearing into his office.

He sat down heavily at his desk, swivelled his chair so he was facing away from the door, and looked unwillingly at the details. While he'd been writing them up, he'd practically managed to convince himself that his valuation was accurate. Taking a fifth, or a third, or even half off every figure had become an automatic calculation, almost as though he were deducting some unavoidable surcharge or tax.

But now, seen in the cold light of day, it was obvious that the asking prices were far too low. When Leo came to sell the place on, he would get at least his extra million. Perhaps a couple of million. Marcus's thoughts flickered uncomfortably to the beneficiaries of the estate. The unsuspicious daughters in America. Between them, he and Leo had done them out of a good chunk of their inheritance. Did he now feel guilty? he wondered. Remorseful? He gingerly tested his feelings. But the only emotion he could identify was alarm. From having once seemed utterly failsafe, the whole affair now seemed wrought with holes.

He told himself firmly that Ginny had probably already forgotten about the whole thing. But in a small part of his mind, a stream of worrying pictures had started to flow. Ginny exclaiming to the world over the price of Panning Hall. Miles asking interestedly to see the details. That dreadful old character from the village deciding to phone the police. Miles would find out. Miles would be devastated. Marcus felt his shoulders hunch uncomfortably. Once, that thought would have spurred him on even further. But now it only made him feel more anxious.

He stared out of the window at the cheerless grey sky, and felt a shiver go through him. Suddenly he wondered why he had agreed to it in the first place. The money wasn't worth it; *really* wasn't worth it, he suddenly thought with fervour. His income from Witherstone's was ample; he had enough capital to be comfortable; what did he need more for? And how, it occurred to him for the first time, was he going to spend this sudden windfall? Nothing went unnoticed in Silchester, not a new car, nor a glamorous holiday, not even a new suit. Besides, he thought tetchily, he didn't want a new suit. Nor a new car.

'Your coffee, Mr Witherstone.' Suzy's voice interrupted his thoughts.

'Thank you, Suzy.' Marcus waited until she had left the room before he swivelled round to face his desk and took a sip of coffee. The solution was simple and obvious, he told himself. He could just turn down his cut. Turn down the twenty per cent. Let Leo sell the estate at a huge profit, and if anybody started asking questions, blame the markets. No one would be able to pin anything on him.

He sat for a couple of seconds, trying to convince himself that this was what he would do; trying to make up his mind to write a quick note to Leo; trying to conjure up a feeling of relief at extricating himself from the situation.

But he couldn't do it. He simply couldn't turn down

that kind of money. It wasn't humanly possible to let a sum like that just go, even if it did come with associated guilt and worry.

Abruptly he opened a drawer of his desk and shoved the details inside. The sooner the place was sold and he'd received his cheque and the whole business was closed, the better. He glanced at the closed door of the office, then hurriedly dialled the number of Leo's office.

'Leo,' he said, as soon as he was put through, 'what's happening?'

'In regard to . . . ?' Leo's voice was smoothly questioning.

Marcus gritted his teeth. 'The sale,' he said irritably. 'You know.' He took a breath. 'Have you found a buyer? You're not planning to delay things for any reason?'

'It will go through in due course.' Leo's voice was bland and courteous, and Marcus wondered whether someone else was in his office with him. He suddenly felt annoyed by Leo's calm.

'Yes, well, people have been asking questions,' he said curtly. That might galvanize the sod, he thought.

'What?' Suddenly Leo's voice had an edge to it. 'What do you mean?'

'Nothing, really,' said Marcus quickly. He lowered his voice. 'Just some PR girl poking around in the files.'

'What fucking PR girl? Marcus, I don't like what I'm hearing.' Leo paused, and Marcus felt his face growing hot. He shouldn't have said anything. 'If you've fucked this up . . .' added Leo, in light, menacing tones.

'It's fine,' said Marcus. His heart was thumping. 'No harm done. Honestly. It's all under control.'

'It had better be,' said Leo shortly. 'For your own sake.' And the line went dead.

Marcus put the receiver down and distractedly took a gulp of lukewarm coffee. He felt shaken up by the exchange, in spite of himself. He had sought reassurance that everything was under control; that he'd soon be safe. But he didn't feel safe. He felt exposed; vulnerable to discovery at any moment. The phone rang, and with a foolish pang of fright he picked it up.

'Hello?' Christ, even his voice was shaking.

'Marcus, it's Liz.'

Marcus closed his eyes. A vague resentment filled his body. Liz. His mistress. Phoning him at work. More deception; more trouble; more risk of discovery. It came to him that Liz was just another part of the whole mess he'd got himself into.

'Marcus, we're about to go to our meeting with the bank,' she said. She sounded tense.

'Oh yes?' he said unhelpfully.

'Have you managed to speak to anyone there?'

'I'm afraid not,' said Marcus shortly. Her voice grated on his nerves, and he felt suddenly restless, as though the receiver of the phone had been pressed against his ear all day. 'Was that all you wanted?' he said.

'I suppose it was.' Liz sounded crestfallen.

'Well, I'm afraid I'm rather tied up at the moment. Can I call you back on that one?'

There was a puzzled pause. Then Liz said, 'Oh, is someone in your office?'

'Yes, that's right,' said Marcus, looking around the empty room.

'Oh dear. Well, I'll call you later if I can. Wish us luck!'

'Goodbye,' said Marcus formally, and was about to put the receiver down.

'Marcus, wait!' Suddenly her voice was soft and tremulous. 'I just wanted to say thank you again. For your lovely Christmas present.'

'I told you. It's nothing.'

'It's not nothing! It's beautiful!'

'Yes, well.' He did nothing to disguise the impatience in his voice.

'I'm sorry,' she said. 'I'll go. I just wanted to say thank you.'

'Goodbye,' said Marcus, and thrust down the receiver before she could reply.

He pushed the phone away and stood up. He didn't feel pleased with himself. Neither did he feel pleased with Liz. She seemed to be encroaching more and more on his life; a life that seemed to be getting complicated and secretive where once it had been safe and blameless. The present had been a mistake, he saw that now. He paced over to the door and looked out through the glass panel at Ginny and Suzy, both now sitting happily on the floor, leafing innocently through endless details of properties. Suddenly he wished he could join them; join their pleasant chat and simple, guiltless existence. He doubted a single worry ever entered Ginny's head, let alone Suzy's.

And suddenly his thoughts turned to Anthea. Anthea, who was, in her own way, as simple and innocent as those two. He pictured her pale face, turned to him in a frown of anxiety; her thin hand, pushing its way uncertainly through her newly shorn hair; and a fierce affection filled his heart. He turned on his heel and went back to the phone. When Hannah answered he didn't hesitate.

'Tell my wife,' he said, 'that if she likes, I'll pick up Daniel from his coaching, and then we can go out to dinner.'

'Wow!' Hannah's strident voice travelled down the phone lines and hit Marcus's ear drum with some force. 'That sounds nice! I'll ask her. She's just in the other room.' As he listened to Hannah loudly relaying the message, Marcus could imagine Anthea wrinkling her brow in annoyance. She was forever telling the boys to use their legs rather than their voices, and hoping that Hannah would take the hint. But even this thought made him smile.

'She says that's fine,' said Hannah. She lowered her voice. 'Actually, I think she's quite chuffed.'

'Good,' said Marcus. He felt suddenly happier. 'So am I.'

Liz and Jonathan arrived at Brown and Brentford ten minutes early, and sat silently side by side in a small waiting area on brown foam-upholstered chairs. Liz felt wary and anxious. She had never really believed that Marcus wouldn't provide a solution for them; had not given any thought to what would happen if he didn't. She had no idea what to expect from this meeting; no idea of what she was going to say.

When the door of the office ahead opened, she gave a nervous start. A comfortable, middle-aged face appeared round the door.

'Mr and Mrs Chambers? I'm Barbara Dean.' Liz looked at Barbara Dean and felt relieved. She had hair in a cosy bun and spectacles on a gold chain, and a mild expression. Nothing can be too awful, thought Liz, in a meeting with this woman.

Half an hour later, she felt shattered. The summary financial position of her and Jonathan and the tutorial college stared accusingly up at her in its plastic folder. Barbara Dean's meticulous assessment of the situation sat snugly underneath. The confident promises they had made in their original business plan lurked somewhere in the middle of the heap of papers in front of her; Liz didn't want to look.

Now Barbara Dean was talking about cashflow, about overdrafts and restructuring and personal loans. Loans everywhere. Liz hadn't realized they had so many loans. Just the idea of them made her feel cold. She stared miserably downwards, and avoided the eyes of Barbara Dean. Which didn't matter, because Barbara Dean was talking directly to Jonathan; it had soon become apparent that Liz either could not or would not join in the discussion. Apart from one voluble outburst at the beginning, during which both Barbara Dean and Jonathan had sat politely waiting for her to finish, she had contributed nothing.

It was Jonathan who was doing all the talking. Liz was amazed; both amazed and ashamed of herself for being amazed. It came to her that she had underestimated Jonathan. She listened, chastened, as he displayed a startling familiarity with the accounts of the tutorial college; as he outlined the improvements in efficiency which had been already made; as he quoted staff–pupil ratios and man-hours and administration costs.

'And what about the modern languages summer school?' enquired Barbara Dean, drawing a page from her folder and looking at it over her gilt spectacles. Liz felt a shock of panic go through her body. She had done nothing about the modern languages department. The meetings with the staff; the rhetoric; the sketching out of course outlines, had all disappeared after a few weeks. After the arrival of Marcus in her life. Her mind flew back to the specialized language teaching computers that had been unpacked neatly in one of the classrooms. She had been meaning for weeks to start using them; to start planning a course. But somehow there hadn't been time . . .

'That's your field, isn't it, Mrs Chambers?' Barbara Dean said, looking straight at Liz.

'Oh, yes,' said Liz faintly. She picked up the folder in front of her and began to flick through the pages as though searching for some vital piece of information. What was she going to say to this woman? What the hell was she going to say? She could feel her lips trembling slightly and her cheeks starting to turn pink, and still she could think of no confident phrases to match Jonathan's. All her passion and enthusiasm for the tutorial college seemed to have vanished, and with it, so had her eloquence. Jonathan cast a covert, apologetic glance at her, almost as though he knew what was going through her mind.

'Liz has been doing as much preparation for the

languages department as her busy schedule allows,' he said loyally. 'She's even been spending some evenings perfecting her Italian. Haven't you, darling?' He smiled at Liz, and for an awful moment she couldn't think what he was talking about. Then she remembered. Oh Christ. Her pathetic alibi for evenings with Marcus was actually being used to bolster their case at the bank. She felt a small stab of guilt in her chest, and smiled cravenly at Barbara Dean as though to make amends. But Barbara Dean looked sternly back at her, and Liz felt nettled. *I bet you'd be different with me if I was here with Marcus*, she suddenly found herself thinking. *If I was his wife.* She imagined sweeping into the bank, attired in an expensive coat, Mrs Marcus Witherstone of Silchester. Rich. Well known. Respected. None of this interrogation. It would actually be worth marrying Marcus, she thought, just for all of that.

Ginny spent the afternoon frantically shopping. She bought fresh pasta, wine, garlic, wild mushrooms, a pale yellow suede skirt, some scented bubble bath, and two large pottery plates decorated with tulips. Then she bought a double chocolate muffin to have with her tea, and carried the whole lot home, her energy still not dissipated.

She couldn't stand the waiting. It was driving her mad. During the morning, it had been just about bearable; a distilled, concentrated version of the exhilarated yearning that she'd carried about with her for the last two months. But as the hour of Piers's audition drew near, she became more and more jumpy. At half-past one she started looking at her watch; imagining Piers—where? In a studio? In a rehearsal room? In a canteen, waiting for his turn? And at two o'clock she began to feel painful, jolting pangs of nerves, combined with a thrilling, unbearable excitement, all the stronger because it was illicit. She wasn't supposed to be getting worked up about this audition; she'd promised Piers that she'd really got to the stage where she could see both the advantages and the disadvantages of getting the part.

But it wasn't true. All she could see was advantage. A new life for them both; the end of uncertainty, the end of money troubles and telling people she found the ups and downs of Piers's career exciting really, and that, no, they didn't feel ready for children yet. A new house, with a garden and plenty of bedrooms. A new circle of friends in television. Celebrity status.

And the disadvantages . . . she couldn't even remember the disadvantages. Some list of moans which Piers had fabricated for himself in an attempt to rationalize the whole thing. Typecasting was one of them. Selling out. Something else about doing too much television. They meant nothing at all to Ginny.

When she got back home, she deliberately put all her shopping away, carefully hanging up her new skirt, and tenderly placing the plates on her little antique pine dresser, before she even looked at the answer machine. Two messages. She sat down unhurriedly, picked up a note-pad and pencil, and began to listen. The first was Marcus Witherstone. 'Ginny? Something I meant to tell you earlier. The estate you were interested in—I should have mentioned that the owners requested that the sale be kept anonymous.' There was a pause, and

Ginny cocked her head politely, suppressing an urge to scream with impatience and press the fast-forward button. 'So if you could avoid mentioning it,' Marcus was saying, '. . . I'm sure you understand . . .'

'Shut up, shut up!' said Ginny out loud. 'Shut up!' And then, all of a sudden, while she was speaking, the beep went, and it was Piers, sounding out of breath and far away. Ginny's heart gave a painful lurch.

'Ginny? Are you there? Ginny? Oh, I suppose you must be out. Well . . .' He stopped, and Ginny jumped. She clenched the pencil tightly, poised over the notebook as though she was about to take dictation. 'Well, actually, it was really good!' Suddenly there was laughter in his voice. 'They liked me! At least I think they did, and the read-through went really well, and so did the prepared bits, and I did a really good scene with the grandmother—you know—in that set out in the summer house. We did quite a lot of it on set. And then we all went for some tea, and they were all really friendly, and, well . . . Oh God, Ginny, why aren't you there? I want to tell you about it. The phone's crap. Look, I'm coming straight home. I'll see you there. Ginny, I love you.'

Daniel was, to his surprise, enjoying his coaching sessions with Jonathan. They happened in a small, bay-windowed room at the front of the tutorial college. Daniel sat on one side of a big table, and Jonathan sat on the other side, and they always spent the first five minutes chatting pleasantly before starting work.

Mr Chambers was one of the best kind of teachers, Daniel decided, because he didn't spend the whole time talking. And he didn't get cross when Daniel said something that was wrong, or made a mistake in the work he did. Sometimes he actually seemed pleased. He said things like, 'I *thought* you had a confusion there. Let's clear it up straight away.' Then he always made Daniel tell him what he thought he'd done wrong; and he screwed up his face and listened really hard; and then he smiled and said, 'Let's start from scratch, shall we?'

Today they were looking at an old scholarship paper from Bourne. It was the General Paper.

'Try number six,' said Jonathan. Daniel's eyes ran down the list of questions, and stopped. *Swiss cheese has holes in it,* he read. *The more cheese you eat, the more holes you eat. The more holes you eat, the less cheese you eat. So the more cheese you eat, the less cheese you eat. Is this true?* Daniel's brow creased, and he wriggled around on his chair.

'No!' he said eventually. 'It's not true!' He gave a questioning grin to Jonathan.

'Good,' said Jonathan. 'I'm glad you said that.' He grinned back at Daniel. 'I would have been worried if you'd said "Yes".' Daniel giggled. 'But you can't just write "No" on a scholarship paper, can you? You have to present your argument.' Daniel stared at Jonathan, wide-eyed.

'I haven't got an argument,' he said.

'Yes you have,' said Jonathan. 'It's in your head. You just don't quite know how it goes yet. But you will.' He paused. 'Do you have lessons on the General Paper at school?'

'Not really,' said Daniel. 'Mr Williams just says, "Use your brains and you'll be all right." '

'Hmm,' said Jonathan. 'Well, I think we can improve on that. There's an art to these things, you know. And when you're in an exam, you need all the help you can get.' He held out a pencil to Daniel, 'The first thing you do,' he said to Daniel, 'is make an essay plan.' Daniel pulled a face.

'Essay plans!' he said. 'I hate them!'

'By the end of today,' retorted Jonathan, who was busily drawing a row of boxes on the sheet of paper in front of him, 'you're going to love them.'

Marcus arrived at six o'clock to find Daniel and Jonathan surrounded by sheets of paper, each covered with boxes filled with writing. As he entered the room, he looked curiously at Jonathan, at his narrow shoulders and his threadbare shirt, and his kindly face. So this was Liz's husband, he thought, working so cosily with his son. He looked at the two of them and felt uncomfortable. The situation seemed wrong, somehow, even though both Jonathan and Daniel were patently innocent.

'Look at these, Daddy!' said Daniel, picking up a sheaf of papers. His cheeks were glowing and there was a huge grin on his face. 'They're all my essay plans. You know, you can make an essay plan for any question under the sun. Ask me a question. Go on, ask me.' Marcus glanced at Jonathan, who nodded.

'OK then,' said Marcus. 'Why do you always look such a mess?'

'Easy!' trumpeted Daniel, and began writing the question out at the top of the page in front of him. Marcus smiled at Jonathan.

'I've no idea what all of this is,' he said quietly. 'But it's obviously doing the trick.'

'We got a bit side-tracked today,' said Jonathan apologetically. 'But I think it's been a very useful session. Knowing how to do a good essay plan is invaluable in exams. He'll get marks for a good plan even if he doesn't have time to write the essay.' Marcus looked at Jonathan blankly for a second, then nodded in what he hoped was an intelligent manner. He gazed around the room. 'I used to come here,' he said reminiscently. 'For O level cramming.'

'Yes, well, we still offer that,' said Jonathan. 'Although it's GCSEs now.' His voice was a bit strained, and Marcus abruptly remembered Liz's phone call. Of course. Today they'd had the meeting with the bank. Suddenly he very much wanted to know how it had gone. He took in the shadows under Jonathan's eyes, and the banked-up coffee cups on the shelf behind him. 'Business going all right?' he risked, and then wondered whether Jonathan would think him impertinent. But Jonathan smiled at him—a charming, lopsided smile that took Marcus by surprise—and shrugged slightly, and said, 'Everyone's having it a bit tough at the moment. You know how it is.' His attention shifted to Daniel. 'Come on, young man,' he said. 'Your father wants to be off.'

'Nearly finished,' said Daniel, who was writing furiously. He scribbled in the last box, then leaned back in his chair and dramatically wiped imaginary sweat off his brow. 'Phewee!' he said.

'Take that one home with you,' said Jonathan, 'and pin it on your wall, and look at it whenever you want to remember how to do an essay plan.'

'I'm taking them all home,' retorted Daniel, gathering up the sheets of paper. 'I want to keep them all.'

Jonathan showed Marcus and Daniel to the door, and gave a wave as they got into the car.

'Poor sod,' muttered Marcus, as they drove off.

'Why poor?' said Daniel at once. 'I really like Mr Chambers,' he added.

'So do I,' said Marcus, to his surprise.

'Why is he poor?' persisted Daniel. Marcus indicated and smoothly turned left.

'Nothing,' he said.

'What?' said Daniel. 'Is it a secret? Tell me.' Marcus sighed.

'There's nothing to tell,' he said. 'I suspect there isn't a lot of business around for them, that's all. But that's just my thoughts,' he added firmly. 'I'm probably all wrong. They're probably doing splendidly.'

Daniel looked at his father. He looked down at the pile of essay plans on his lap. Then he looked out of the window and began to think hard.

CHAPTER TWELVE

Two days later, Daniel hurried out of school to see his mother waiting in the forecourt, surrounded by a gaggle of mothers. He paused briefly, to decide exactly what he would say. Then he frowned, nodded, and marched over to the bunch of women. His mother was, as usual, holding court.

'Of course,' she was saying, 'we wouldn't want to put Daniel under any pressure. After all,' she gave a little laugh, 'a scholarship isn't everything.'

The other mothers nodded earnestly.

'That's absolutely right,' said Mrs Lawton.

'I quite agree,' said Mrs Eadie.

'It's not worth taking these things too seriously,' volunteered Mrs Robertson, beaming around the group. Daniel looked at her in amazement. Adam Robertson was in his class, and he'd told them all that his mother made him get up early and read the paper from the front to the back *before* he did his cello practice, just so that he would know about politics and stuff for the interview. Mrs Robertson's gaze fell on Daniel.

'I suppose your scholarship must be quite soon,' she said. 'I don't know why Bourne has to have all its exams so long before the others. That was one reason why we decided not to sit Adam for the Bourne scholarship,' she informed the assembled company. Daniel looked at her sternly. He knew it was because Mr Williams had told Adam the competition was too stiff and he'd do better to try for smaller schools. But there was no point saying things like that to mothers. They just got angry.

'My scholarship's in a couple of weeks,' he agreed. He stopped, and looked cautiously at his mother. He had thought it absolutely amazing at first when she'd told him to keep his coaching a secret from the others at school. Then he'd realized it was just because she didn't want everyone else having the same idea. But she was just going to have to put up with it. 'My scholarship's in a couple of weeks,' he repeated. He looked around the faces impressively. 'But I've been really well prepared for it.'

'By Mr Williams,' put in his mother quickly. 'He's so thorough—' Daniel interrupted her.

'With all my special coaching,' he said in clear tones. 'Special scholarship coaching.'

'Special coaching?' The mothers' voices rose as one, in an outraged screech that carried right across the forecourt. Daniel looked over to the door of the school and winced. Some of the others from his form were coming out, and they'd absolutely kill him if they knew what he was doing.

'Where?'

'Who?'

'What do you mean?'

'I go,' said Daniel deliberately, 'to the Silchester Tutorial College. I have Mr Chambers. He's brilliant. I go every day,' he added. 'I'm going there now, aren't I, Mummy?'

'It's not really coaching as such, is it, darling?' said his mother in brittle tones. She looked at him furiously, then flashed a bright smile around the group. 'More like supervised homework.' Daniel thought for a moment.

'We go through loads of exam papers,' he said, smiling at Mrs Robertson, 'and sometimes we do things that Mr Williams never told us about.' He felt a fleeting pang of guilt towards Mr Williams as he said this. Mr Williams was definitely a brilliant teacher; Mr Chambers said he couldn't be in better hands. But he had to say something like that to impress the mothers. 'It's the Silchester Tutorial College,' he said again, just to make sure.

As his mother dragged him off to the car, he could hear a babble of talking break out behind him. Andrew was leaning against the passenger door, waiting for them, and he looked interestedly over at the gaggle of mothers.

'What did she say?' he mouthed at Daniel, jerking a thumb towards their mother.

'Nothing,' mouthed Daniel back. He hoped his mother wouldn't mention it when they were in the car. But as soon as the doors were safely closed behind them, she turned round in her seat, a spot of colour on each cheek.

'I told you, Daniel,' she said, 'not to tell everyone about your coaching.'

'I didn't tell everyone,' said Daniel mildly. 'I just told a few people.' Anthea gave him an angry look, then turned round again and began to manoeuvre the car out of its parking space.

'There are times,' she said jerkily, 'when it is better to be discreet. Do you know what that means?' Andrew gave him an astounded look.

'Did you tell the mothers about your coaching?'

'Yes,' said Daniel. 'I'll tell you why later,' he whispered.

'What are you whispering?' called Anthea sharply.

'Nothing,' called back Daniel cheerfully. He felt buoyed up and, for the first time in his life, impervious to Anthea's anger. Somehow he just knew that he'd done a good thing. Whatever his mother thought.

Alice had not looked Jonathan properly in the eye since the ECO parade. Her initial shuffling guilt and embarrassment had gradually hardened into a shell around her, until she couldn't see or think of her father without inwardly turning away. And usually outwardly, too.

It had been the worst Christmas Day she could remember. She'd left buying Christmas presents for her parents until far too late, and then she'd panicked and bought her father a huge book on birds that she couldn't really afford. It was only when she saw it actually in his hands, half out of the wrapping-paper, that she realized why it looked familiar.

'I'll get you something else!' she exclaimed, cutting across his thanks. 'I forgot you had it already.'

'Don't be silly!' her father retorted, opening the book

and running his finger across the glossy pages. 'This is a new edition. What a super present!'

But what good was a book that you'd already got? He was just being polite. And, obscurely, Alice resented it. She would almost rather he'd shouted at her. At least she could have shouted back. But her father never shouted. It was her mother who usually shouted. Except that this Christmas her mother had been on another planet. She'd forgotten to buy the crackers, so they had to do without, and she hadn't joined in decorating the tree, and she'd hardly taken any notice of her presents.

Altogether, thought Alice, as she made her way that evening to Russell Street, Christmas had been a disaster. Not like bloody lucky Genevieve, who had just written her a letter, telling Alice all about their Christmas in the sunshine, by the swimming pool. It wasn't fair. Their life out in Saudi sounded like one long holiday. Genevieve had sent Alice a photo of herself on Christmas Day, wearing a tiny white bikini, and looking really brown, with hair even blonder than before, and a huge smile. She suddenly looked all grown-up and glamorous, and when Alice had first seen it, she had felt an extraordinary pang of envy.

But Genevieve had things to be envious of, too, she'd told herself. She'd already started her own letter back to Genevieve, starting, 'Do you remember I told you about Piers? Well, guess what! He's going to be in *Summer Street*.' That would impress Genevieve, who was always going on in her letters about how crap the telly was in Saudi. To know someone who was actually in a soap opera was really cool.

But after she'd written that first bit, she stopped.

Because it still wasn't actually quite true. Ginny had told her that the first audition had gone brilliantly, and they'd loved Piers, but they had to see him again with the chief producer there, or something. That was in three weeks' time. There wasn't any doubt, really, that he was going to get it, Ginny had assured Alice. But these big television companies were always the same, she said. It took forever for them to make things official.

Until then, Alice supposed, it wouldn't really be strictly right to say that Piers was definitely going to be in *Summer Street*. But she didn't want to write anything less in her letter to Genevieve. So it lay, abandoned, on top of a pile of magazines in her bedroom, with a pale brown ring at the bottom where she'd put a cup of coffee down on it.

When she got to Twelve Russell Street, she found Ginny in sparkling mood. She and Duncan were sitting at the kitchen table, drinking something that looked like mulled wine, and Ginny was writing out names and addresses on envelopes.

'Have some!' she said, gesturing to a saucepan gently steaming on the stove. 'It's Norfolk punch! Completely non-alcoholic!'

'Oh, right,' said Alice. 'Thanks.' She ladled some into a glass, and gingerly tasted it. 'It's nice!' she said, in surprise.

'Isn't it?' Ginny beamed at her. 'I'm cutting back on alcohol completely. We drink far too much,' she added, a slight flush coming to her cheeks. 'It isn't healthy.'

Duncan winked at Alice, who wondered what the joke was.

'So, Alice,' he said, 'did you have a merry Christmas?'

'Brilliant, thanks,' said Alice automatically. 'And you?'

'Comatose, thanks.' Alice giggled.

'Isn't it great about *Summer Street*?' she said.

'Don't!' commanded Ginny firmly. 'We're *not* going to talk about *Summer Street*! We're going to talk about our party.'

'Party?' said Alice. Duncan slumped theatrically in his chair.

'I come back here for some clean, quiet, country living,' he complained. 'And what do I find but manic celebrations—'

'It's not a celebration,' said Ginny sharply. 'It's just a party. To get to know some people in Silchester.'

'What for?'

'Duncan!'

'We already know Alice. And the rest speak for themselves.'

'The rest,' said Ginny reprovingly, 'are very nice people like Alice's parents. Whose invitation is here.' She searched through the pile, then looked up at Alice with a smile, and handed her two white envelopes. One was addressed to Miss Alice Chambers and the other to Mr and Mrs Jonathan Chambers. 'D'you think your parents will come?' she said. Alice shrugged.

'Dunno.' Not if I can help it, she thought.

Ginny looked around the kitchen, pen in hand.

'This house'll be great for a party,' she said idly. 'It's got such a nice feel to it—' She broke off, and suddenly turned to Alice.

'Do you find it strange? Spending all this time in your old house?' Alice stared back, confused.

'I . . . I don't know.' She thought for a while. 'It's like it's a different place. It's like . . .' She paused. 'You know like when you go to a friend's house, and it's the same sort of house as yours, and you already know where the kitchen is, and where the loo is? You just kind of know it, even though you've never been there before? Well, it's a bit like that.' She gestured around. 'I mean, your stuff's so different . . .'

'Yes, but a lot of this furniture was yours,' persisted Ginny. 'Is yours, I should say. Doesn't it make you feel a bit strange?' Alice looked at the pine table, and, with a pang, suddenly remembered it at breakfast-time in the winter, covered with bowls and plates and boxes of cereal, and Ready Brek, and the toast rack, which always had one cooling piece of toast left in it that everyone ignored. And outside it was usually still dark, but the kitchen was always warm and light, and filled with the sound of the radio and her mother answering the presenters back. And there was always Oscar, mewing for attention and jumping up onto the table and being patiently scooped up and put back onto the floor before he got to any unguarded bowls of cereal.

She could feel a sudden stinging at the back of her eyes, and looked hastily out of the window. But there was the garden. Where they'd had birthday parties every summer until she was twelve and started taking friends to the cinema instead. Where they'd had a paddling-pool one year, and a tent another year, and, for a while, a dreadful second-hand swing that they'd bought from another family and that kept coming out of the ground when she swung too high.

For an awful moment, she thought she really was go-

ing to cry. But somehow, by staring straight up at the
sky, and holding her breath, and digging her nails into
the palm of her hand, she managed to get over the moment. When she was sure she was OK; when her eyes
were nearly back to normal and she was breathing properly again, she turned back to Ginny, allowing herself to
see only the lovely things of Ginny's that she admired:
the pottery jugs, the cast-iron recipe book stand, the
weird chrome kettle; blocking out from her vision the
old, familiar, memory-ridden bits of the kitchen. Let
alone the rest of the house. Eventually she met Ginny's
eyes, and shrugged. 'I don't really ever think about it,'
she said casually, and took a sip of punch.

Ginny looked at Alice and felt a small rush of sym-
pathy for her. How awful to have to move out of the
house where you'd grown up. When she and Piers had
children, she found herself thinking, she would make
sure they had a stable, happy family home, all their
lives. A farmhouse, perhaps. Or a converted rectory.
Or even a house in London like Clarissa's new place . . .

Ginny had phoned Clarissa that morning to invite
her to the party.

'Ooh, yes, how lovely!' Clarissa had gushed. 'But
I . . . I won't be drinking! Guess what?'

Of course, she was happily pregnant. Of course, they
had put in an offer on a large house with a garden in
Kensington, and she was having a nanny, and was really
hoping to go back to work straight away afterwards, but
actually, it didn't awfully matter if she did or not, did it?

'I mean, Ginny, you can keep Prentice Fox PR going
for me, can't you? Until I'm ready to come back?'
As she listened, Ginny imagined Clarissa at her desk,

twisting the telephone cord winsomely round her wrist,
blooming in a designer maternity dress.

'Actually, Clarissa,' she found herself saying, 'you
never know. We were thinking we might have a baby, too.'

'Really? Oh Ginny! That's brilliant!'

'Yes,' said Ginny, feeling emboldened by Clarissa's
enthusiasm. 'Piers has got this brilliant television part
practically in the bag. Loads of money. It's perfect
timing.'

'How thrilling!' Clarissa's voice came lisping be-
guilingly down the line. 'Oh, Ginny, you are lucky to
be married to an actor, instead of a boring old banker!'

'I know! It's so exciting.' And Ginny had smirked
and giggled for a few minutes, and felt a glow of fame
and achievement and the exhilarating feeling that she'd
taken a risky gamble, and won hands down.

Now her hands trembled slightly as she continued
addressing envelopes. Piers in *Summer Street*. It felt so
real; as though it had already happened. She almost
thought he *was* in *Summer Street*; that she would turn
on the television and there he'd be. She couldn't imagine that it wouldn't happen. Piers was going to get that
part. He had to. It was just a question of waiting.

Later on that night, Liz sat at the table in the sitting-
room, pretending to go through her plans for the modern languages department at the tutorial college. A pile
of notes was in front of her, and she'd written 'Course
Subjects' at the top of her pad of paper and underlined
it twice. But she hadn't written anything underneath

yet, and was now sitting, staring blankly ahead, filled with a dispirited torpor.

She had felt like this ever since the meeting at the bank. Blank; numb; lacking the energy to tackle any new projects; able only to keep day-to-day life ticking over. The tutorial college no longer filled her with a proprietorial excitement, but seemed suddenly an unwanted burden which she had inadvertently lumbered herself with.

It wasn't that the bank had been wholly negative. Barbara Dean had turned out to be quite a pleasant woman, and had seemed as keen for the enterprise to succeed as they were—or, rather, as Jonathan was. But, as she had repeatedly reminded them, the amount of capital they had invested in the venture was worryingly small. The mortgage on the business had, she explained, been granted on the basis that when they sold the house in Russell Street, they would put another, larger chunk of money into the tutorial college. And, of course, that hadn't yet happened.

In the short term, she'd told them, she quite understood that renting the house out was the most sensible thing to do. But longer term, they would simply have to sell the house. Simply have to. Otherwise . . . And Barbara Dean's eyebrows had disappeared above her gilt spectacles, almost into her hair, at the horror of what might happen. Then she'd relented, and the eyebrows had fallen back into place. In the meantime, she'd assured them, things could be a lot worse. And with a bit more work and a few more initiatives, they could soon be looking at a nice profit.

But her encouragement was too late for Liz. She didn't feel like putting in any more work. She didn't, as Barbara Dean had suggested, relish the challenge. She would almost rather they'd been forced to give up the ghost there and then, and put the tutorial college back on the market. It seemed preferable to the long slog that inevitably lay ahead.

She looked around her and shuddered. Somewhere along the line, her entrepreneurial drive, her enthusiasm, her will to make this venture work, had all ebbed away. She felt as though the harness had slipped from her shoulders; as though Jonathan was now singlehandedly powering the business's progress. And, try as she might, she couldn't force herself to join in again. It all suddenly seemed pointless; a lot of work for very dubious and uncertain rewards.

Surreptitiously, she fingered the gold bracelet which lay snugly below her sleeve; feeling its heavy links warm against her skin; estimating yet again what on earth it must have cost. When Marcus had, rather sheepishly, produced a small, gift-wrapped box one evening just before Christmas, she had been surprised. When she had seen what was inside, she had been stunned. Proper jewellery, from a smart London jeweller. And she hadn't even thought to buy him anything. But he had shrugged off her faltering thanks, her promises of a present after Christmas.

'It's nothing,' he said. 'Just a little something.' He grinned at her. 'Just a little treat. To remind you of me.'

She'd told Jonathan it was only gold-plated; a present for Alice which she'd decided to keep for herself—and as far as she could tell, he believed her. So she'd been able to wear it all Christmas, watching its shiny surface under the Christmas tree lights; playing with it as she watched television; careless of the warm, flowered nightie that Jonathan had bought her and the tapestry kit that Alice had bought her and the other assortment of well-meant, ill-chosen, utterly insignificant gifts. Everything suddenly seemed meagre, inadequate, scarcely worth bothering with. Nothing in comparison with the presents that Marcus and his family must surely be exchanging.

Even while she was tearing open the bottle-shaped parcel from Jonathan's father and wondering loudly, in the traditional family fashion, what on earth it could be, part of her mind was greedily imagining the scenes of gift-opening at the house of Marcus Witherstone. If he had given her a gold bracelet as a little something, what on earth had he given Anthea? Diamonds? Cashmere? A designer handbag? Whatever it was, it obviously wasn't doing anything for their relationship, she thought a little sourly. Marcus had phoned her the night before to put off their next couple of meetings. Anthea was getting a bit tetchy, he'd explained. Liz thought Marcus sounded pretty tetchy himself. It must be hell for him.

She'd seen Anthea from afar quite a few times now, coming to pick her son up from his interminable coaching sessions. Liz had normally finished teaching by that time of day, and she would watch from an upstairs window as Anthea's car came to a stop on the other side of the road; as her long, skinny legs emerged; as she hurried to the front door. She would sometimes spend twenty minutes or half an hour talking to Jonathan, then it was out again, talking over her shoulder to the poor boy; telling him to hurry up and look both ways; bundling him into the car and driving off. What a nightmare she was. No wonder Marcus was unhappy.

A very few times, it was Marcus himself who came to pick the boy up, and Liz would watch wistfully as he marched in and marched straight out again. No hanging around. No time for her to run downstairs and pretend to be passing the classroom. Sometimes she longed to tap on the window, like an imprisoned princess, and see him look up at her; see his smile of delight. But she never did. She would watch as he drove smartly off, then leap up, ready to be engaged in some other activity, far away from the window, when Jonathan came in.

Now she pulled her bracelet out from under her sleeve and stared at it, turning it this way and that under the light. She wanted more of this, she found herself thinking. More of him. She deserved more. She leant back in her chair and stared up at the ceiling. Strange thoughts were circulating in her head. Thoughts which had appeared vaguely at the back of her mind before but which she had never articulated. What would she do, she found herself asking herself, if Marcus ever asked her to leave Jonathan and come and live with him in wealthy bliss?

Well, of course, he never would, a loud voice inside her mind rudely told her.

Yes, but what if he did? What if he begged? After all, he'd almost hinted at it already. She remembered with a tremble of pleasure his voice, his exact words in that horrible hotel room: 'All this lying is getting to me.' What if he said he'd had enough of deception; he couldn't live without her? A scene popped into Liz's head; an image of Marcus entreating her, desperately; arms outstretched, telling her he loved her more than anything else. Telling her that he wanted to walk down the street with her, arm-in-arm, in front of the entire world. That he would be honoured to make her his wife. A glittering feeling of pleasure and excitement fluttered up her body. It was a bit unlikely . . . but it was still possible. Utterly possible. After all, men did leave their wives. They did marry their mistresses. And unlikely things did happen. A year ago, she'd never have thought she would have an affair, and now, look, she was in the middle of one. Incredible. And who knew what could happen next?

Beguiling images entered her mind: of herself, sweeping into a shop full of designer clothes; choosing items for a packed social diary; putting down a charge card on the counter with an air of nonchalant confidence. Or cooking supper for Marcus in an expensively designed kitchen, with terracotta tiles and dried flowers hanging from the ceiling; opening a bottle of rich red wine; leaving the washing-up for the cleaner to put in the dishwasher. They would retire to a thickly carpeted bedroom. With an *en suite* bathroom. Two glossy cars parked in the drive outside. No more work; no more worry. Nothing to do each morning except wake up.

There was a sound at the door, and Liz jumped.

'Oh hi,' said Alice, coming halfway into the room and stopping. She screwed up her face and blinked at Liz. 'It's a bit bright in here, isn't it?'

'Is it?' said Liz vaguely. She looked at Alice's scruffy form and saw her in a year or two; hair longer and glossy; dressed in casually elegant clothes; conversing with guests across a gleaming dinner table. Smiling at Marcus as he poured her half a glass of wine. She would be able to have her own car as soon as she learnt to drive. She would go to a smart school for her sixth form. Perhaps even be a deb . . .

'What we should have,' said Alice with more animation, 'is lamps. Like, really soft lamps everywhere. With cream shades. Not this old thing.' She gestured to the beige ceiling light-fitting disparagingly. Liz stared at Alice blankly for a while. Then a look of realization passed over her face.

'I suppose,' she said, 'your friend Ginny has lamps everywhere.' Alice shrugged, and went slightly red.

'Dunno,' she said. 'A few. One or two.' She looked around as though to find a new subject. 'What're you doing?' she said eventually.

'Planning courses for the tutorial college,' said Liz briskly. She picked up her pen and began to write a series of meaningless subheadings on her page; fruitlessly numbering and underlining them; anything to give an air of industry. Alice watched silently for a few minutes. Then, with a sigh, she felt around in the pocket of her jacket. She paused, then slowly, reluctantly, withdrew a white envelope.

'This is for you,' she said.

'For me?'

'Both of you,' said Alice discouragingly. 'It's an invitation,' she said, as Liz pulled out the card. 'You don't have to come,' she added.

'We might want to come!' Liz looked up at Alice. 'How nice of them to ask us. But won't we be too old?' Alice struggled briefly with a desire to say, Yes, you will.

'Not really,' she admitted eventually. 'There will be some oldies there. Like the people Ginny works with.'

'We're not exactly oldies,' began Liz. Then she stopped. 'Do you mean people at Witherstone's?' she said.

'Dunno. Yes. God, I don't know!'

'You know, our house was let to Ginny and Piers through Witherstone's,' said Liz, more for her own amusement than anything else. Alice's bored face remained motionless. 'Mr Witherstone himself organized it. Marcus, I think his name was. Marcus Witherstone.' She could hardly believe she was saying his name aloud in her own sitting-room. A dim light came into Alice's eyes.

'Yeah,' she said. 'I think he's been invited. Somebody Witherstone.' She shrugged. 'Anyway, you'll probably be too busy or something,' she said hopefully.

'On the contrary,' said Liz. 'I'm looking forward to it.' She balanced the white card carefully on the pale blue tiles of the fireplace and stood back to admire the effect. 'I'm looking forward to it very much.'

CHAPTER THIRTEEN

In the next three weeks, Jonathan took twenty-three calls enquiring about Common Entrance and scholarship coaching. By the time Daniel came for his last session, two regular after-school classes had been set up, containing most of his form-mates, as well as assorted other eleven- and twelve-year-old boys whose mothers had heard on the grapevine about the Silchester Tutorial College.

Jonathan was in his element. The boys were, by-and-large, an intelligent bunch, he had explained to Liz, which meant that there was something there worth working with. And several of them were extremely promising. Several of them might well win scholarships to major schools. The only slight disadvantage with teaching such clever boys was the high expectations of the parents. They hung around after every class with questions, comments and complaints pouring off their lips, until eventually he had to make a system of consultation appointments—for which, he told Liz, he charged a reasonable fee for his time. All in all, they should do very nicely out of it. And if any of the boys did well—it could only help their reputation.

Liz nodded lackadaisically while he told her all this. She could see that the Common Entrance coaching was a triumph; she had looked at the burgeoning lists of pupils, and could appreciate what it would do for their figures. Barbara Dean would no doubt be thrilled. But still Liz could not drum up any enthusiasm for the tutorial college. It was still a burden. It was still mortgaged up to the hilt. They were still under instructions to sell the house in Russell Street. They were still going to be poor for ages and ages before they started making a decent profit.

In her own mind, she was no longer associated with any of it. She was above the sordid workings of banks and loans and mortgages and repayments. She was on another, more comfortable, more carefree level. Or at least . . . she would be. She would be soon. It now seemed to her that during these last few weeks she had simply been marking time; before long, her real life would begin. She looked kindly at Jonathan as he explained his small success; perused obediently the figures that he thrust before her. But it all seemed irrelevant and footling. A hundred pounds here and a hundred pounds there. When Marcus regularly paid much more than that simply for a night in a hotel room.

She hadn't seen Marcus since Christmas. That wife of his was obviously becoming more demanding. Poor Marcus. Liz had never met Anthea, but from what Jonathan said, she seemed a neurotic woman; half-blind with love for Marcus no doubt, and beginning to sense that something was wrong. Liz thought of Marcus at home, trying to reassure his nervy, possessive wife, and shivered. It was no good. Things would have to be put straight soon. They couldn't go on snatching meetings in secret like this. Their relationship was going to have to be put on a different footing. Exactly what, Liz wasn't sure, but she had a strong, certain feeling in her stomach that things were coming to a head. She would see Marcus at the party. If she got the chance, she thought, she would talk to him about it all then.

Ginny couldn't believe her ears.

'What?' she exclaimed, and stared at Piers in outrage, as though it was his fault.

'They said it was some admin problem,' said Piers, attempting to sound cheerful. 'It doesn't mean anything.'

'It does mean something! They can't just mess you around like this! What's wrong with tomorrow?' Piers shrugged.

'Dunno. They didn't say. Maybe the chief honcho's busy.'

'Honestly!' Ginny pushed a hand exasperatedly through her hair. 'I thought it was just a formality. I mean, you've got the part. They've said they like you. Whoever this bigwig is, he's not going to go against the producer, is he?' Piers shrugged again.

'Who knows?' he said in deliberately flat tones. Ginny stared at Piers, suddenly deflated.

'But next week's the party,' she said hopelessly. 'You can't do an audition on the same day as the party.'

'Of course I can,' said Piers. 'Easy. We'll get everything ready the night before.'

'But—'

'What?' Ginny stared at Piers silently. She couldn't tell him that her secret plan had been to announce the news of the part at the party; that she had envisaged buying herself a stunningly expensive dress for the occasion; that she wanted everything to be in the bag *this* week, not next. 'I just think it's really bad, that's all,' she said eventually. 'They should treat you with more respect. I mean, what if you hadn't been free next week?'

'Then I expect,' said Piers, 'they would have given the part to someone else.' He walked out of the room, and Ginny stared after him with a pounding heart and a clouded face.

That afternoon, Marcus and Anthea together took Daniel to Bourne for his three-day scholarship. As he neared the impressive gates of Bourne College, Marcus realized, to his amazement, that he was actually feeling nervous. He swivelled around in his seat as they began the sedate drive along the speed-bumped, tree-lined avenue leading to the school, and grinned at Daniel.

'Feeling OK?' he said.

'Fine,' said Daniel, clutching his pencil case rather tightly, and grinned back. Marcus felt a sudden, overwhelming stab of painful pride. Daniel had worked bloody hard for this exam. He bloody well deserved to do well. He was a bloody hero. He grinned harder at Daniel, and wished he could give him a hug, there and then.

'Marcus!' said Anthea. 'Look out! You're going into a tree!' She was sitting next to Marcus, staring grimly ahead, her face taut and her hands clenched in her lap.

'What have they done?' said Marcus in amazement, as they drew near the school buildings. 'What's that building?'

Anthea replied without pausing. 'It's the new arts and media building. I told you about it. You would have seen it if you'd come to the parents' open day.'

'Yes, well.' Marcus had, for reasons which were obscure to himself as well as to Anthea, refused to go back and walk round his old school as a prospective parent. 'I know the place,' he'd said. 'What's the point in seeing it again?' Now he felt an affecting mixture of nostalgia and curiosity at the combination of old, familiar buildings and new, state-of-the-art constructions. For the first time, with a strange sensation in his stomach, he imagined Daniel wearing the school uniform that he used to wear; playing rugby on the same pitches; perhaps even sleeping in the same dormitory.

Then it occurred to him that if Daniel did win a scholarship he wouldn't be in Marcus's old house. He would be in the Headmaster's House. He would be one of the élite of the school, who strode around in black gowns and were regularly photographed by the press. One of the chosen few. He would be like Edwin Chapman, who had been a scholar in Marcus's year and was now a junior cabinet minister. Or William Donaghue, who had been in the year below and was now a rampantly, famously successful barrister.

Marcus looked at Daniel with a new respect as he parked the car. Could his son really slip into that world of excellence? His own son? The son of a parochial estate agent?

'Daniel,' he found himself saying, 'just do your best. Try to remember everything that Mr Chambers has told you. And remember, we'll be proud of you whatever happens—'

'Have you got enough ink cartridges?' interrupted Anthea anxiously. 'Have you got your pencil sharpener? Have you—'

'Anthea,' said Marcus gently. 'I should think that the mighty Bourne College could probably come up with the odd ink cartridge if it's needed.' He caught Daniel's eye and they both grinned. Then Marcus leant over and ruffled Daniel's hair affectionately. 'Come on,' he said. 'I want to show you my old school.'

Later on, when Daniel had gone in, he and Anthea strolled around the grounds of the school, arm in arm. Anthea covered up her nerves by talking incessantly: pointing out interesting-looking architectural features; speculating on the number of boys applying for the scholarship; exclaiming at the interior of the chapel; wondering again and again and again how Daniel was getting on. Marcus simply smiled and walked peacefully along beside her.

They stopped eventually by the man-made lake, which was used for water sports and rowing, and looked back at the school. Marcus put his arm around Anthea's thin, tense shoulders, fragile like porcelain.

'You know,' he said slowly, 'if Daniel does get this scholarship, it'll be completely down to you.' Anthea looked up at him with wide, questioning eyes. 'He's got your intelligence for a start,' continued Marcus ruefully. 'I never came near any kind of scholarships. And it's you who encouraged him to do well. You're the one who's put in all the work.' Anthea stiffened slightly.

'I thought you disapproved of him doing the scholarship,' she said. She looked away into the distance. 'I thought it was all such a waste of time.'

'Yes, well, maybe I was wrong,' said Marcus, after a pause.

'Maybe I was wrong too,' said Anthea, surprisingly. She swallowed. 'I know I sometimes work the boys too hard. I know everyone thinks I'm too pushy.' She pushed a hand through her thin red hair. 'But I just want them to reach their potential. I'm just doing it for their sakes.' She looked at him with worried eyes. 'I do mean well, you know.' A flood of affection filled Marcus's heart.

'I know you do,' he said gently; 'I know you do.' He put his arms around her and pulled her slender body towards him.

'Marcus!' she exclaimed, trying to wriggle free, her eyes darting anxiously about. 'You can't do that here!'

'I'm an Old Boy of this school,' said Marcus firmly, 'which means I can do whatever I like, wherever I like.'

Alice was getting more and more panicked about what to wear to Piers's and Ginny's party. When they'd originally talked about it, she'd assumed that she was going to wear her usual pair of torn jeans and perhaps her Indian silver necklace. But then, at home, she'd looked properly at the invitation, and seen that it said, 'Dress: Black and Red.' Alice had lots of black clothes, but they were all things like faded T-shirts and woolly tights; not the sort of thing you could wear to a party like this one.

And then, today, Ginny had shown her the dress she had bought for the party. It was bright red silk, very short, with black squiggles on the front. If Alice had seen it in a shop she would immediately have said, Yuck, gross. But when Ginny put it on, Alice had to admit she looked pretty good. And then, twirling in front of her bedroom mirror, Ginny had said to Alice, 'And what are *you* going to wear?' Alice had shrugged nonchalantly, and said she hadn't thought about it.

Since then she hadn't thought about anything else. Black and Red. Black and Red. Black jeans and a red T-shirt? No. Awful idea. *Awful.* Black jeans and black polo-neck? No. Too dull. She imagined herself at the party. Piers would be there, looking admiringly at Ginny's shiny squiggles. She had to wear something that he would like. Something grown up.

She marched into the kitchen, where her mother was leaning against the side, dreamily drinking a cup of tea.

'I need something to wear to this party,' she said without preamble. 'I haven't got anything black and red.' She looked at her mother without much hope, and waited for her to say that surely Alice had plenty of clothes. But Liz's face lit up.

'Of course!' she said. 'We should get you something nice.' Alice looked at her suspiciously.

'It has to be black,' she said. 'Or red. That's what the invitation says.'

'Does it really?' said Liz. 'Goodness. Well, then, perhaps I'd better get something new as well.' She beamed at Alice. 'I think we both deserve a treat, don't you?'

'I suppose so,' said Alice. 'Can I have some money, then?'

'We'll go shopping together,' said Liz firmly. 'We'll go into Silchester on Saturday and each buy something nice for the party and then have lunch out. How about that?'

'Yeah, I suppose,' said Alice. 'Or I could go on my own, after school,' she added casually.

'No you couldn't,' said Liz. 'You could come with me on Saturday, or you could go in your black jeans and my red corduroy shirt.' Alice grinned mistrustfully at her.

'All right,' she said. 'Saturday.'

Silchester on Saturday was always packed. As they strode into the market square, Liz groaned.

'We should have come at nine o'clock,' she said. 'It'll be hell.'

'Never mind,' said Alice, glancing around at the heaving crowds. She looked at Liz and thought that possibly it could be OK going shopping with her. As long as she didn't try and force her into a pair of disgusting shoes like last time . . .

'Excuse me! Might I have a minute?' Alice looked up. A young man with a quiff and a clipboard was bearing down on her. She hesitated. Someone at school had said yes to one of these people recently and got to taste loads of different chocolate cake. 'All right, then,' she said. She looked at her mother. 'It won't take long?'

'No time at all,' said the man. 'Just a few simple questions. Do you live or work in Silchester?'

'Yes. Live, I mean.'

'Are you married, single or attached?'

Alice blushed. 'Why do you need to know that?' she said.

'We're offering a new dating service in Silchester,' said the man. 'Lots of lonely people out there, you know.'

Alice blushed harder. 'I'm still at school,' she said. 'I don't think—'

'Oh!' The man looked more closely at her. 'You're quite right,' he said. 'Eighteen and over only. My apologies.' He began to walk off. But Liz's voice arrested him in his tracks.

'Hang on a minute! Why didn't you ask me?' The man turned back.

'Well,' he said uncertainly. Alice gave a flabbergasted look at Liz.

'Why didn't you ask me?' repeated Liz. 'You never know; I might be interested in your service.' The man glanced at her gloved left hand.

'I assumed . . .' he began.

'Assumed I was married? Assumed I was too old for that kind of thing?' Liz shook back her hair, and smiled at the man. 'How do you know I'm not young, free and single? Or, at least, free and single?' The man grinned back, and patted his quiff.

'I suppose I don't. Are you?'

'Young? Not very, I'm afraid.'

'Rubbish,' said the man gallantly. He winked at Alice,

and she cowered inside her collar, hot with embarrassment and outraged at Liz. What was going on with her? Why was she talking like this to a stranger? She must be getting old and eccentric or something. She should have known, Alice thought miserably to herself, that coming out shopping with her mother would be a mistake.

'OK then,' said the man cheerfully. 'Let's start again.' He turned over to a new sheet of paper with a flourish. 'Do you live or work in Silchester?'

'Yes. I live here.'

'And are you married, single or attached?'

'Sometimes I feel all three,' said Liz conversationally.

'Mum . . .' said Alice in an agonized voice.

'All right.' Liz relented. 'I'm married. Attached. Whatever. And I'm not interested in a dating service.' She paused. 'But I've made you think a bit, haven't I?'

'So I was right in the first place!' said the man in mock-indignation. 'I knew you were married.'

'Yes, but I might not have been, might I?' said Liz, raising her eyebrows at him. 'I'd try that woman over there next,' she added, pointing to a grey-haired lady pulling along a tartan shopping trolley. 'You never know. So long!' She began to stride off, and Alice scuttled after her, giving an apologetic look to the man with the clipboard. Sometimes her mother astounded her.

By lunchtime she was even more astounded. They'd gone straight to Sedgwick's, the big department store in Silchester, and up to the designer department. Her mother had talked to the sales assistants as if she was used to buying this kind of stuff all the time, and got three of them to keep bringing clothes to her in the changing-room. In the end she'd bought a pair of black trousers and a red silk shirt and together they came to more than two hundred pounds. Alice couldn't believe it.

And then they'd seen a very short black dress, made out of lots of fringes.

'Alice! That's made for you!' Her mother had sounded exactly like Ginny when she said that. She'd made Alice try it on, and twirl around in it so that the fringes flew out, and got all the assistants to come and have a look, and then said, 'Well, of course, we've simply got to have it. Haven't we?' And they'd wrapped it all up in tissue paper, and there it was, in a shiny carrier bag in her hand.

And now they were walking into a restaurant full of pink cushiony chairs and flowers and someone playing the piano in the corner. Alice couldn't believe it. Her mother was acting like another person today. Like Genevieve's mother, who had once taken her and Genevieve to Harrods, and bought bags and bags full of stuff and then ordered them huge ice-creams for tea. Her own mother *never* bought expensive clothes. And they hadn't been to any restaurants for ages. Not since they'd bought the tutorial college.

'A table for two,' Liz was saying to the head waiter. 'Non-smoking. Oh!' She gave a little cry, and Alice looked up. But it was just some men saying hello to her mother. She surreptitiously reached inside the bag and fondly felt the fringes of her new dress. She would wear shiny black tights underneath it, she decided, and polish up her Doc Martens, and perhaps Piers would ask her to dance . . .

'Alice!' Her mother was looking a bit flustered. 'Come and meet Marcus Witherstone. He's the estate agent who let out the house to Ginny and Piers, you know.'

'Hello,' said Alice politely. She looked interestedly at Marcus Witherstone. Ginny had told her a bit about him, she remembered now. She'd said that he was a bit of a rascal, and his wife was a complete nightmare. He didn't look like a bit of a rascal to Alice. He looked old and boring, and even a bit angry. She switched her attention to the other man; shorter, with reddish hair and a pink face. Her mother was looking at him too, she noticed. Everyone was looking at him.

'Hello,' he said, giving Alice a horrible sickly smile. 'I'm Leo Francis. I'm a business associate of Marcus.'

'Leo is a lawyer,' said Marcus Witherstone quickly. 'He handles some of our day-to-day transactions. Standard conveyancing. Ordinary stuff, really.' Bo-ring, thought Alice. Her attention wandered over to a table in the corner, where the waiter had brought over a dish and was setting it alight. The flames flickered blue, and everybody at the table smiled, even the waiter. She wanted one of those, Alice decided. Whatever it was. And actually, she was feeling quite hungry. She looked up at her mother, waiting for her to say, How nice to see you, and move off. But her mother was still smiling at the boring estate agent man. 'We've been buying clothes for the party,' she was saying rather rushingly. Then, to Alice's disbelief, she actually pulled open her carrier bag for the two men to look inside. Even Alice knew that men were never interested in clothes. Not even the clothes their wives wore. 'You *are* going to the party?' Liz said. 'Piers and Ginny Prentice's party?'

'Yes, I think we are,' said the estate agent in tones of surprise. Then he suddenly scowled. 'I'm afraid I've got to be going,' he said.

'See you there, then!' said Liz gaily. 'See you there,' she repeated slowly to his retreating back. Then she turned and looked at Alice with strangely bright eyes.

'I tell you what,' she said, 'I feel like some champagne. How about you?'

As they walked into the foyer, Leo spoke out of the corner of his mouth.

'That was a rather flustered display you gave there. Your mistress, is she?'

Marcus opened his mouth to make an angry retort. Then he closed it. He didn't want to get into an argument with Leo. He didn't want to communicate with Leo any more than he had to. He wanted Leo out of his life.

His thoughts slid comfortably to the cheque for two hundred thousand pounds sitting in his inside breast pocket. That was some reward for his anxiety; his worry; the mess of the whole affair. But even now, even now he'd got the money and, as far as he could tell, was safe from discovery, he hadn't changed his mind. He would never do it again. He'd told Leo over their Dover sole and beurre blanc that he could bloody well find someone else to put their professional reputation on the line next time.

Leo, of course, had spoken smoothly and reassuringly, then, when he realized that Marcus was serious, switched to a patronizing scorn. But Marcus didn't care. Neither did he care that he was saying goodbye to what was, in effect, easy money. It simply wasn't worth the risk. Two hundred thousand pounds—but what, he thought yet again, was he going to do with it? Pay the school fees? But there was a family trust already set up for that purpose. And anyway, he thought, smiling as he remembered Daniel's excited face last night, if the scholarship exams had gone as well as everybody seemed to think, perhaps he wouldn't be paying any school fees for Daniel. So what else? A country cottage? A house in France? But the rest of the family would want to know where he'd got the money.

The trouble with family money, their family money in particular, he thought, was that it was all so transparent; so well documented. They all knew exactly the sums of capital each other possessed; they all knew exactly how much the others had paid for their houses; they knew how the family firm was doing. It would be less scandalous to confess to being broke than to having sudden large amounts of unexplained cash.

Marcus felt a cold feeling at the base of his spine, as he imagined admitting everything to Miles; watching his honest face creasing into a horrified frown. Dear Miles, who valued family loyalty above almost anything else, who quite clearly wanted to believe the best of Marcus, whatever his suspicions were. Since that phone call on the day of the ECO parade, Miles had said nothing to Marcus about Leo Francis. And yet he must have been wondering, and worrying . . . Marcus shivered. At least some of this money, he suddenly thought fiercely, would go on a long boozy lunch at Le Manoir for himself and Miles. A good bottle of claret, brandy, the works. An all-afternoon job. Just like in the old days . . . the days before Leo. And before Liz . . .

'Well, goodbye, Marcus,' said Leo smoothly, as they were handed their coats. 'Good to do business with you.' Marcus nodded curtly, pulled on his herringbone coat, and hurried down the thickly carpeted stairs towards the exit of the restaurant. He suddenly wanted to get out of the place; to leave all of them behind. Leo, Liz, the lot of them. He could barely believe that he'd bumped into Liz like that. Christ knew what might have happened, what might inadvertently have come out. The thought made him shiver, and curse himself unreasonably. He shouldn't have agreed to going to the restaurant in the first place. They should have met at Leo's place instead. Really, he might have known he would bump into someone he knew, he told himself angrily. And he might have known it would be Liz.

He recalled Leo's teasing comment, and felt a tingle in the base of his spine. Did Leo really suspect something? Had he guessed at the truth? And would he, out of some sort of malice, make his suspicions known to Anthea? Marcus suddenly, irrationally, pictured Leo picking up the phone; speaking to Anthea; smoothly insinuating and hinting, while Anthea's bewildered frown got deeper and deeper. The bastard. He would fucking kill him if he said anything.

Then common sense took over. Leo hadn't meant anything. He wouldn't say anything. He had no reason to make an enemy of Marcus. As his steps took him further away from the restaurant; further away from the danger, Marcus was able to reassure himself that it had just been bad luck.

But the encounter had left him feeling wary and on guard. What if he bumped into her again? What if Anthea had been with him? She would have been bound to notice something, with Liz getting so flushed and animated. He recalled Liz's pink cheeks and sparkling eyes, and shuddered. Once upon a time the sight of those would have made him excited, made him look forward even more to their next encounter. Now it just made his heart sink slightly. Obviously she thought everything was still the same between them. Didn't she realize why he kept cancelling their meetings? Had she unwittingly misunderstood the message he was trying to give? Or even deliberately?

It came to Marcus that he had to make things plain to her soon, very soon. He couldn't let her think things were going to carry on as they had done; couldn't run the risk of bumping into her again before they'd got everything straightened out. It shouldn't be too difficult, he told himself. After all, he reasoned, she had a husband to think about, just as he had a wife. A very nice husband, too.

Probably, he thought comfortingly to himself, as he reached his car and flicked the door open with his remote control, probably Liz was thinking the same as him. Probably she'd had quite enough of the affair, too. He thought back to her flushed cheeks. He'd probably got it all wrong. Probably she'd just been embarrassed to see him when she was with her daughter. He switched on the engine and relaxed back into his seat. What a fuss over nothing, he thought to himself. It was all going to be absolutely fine.

CHAPTER FOURTEEN

On the day of the party, Alice woke early. She got out of bed, put a sweatshirt on over her pyjamas, and padded into the kitchen. Outside the sky was grey and menacing, and the whole room looked even more depressing than usual. She looked at the clock. Seven o'clock. And today her morning started with a double free period so she didn't have to be in school till ten. Normally she would have had a lie-in and then a leisurely breakfast in front of the television. But she was too excited to go back to bed. She wanted it to be this evening *now*.

She thought lovingly of her new dress, hanging up ready in her wardrobe, and her new, very expensive tights, and her new, purplish-brown lipstick that had taken an hour after school to choose. Ginny had said Alice could come round early, before the party, and she'd help her put on her make-up and do her hair. Alice was almost looking forward to that bit best. She adored people putting make-up on her and fiddling with her hair, and she adored being in Piers's and Ginny's bedroom, which always seemed to smell of Ginny's lovely scent and be full of new and interesting things. Sometimes she looked around when she was in there and could hardly believe that it used to be her parents' bedroom, smelling of nothing in particular, and full of books and newspapers and clutter.

She wandered over to the kettle, automatically switched it on, and leaned against the counter, impatiently tweaking the electrical cord as though that would make it boil quicker. Twelve whole hours till the party. It was going to be unbearable. Then, with a sudden thrill, she remembered what else was happening today. It was Piers's second *Summer Street* audition. Or whatever it was. Piers always talked of it as an audition, but Ginny always wrinkled up her nose and said, 'It's not really an *audition*, is it? More like a meeting.' Alice didn't really know what the difference was. But it was definitely happening today. They would be getting up earlier than usual, in time for Piers to catch the mid-morning train to London. Alice pictured them all— Piers, Ginny and Duncan—sitting round the breakfast table, making jokes about *Summer Street*, planning last-minute details for the party, and pouring out deliciously strong coffee for each other. She looked disparagingly at her own mug, ready for a spoonful of Nescafé. Suddenly she wanted to be there with them. It would be so cool to drop in before school and wish Piers luck. Then, whenever *Summer Street* was on, she would be able to point to Piers on screen and say things like, 'God, I remember the day he got the part. We were having breakfast together.'

She savoured the image for a moment, then switched the kettle off, and hurried back to her room. On the way, she passed her mother, coming, bleary-eyed, along the corridor.

'The kettle's hot,' said Alice kindly. 'I'm going out for breakfast.' She registered with satisfaction her mother's look of surprise, and then disappeared behind her door to choose the least gross of her grey uniform skirts and put on as much eyeliner and mascara as she would be able to get away with.

When she got to Russell Street, she momentarily hesitated. She often dropped in on Ginny and Piers, but not on weekday mornings. Still, today was a special day, she thought to herself. And when she peered in through the kitchen window of number twelve, she was delighted to see them all there as she had imagined, sitting round the table, holding those gorgeous painted mugs, looking like something in an advert. Duncan caught her eye, and waved, saying something to Ginny and Piers. Ginny's head immediately shot round. She didn't look that pleased to see Alice; in fact, she was looking really tense. But Alice supposed that was just because of the audition. Meeting. Whatever.

'You look wonderful!' she said enthusiastically to Piers as he opened the kitchen door for her. 'Really brown! How come?'

'He doesn't look that brown,' snapped Ginny. 'It's just a bit of a glow. Just to liven him up.' The sunbed had been her idea, and now a tingle of worry was growing in her stomach. Did he look too tanned? *Summer Street* was, after all, a very British soap opera.

'Well, I think it looks brilliant,' said Alice honestly.

She stared at Piers. 'And that blue shirt looks really good.'

'This shirt is great,' said Piers, tugging at it fondly. 'I always do well in this shirt.' He caught Ginny's eye and grinned. For a moment her expression remained tense. Then suddenly she broke into a smile.

'Sit down, Alice,' she said, patting a chair. 'Are you on your way to school?'

'Yes,' said Alice. 'I just thought I'd come and say good luck. Not that you need it,' she added hastily.

'Oh, I don't know,' said Piers, grinning. 'You can never have too much luck.'

He looked really good, thought Alice wistfully. Really good-looking and confident, just like a famous actor . . .

'Have you had breakfast?' enquired Duncan, standing at the stove. 'Would you like my famous scrambled eggs?'

'Yes please,' said Alice joyfully.

'And some coffee,' added Ginny, passing her the cafetière. 'Help yourself to a mug,' she added, gesturing to the shelf behind Alice.

Afterwards, Alice couldn't work out how it could have happened. One minute, she was grasping firmly hold of the handle of the cafetière and turning round in her seat to pick up her favourite mug with a mermaid painted on it. The next, Piers was yelling furiously, and clutching a sleeve dripping with hot coffee.

'Alice!' yelled Ginny and Duncan simultaneously. Then Duncan, seeing Alice turn very pale and then very red, added, 'What a shame! Quick, Piers, off with that shirt. Is your arm OK?'

'It's fine,' said Piers shakily. He gave Alice a smile. 'Don't worry!'

Alice stared at him in shattered disbelief.

'I'm sorry,' she whispered. She looked at his wet, red-dened arm in horror as he peeled back his sleeve. His shirt was stained brown in patches. She didn't know what to say.

'How could you do something so stupid?' Ginny's voice hit her ears like whiplash.

'Ginny!' Piers's voice filled the kitchen with reproof. Alice shrank in her chair. She couldn't believe she'd done such an awful thing. She should have stayed safely at home. 'It's not a problem,' Piers was saying. 'I'll just go and change my shirt.'

'But is your arm OK?' Alice didn't dare look at Ginny's face. She sounded absolutely furious.

'My arm's fine,' said Piers firmly. Alice risked a glance at him. His mouth was set straight, and his eyes were forebodingly dark.

'I'm so sorry,' she whispered. 'I'm so, so sorry.'

'For God's sake!' said Piers in mock-irritation. 'It's not such a disaster.' He looked at his watch. 'I'd better go and find another shirt.'

'But that was your lucky shirt,' wailed Ginny as he stood up.

'Well, I'd better wear one of my unlucky ones then,' said Piers evenly. Ginny sagged down into her chair when he had gone.

'I don't believe it,' she said brokenly.

'Come on, Ginny!' said Duncan. 'Brace up! Piers is fine.'

'But it's such a bad omen,' persisted Ginny.

'Bullshit!' said Duncan robustly. 'It could have been a lot worse. What if he'd spilled coffee over himself in the waiting-room at the television studios?'

'Yes, but . . .' began Ginny. She stopped. Alice knew what she was thinking. *But he didn't spill the coffee over himself, did he?*

'Ginny, I'm really sorry,' she said tremulously. 'I don't know how it happened.'

'It's OK,' said Ginny, relenting slightly. 'It was just an accident. Accidents happen.' She looked at her watch. 'Piers is going to miss his train if he doesn't hurry up,' she said fretfully.

'I thought he was catching the eleven o'clock?' said Alice without thinking.

'Yes, well, he decided to catch the earlier one, didn't he?' said Ginny shortly. She sighed. 'Look, Alice, I'm sorry. I shouldn't have shouted at you. It's just . . .' She swallowed, and pushed a hand through her hair. 'This is quite an important day for us.' Alice nodded mutely, and looked miserably at the coffee still puddling on the table, dripping down onto Piers's chair and the wooden floor. Should she offer to clear it up? Might she not then knock something else over? She felt as though her own hands and limbs were no longer to be trusted.

'Look, Ginny,' said Duncan gently, 'why don't you go upstairs and sort Piers out, and Alice can help me clear this lot up. What about it?' For a few moments, Ginny sat immobile, staring blankly at the table. Then she seemed to shake herself, and looked up.

'OK,' she said. 'Perhaps I'll go and see if Piers has got another shirt he can wear.' Without looking at Alice, she abruptly stood up, and left the kitchen.

Alice watched her go, then promptly, and to her great shame, burst into tears.

'Oh Alice,' said Duncan. 'Don't do that. We've got enough surplus liquid in this kitchen already.' Alice's sobs increased. 'Look,' he said, sitting down next to her and putting an arm round her shoulders, 'Ginny's just ratty this morning. Don't take any notice of her. You couldn't help it.'

'I'm so stupid,' sobbed Alice. 'I've ruined it all for Piers.'

'No you haven't,' said Duncan. He thought for a minute. 'It was probably just what he needed, to take his mind off things,' he added.

'You're just saying that,' shuddered Alice, but with a note of hope in her voice.

'I'm not,' said Duncan. 'Anyway, Piers is tough as old boots. You don't need to worry about him. Now, if you'd spilled a pot of coffee over me, it would have been a different story, I can tell you!' His voice rose on an indignant note, and Alice gave a half-giggle in spite of herself.

'That's right,' said Duncan. 'Now, what I think you should do is go to school.' Alice looked up woefully.

'But what about the kitchen?' she said.

'I'll clear up the kitchen,' said Duncan, putting on his actor's voice, 'with my super-speed extra power Mr Clean-Fast. Did I tell you I got a commercial, by the way?' he added. 'Filming next month. Lots of dosh.'

'No,' said Alice, momentarily diverted. 'That's really good! What for?'

'Tooth powder,' said Duncan. 'I play a tooth.'

'Wow!' Alice giggled, and pushed her hair back.

She rubbed her face with her sleeve, and gave a huge sniff.

'Good girl,' said Duncan approvingly. He picked up her school bag and handed it to her.

'Now,' he said, 'we'll see you later on at the party. Come nice and early.'

'Ginny was going to do my make-up,' said Alice, in a woebegone voice. 'I don't suppose she'll want to do it now.'

'Of course she will,' said Duncan. 'But if she's too busy,' he added diplomatically, 'I'll do it.'

'You?' Alice looked at him sceptically. 'Can you do make-up?'

'Can I do make-up?' echoed Duncan indignantly, shooing her out of the kitchen door. 'Can I do make-up? What on earth do you think I went to drama school for?'

Anthea spent breakfast standing up, sitting down, making slices of toast and cutting them into smaller and smaller pieces till they disintegrated. She was watched by a resigned Hannah, who followed her about the kitchen with a jay-cloth, an unconcerned Daniel and Andrew, and an amused Marcus. When Hannah had chivvied the boys off to get ready for school, she turned agonized eyes on Marcus.

'Do you think we could phone them up?'

'No,' said Marcus cheerfully. 'I don't. They said they'd contact the school.'

'I know.' Anthea put her nail anxiously to her mouth, began to bite it, then thought better of it. 'They're having the meeting this morning,' she said slowly, as though trying to memorize lines. 'They'll make a decision by lunchtime.'

'Unless they can't decide,' suggested Marcus. 'Or unless they decide not to give any scholarships this year.' Anthea shot him a look of annoyance.

'Then they'll phone the school.'

'And then the school will phone us,' said Marcus. 'There's nothing we can do until then.'

'But you know what these organizations are like,' said Anthea desperately. 'Last year it was days before anyone heard.' She pulled her dressing-gown comfortingly around her. 'There must be some way we can find out sooner.'

'We're not even sure the meeting's today,' said Marcus soothingly. 'I really don't think there's any point worrying about it.'

'Mr Chambers told me the meeting was definitely today,' said Anthea crossly. 'He knows about these things. He's a friend of the headmaster of Bourne.' A strange look passed her face. 'Of course!' she exclaimed suddenly.

'What?' said Marcus. He looked at her suspiciously.

'We'll get Mr Chambers to phone up the headmaster this afternoon and ask.'

'No we won't!' said Marcus. 'We can't ask him to do a thing like that!'

'Why not?' Anthea stuck her chin out at him. 'He'll be just as concerned to know as we are.' She picked up the cordless phone and began to jab at the buttons.

'I don't want to hear this,' said Marcus. 'I'm going to

clean my teeth.' He stood up, and shook his newspaper at Anthea. 'He won't do it. I can tell you that now.'

But when he came back down into the kitchen, holding his briefcase and ready to go to work, Anthea was simpering down the phone.

'Thank you so much,' she said. 'Goodbye.' She put down the receiver and smirked at Marcus.

'Did he agree to it?' said Marcus in amazement.

'Yes,' said Anthea triumphantly. 'I knew he would. He said if we want to pop round after work, he should have got through to Bourne by then.'

'Do we both have to go?' said Marcus grudgingly.

'Yes,' said Anthea. 'And then we'll go on to the party. Apparently Mr Chambers and his wife are going to it, too. I said we could take them.' She raised innocent eyes to Marcus. 'The Prentices' party. You remember.' Marcus scowled.

'Why don't we just forget the party?' he said impulsively. 'Why don't we go out to dinner instead? Either way. To celebrate or commiserate.'

'Oh no!' said Anthea. 'I've arranged my appointment at the hairdresser's now. And I've bought a new dress. We can't not go. And anyway, it'll be fun.' She wrinkled her nose at Marcus. 'Why don't you want to go?'

'Oh, I do,' said Marcus quickly. 'I do. It'll be tremendous fun.' He picked up his briefcase and gave Anthea a warmer-than-usual kiss. He would be very glad, he thought darkly, when the day was over, and everything had been settled. One way or the other.

Piers arrived at the television studios five minutes early for his appointment. Usually he would have been at least fifteen minutes early, but today he liked to think he could be a bit more relaxed. He smiled disarmingly at the girl on reception, and gave her his name self-deprecatingly, as though he were already an established member of the cast; a well-known figure at the studios. *This time in a couple of months*, he thought, then, out of habit, stopped himself. But he couldn't stop his heart jumping a little as the girl nodded a couple of times on the phone, then beamed at Piers and said, 'Alan Tinker will be out presently.'

When Alan appeared, he greeted Piers like an old friend.

'Great to see you, Piers. Marvellous.' He swept Piers through a pair of double doors and down a corridor and into a waiting-room. 'Be back in a second. Explain everything then. Help yourself to coffee. Ciao for now!' He winked at Piers, then disappeared out of the door. Piers flashed him a smile, turned around, and froze. Sitting on a plushy chair in the corner, sipping at a polystyrene cup, was a young man. He was tall and dark, and wearing smart-casual clothes together with an elaborate air of confidence. He looked, Piers realized with a shock, not unlike Ian Everitt.

'Hi there,' he said, in a voice which could only belong to an actor. Piers felt his heart begin to thud. What was going on?

The door opened, and Alan Tinker ushered another young man in. He was tall, and dark, and wearing a blue shirt just like the one Alice had spilled coffee over.

'Bear with me,' said Alan Tinker, addressing the three of them cheerfully.

'You're all here now, but we've just got a bit more setting-up to do. I'll be two ticks.' And he disappeared again.

'Hello there,' said the third man nervously. 'Are you here to audition for Rupert in *Summer Street*?'

'Aren't we all?' said the man in the corner. 'Bloody cheek, I call it. I thought I was the only one up for it. That bastard practically said the part was mine. I couldn't believe it when he said there were three of us.'

'Me too,' said the man at the door in fervent tones. 'I thought I'd got the job weeks ago.' He looked at Piers. Then he looked back at the man in the corner. 'Gosh,' he exclaimed, walking into the room. 'Don't we all look similar?'

CHAPTER FIFTEEN

At six o'clock, Ginny heard the sound of the key in the front door lock. She rushed to the top of the stairs, her head half full of heated rollers, in time to see Piers enter the house, not with the triumphant swagger of success, but quietly; almost deferentially. A disastrous pounding began in her chest.

'Well?' she almost shouted. Piers looked up at her and gave an eloquent shrug. 'What? They still haven't told you?'

'They're going to phone tonight,' said Piers. 'At least, that's what they said.'

Ginny stared at him. 'What do you mean?'

'I need a drink,' said Piers. 'Is there any gin?'

'In the kitchen,' said Ginny. She looked at her watch. 'Shit. I've still got to do my hair.'

She nevertheless followed Piers anxiously into the kitchen, watching him as he poured out a large gin and tonic; shaking her head when he offered her some. He cracked a couple of ice-cubes into the glass, then took a large swig. He took another. Then he wiped his mouth.

'Bastards,' he said.

'What?' A painful stab of panic went through Ginny's chest. She stared at Piers, nervously twisting a stray strand of hair round and round in her fingers. 'What did they do?'

'It wasn't just me auditioning,' said Piers.

'What?'

'There were three of us. We had to go on one after another. They wanted to be able to compare us easily, they said.' Piers's voice held mocking scorn. Ginny looked at him blankly.

'I thought it was just you.'

'So did I. So did the others.' Ginny's heart began to thud.

'And what were the others like?' she asked, trying not to sound too urgent.

'One of them looked a bit like Ian Everitt. He was called Sean something. The other one was a bit of a wimp. Fresh out of drama school, I think.'

'Did you see them auditioning?'

'No, thank God. At least we didn't have to watch each other.' But then at least you'd know what the others were like, thought Ginny impatiently.

'And then what happened?'

'Well, it was a bit strange. We'd all done our bits, and we were sitting in the waiting-room.' Piers took a final swig, and poured himself another drink. He cast his mind back to the scene; the unbearable tension between the three of them; the false smiles and idle, distracting pieces of gossip.

'And then,' he said, 'Alan Tinker came in, and asked Sean to come back and do another little bit. And he told me and the other bloke to go.' A dead weight dropped to the bottom of Ginny's stomach. 'But then he said,' added Piers, 'that we mustn't read anything into it. And that they'd let us all know this evening.' He scowled, and took another huge gulp of gin. Alan Tinker's voice floated back into his mind. *Now, don't get alarmed, you two. Don't think this means we're reject-ing you.* And he'd smiled at them both. Had he smiled especially hard at Piers? Piers couldn't tell.

'Oh God.' Ginny sank into a chair. 'I don't believe it. Why would they have wanted to see the other guy again?'

'I don't know.' Piers looked at her with dark, unhappy eyes. 'I asked myself that all the way home. Were they just bullshitting me? Have they given it to him?'

'Well, if they have,' said Ginny indignantly, 'why couldn't they have just told you on the spot?'

'God knows. The bastards. Oh Christ!' Suddenly he crashed his glass down on the table. 'This fucking au-dition's been hanging over me for months. I just want to fucking well know!' Ginny looked at her watch.

'Did they say when they'd phone?' Piers shook his head.

'Of course they didn't,' he said sarcastically. Ginny looked at his taut face.

'What do you really think?' she said carefully. It al-most killed her to say it. 'Do you think they gave it to the other guy?' Piers shrugged. He didn't want to think about it.

'I don't know,' he said. 'I really don't know.' He looked up at Ginny and forced himself to smile. 'You look great,' he said. 'I'd better start getting ready for the party, I suppose.' Ginny smiled back and took his hand. Inside her, a heavy misery battled with a piercing, desperate hope. It was unbearable. She felt drawn-in, unable to face the outside world. What's the point of having this stupid party? she thought. What's the point of it all now?

Liz had told Alice at tea-time that if she liked, she would do her hair and make-up for her. And Alice, who felt rather unwilling to go back and face Ginny after the coffee episode, had eventually agreed. Now she sat on her mother's bed, feeling the soft brushes and pencils tickling her face, telling herself that if it looked too gross she could always put loads of black eyeliner on top. Her mother seemed in a really good mood. She had opened a bottle of wine for them to drink while they got ready, and she was humming, and kept telling Alice she was going to look stunning.

Eventually she told Alice to look in the mirror. Alice stared at herself in agreeable surprise. She couldn't put her finger on what was different, but her face seemed much brighter than usual. Even her hair looked shiny.

'Go and put on your dress,' said Liz, beaming at her. 'You're going to be the belle of the ball.' Alice stared at her mother. Usually she told Alice she was too young to be wearing such a lot of make-up. But today she seemed really keen for Alice to wear it. And actually, thought Alice, looking more carefully at her mother's face, she herself was wearing a lot more make-up than she normally did.

'You look nice,' she offered. 'Your make-up.'

'I had it done at Sedgwick's,' said Liz gaily. 'At one of the counters.' Alice stared at her mother, flabbergasted.

'You sat on one of those little chairs? In front of everybody?'

'Yes,' said her mother. 'Why not? It's free. And I can't afford to buy all those expensive things myself.' Not yet, anyway, she added to herself.

When Alice had disappeared to her room, Liz pulled out her new party clothes from the wardrobe. She dressed carefully, brushed her hair until it was gleaming, and then looked at herself appraisingly in the mirror. Was it her imagination, or did she already give off a slight veneer of being well-to-do? Was she picking up Marcus's confident bearing; his easy manner with luxurious things? She walked up and down a few times in front of the mirror, admiring the way her new silk shirt skimmed gracefully over her trousers. All her bulges seemed magically to have disappeared.

When Jonathan knocked on the door, she looked over unhurriedly and, in an elegantly enquiring voice, said, 'Yes?'

'I didn't want to disturb you,' said Jonathan, heading for his bedside cabinet and picking up a book. He turned back and looked admiringly at Liz.

'You look wonderful!' he said. As if you'd know, thought Liz scathingly. 'I've just been speaking to Daniel

Witherstone's mother,' added Jonathan. 'I haven't managed to get through to Geoffrey yet.'

'Oh, what, this scholarship thing?' Liz paused. 'What time are you phoning the . . . the parents?' she asked carefully.

'I'm not. They're coming here. It turns out they're going to this party too.' Jonathan smiled at Liz. 'It's a small world, isn't it? Mrs Witherstone said they'd be able to give us a lift. But they're very keen to find out the result first.'

'Oh gosh,' said Liz. Her heart began to flutter. She didn't want to see Marcus yet. Not here. Not with his wife.

'Actually,' she said rapidly, 'it's probably more sensible if Alice and I go separately.' A stroke of inspiration hit her. 'After all, we'll need to have the car there to get back.'

'That's true,' said Jonathan thoughtfully. 'And, now I think about it, I didn't mention Alice. There may not be room for all of us.'

'I shouldn't think that would be a problem,' said Liz tersely. 'I mean,' she amended, 'that Witherstone boy seems to get picked up in huge cars. They seem pretty well-loaded to me.' She lay the statement down like a challenge. Jonathan shrugged.

'I guess they are.' Liz looked at him crossly. Wasn't he even going to express the smallest amount of jealousy?

'In fact,' she said, 'I can't think why they need a scholarship at all.'

'It's not just the money,' said Jonathan mildly. 'A

scholarship to Bourne is very prestigious in academic terms. That's partly why I'm staying behind to telephone. I'd very much like to know how young Daniel has done. You know,' he looked at Liz, 'if he does well, it could be very good for us. For the tutorial college. News travels fast in Silchester.' But Liz wasn't listening. She was suddenly anxious to be gone, before Marcus and Anthea rolled up in their smart car and smart clothes and smart veneer of togetherness.

'OK then,' she said. 'You come along later.' She picked up her bag and went out onto the landing. 'Alice,' she called, 'are you ready yet?' Jonathan sighed. He looked at her clothes strewn in careless haste around the room. He picked up a crumpled shirt and gazed at it. Then he shrugged, threw it back onto the floor where it had lain, followed Liz out, and stopped in amazement. Alice was coming out of her bedroom, looking like a twenties flapper in a short, flirty dress and dark-lashed, shining eyes.

'You look beautiful!' said Jonathan with conviction. 'Really stunning.' His eyes rested on her Doc Martens. 'I take it those are part of the ensemble?' he added humorously.

'Yeah,' muttered Alice. She looked at him, at his battered grey trousers and faded shirt. 'Is that what you're wearing?' she began in alarm.

'No,' said Jonathan patiently. 'I'm going to change. Don't worry, Alice,' he added, in a light, toneless voice, 'I won't embarrass you in front of your friends. I'm not going to come as a duck.' He tried to catch her eye, but Alice flushed and looked away. Liz, who had been applying a last coat of lipstick and not listening, looked up.

'Right, come on, Alice,' she said. 'See you there, Jonathan.' And with a schoolgirl-light step, she hurried down the stairs. Alice followed slowly, dragging her feet, half wanting to smile at her father and say, 'See you there!' and half hoping he would decide at the last minute not to come. She turned at the bottom of the stairs, and looked up, thinking she could compromise by saying a friendly, 'Goodbye!' But he had gone.

When Alice and Liz arrived at Twelve Russell Street, the lights were on, and music was pounding through the walls. Liz hesitated momentarily.

'Is this my sort of party?' she said, more to herself than Alice.

'Of course it is! Come on!' Alice looked crossly at Liz. She was feeling a bit nervous, too, and didn't need her mother making her feel worse.

But when Duncan opened the door, suddenly everything seemed OK. He was dressed, like Liz, in a red silk shirt, with rosy cheeks to match. Music flooded out and around him like a warming wave of water, and he kissed each of them elaborately before allowing them past the threshold.

'Welcome, welcome!' he exclaimed. 'Some honest Silchester residents! You're the only people from Silchester so far,' he added in a stage whisper.

'Who are all those people in there, then?' asked Alice, giggling.

'Horrible Londoners,' replied Duncan confidingly. 'Not our sort at all. But they insisted on coming, so what can you do . . . ?' As he led them into the crowded sitting-room, Liz looked at Alice and laughed.

'He's quite a character!' she said, raising her voice above the music.

'I know,' said Alice, feeling suddenly superior. These were *her* friends. She looked around for Piers. But although there were plenty of men in the room who looked a bit like Piers, he didn't seem to be one of them.

'Hello, you two!' Ginny bore down on them, eyes glittering. 'Have a drink! Have two!' Alice looked at Ginny uncomfortably.

'I'm sorry about this morning,' she began.

'Oh that!' Ginny waved her hand rather manically in the air. 'No problem! No problem!' She grinned fiercely at Alice.

'What happened? At the audi . . . meeting?'

'They're still in conference,' said Ginny airily. She thrust the bottle she was holding at Alice. 'Here, help yourself. I must just go and say hello to my business partner.' She strode off, and Alice looked at Liz helplessly.

'Well!' said Liz. 'What's with her? Is she on drugs?'

'I don't think so,' said Alice puzzledly. 'I don't know what's wrong. She's not normally like that.'

Ginny felt as though she was about to fall over the edge. As she swooped down on Clarissa, glamorous even in pregnancy, shrieked over the sight of her swelling stomach with unbearable gaiety and engaged in the obligatory treble kiss, her eyes were darting feverishly around the room. She wanted to scream. Bloody Duncan seemed to have invited everyone they knew to this party, friends and enemies alike. They'd all come down from London in a convoy of cars, and all the property people were yelling about provincial house prices, and all the actors were asking if it was true that Piers was up for a part in *Summer Street*.

And still the phone hadn't rung. For a while, Piers had come down and talked to people, always with one eye permanently on the telephone, parrying questions about *Summer Street* until people gave up. Now she didn't know where he was. And that bloody little Alice, with her dowdy mother, turning up and asking so blatantly about the audition. If she'd asked any louder, somebody might have *heard*. Ginny looked across the room at Alice, already being chatted up by some flash London friend of Clarissa's, and suddenly regretted having been so confiding with her. One way and another, she had basically told Alice everything—about the audition, about Piers's career, even about wanting to start a family, for Christ's sake. She'd told all her secrets to a bloody *schoolgirl*. It was too much.

Alice looked over at Ginny and wished that she would come across and talk to her. The man she was talking to had a balding head and a pony-tail and looked really old and gross, but he kept trying to make out to Alice that he was really cool, and going on about what labels were in and had she been to any gigs recently? She'd already told him that she couldn't afford to go to gigs, she was only fourteen, but he didn't seem to understand. And now he was talking about club life in New Orleans. What did she know about New Orleans? She really felt like having a cigarette, but no-one else seemed to be smoking and it would be really obvious if she started. Perhaps, in a minute, she could get away and have one in the garage. If she could make sure her mother wouldn't see her. Alice hadn't acknowledged her mother's existence since those first few minutes of the party. It was bad enough only being fourteen. But having your *mother* at the same party . . .

As Marcus pulled the car up in front of the tutorial college, Anthea suddenly clutched his arm.

'Perhaps we should wait,' she said. 'Perhaps we should just let them phone us.' Marcus looked at her. Her face was drained of all colour, except for two patches of blusher carefully applied earlier in the evening.

'Come on,' he said comfortably. 'Now we're here, we might as well know.'

'I can't bear it,' whispered Anthea. Marcus leant over and kissed her neck.

'Whatever happens,' he said, 'we love Daniel and we love each other. Don't we?'

'Yes,' faltered Anthea.

'Well then,' said Marcus, 'nothing else is really important. Come on!' And he opened the car door.

Jonathan was waiting for them. He had just tried Geoffrey's number, only to be rewarded with the engaged tone.

'I'll give him a couple of minutes, then try again,' he said. He looked at Anthea, in her smart coat and sheer tights; at Marcus, solid and opulent. He swallowed.

'Could I offer . . . ?' he began. 'Could I offer either of you a drink?'

As they entered the flat, Marcus looked about him with an appalled fascination.

'It's not much,' called Jonathan from the kitchen, 'but

it keeps us warm. Here!' He ushered them into the sitting-room and poured out three little glasses of sherry. Anthea sat down delicately on the sofa; Marcus strode to the far corner of the room. It only took him three strides. He couldn't believe the cramped size of the rooms in this little flat; the awkward corners and the dingy atmosphere. No wonder Liz was miserable here.

'I'll have another go, shall I?' said Jonathan cheerfully. 'The phone's out on the landing.' As he left, Marcus looked at Anthea for a reaction similar to his own. But she was staring broodingly into space.

'Delicious sherry,' he said out loud. 'Could I have a top-up?' He suddenly wanted to see more of this grim little dwelling.

'Help yourself,' said Jonathan. 'In the kitchen.'

The kitchen seemed, to Marcus, even worse than the sitting-room. He peered at the Formica counter; noted the packets of breakfast cereal on the side, and wondered which mug was Liz's. But then Jonathan's voice galvanized him.

'Hello, Geoffrey? Jonathan Chambers here.'

Marcus couldn't bear to listen. He rejoined Anthea in the sitting-room and closed the door.

'If it's bad news,' he said rapidly to Anthea, 'try not to be too disappointed. Especially to Daniel. I mean, he worked bloody hard for it. He worked as hard as he could. And it's not the end of the world, is it? It's not . . .' He stopped abruptly.

'I see,' Jonathan was saying. 'Well, thanks very much, Geoffrey. Thanks for letting me know.' Marcus and Anthea looked at each other. A premature feeling of disappointment began to spread over Marcus's chest, and he gave Anthea a broad smile to compensate for it. She looked at him mutely, pale and shaking.

The door opened. Jonathan stood, a curious expression on his face.

'Your son,' he began. Anthea gave a sharp intake of breath. 'Your son,' he continued slowly, 'has been awarded the honour,' he swallowed, 'the honour . . .' There was a short agonized pause. 'Of this year's top scholarship to Bourne College.'

CHAPTER SIXTEEN

When she saw Marcus arriving at the party with Jonathan and Anthea, Liz didn't move. She carried on her
conversation with the rather dull young surveyor who
had offered to get her a drink, and waited for Marcus to
come to her. She knew he would come to her. It was
inevitable; part of the power she had over him. So she
relaxed into her chair—literally her chair, it suddenly
occurred to her, since she was the one who had bought
it—and greedily drank her glass of wine, and laughed
loudly at the young surveyor's jokes, and waited.

And when Marcus caught her eye over the nodding,
bobbing heads of Ginny's friends, and jerked it surreptitiously towards the garden, she smiled to herself in
confirmation, and left it a full three minutes before she
interrupted the young man's lecture on subsidence. As
she made her way towards the back door, she was careful not to catch the eye of Jonathan. She didn't want to

have to talk to him; introduce him as her husband; adopt the wifely role. She was beyond all of that.

She had expected that Marcus would catch her in a desperate embrace as soon as she appeared outside. It had, after all, been weeks since their last union. But instead, he hissed, 'What happened at the bank?'

'The bank?' Liz stared at him uncomprehendingly.

'A few weeks ago. You were going to see the bank. What did they say?'

'Oh yes.' Liz forced herself to recall the meeting. 'They said we had to sell this house. We haven't got enough capital invested in the tutorial college.'

'Or what?'

Liz shrugged. She found this questioning rather irksome.

'I dunno. Repossession, I suppose.' She gave a little giggle. Marcus seized her wrist.

'It's not funny!' Liz stared at him.

'What's all this about? What does it matter?'

'It's your livelihood,' said Marcus furiously. 'Of course it matters. Your business deserves to succeed.' He stopped. When he spoke again, it was in a different voice. 'Daniel got his scholarship,' he said. His mouth twitched a few times. 'Top scholarship to Bourne,' he added. This time, he couldn't help grinning.

'Oh good,' said Liz. 'Listen,' she continued, 'when are we going to see each other properly?'

Marcus stared at her in astonishment.

'Is that all you can say?' he exclaimed. Liz shrugged.

'What do you—' She broke off. The back door had opened, and the voice of Duncan was coming unmistakably across the garden. 'Into the garage,' she hissed.

She hurried Marcus in, closed the door and stood facing him, breathing heavily across the blackness. 'They won't see us if we don't turn the lights on,' she murmured, and tilted her face up to be kissed. But Marcus pulled her chin down irritably.

'Don't you care about your own business?' he exclaimed softly. 'You know, your husband is working wonders.'

'I'm sure he is,' retorted Liz. 'Good luck to him.'

'What's that supposed to mean?'

'Well, you know,' said Liz. A drunken excitement began to grow inside her. It was all going to happen now, she thought. Marcus was going to ask her if she still loved Jonathan. She was going to say no. And he was going to ask her to marry him.

'No, I don't know.'

'Us,' said Liz shyly, and put her hand tenderly up to Marcus's chin. He looked at her in horror, and tore it away.

'Us?' he exclaimed. 'There is no us!'

'Of course there is,' said Liz truculently.

'Not any more,' said Marcus. 'It's over. Over!' His voice filled the small garage with a shocking ferocity. Liz took a small step backwards.

'What do you mean?' she whispered.

'You heard him.' A small, shaking voice came from the corner. Marcus and Liz turned as one, and watched in disbelief as the tiny flame of a cigarette lighter flickered alight. Alice, curled up in the corner, all fringes and long legs, looked with huge eyes from one silent face to the other, then slowly, jerkily, lit a cigarette. She took a few deep drags to get it going properly, then slowly got up, her gaze still darting between Liz and Marcus. She came towards them, threading her way through the piles of boxes and junk, and faced Liz. For a moment she seemed about to say something. Her lips quivered frantically, and she took several drags on her cigarette. Then she seemed to think better of it. She pushed her way roughly between them, out of the garage, and slammed the door behind her. Liz stood completely still for a few minutes.

'Christ,' she said. 'Oh Christ!' Her voice rose to a wail.

'Fucking hell,' said Marcus in more subdued tones. He looked at Liz without particular affection. 'We'd better go and see if we can limit the damage,' he said drily. 'And I suggest you stop that noise first.'

When the phone rang, pealing insistently over the sound of the music, Ginny froze. She looked frantically around for Piers. But she couldn't see him. And Duncan had led a party into the garden. There was only her. She looked over to the telephone and, to her horror, saw a hand reaching towards it.

'Stop!' she screamed. 'I mean, I'll get it.' The owner of the hand, a small chap in PR whose name Ginny had quite forgotten, smiled at her apologetically.

'I thought it might be someone wanting directions,' he said. Ginny ignored him and grabbed the receiver. But Piers had got there first, on the upstairs extension in their bedroom.

'Hello?' he was saying, in the carefully modulated tones he always used to impress.

'Piers? Alan Tinker here.' Ginny thrust the phone down and looked paranoically around the room to see if anyone had overheard the name. But the few odd glances she was attracting were not those of curious actors. Nobody had guessed.

She stood immobile for a few seconds, balancing lightly on the soles of her feet, thinking light-headedly that their entire fate was being decided in this one telephone call. The thought almost made her want to laugh. Then, slowly, she began to thread her way unobtrusively through the crowded room, marvelling at her own ability to smile gaily at people, blow kisses, even spontaneously compliment some dim actress girl on her jacket. At last she reached the hall. Slowly, silently, she climbed the stairs, counting the steps to herself. At the sixteenth step was Piers and the answer.

She reached the top just as he reached the door of their bedroom. One look at his face was enough. He hadn't got it. He hadn't got the part.

A searing pain seemed to rip her stomach in two, and she smiled brilliantly at him.

'Well, never mind,' she said. A pair of tears forced themselves to the surface of her eyes. 'You didn't want that crappy job anyway.'

'No,' said Piers, 'I didn't.' He looked at her expressionlessly for a few seconds; then suddenly his face crumpled, and he gave a heaving, shocking sob. Ginny stared at him, aghast. 'I did want it,' he cried. 'Christ, I wanted it more than you wanted it. I was scared at how much I wanted it.' He sank to the floor. 'They gave it to Sean. The one they asked back. I fucking knew it. The bastards.' He thumped the ground. 'Why did they make us wait?' Ginny crouched down beside Piers and took him in her arms. Another pair of tears forced their way out onto her face. She couldn't think what to say; what to think. All her thoughts, for the last three months, had been anchored in *Summer Street*. Oh God. No. It couldn't be true. Another pain in her stomach made her double up.

'Ginny?' A voice made her head jerk up. Alice was standing on the stairs, looking worriedly at her, puffing furiously at a cigarette. Her face was deadly white, and her hands were trembling. 'Ginny, something awful's just happened.' Ginny looked up at her. Bloody little Alice. The timing almost made her smile.

'I was in the garage—' Alice was saying.

'Alice?' Ginny interrupted brightly. 'I don't want to know, all right?' She crawled over until her face was close to Alice's. 'I bloody well don't want to know, do you hear?' Her voice rose to a scream. 'As far as I'm concerned, you can bloody well fuck off and die!' Alice physically jumped.

'What . . . ?' she began in a quavering voice.

'If you hadn't been so fucking clumsy this morning,' yelled Ginny; 'if you hadn't come round here; if you didn't have such a fucking crush on Piers, then perhaps you wouldn't have ruined his audition! Now just go! Go!' And she burst, at last, into wrenching sobs.

Alice didn't hesitate. Her heart thumping wildly, eyes darkened in shock, she scrambled as best she could down the stairs, through the front door and out into the night.

'What's wrong?' said Clarissa in surprise, poking

her head into the hall. 'Is something wrong with that little girl? Should someone tell her parents?'

Liz tottered into the house with a quailing heart, and went up to Jonathan with what she hoped was a normal expression on her face.

'I'm a bit worried about Alice,' she said, her voice shaking. 'Have you seen where she's got to?'

'No, I haven't. Has she been drinking too much?' Jonathan looked anxiously at Liz. 'Honestly, she is a silly girl!'

'No, that's not it,' faltered Liz. She looked frantically around. 'Haven't you seen her anywhere?'

'Excuse me!' A bright, blond, slightly pregnant baby-faced girl tapped Liz on the shoulder. 'Are you the mother of the little girl in the fringes? I thought you should know, she's just run out into the street. She looked a bit upset.'

'I'll go,' muttered Liz, and started to push her way past Jonathan. But he put his arm out to stop her.

'No, I'll go,' he said firmly. 'You stay here and enjoy the party. And talk to Anthea. I don't think you two have properly met, have you?' Liz stared, dumbfounded, at Anthea, who smiled vivaciously at her. 'Thank you,' added Jonathan to Clarissa, who waved her glass merrily back. 'I won't be long,' he added, and suddenly was gone.

Liz looked at Anthea. She had nothing to say to her. But Anthea was brimming over.

'Your husband is a genius,' she began. 'I can't tell

you how wonderful he is. I've never seen anything like it. His patience, his sense of humour . . . and he's so good at explaining things so that children understand them!' She paused. 'Of course, you know about our son's scholarship?'

'I heard,' murmured Liz, staring at the floor. 'Tremendous.'

'Isn't it? We're absolutely thrilled. Aren't we, darling?' Liz looked up in surprise, and through a horrified daze, saw that Anthea was gazing up at someone. And the someone was Marcus. And he was putting his arm affectionately around Anthea's shoulders, and bending over and kissing her as though he still loved her.

A black hatred settled in Liz's chest, threatening to break into heaving tears at any moment. She would stay for one more minute, she told herself, then go. But go to what? To Jonathan? To Alice?

'I've told all my friends about your tutorial college,' Anthea was saying. 'And lots have signed up. They all think it's wonderful. When I tell them about Daniel . . .' She paused significantly. 'And do you do Common Entrance coaching too, Mrs Chambers?'

'No, I don't,' said Liz. She looked directly at Marcus's unflinching eyes. 'I'm not sure what I do these days.'

Jonathan found Alice running along the street, panting and wheezing and sobbing, with make-up smeared across her face and a trail of cigarettes behind her. As he caught up with her, she was flicking her lighter frantically, swearing and crying out as the wind blew it out again and again.

'Alice!' he called as he caught up with her. 'Alice! Slow down!' Alice turned, saw her father's face, then burst into a frenzy of sobs. 'Come on!' said Jonathan. He hooked an arm round her, then when she had slowed down enough, put another arm round her. 'It's all right,' he said. 'Really. Everything's OK.' For a few moments, Alice shuddered silently against his shirt. Then she looked up at his face and gave an anguished cry.

'Oh, Dad! I'm so sorry!' Her voice tailed away into a wail.

'There's nothing to be sorry for,' said Jonathan calmly. 'It was a boring party anyway.' He grinned at Alice.

'But you don't understand!' she began. She looked around her at the dark, empty street. 'Oh God! It's so awful!' A fresh stream of tears spurted from her eyes.

'What *I* think is so awful,' said Jonathan, regarding the thin white trail of cigarettes behind them, 'is that you've been smoking for so long without telling us.' Alice gasped.

'How do you mean?' she said, a note of resentment creeping shakily into her voice.

'I thought when Genevieve went away, you might stop. But obviously not.' Alice gaped at him.

'Did you know? All that time?'

'Subtlety, Alice,' observed Jonathan, 'is not your strongest point. The cigarette butts in the garage were a bit of a give-away.'

'But you never said anything!' There was a long pause.

'Just because you know something,' said Jonathan clearly, 'it doesn't mean you have to tell it to everybody. Or, indeed, anybody.' He looked at her. 'Do you always put your hand up in class when you think you know the answer?' Alice shook her head mutely.

'Exactly. Sometimes you leave it to someone else. Sometimes you're not quite sure. Sometimes you decide the best thing is to wait, listen, and learn.' Alice looked at him. Thoughts were buzzing around in her head.

'Dad . . .' she began, then stopped.

'Yes?' He looked at her anxiously. There was a moment's silence. Alice pushed a hand through her hair, and forced a shaky grin onto her face.

'Can I have a cigarette?'

Duncan went upstairs to find Ginny and Piers, and heard muffled sobbing coming from their bedroom. Oh Jesus, he thought, realizing immediately what had happened. His face sagged, and suddenly his whole body felt heavy. Although he had never confessed as much, he had hoped and wished as much as they had. For a few moments, he stood outside the door, stupidly wishing he could go in; share his disappointment; give his commiserations. At least they had each other.

Then a sound from downstairs galvanized him. The party. No one at the party must be allowed to find out. He turned briskly on his heel, ran lightly down the stairs, and picked up two open bottles of wine that stood on the hall table.

'Who needs more booze?' he cried. 'Turn the music up!'

'Duncan?' Ginny's friend Clarissa was tugging sweetly at his sleeve. 'Do you know where Ginny is?

We want to say goodbye.' Duncan hesitated only for a second.

'Well, between you and me,' he said, grinning wickedly at her, 'I think Ginny and Piers would rather not be disturbed just at the moment.' He winked at Clarissa, and she gave a delighted peal of laughter.

'Oh, all right then,' she said. 'Do tell them we said goodbye, won't you?'

Liz stayed at the party until Duncan started bringing in cups of tea on trays. Then, realizing how late it was, and with only a little reluctance, she gathered together her coat, her scarf, her gloves, and went out into the freezing night air. Her resentment against Marcus; her apprehension at seeing Jonathan; her fear as to what Alice might have blurted out; all seemed to have evaporated. She walked home swiftly and evenly, thinking that what she would do when she got in was make a mug of tea and put plenty of sugar into it, and sip it, warming her hands against the sides of the mug. Beyond that, she couldn't think.

But as she crept into the kitchen, she gave a gasp of shock. Leaning against the side, sipping from the very mug she had envisaged using, was Jonathan.

'Did you enjoy the rest of the party?' he said in a low but friendly voice. 'You've just missed Alice. She was a bit tired, I think.' Liz stared at him as though in a stupor. Was he suddenly very stupid? Was he playing games with her?

'I suppose Alice told you everything,' she said in a

voice roughened by worry. Jonathan clutched the mug more tightly, but his expression didn't change.

'Alice told me nothing,' he said evenly. 'I don't think there was anything to tell.' He smiled. 'Now sit down, and I'll make you a nice mug of tea. With sugar.'

CHAPTER SEVENTEEN

Two weeks later, Jonathan sat in Marcus's office and looked at him with a clear, enquiring gaze. Marcus met his eyes, coloured slightly, and looked away.

'It's very good of you to come in,' he said. 'Especially on a Saturday. I can appreciate how busy you must be.' He paused, and his eyes fell on the local paper, open on his desk for reference at the display property advertisements. 'Did you see the piece in here about the scholarship?' he asked, picking it up and turning to an inside news page. 'Quite a nice item, I thought. Anthea's idea,' he added.

They both looked at the grainy photograph of a grimly smiling Daniel; at the headline LOCAL PRODIGY WINS TOP AWARD. 'I don't think Daniel was too wild about it,' continued Marcus. 'But I hope it's been some good publicity for the tutorial college.'

'It has, as a matter of fact,' said Jonathan, giving a small smile. 'I had no idea there were so many children taking Common Entrance in Silchester who needed coaching.' He looked at his watch. 'In fact, I've got a class a bit later on. We're fitting them in at all times.'

'Oh, right you are,' said Marcus, abruptly closing the paper. 'I've got to shoot off myself, actually. But this won't take long. I just wanted to tell you, first of all, that Ginny and Piers Prentice have given notice on the house in Russell Street.'

'Oh dear,' said Jonathan, his face falling. 'That didn't last long.'

'Yes,' said Marcus, frowning. 'I'm not sure what the reason is. They've already left, with quite a lot of their stuff, and they're having the rest sent on. Some friend of theirs is sorting everything out. They'll pay the rent due in full,' he added hastily. 'But to all intents and purposes, the property is now vacant.'

'What a shame,' said Jonathan. 'I had gathered from my daughter that they'd left Silchester for the moment. She was rather upset when she found out that they'd gone.' His brow wrinkled. 'But I didn't realize it was for good.' He looked up anxiously at Marcus. 'We really needed the income from their rent, you know. How long do you think it'll be before you find another tenant?'

'Well, there may be no need for that,' said Marcus breezily. 'As it turns out, it's not such bad news for you after all.' He paused, and studied his fingernails for a few seconds. When he looked up, his face was blank. 'I believe,' he said slowly, 'that I may have found a buyer for your house.'

'What? Really?' Jonathan looked at Marcus in amazement. 'I'd almost given up on that front.'

'The buyer,' said Marcus steadily, 'is a foreign purchaser who wishes to make an investment in the Silchester area. I have advised him to make an offer of two hundred thousand pounds for the property.' There was a short silence. He looked up. Jonathan was gaping at him in astounded disbelief.

'I should add that the buyer wishes to remain anonymous,' added Marcus quickly. 'So all the dealing would be done with myself. If you were to find the offer satisfactory.' Jonathan recovered himself.

'Find the offer satisfactory?' he said, in an incredulous voice. 'My God, it would solve everything.'

'Good,' said Marcus in neutral tones, needlessly rearranging the pile of property details on his desk. 'So I can take it that you accept?' He glanced up. Jonathan still looked stunned. Unsuspicious, but stunned.

Marcus thought rapidly, then said lightly, 'It's been a very fortunate turn of events for a number of vendors in your position.' He smiled at Jonathan. 'This particular buyer is planning a number of purchases in the area. He wishes to take advantage of current depressed prices.'

'I wouldn't call two hundred thousand pounds a depressed price for our house!' said Jonathan. His eyes were faintly shining.

'Relatively speaking,' said Marcus smoothly. 'I take it the sale will help you out financially?' he added in unconcerned, polite tones.

'I'll say,' said Jonathan. 'You may not realize it, but the tutorial college is mortgaged up to the hilt.'

'Really?' said Marcus. 'Well, then, this is good news.' He beamed at Jonathan.

'It certainly is,' said Jonathan in heartfelt tones. 'How

can I begin to thank you? We thought we'd never sell the place.' Marcus waved a self-deprecating hand.

'Just our job,' he said, in professional tones. 'There is one other thing,' he added lightly. 'It may not be of interest to you.'

'Oh yes?'

'The purchaser,' said Marcus carefully, 'has expressed a willingness to let the house out. At very reasonable terms, if he can find the right tenants.' He paused. 'Before advertising it, I thought I would give you first refusal.' He shrugged. 'I don't know if you're interested in the idea. Perhaps you'd prefer to stay where you are.'

'I don't know about "prefer to",' said Jonathan, giving him a rueful grin. 'Try "have to". Until the business is really off the ground—'

'You may find that the rent is sufficiently low for you to consider it,' said Marcus. 'The buyer has expressly said that he values quality of tenant over rental income. He is, after all, purchasing the property primarily for capital gain.'

'Goodness,' said Jonathan. 'Well, I don't know. I mean, what sort of sums are we talking? Per month?'

Marcus got up from his chair. He wandered over to the window, and stared out at the courtyard for a few seconds. A lone daffodil stared bravely back at him. Then he turned round and named a sum.

For a moment, he thought he'd got it hopelessly, disastrously wrong. Then Jonathan's brow cleared.

'Well, I'm not sure,' he said. 'But I think we might be able to manage that.'

'The buyer is open to negotiations,' said Marcus hastily. 'If necessary.'

'I don't think they will be necessary,' said Jonathan. He beamed at Marcus, and Marcus, after a moment, smiled back. 'I'm going to have to talk about this with my wife, of course,' Jonathan added.

'Of course,' said Marcus sagely. 'She might, perhaps, prefer to stay where you are?' he risked. Jonathan gave him a rather strange look.

'I don't think so,' he said. 'But I'd better talk to her, anyway.'

Liz felt grey. Grey in body and grey in soul. Outside, a pale spring sunlight served not to cheer her spirits, but simply to thrust her melancholy into sharp relief. She sat gloomily in one of the classrooms, trying yet again to drum up some inspiration for the modern languages department, shrinking into her chair as she heard tutors and stray pupils passing cheerfully by the door; wincing as the sound of Alice's pop music penetrated the walls with its dull thudding.

It had taken Alice a mere week to recover her spirits. For seven days she had refused to eat, refused to look Liz in the eye, burst into tears at the slightest provocation, and sat most of the time, holed up in her room, wrapped in her duvet, listening to music which seemed to get louder and louder and gloomier and gloomier by the day. It had taken all Liz's self-control not to go in there and pick a fight. But the knowledge that a row would probably only augment the problem, allied with an inarticulated fear of what secrets Alice might choose to divulge, had kept her from saying anything. And, in part, she had sympathized with Alice's blatant, public

display of woe. Her own dull misery was something to
be hidden, fought and, if possible, one day overcome.

Which was why she was so outraged to hear Alice
now, giggling and shrieking behind her closed door, as
though nothing had happened. A pang of envy filled Liz
as she imagined the hilarious scenes in that little room;
the jokes; the stories; the inexhaustible capacity for giggling. Alice and Genevieve, back together again.

The arrival of Genevieve for a month's home leave
had taken them all by surprise. Her manically giggling
phone call from Heathrow had turned Alice's black scowl
into a cautious smile; within half an hour of hearing Genevieve's voice she was grinning again. Now she bubbled
over with excitement every day. Liz marvelled at her
rubber-like resilience. And, at the same time, resented
her for it. Now she was alone in her apathetic misery.

The classroom door suddenly opened, and Genevieve's face appeared around it. It still managed to take
Liz slightly by surprise. Genevieve was now deeply
tanned and a good half-stone lighter than before going
away, and her face was decorated with a newly acquired
nose-ring.

'Mrs Chambers?' she said. Her voice had acquired a
slight American twang which Liz found alternately
charming and trying. 'Is it OK if we make peanut butter?' Liz looked at her blankly. What for? she wanted
to ask, but instead, she nodded.

'I don't see why not.'

'Cool.' Genevieve's head disappeared.

'Don't make too much mess,' added Liz automatically. But it was too late. She thought about going after

Genevieve and saying it again. Then she decided that she simply couldn't be bothered to.

As Jonathan walked with Marcus into the foyer of Witherstone's he saw Anthea and the two boys sitting in the waiting area.

'Mr Chambers!' Anthea rose and charmingly took both hands in hers. 'Did you see the piece in the paper?'

'Yes,' smiled Jonathan.

'I showed it to him,' said Marcus.

'We're still so thrilled about it all!' continued Anthea. Daniel was trying to catch Jonathan's eye.

'Do you think,' he said, 'that the article in the paper will get you more pupils at the tutorial college?'

'I should think so,' said Jonathan. Daniel immediately looked at Andrew, as though to say, *You see* . . .

'You still looked like a nerd,' said Andrew placidly to Daniel. Jonathan's mouth twitched, and he looked at his watch.

'I've got to dash,' he said apologetically.

'Of course,' said Marcus. 'Well, just let me know about the house. No hurry,' he added. 'No hurry at all.'

When Jonathan arrived back from Witherstone's, Liz was standing in the kitchen of the flat, disconsolately stirring a mug of coffee. Alice and Genevieve were pouring peanuts into the weighing dish of the scales, giggling helplessly as they bounced off the plastic, onto the counter and onto the floor.

'Not enough,' announced Genevieve. 'Let's go and buy some more.'

'OK!' said Alice. She looked up at Jonathan with bright eyes. Her cheeks were flushed and she looked utterly happy.

'Before you go, let me tell you the good news,' said Jonathan. 'We've had an offer on the house in Russell Street.'

'Oh, right,' said Alice, picking a peanut off the floor and nibbling at it.

'Cool,' said Genevieve politely. Liz said nothing. She felt as though their life had been taken out of her control.

'And there's a possibility,' said Jonathan, 'that we may be able to rent it back off the new owners.'

'Wow!' said Alice. 'Like, live there again?'

'Yes.'

'Excellent!'

'I think that's really good,' said Genevieve surprisingly. 'I mean, this flat's really nice, and everything,' she looked around kindly, 'but your old house was better.'

'Thank you for that insight, Genevieve,' said Jonathan, his eyes crinkling humorously. He tried to catch Liz's eye, but she was staring blankly ahead.

'That's OK,' said Genevieve equably. 'C'mon, Alice.'

When they had gone, Jonathan looked at Liz.

'You haven't said anything,' he said. 'Aren't you pleased?' Liz shrugged despairingly.

'I don't know. I mean, moving back to our old house. Isn't it a bit of a backwards step? Will we really be happy there?'

'No, it's not a backwards step,' said Jonathan. 'And

yes, we will be happy there.' He regarded her plainly. 'We will move back there and we will be happy.'

'Is that an order?'

'If you like.' Liz gave a resentful, heaving sigh.

'I can't just start being happy. Just because you want me to.'

'You could,' said Jonathan, 'if you really wanted to.' Liz gave him a baleful look.

'I could *pretend* to be happy, if you like,' she said in sarcastic tones. 'If that would help.'

'Yes, actually it would,' said Jonathan. 'It would help a lot. Why don't you start straight away?' And he picked up a peanut, popped it in his mouth, and walked out of the kitchen, leaving Liz staring after him in nonplussed silence.

Keep reading for a sneak peek of
more Madeleine Wickham novels
you won't want to miss!

40 love

Patrick Chance has the perfect setting for a tennis
party—his beautiful new country house complete with
stable, cocktail bar, Jacuzzi, and, of course, the tennis
court. As his guests gather on the sunny terrace, it
seems obvious who is winning in life and who is
losing. But by the end of the party, nothing will be
certain. As the first ball is served over the net it
signals the start of two days of tempers, shocks,
revelations, the arrival of an uninvited guest, and the
realization that the weekend is about anything but
tennis. In this funny, penetrating, and perceptive
novel, Madeleine Wickham is in stellar form, sure to
please her many fans and gain new ones as well.

the wedding girl

Engaged to a man who is wealthy, serious, and
believes her to be perfect—she is facing the biggest
and most elaborate wedding imaginable. Milly's past
is locked away so securely she has almost persuaded
herself that it doesn't exist—until, with only four
days to go, her secret catches up with her. . . . And
when 'I do' gives you déjà vu it could be a problem.

A delightful comedy that will leave readers desperately wanting more wonderful Wickham!

sleeping arrangements

When two families arrive at a villa in Spain for their vacation, they get a shock—it has been double-booked. An uneasy week of sharing begins, and tensions soon mount in the soaring heat. But the temperature isn't solely to blame: there's a secret history between the families—and as tempers fray, an old passion begins to resurface. . . . Sit back, grab a cool drink, and get ready for a wonderfully wicked trip you'll not soon forget!

the gatecrasher

Fleur Daxeny goes through more rich men than she does designer hats. Beautiful, charming, and utterly irresistible, her success at crashing funerals to find wealthy men is remarkable. Fleur is not one to wear her heart on her Chanel sleeve, but she soon finds her latest conquest, the handsome and rich widower Richard Favour, more loveable than she could have thought possible. Can she trust her heart or will she cut ties and run away as fast as her Prada pumps can take her?

cocktails for three

Each month, three staffers of *The Londoner* gather
at a nearby lounge for a night of cocktails and
gossip. But the events of one April evening will have
permanent repercussions for the trio. Madeleine
Wickham combines her trademark humor with
poignant insight to create an edgy, romantic tale of
secrets, strangers, and a splash of scandal.

40 love

It was the sort of warm, scented evening that Caroline Chance associated with holidays in Greece; with glasses of ouzo and flirtatious waiters and the feel of cool cotton against burnt shoulders. Except that the sweet smell wafting through the air was not olive groves, but freshly mown English grass. And the sound in the distance was not the sea, but Georgina's riding instructor, intoning— always with the same monotonous inflection—'Trot *on*. Trot *on*.'

Caroline grimaced and resumed painting her toenails. She didn't object to her daughter's passion for riding— but neither did she comprehend it. The moment they had moved to Bindon from Seymour Road, Georgina had started clamouring for a pony. And, of course, Patrick had insisted she should be given one.

In fact, Caroline had grown quite fond of the first pony. It was a sweet little thing, with a shaggy mane and a docile manner. Caroline had sometimes gone to look at it when no-one was about and had taken to feeding it Ferrero Rocher chocolates. But this latest creature was a monster—a huge great black thing that looked quite wild. At eleven, Georgina was tall and strong, but Caroline couldn't understand how she could even get onto the thing, let alone ride it and go over jumps.

She finished painting her right foot and took a slug of white wine. Her left foot was dry, and she lifted it up to admire the pearly colour in the evening light. She was sitting on the wide terrace outside the main drawing-room of the house. The White House had been built—rather stupidly, Caroline felt, given the English climate—as a suntrap. The stark white walls reflected the sun into the central courtyard, and the main rooms faced south. A vine bearing rather bitter grapes had been persuaded to creep along the wall above Caroline's head; and several exotic plants were brought out of the greenhouse every summer to adorn the terrace. But it was still bloody freezing England. There wasn't much they could do about that.

Today, though, she had to concede, had been about as perfect as it could get. Translucent blue sky; scorching sun; not a gust of wind. She had spent most of the day getting ready for tomorrow, but luckily the tasks she had allotted herself—arranging flowers, preparing vegetables, waxing her legs—were the sort of thing that could be done outside. The main dishes—vegetable terrine for lunch; seafood tartlets for dinner—had arrived from the caterers that morning, and Mrs Finch had already decanted them onto serving plates. She had raised an eyebrow—*couldn't you even bring yourself to cook for eight people?*—but Caroline was used to Mrs Finch's upwardly mobile eyebrows and ignored them. For Christ's sake, she thought, pouring herself another glass of wine, what was the point of having money and not spending it?

the wedding girl

A group of tourists had stopped to gawp at Milly as she stood in her wedding dress on the registry office steps. They clogged up the pavement opposite while Oxford shoppers, accustomed to the yearly influx, stepped round them into the road, not even bothering to complain. A few glanced up towards the steps of the registry office to see what all the fuss was about, and tacitly acknowledged that the young couple on the steps did make a very striking pair.

One or two of the tourists had even brought out cameras, and Milly beamed joyously at them, revelling in their attention; trying to imagine the picture she and Allan made together. Her spiky, white-blond hair was growing hot in the afternoon sun; the hired veil was scratchy against her neck, the nylon lace of her dress felt uncomfortably damp wherever it touched her body. But still she felt light-hearted and full of a euphoric energy. And whenever she glanced up at Allan—at her husband—a new, hot thrill of excitement coursed through her body, obliterating all other sensation.

She had only arrived in Oxford three weeks ago. School had finished in July—and while all her friends had planned trips to Ibiza and Spain and Amsterdam, Milly had been packed off to a secretarial college in Oxford. 'Much more useful than some silly holiday,' her mother had announced firmly. 'And just think what an advantage you'll have over the others when it comes to job-hunting.' But Milly didn't want an advantage over the others. She wanted a suntan and a boyfriend, and beyond that, she didn't really care.

So on the second day of the typing course, she'd slipped off after lunch. She'd found a cheap hairdresser and, with a surge of exhilaration, told him to chop her hair short and bleach it. Then, feeling light and happy, she'd wandered around the dry, sun-drenched streets of Oxford, dipping into cool cloisters and chapels, peering behind stone arches, wondering where she might sunbathe. It was pure coincidence that she'd eventually chosen a patch of lawn in Corpus Christi College; that Rupert's rooms should have been directly opposite; that he and Allan should have decided to spend that afternoon doing nothing but lying on the grass, drinking Pimm's.

She'd watched, surreptitiously, as they sauntered onto the lawn, clinked glasses and lit up cigarettes; gazed harder as one of them took off his shirt to reveal a tanned torso. She'd listened to the snatches of their conversation which wafted through the air towards her and found herself longing to know these debonair, good-looking men. When, suddenly, the older one addressed her, she felt her heart leap with excitement.

'Have you got a light?' His voice was dry, American, amused.

'Yes,' she stuttered, feeling in her pocket. 'Yes, I have.'

'We're terribly lazy, I'm afraid.' The younger man's eyes met hers: shyer; more diffident. 'I've got a lighter; just inside that window.' He pointed to a stone mullioned arch. 'But it's too hot to move.'

'We'll repay you with a glass of Pimm's,' said the American. He'd held out his hand. 'Allan.'

'Rupert.'

She'd lolled on the grass with them for the rest of the afternoon, soaking up the sun and alcohol; flirting and giggling; making them both laugh with her descriptions of her fellow secretaries. At the pit of her stomach was a feeling of anticipation which increased as the afternoon wore on: a sexual frisson heightened by the fact that there were two of them and they were both beautiful. Rupert was lithe and golden like a young lion; his hair a shining blond halo; his teeth gleaming white against his smooth brown face. Allan's face was crinkled and his hair was greying at the temples, but his grey-green eyes made her heart jump when they met hers, and his voice caressed her ears like silk.

When Rupert rolled over onto his back and said to the sky, 'Shall we go for something to eat tonight?' she'd thought he must be asking her out. An immediate, unbelieving joy had coursed through her; simultaneously she'd recognized that she would have preferred it if it had been Allan.

But then Allan rolled over too, and said 'Sure thing.' And then he leaned over and casually kissed Rupert on the mouth.

The strange thing was, after the initial, heart-stopping shock, Milly hadn't really minded. In fact, this way was almost better: this way, she had the pair of them to herself. She'd gone to San Antonio's with them that night and basked in the jealous glances of two fellow secretaries at another table. The next night they'd played jazz on an old wind-up gramophone and drunk mint juleps and taught her how to roll joints. Within a week, they'd become a regular threesome.

And then Allan had asked her to marry him.

sleeping arrangements

It was too hot to work, thought Chloe, standing back and pushing tendrils of wispy fair hair off her forehead. Certainly too hot to be standing in this airless room, corseting an anxious overweight girl into a wedding dress which was almost certainly two sizes too small. She glanced for the hundredth time at her watch, and felt a little leap of excitement. It was almost time. In only a few minutes the taxi would arrive and this torture would be over, and the holiday would officially begin. She felt faint with longing; with a desperate need for escape. It was only for a week—but a week would be enough. A week had to be enough, didn't it?

Away, she thought, closing her eyes briefly. Away from it all. She wanted it so much it almost scared her.

'Right,' she said, opening her eyes and blinking. For a moment she could barely remember what she was doing; could feel nothing but heat and fatigue. 'Well, I've got to go—so perhaps we could leave it there for today? If you do want to go ahead with this particular dress—'

'She'll get into it,' cut in Mrs Bridges with quiet menace. 'She'll just have to make an effort. You can't have it both ways, you know!' Suddenly she turned on Bethany. 'You can't have chocolate fudge cake every night and be a size twelve!'

'Some people do,' said Bethany miserably. 'Kirsten Davis eats what she likes and she's size eight.'

'Then she's lucky,' retorted Mrs Bridges. 'Most of

us aren't so lucky. We have to choose. We have to exercise self-control. We have to make sacrifices in life. Isn't that right, Chloe?'

'Well,' said Chloe. 'I suppose so. Anyway, as I explained earlier, I am actually going on holiday today. And the taxi's just arrived to take us to Gatwick. So perhaps if we could arrange—'

'You want to look like a princess! Every girl wants to make the effort to look their best on the day they get married. I'm sure you did, didn't you?' Mrs Bridges' gimlet gaze landed on Chloe. 'I'm sure you made yourself look as beautiful as possible for your wedding day, didn't you?'

'Well,' said Chloe. 'Actually—'

'Chloe?' Philip's mop of dark curly hair appeared round the door. 'Sorry to disturb—but we do have to get going. The taxi's here . . .'

'I know,' said Chloe, trying not to sound as tense as she felt. 'I know it is. I'm just coming—'

—*when I can get rid of these bloody people who arrive half an hour late and won't take a hint,* her eyes silently said, and Philip gave an imperceptible nod.

'What was your wedding dress like?' said Bethany wistfully as he disappeared. 'I bet it was lovely.'

'I've never been married,' said Chloe, reaching for her pinbox. If she could just prise the girl out of the dress . . .

'What?' Mrs Bridges' eyes darted to Bethany, then around the room strewn with snippets of wedding silk and gauze, as though suspecting a trick. 'What do you mean, you've never been married? Who was that, then?'

'Philip's my long-term partner,' said Chloe, forcing

herself to remain polite. 'We've been together for thirteen years.' She smiled at Mrs Bridges. 'Longer than a lot of marriages.'

And why the hell am I explaining myself to you? She thought furiously.

Because three fittings for Bethany plus six bridesmaids' dresses is worth over a thousand pounds, her brain swiftly replied. And I only have to be polite for ten more minutes. I can bear ten minutes. Then they'll be gone—and we'll be gone. For a whole week. No phone calls, no newspapers, no worries. No-one will even know where we are.

the gatecrasher

Fleur Daxeny wrinkled her nose. She bit her lip, and put her head on one side, and gazed at her reflection silently for a few seconds. Then she gave a gurgle of laughter.

'I still can't decide,' she exclaimed. 'They're all fabulous.'

The saleswoman from Take Hat! exchanged weary glances with the nervous young hairdresser sitting on a gilt stool in the corner. The hairdresser had arrived at Fleur's hotel suite half an hour ago and had been waiting to start ever since. The saleswoman was, meanwhile, slightly beginning to wonder whether she was wasting her time completely.

'I love this one with the veil,' said Fleur suddenly, reaching for a tiny creation of black satin and wispy netting. 'Isn't it elegant?'

'Very elegant,' said the saleswoman. She hurried forward just in time to catch a black silk topper which Fleur was discarding onto the floor.

'Very,' echoed the hairdresser in the corner. Surreptitiously, he glanced at his watch. He was supposed to be back down in the salon in forty minutes. Trevor wouldn't be pleased. Perhaps he should phone down to explain the situation. Perhaps . . .

'All right!' said Fleur. 'I've decided.' She pushed up the veil and beamed around the room. 'I'm going to wear this one today.'

'A very wise choice, madam,' said the saleswoman in relieved tones. 'It's a lovely hat.'

'Lovely,' whispered the hairdresser.

'So if you could just pack the other five into boxes for me . . .' Fleur smiled mysteriously at her reflection and pulled the dark silk gauze down over her face again. The woman from Take Hat! gaped at her.

'You're going to buy them all?'

'Of course I am. I simply can't choose between them. They're all too perfect.' Fleur turned to the hairdresser. 'Now, my sweet. Can you come up with something special for my hair which will go under this hat?' The young man stared back at her and felt a dark pink colour begin to rise up his neck.

'Oh. Yes. I should think so. I mean . . .' But Fleur had already turned away.

'If you could just put it all onto my hotel bill,' she was saying to the saleswoman. 'That's all right, isn't it?'

'Perfectly all right, madam,' said the saleswoman eagerly. 'As a guest of the hotel, you're entitled to a fifteen per cent concession on all our prices.'

'Whatever,' said Fleur. She gave a little yawn. 'As long as it can all go on the bill.'

'I'll go and sort it out for you straight away.'

'Good,' said Fleur. As the saleswoman hurried out of the room, Fleur turned and gave the young hairdresser a ravishing smile. 'I'm all yours.'

Her voice was low and melodious and curiously accentless. To the hairdresser's ears it was now also faintly mocking, and he flushed slightly as he came over to where Fleur was sitting. He stood behind her, gathered together the ends of her hair in one hand and let them fall down in a heavy, red-gold movement.

'Your hair's in very good condition,' he said awkwardly.

'Isn't it lovely?' said Fleur complacently. 'I've always had good hair. And good skin, of course.' She tilted her head, pushed her hotel robe aside slightly, and rubbed her cheek tenderly against the pale, creamy skin of her shoulder. 'How old would you say I was?' she added abruptly.

'I don't . . . I wouldn't . . .' the young man began to flounder.

'I'm forty,' she said lazily. She closed her eyes. 'Forty,' she repeated, as though meditating. 'It makes you think, doesn't it?'

'You don't look . . .' began the hairdresser in awkward politeness. Fleur opened one glinting, pussycat-green eye.

'I don't look forty? How old do I look, then?'

The hairdresser stared back at her uncomfortably. He opened his mouth to speak, then closed it again. The truth was, he thought suddenly, that this incredible woman didn't look any age. She seemed ageless, classless, indefinable. As he met her eyes, he felt a thrill run through him; a dart-like conviction that this moment was somehow significant. His hands trembling slightly, he reached for her hair and let it run like slippery flames through his fingers.

'You look as old as you look,' he whispered huskily. 'Numbers don't come into it.'

'Sweet,' said Fleur dismissively. 'Now, my pet, before you start on my hair, how about ordering me a nice glass of champagne?'

The hairdresser's fingers drooped in slight disappointment, and he went obediently over to the telephone. As he dialed, the door opened and the woman from Take

Hat! came back in, carrying a pile of hat boxes. 'Here we are,' she exclaimed breathlessly. 'If you could just sign here. . . .'

'A glass of champagne, please,' the hairdresser was saying. 'Room 301.'

'I was wondering,' began the saleswoman cautiously to Fleur. 'You're quite sure that you want all six hats in black? We do have some other super colours this season.' She tapped her teeth thoughtfully. 'There's a lovely emerald green which would look stunning with your hair. . . .'

'Black,' said Fleur decisively. 'I'm only interested in black.'

cocktails for three

Candice Brewin pushed open the heavy glass door of the Manhattan Bar and felt the familiar swell of warmth, noise, light and clatter rush over her. It was six o'clock on a Wednesday night and the bar was already almost full. Waiters in dark green bow ties were gliding over the pale polished floor, carrying cocktails to tables. Girls in slippy dresses were standing at the bar, glancing around with bright, hopeful eyes. In the corner, a pianist was thumping out Gershwin numbers, almost drowned by the hum of metropolitan chatter.

It was getting to be too busy here, thought Candice, slipping off her coat. When she, Roxanne and Maggie had first discovered the Manhattan Bar, it had been a small, quiet, almost secretive place to meet. They had stumbled on it almost by chance, desperate for somewhere to drink after a particularly fraught press day. It had then been a dark and old-fashioned-looking place, with tatty bar stools and a peeling mural of the New York skyline on one wall. The patrons had been few and silent—mostly tending towards elderly gentlemen with much younger female companions. Candice, Roxanne and Maggie had boldly ordered a round of cocktails and then several more—and by the end of the evening had decided, amid fits of giggles, that the place had a certain terrible charm and must be revisited. And so the monthly cocktail club had been born.

But now, newly extended, relaunched and written up in every glossy magazine, the bar was a different place. These days a young, attractive after-work crowd came flocking in every evening. Celebrities had been spotted at the bar. Even the waiters all looked like models. Really, thought Candice, handing her coat to the coat-check woman and receiving an art deco silver button in return, they should find somewhere else. Somewhere less busy, less obvious.

At the same time, she knew they never would. They had been coming here too long; had shared too many secrets over those distinctive frosted martini glasses. Anywhere else would feel wrong. On the first of every month, it had to be the Manhattan Bar.

There was a mirror opposite, and she glanced at her reflection, checking that her short cropped hair was tidy and her make-up—what little there was of it—hadn't smudged. She was wearing a plain black trouser suit over a pale green T-shirt—not exactly the height of glamour, but good enough.

* * *

Maggie Phillips paused outside the doors of the Manhattan Bar, put down her bulky carrier bag full of bright, stuffed toys, and pulled unceremoniously at the maternity tights wrinkling around her legs. Three more weeks, she thought, giving a final tug. Three more weeks of these bloody things. She took a deep breath, reached for her carrier bag again and pushed at the glass door.

As soon as she got inside, the noise and warmth of the place made her feel faint. She grasped for the wall, and stood quite still, trying not to lose her balance as she blinked away the dots in front of her eyes.

'Are you all right, my love?' enquired a voice to her

left. Maggie swiveled her head and, as her vision cleared, made out the kindly face of the coat-check lady.

'I'm fine,' she said, flashing a tight smile.

'Are you sure? Would you like a nice drink of water?'

'No, really, I'm fine.' As if to emphasize the point she began to struggle out of her coat, self-consciously aware of the coat-check lady's appraising gaze on her figure. For pregnancy wear, her black Lycra trousers and tunic were about as flattering as you could get. But still there it was, right in front her, wherever she moved. A bump the size of a helium balloon. Maggie handed over her coat and met the coat lady's gaze head on.

If she asks me when it's due, she thought, I swear I'll smother her with Tinky Winky.

'When's it due?'

* * *

Roxanne Miller stood in the ladies' room of the Manhattan Bar, leaned forward and carefully outlined her lips in cinnamon-coloured pencil. She pressed them together, then stood back and studied her reflection critically, starting—as she always did—with her best features. Good cheekbones. Nothing could take away your cheekbones. Blue eyes a little bloodshot, skin tanned from three weeks in the Caribbean. Nose still long, still crooked. Bronzy-blond hair tumbling down from a beaded comb in her hair. Tumbling a little too wildly, perhaps. Roxanne reached into her bag for a hairbrush and began to smooth it down. She was dressed, as she so often was, in a white T-shirt. In her opinion, nothing in the world showed off a tan better than a plain white T-shirt. She put her hairbrush away and smiled, impressed by her own reflection in spite of herself.

Then, behind her, a lavatory flushed and a cubicle door opened. A girl of about nineteen wandered out and stood next to Roxanne to wash her hands. She had pale, smooth skin and dark sleepy eyes, and her hair fell straight to her shoulders like the fringe on a lampshade. A mouth like a plum. No make-up whatsoever. The girl met Roxanne's eyes and smiled, then moved away.

When the swing doors had shut behind her, Roxanne still stayed, staring at herself. She suddenly felt like a blowsy tart. A thirty-three-year-old woman, trying too hard. In an instant, all the animation disappeared from her face. Her mouth drooped downwards and the gleam vanished from her eyes. Dispassionately, her gaze sought out the tiny red veins marking the skin on her cheeks. Sun damage, they called it. Damaged goods.

Then there was a sound from the door and her head jerked round.

'Roxanne!' Maggie was coming towards her, a wide smile on her face, her nut-brown bob shining under the spotlights.

'Darling!' Roxanne beamed, and gaily thrust her make-up bag into a larger Prada tote. 'I was just beautifying.'

'You don't need it!' said Maggie. 'Look at that tan!'

'That's Caribbean sun for you,' said Roxanne cheerfully.

'Don't tell me,' said Maggie, putting her hands over her ears. 'I don't want to know. It's not even approaching fair. Why did I never do a single travel feature while I was editor? I must have been mad!' She jerked her head towards the door. 'Go and keep Candice company. I'll be out in a moment.'